The warrior shot an arrow and Thane felt it slam into the war shield with the power of a large stone. The arrow hit a glancing blow and shot off into the air. His arm went numb but he held onto the shield and turned his pony as the second arrow came and sliced through the upper part of his thigh. Blood spurted like splashed water and a fire welled up that brought a dizziness to him. He felt his pony slow down as he nearly lost control and fell, waiting for the final, fatal arrow to come.

But the warrior had fallen from his pony and lay twisted on the ground, writhing and holding his hip. He was chanting in a loud voice, a high call that sounded not unlike a keening for the dead. His pony, the swift pinto, stood beside him, its sides heaving for air. In the near distance a cloud of dust signaled the coming to other Piegan warriors. Thane turned his pony, holding tight to keep from falling, and rode for his life.

HIGH FREEDOM

EARL MURRAY

TOR

A TOM DOHERTY ASSOCIATES BOOK

ACKNOWLEDGMENT

Thanks to Magdalene Medicine Horse and
Dan and Mardelle Plainfeather for their help and
guidance.

HIGH FREEDOM

First printing: July 1988

A TOR Book

Published by Tom Doherty Associates
49 West 24th Street
New York, N.Y. 10010

ISBN: 0-812-58596-8
CAN. ED.: 0-812-58597-6

Printed in the United States

0 9 8 7 6 5 4 3 2 1

Should you ask me whence these stories?
Whence these legends and traditions,
With the odors of the forest,
With the dew and damp of meadows . . .

Should you ask where Nawadaha
Found these songs so wild and wayward,
Found these legends and traditions,
I should answer, I should tell you,
"In the birds' nests of the forest,
In the lodges of the beaver . . ."

Henry W. Longfellow
The Song of Hiawatha

Prologue

Charlotte County, Virginia
Just before Dawn, January 1, 1824

THANE THOMPSON PEERED INTO THE STREET THROUGH THE window bars of his cell, to where the gallows stood like a black tower in the shadows of the moon. The noise of the New Year's celebration had subsided and morning was near. Everyone was waiting for the hanging on New Year's Day. All was quiet, and he could hear the hooting of a distant owl.

Thane's neatly trimmed red-brown hair was now matted and tangled from nervous fingers. His topcoat and hat had been torn away and left lying in the street. Though the cell was cold, his pleated dinner shirt hung damp with perspiration. He turned away from the cell window and muttered a curse, then flipped his bed over and kicked the thin feather tick against the wall. The noise roused the jailer, who coughed himself awake from his drunken stupor and rose to his feet.

Thane smashed the wooden frame of the bed against the cell bars. Wood splinters flew in the darkness and the jailer cursed. He wobbled unsteadily as he grabbed his lantern and made his way over to the cell.

"What the hell do you think you're up to?" he asked

Thane. His voice was raspy from liquor and sleep, and he drooled.

Thane paid him no attention, but continued to destroy the bed. Each blow was against his uncle, William Chapman, who had murdered his father on Christmas Day. Chapman had made the authorities believe Thane had killed his own father in order to take over the family plantation. Thane was again feeling the shock and anger at seeing his father tumble from his chair at the dining room table after drinking a glass of wine Chapman had given him. Thane again saw himself trying to shake his father out of the convulsions while Chapman smirked and rushed from the room to notify the authorities.

It had all happened so fast: the sheriff's speedy arrival, followed by the harried trial and conviction. No conspiracy could have been better planned. Perhaps it would have been more difficult for Chapman had Thane's mother still been alive. Now, with dawn soon to come, Thane would be led to his death at a gallows and William Chapman would take sole possession of a tobacco fortune.

The jailer watched Thane continue to destroy the inside of the cell. Finally he went back to his desk and grabbed a flintlock pistol. The lantern's light flickered against his puffed face as he flipped a loose suspender back onto his shoulder and fumbled with the gun. He worked to load it with shaking hands, spilling through his fingers grains of powder that danced like fine sand against the floor. Finally, he cocked the pistol and returned to Thane's cell.

"By God, I told you to stop!" the jailer yelled. He pointed the pistol at Thane.

Thane stuck his face through the bars. He held up a broken piece of bedpost for the jailer to see.

"I'm going to run this through Chapman's heart."

The jailer stepped back from Thane, wide-eyed. Then he squinted and his breathing grew more intense. He worked to steady the pistol in his grasp.

"Mr. Chapman warned me you'd be trouble," he said. "He told me not to stand for nothing from you."

"Chapman hasn't seen the last of me," Thane said. His voice was firm and under control.

"Oh, no," the jailer insisted. "You'll hang come first light. You got a proper trial."

"I got a trial. It wasn't proper." Thane pointed the sharp piece of wood at the jailer.

"You just stand back now," the jailer said. He stuck the pistol out. "I'll use this."

Thane laughed. "No you won't. You surely won't. If you shot me and spoiled Chapman's show, he'd hang *you* instead."

The jailer studied Thane through the bars. The lantern showed Thane's determined face. He knew Thane was right: William Chapman wanted to see his nephew hang, neat and secure. Thane Thompson could destroy the cell if he so wished, but before very long he would be dead at the end of a rope.

"Say what you want," the jailer said, "but it's the end for you." The dandy of his father's eye, schooled in the best of schools, and still a wanderer, a whelp of the woods. "You should have been born a tramp. You didn't deserve to have what your father built for you, no sir. There wasn't much but wanderlust in your blood."

"It's bad luck to speak in the past tense," Thane said, tapping the sharp piece of wood against the bars. "I'm still here. And I will be alive when the sun is high tomorrow."

"Oh no, my boy." The jailer laughed. "I'm afraid not."

As the jailer spoke, Thane reached way out and rammed the broken piece of wood into his face. The point gouged the jailer's right eye and he screamed and dropped to his knees. A stream of blood and matter trailed out through his fingers and both the pistol and the lantern clattered to the floor. The

lantern shattered into flame and whooshed into
Thane's cell, a dancing red wave.

Thane reached through the bars and grabbed the
jailer by the sleeve of one arm. The jailer cursed and
struggled, but Thane was too strong. He soon had the
jailer's arm twisted behind him. Thane then grabbed
the man's hair and slammed his head backward into
the bars until his tongue rolled out and he slid down
into a sitting position.

The flames roared through the cell and across the
floor of the jail. Thane coughed from the smoke and
struggled to free the keys from the jailer's belt. He
shook his arm as flames caught his shirt and spread a
searing pain from his wrist to his elbow. He quickly
tore the sleeve free and threw it aside, fighting nausea
from shock and weakness.

Thane told himself he must ignore the burn. He put
his good arm through the bars and jammed the key
into the lock. When the latch clicked he jumped out of
the cell and away from the flames, struggling to see
through the smoke while he pulled the unconscious
jailer along by the collar.

Outside the sky was just beginning to lighten.
Thane left the jailer face up in the street while he went
back in and found a fine Kentucky-style flintlock rifle
with a horn of powder and a pouch of lead balls. He
fought the pain in his arm and searched until he found
a jar of lamp oil. Then he wrestled a piece of burning
wood from the flames and ran back out into the street.

The jailer had not moved. He lay groaning, his
hands held over his injured eye. Thane doused the
lamp oil over the gallows and tossed the flaming wood
onto the deck. Fingers of fire quickly leaped up the
oak frame, engulfing a small cracked bell that hung
from the uppermost cross member. The light showed
neatly carved words in the cross member, a phrase
which read: "For God and Country."

Now the jail and gallows were both ablaze, bringing
people from all directions. Gripping the flintlock in

his right hand, Thane cradled his burned arm at his side and bolted into the shadows. The stables were not far and his opportunity to escape was now, while the townspeople milled about in confusion. Thane found the stables unmanned and had his pick of horses. He led a big bay stallion out and caught a glimpse of Chapman, who was ordering men to spread out around the town and be sure Thane couldn't escape. Thane decided he had one thing left to do before he escaped.

William Chapman waved his arms and yelled while Thane took aim from the shadows. The flintlock jumped in Thane's hands and his burned arm screamed with pain. Smoke and flame licked from the rifle barrel and William Chapman jerked sideways in the street, then fell to the ground. Thane jumped on his horse as men mounted up after him.

Thane's arm throbbed and he continued to fight shock as he kicked the horse into a run toward the woods. As the sun began to rise he crossed the river and turned the horse off the main trail and followed the game trails through the deep woods, ducking limbs and jumping fallen trees while the sounds of his pursuers grew ever fainter. Finally, at a safe distance, Thane soaked his burned arm in the cold water and dressed it in mud. He was gone now, away from the life he had once known. They would never catch him. They had already given up. William Chapman, if he lived, would never see him hang. But he would have to go as far away as he could now, and never return.

Thane rode into the Blue Ridge country, the land of his boyhood. It was there he had first tasted the sweet feel of freedom and the wondrous excitement of following trails through wild country. Though Thane's father had always insisted on his education with books first, he'd never said no to Thane's occasional travels out and away from society. There was never any insistence that Thane maintain his aristo-

cratic manners and dress at all times. Thane's father
had understood that a boy needs room to grow and
become an individual on his own. He'd also realized it
would have been impossible to keep Thane out of the
woods.

Maybe the jailer had been right. It might have been
better had he been born to a pioneer family, living at
the edge of the settlements. Though the civilized
world was interesting to learn about, Thane had
always wanted to know more about the untamed
lands. The country to the west, yet uncharted, captured his fascination.

Now Thane was ready for such a land. The Blue
Ridge country had educated him as a boy. Trails
through deep and sudden pockets of wild land had
taught Thane well. Lessons of Old England had come
easy, as well as the grace of acceptable speech, but his
first love was the freedom of the woods. As a boy he
had always kept a snowy owl feather in his cap for
good luck. Each successive summer would find him
better schooled in both the wilderness and aristocratic
manners. Thane had come to enjoy the contrast in his
two lives. He could sit at a table engraved with gold
while servants served the best of imported wines and
food, or he could fend for himself in the wilderness.
Squirrels and raccoons and rabbits, as well as various
game birds, had all fallen to his early efforts with a
flintlock.

But his boyhood had long since passed. And now
his father was gone as well. It was time to bid one last
farewell to this land. He must move on out of Virginia
altogether, through the Cumberland Gap and then
down the Ohio River to the state of Missouri. The
country's edge. He had heard scattered talk of the
Rocky Mountains far to the west, the new land of the
Louisiana Purchase. It was a different world there, a
changing world where a man could be a part of a new
and growing territory. It was a place of new begin-
nings.

That land would suit him fine, wild and free from the ties of civilization. Thane had no worries about making it there: he could handle a rifle and carry a hundred pounds with ease. He could sleep on the ground and go with little to eat; he had done so as a boy for the better part of a week while lost on the Blue Ridge. He had found his way out and had certainly learned from it.

St. Louis was a good distance to the west. A long ways through land heavily wooded and with few trails for travel. But Thane cared little how far it was. He would work his way through the mountainous backcountry away from the settlements, and take a flatboat with other travelers up the Ohio. Rain and damp ground would surely find him, but in time he would look up the Missouri River where it fed the Mississippi and head for the high freedom of the mountains.

Great Falls of the Missouri River
February 1, 1824

AMONG THE PIEGAN BLACKFEET, MORNING SWAN WAS considered a rare woman. Though she had been taken as a small child during a raid on a Crow village, Morning Swan had grown up to be as good a Piegan as any other among the Small Robes band. She worked long and hard during each day, despite the weather, and seemed always to sing a cheerful song.

A strong warrior named Long Hand had taken her as his wife during her sixteenth winter. Long Hand was a good provider and allowed Morning Swan many luxuries usually out of bounds to a working woman. He allowed her access to his prize buffalo pony, a brown pinto he called Whirlwind, so that she might enjoy herself racing across the vast grasslands below the mountains and know the feel of chasing buffalo. These animals provided the bulk of the food for the Piegans, and now that the horse was their major means of transportation, great numbers of buffalo could be killed at once. It was important, Long Hand often told Morning Swan, that she be self-supporting if ever the need arose.

So Morning Swan had taken full advantage of her

husband's generosity and had come to learn all she could about providing those things usually reserved for a warrior's status. She had learned the use of the bow and arrow and how to fire the thundersticks that shot flame and a little round ball that killed when it struck. These had come from the Hudson's Bay people to the north, the white men with whom the Blackfeet people traded furs and buffalo robes in exchange for guns and knives and various tools, as well as blankets and beads and pots for the women. Now, in addition to the many chores the women performed on a daily basis, Morning Swan had come to be able to do most of the things a warrior must do to bring meat in for the pots. Morning Swan could do all that was needed to sustain life. She had Long Hand to thank for her good fortune.

Despite the good relationship between Morning Swan and Long Hand, there was one problem in their lives. There was one thing she sorely wanted to do for him. She and Long Hand had now shared a lodge for five winters and Morning Swan had but one girl child. Rosebud was now three and like her mother, a daring and adventuresome sort. But in the lodge of Long Hand and Morning Swan there was an undercurrent of unrest. She felt she must bear him a son.

Morning Swan did not let this problem overshadow her daily life. She held her head high and her dark eyes flashed with confidence. Her courage was without question, as was shown when she once frightened a black bear away from a large bag of chokecherries she had collected and did not want to give up. She was not afraid to speak her mind when the need arose and there was no one in the village who questioned her intelligence. But it was not a matter of wit or courage that made her feel insecure among the Piegan people: among warring peoples, wives were expected to produce sons who would some day become strong warriors and provide for the good of the band and give credit to their nation. Morning Swan knew her purpose and felt confident that the day would come when she would give Long Hand a boy child.

Now the people in the Small Robes village along the waters of the Big Muddy River rested in the warmth of their lodges as the first light of day broke into a sea of crisp blue sky. A gusty breeze mourned along the river and carried crystals of frozen snow across the surging Great Falls and into the village, where they danced their whirling, frozen steps to the whine of the wind. Morning Swan made sure Rosebud was covered and sleeping well before she wrapped herself in a bearskin robe and stepped out into the new day. She walked through the sleeping village and out from the lodges to stare toward the sun and into a range of mountains with white peaks glimmering in the frosty dawn.

The Highwoods marked the unspoken boundary between the Blackfeet nation and their enemies, the Crows, whose principle home was south along the great flow of water known as Elk River, called the Yellowstone by the white traders, the Long Knives, who had come to these lands to trap the beaver. The Long Knives and the Crows were now allied in an effort to come into Blackfeet lands and take the beaver from the streams. Ancient enemies of the Blackfeet, the Crows welcomed the Long Knives if for nothing more than strength against their enemies.

Morning Swan was greatly worried as she peered into the distance and tried to make her eyes see a column of warriors, led by Long Hand, amidst the swirling fog of snow that the wind brought to life along the broad plain between the Highwood Mountains and the river. Long Hand was out there somewhere, leading a group of warriors against the Crows and a party of Long Knives.

Long Hand's medicine was the snowy owl, the winged warrior from the far north who came to these lands during the time of terrible winters. In the middle of the last moon Long Hand had watched while several of these white owls passed overhead, and when one in particular had settled in the top of a cottonwood, Long Hand had told Morning Swan it was a sign that he was to gain power among the Small Robes. That evening Long Hand had gone before the village council to request a party of warriors to drive the Crows and Long Knives back to the Elk River, and take horses from them.

It had seemed like a good idea then, but now Morning Swan was extremely concerned. For the past two nights her dreams had brought her visions of Long Hand with only half a body. His torso, from the navel and below, was missing and he was floating above the ground in great pain. She did not know what this meant but she had an idea his medicine had gone bad.

When Long Hand had led the warriors out of the village the white owls had been in the trees along the river—a good sign. But three suns past they had disappeared back into the north, forecasting a change of weather. It was still bitter cold now as the sun climbed over the rim of the world, but across the western sky the clouds were thin and windblown. Morning Swan knew the warm winds had started and that they would come again.

Morning Swan did not have to wait long for the appearance of Long Hand and the war party. In the glowing light of the morning they appeared on the grassy flats out from the river. They came slowly, not riding their ponies in glory and honor. As they came closer Morning Swan could see that Long Hand was doubled over his pony, barely able to ride. His medicine had indeed gone bad.

Many of the people now gathered while the warriors rode into the village. There were five bodies draped over the backs of ponies and other riders besides Long Hand who had sustained serious wounds. Four additional horses were riderless, the riders no doubt killed and not recovered. Wailing among the women began immediately, and as Morning Swan looked into the eyes of her husband, she could tell he was badly injured.

"It was the Long Knives' thundersticks," he told her as he got down from his pony and struggled through the snow toward their lodge. "Their aim was deadly. We had no chance."

"Where is your wound?" Morning Swan asked.

"It is my hip," Long Hand explained. "One of the balls went through it. I did not bleed badly but I am afraid some bone is broken loose inside."

Rosebud was awake when they got to the lodge and she asked her father what the matter was, her little eyes wide with concern. She insisted on seeing the wound and touching it. Then she leaned over her father and gave him a kiss.

"Are you going to be better soon?" she asked. There were tears in her small eyes. She was concerned that her father's face was contorted from pain.

"He will be better soon," Morning Swan said, comforting her daughter. "We must let him rest now."

Just North of St. Louis, Missouri
March 1, 1824

THE SKY WAS BREAKING LIGHT AND THANE CONTINUED TO
walk. He had been on the go most of the night, eager
to reach St. Louis. The trip down the Ohio had been a
succession of cold and miserable days on barges and
flatboats. Only the boatmen's stories of the fur trade
had broken the insane boredom.

One of them had directed Thane to this area, where
an old mountain man from the early days of the trade
had a general store. It was said he had been with
Major Andrew Henry way back in 1809 and 1810,
when the trade had suffered severe losses from the
Blackfeet Indians at the head of the Missouri River.
The old mountain man had returned with an arrowhead in his knee. The boatman had told Thane he
could tell this old trapper easily: look for Old Eli, who
hated settlements and swung a diamond willow cane
with the force of a club.

Thane continued to walk. A cold mist hung over the
river and the only sounds were birds awakening in the
trees. Thane's hair had grown to near shoulder length
and his burn was now a dark and oblong patch,
resembling a ragged birthmark. There were many who
would ask about it. They all heard a story about how

13

his farm had gone up in smoke and now he wanted to start a new life.

He looked different now, more as if he belonged on the frontier. Just out of the Blue Ridge country, he had met a farmer and his family and had traded the bay stallion for a knife and some new clothes. The farmer's wife had made them to fit—homespun cotton, loose and comfortable. He also had a broad-brimmed frontiersman's hat, which he had shaped to suit himself. He had yet to find a snowy owl feather for it.

The mist over the river began to rise with the sun. Thane heard someone's voice—a kind of singing—and saw him sitting on top of a hill. From a distance he looked like an Indian. His arms were raised skyward, his eyes steady on the streak of light in the east. The man was chanting and his voice ranged in tone from high to low. Thane stopped walking for a minute and looked to the top of the hill, thinking this had to be the old mountain man he sought.

Thane continued to watch the man at the top of the hill. This *had* to be Elias Kleinen, Old Eli, the trapper the boatman had told him about. He would surely know about any expeditions into the mountains. He might possibly even introduce him to someone going upriver, someone who needed men.

At the top of the hill, Thane stood for a time and watched while the old trapper continued chanting to the sun. There was nothing about it Thane could understand, and it reminded him of temple rituals performed by early European cultures he had read about during his educational years.

The old trapper turned to Thane and scowled.

"What might you be gawkin' at?" he asked.

His buckskins were dark from wear and a cap of otter fur lined with beads and wolf teeth held two red-tipped eagle feathers that fluttered in the morning breeze. His hair was gray as slate stone and offset a grizzled face ruffled with a beard and lined from battle against time and wind. He continued to stare at Thane through blue-gray eyes while his mouth moved in little circles.

"Don't you know better than to spoil a man's daily talk with the powers that be?" he asked Thane. He started to rise to his feet.

"I meant no offense," Thane told him, offering a hand to help him up.

The old trapper pushed Thane's hand aside and struggled to his feet. He hauled himself up with a hand-crafted diamond willow cane lined with eagle feathers and various tassels. Midway down the cane hung three locks of long black hair attached to dried skin—scalps, no doubt, from the heads of Indian warriors. When he was finally to his feet the old trapper leaned heavily on the cane and looked at Thane with narrowed eyes.

"The day's a long ways off when I can't get myself up, young feller. Nothin' grates my soul like a do-gooder. So what is it you come for?"

"Would you by chance be Elias Kleinen?"

"And what if I am?"

"I was told you might know about trips into the mountains for beaver."

"I've not been to those mountains for nigh on to fifteen years," he said. "Can't a body leave a man to rest?"

"I got off a barge a few days back," Thane explained. "One of the boatmen told me you own a trading post up here, that you've been to the mountains and know them. And maybe that you knew of some men who were headed out this spring."

The old trapper studied Thane for a time and grunted. "There's a passel who think they could go up for beaver, but I'm one who says they'll all lose their hair. Slick as that, have it skinned clean off." With surprising quickness the old trapper pulled a knife and with a twist of his wrist, turned it slicing through the air.

Thane looked at him. "I've seen a scalp or two taken before," he said. "The Blue Ridge country's not tame by any means."

The old trapper put his knife away and his thin mouth poked out of his beard. His lips were tight. "You'll travel no country with Injuns worse than the Blackfeet," he said. "The Blue Ridge is picnic grounds."

"Some would argue that," Thane said. "When your time's up you go. A man can die just once."

"But if he's to die, he'd best have other than the Blackfeet do it. They'll take a man clean past hell."

"I aim to head west," Thane said firmly. "Blackfeet or hell or whatever. I'm not looking to have anybody teach me anything about the mountains; I can take care of myself." He now looked at Eli with confidence. "You might be surprised what a young whelp like me could teach someone as seasoned as you."

The old trapper brushed his hand across in front of him as if shooing a fly. "Son, the day won't come when you can teach me a thing or two."

"Can you read or write?" Thane asked him. "Did you ever learn about continents and armies across the ocean? Or do you know the placing of the stars in the sky, their names, and when they move? Maybe there are things you've seen and wondered about and maybe I could explain some of them to you."

"School don't keep a man alive in Blackfeet country," the old trapper insisted.

Thane could see how set in his ways this old buckskinner was and there seemed little reason to argue further. "Sorry to bother you," Thane finally said. "I only thought you might know where I could sign up with somebody."

The old trapper was silent, his eyes narrowed beneath the bush of eyebrows and the mouth working through his mass of gray beard. He had noted that Thane was dressed in homespuns, but had the manners and speech of an aristocrat, one of the businessmen—mainly French and English—who were taking up residence in St. Louis and investing in the fur trade. They often went for rides in the country, but few of them had a feel for the land as this young man had.

Finally he asked Thane, "Why would you be headed to the mountains? An Eastern dandy like you, no doubt with plenty of women in fancy beds, just don't come out into country like this. Schooled and fed proper and all. Why is it the likes of you would leave the soft life?"

"I didn't ask you about your life. I just asked if you might know somebody headed out to the mountains I could hire on with."

The old trapper studied Thane for a short time longer and finally said, "You figure you could make a go of it in those mountains yonder with or without someone who's been there?"

"Without question," Thane said with a convincing nod.

"You're a long ways from proper dress and manners."

"The farther away I get, the better."

A grin sprouted through the tangle of beard. "Maybe there was a time when you was fat, but it looks like you could use a meal now."

Thane nodded. "That I could."

"Folks call me Eli," he said. He extended a weathered hand to Thane.

"Thane Thompson. Glad to know you."

Eli pointed his cane down the hill toward a cabin tucked among the trees off the main road. "That's my store. I hate the son of a bitch. I ain't no storekeeper but I'm not much good for otherwise now. I've got some work down there for you, if you've a mind to stay a day or so. I reckon a strong young bull like you could help out some. Maybe I can think of someone who needs men to go upriver."

While they walked together down the hill, Thane

noticed Eli favored his right knee heavily and wondered how he had made it out of the mountains at all.
The chance of infection must have been immense. Eli
told him he had been lucky is all. He said his luck
wasn't holding, though. There were too many outsid-
ers coming into the area around St. Louis. There were
farmers and a lot of people looking to start again. And
there were the "hangers-on," as Eli called them. These
were mostly traveling scoundrels who hoped to make
money by preaching or dealing in false cures and
remedies.

"There's a bunch that just moved in here not long
back," Eli said, "who claim to have come from God.
They want money from everybody so's they can be
saved. I've told them to get out of my store a couple of
times. They got folks around here thinking I'm an
Injun heathen. Don't know how long I can stay."

"They can't just run you out," Thane said.

Eli raised an eyebrow. "I ain't no spring chicken no
more. I can't fight like I could once, you know."

Thane got into the chores Eli laid out for him. The
afternoon went quickly and the thought of heading
into the West made Thane work that much harder.
Evening brought clouds that rolled in dark and
brought a deep rumble with them. Soon rain began to
drum on the roof of the store. Thane finished opening
some kegs of goods for Eli and the two sat down to
biscuits and bacon.

"Tell me about the mountains out there," Thane
said.

"Ah, that's some country, it is," Eli said with a nod.
"No better life. Open sky and fat buffler as far as the
eye can see. I'd be out there now if it weren't for my
knee." He popped his cane violently against a nearby
keg of apples. "Damn the Blackfeet!"

"How did it happen?" Thane asked.

"Up on the Three Forks. Heaven for Blackfeet, hell
on everyone else. A bunch of good men went under
that day. I saw him draw back his bow, never forget it.

I couldn't move fast enough." Eli pointed to his knee and used his finger as if it were a knife he meant to pry his kneecap back with. "The shaft came loose when I fell but the flint head stayed put, lodged in under. Now it'll grate there until hell turns to gold."

"Have a doctor remove it," Thane suggested.

Eli frowned. "Wagh! They'd take my leg quicker 'n you could spit. There's no white medicine for this old hoss."

Suddenly two men appeared in the doorway, both small and dressed in fine black clothes, with wide-brimmed black hats. Their approach had been muffled by the storm and Eli grunted with disgust at not having heard them. Outside the sky rumbled and the rain grew heavier on the roof while the two men shook water from their overcoats. One of them had a noticeable limp owing to the fact his left leg was shorter than his right. The other had thinning gray hair that jagged out from under his hat. There was a patch over his left eye, with a deep scar that trailed out and down his face. Without a word the patch-eyed one reached beneath his coat and drew a flintlock pistol.

Eli and Thane both lurched from their seats. The patch-eyed man told them to sit back down, that he had a sermon he wanted to make. His lone eye was squinted into a fine line and his mouth was set with the lips pursed, as if someone had sewed them shut. Thane suddenly felt cold in the pit of his stomach.

"What you two doing back here?" Eli demanded. "I thought I told you I didn't want none of your preaching."

"The Good Lord sent us back," the patch-eyed man answered. The short-legged one pulled a worn Bible from his pocket and waved it in the air. He made a strange, high-pitched sound from his mouth while he waved the Bible.

The patch-eyed one took a few steps forward and his mouth curled like a snake. His good eye settled on Eli and it grew big and round. "You, old man, are a sinner. You wear the clothes of a heathen savage. You bring back the seeds of evil from way out there in those mountains and you seek to destroy us good folks here. Your kind will spoil the righteous. You've been warned, but you've chosen to ignore our warnings. If you will give us the money we demand, we can save you. We can make you good and righteous again. Do you understand?"

Thane looked at Eli. Eli was staring coldly at the patch-eyed man. "There's the door. Go out through it, or I'll carve your guts into strips."

The short-legged one galloped up and waved the Bible again. He pulled a knife from his belt and shook it like a finger. Again came the high-pitched noise, but he did not speak. It occurred to Thane that maybe he couldn't.

The one-eyed man cleared his throat and dark anger rose in his one good eye. He waved the pistol in a little circle as he glared at Eli.

"You've got no concern for the Good Lord's wishes, do you?" he hissed. His good eye brightened with a strange, eager light. Then he looked at Thane and said, "I have little doubt you are of the same mold as this old man. You are a filthy and horrible sinner. The Lord has his ways, though, and there is but one thing you can do. You must pay us, as we asked. Then you must get on your knees and repent. Now!" In a rage he bent down toward Eli and Eli spat in his face.

Thane grabbed the keg between him and Eli and jumped to his feet. He lunged forward as the patch-eyed man's pistol spewed smoke and flame, driving the ball through the wooden slats and into the apples as Thane shoved him back and into the wall. The barrel smashed into his chest, crushing him against the logs. As the patch-eyed man struggled to breathe, Thane slammed a fist into his face and blood spewed from his nose like a geyser.

The short-legged one was just getting ready to drive his knife into Thane's back when Eli's cane cracked against his right temple, just below his hat. The little man jerked sideways and fell to the floor. He began to kick on the floor like a brain-shot dog, scattering blood that streamed from his left ear and eye socket.

Thane now had his flintlock and watched as the patch-eyed one got back on his feet. His face was a mass of red and his good eye was wide and crazed. He reached for an axe that stood nearby and Thane shot from the hip. The ball entered just above the man's left eyebrow and he dropped to his knees with his mouth open, as though someone had chopped his legs at the joints. He let out a sigh and fell face first into the floor.

The short-legged one was now up like a crazed animal that couldn't be stopped, running over kegs of goods and into walls while strange screams made their way from his contorted mouth. The left side of his face was a mass of red and he held his head at an odd angle as if he were trying to regain hearing in his left ear. He had gained incredible strength and suddenly began to tear things apart and hurl them around the room. Thane ducked a keg of apples and then a wooden box of awls that smashed into the wall and scattered like a flock of birds. Then there was an explosion in the room and Eli stepped out of the smoke of a rifle he had found. The short-legged man spun twice as if he were dancing. The last time he turned, his chest seemed to be spewing out over his fingers and he collapsed and lay still.

The room was ragged with heavy breathing and acrid smoke. Eli finally shook his head. "Can't believe the luck, no siree. This country has come to be poor doings, it has."

"It's good you had the cane," Thane remarked. "I was stupid enough not to leave my rifle within reach. What kind of rifle is that you've got?" Thane noticed how it was a stockier rifle with a shorter barrel.

Eli held up his rifle, a custom-made Edward Marshall set in dark walnut and scrimshawed along the stock and butt. There was a string of three ermine tails dangling from the upper stock and Eli caressed it like a child while he spoke.

"This here is Rachel. I might've gone under many a time without her. She's dear to me, she is." He raised a finger and his eyes lit up. "Just hold here a spell," he told Thane.

Eli disappeared in the back room of the store. Shortly he was back with another flintlock rifle. He took Thane's Kentucky-style piece from him and handed him a new rifle with the inscription *S. Hawken St. Louis* upon it.

"What's this?" Thane asked while he inspected the rifle.

"After what just happened here, I owe you more than just a good feed," Eli answered. "Them two might have put me under if you hadn't wandered out here this morning. That there is a new rifle I traded for not more than a week ago from a gunsmith in St. Louis. It's just the right medicine for the mountains."

Thane continued to study the rifle, getting the feel of it in his hands and noticing the distinct differences from his Kentucky rifle with the longer barrel and much smaller gauge. The barrel of this gun was just over thirty inches in length and a heavy 53 gauge, fitted on a half stock as opposed to his Kentucky rifle's full stock. There were other differences, including noticeably less drop in the butt stock and the need for a heavy wrist to control the blast from the barrel. The patch box was not rectangular, but oval in shape, and held more powder. This gun would certainly provide a lot of killing power.

"I thank you greatly, Eli," Thane said. "But I'm just wondering how far this piece will shoot."

"Well, distance don't count out in them mountains. Buffler and big bears is what it was made for. They don't go down with a piddly thirty-three gauge like your Kentucky, and God knows if they don't go down you will. And Blackfeet. One dose of that Hawken medicine and they'll pray to their spirits, they will."

Thane watched Eli make his way over to the door with his cracked cane and stare out into the late evening sky. The rain had stopped and a rainbow trimmed the western horizon. Eli seemed to be straining his eyes to see where the end of the colored bow fell. After a time he turned back into the store and stopped for a moment to study the two men's bodies. The patch-eyed man lay face down with a pool of blood around his head. The short-legged man had fallen so that his legs crossed and his body was twisted at the trunk, his arms outstretched. Now and then the forefinger on his right hand would twitch ever so slightly, as if there were one small ligament that refused to die. Eli stomped the hand with his heel and walked past Thane, his eyes determined. He took a skin bag from behind the counter and began to fill it with various items and goods from his store: powder and shot, knives, a few awls.

"I heard Major Henry needs more men out in the mountains," he said while he worked. "Being that's so, there'll be a boat go up before long, I'm thinking." When he had sacked up all he wanted, he turned to Thane. "A man's got to watch out for varmints of all sorts here, same as in the mountains. So I might just as well be out there where I can at least enjoy the worry."

Thane smiled. "If a man has to put up with trouble, it might as well be where it suits him."

Eli cackled. "Damn sure!" The thought of returning to the wilderness put a gleam in his eyes. His grin was wide through the gray mantle of beard. "We're headed out, we are."

Eli then ushered Thane outside while he poured kerosene fuel throughout the inside of the store, including over the two men's bodies.

"Eli, what are you doing?" Thane asked.

"I figure to leave things here the way I found them," he said. "I didn't bring nothing here and I don't figure to leave it neither."

Thane pointed to the bodies. "What about those two?"

"Ashes to ashes, and then straight to hell."

Eli lit the store and it quickly blossomed into a wall of flame and smoke that billowed up into the evening sky. He turned to Thane and they began to walk south toward St. Louis, where the expeditions for the mountains would soon be getting underway.

Eli was laughing as they walked, limping and swinging the cane at his side. He told of the high country and of Crow and Shoshone women on cold winter nights, and vast seas of buffalo. He talked of white wolves that were big medicine and huge bears that stood as high as two men. Thane listened to him, eager to learn what he could from the old trapper. He told Eli he would teach him to read and write, and anything else he might want to know. They laughed and talked as they reached the top of the hill above the burning store, and never once did either of them look back.

Part One

1824

One

THE FUR BRIGADE NUMBERED FIFTY STRONG, A WINDING formation of horses and mules and buckskinned riders twisting across hills of cured grass layered with thick frost that glistened like diamonds. Summer was gone and the wind spoke of the coming winter. Overhead, geese flew in formation; uneven V's that broke the deep blue of the sky, their voices carrying across the broad land.

Thane rode near the head of the column, his red-brown hair streaming out from under the broad-brimmed hat he favored over the skin caps worn by most of the other trappers. In the hat was a good-luck feather, a tail feather from a snowy owl, pure white with bars of black across it, that he had found two days ago, back along the Judith River. Eli had told him the white owls were a special breed that came down from the far north and only in the dead of hard winters. Good medicine.

The long journey from St. Louis out to the mountains had been largely uneventful. In Thane's mind the trip remained mainly a series of tedious days aboard a large keelboat, days that ran together with

27

blisters and sweat as he and the other hunters found themselves helping the crew of French *voyageurs* man the boat through turbulent waters of the Missouri River. As they neared the mountains and the summer progressed, the river had dropped, causing an endless succession of sandbars and shallows that snared the keelboat's bottom like gummy jaws. Thane had often helped pull by means of the *cordelle,* a long rope fastened to the bow or the lower mast that was manned by a group of workers who lined out along the shore and literally dragged the boat through the water.

There were times of low rations, and occasionally some of the *voyageurs* and hunters would desert when they lost heart in the journey. But the trip was mostly long and wearisome, days of flies and mosquitos that descended like armies, and a river that seemed to twist on ahead into forever. For a time it had seemed to Thane they would never reach the mountains. But after Fort Atkinson it had all changed, and after they'd gotten to the Plains, the land had opened up into a vast panorama unimaginable to someone whose life had never brought them there. The vast herds of buffalo had begun, and his first taste of that meat had brought him a sense of truly entering the wilderness.

The journey had taken them the entire summer and then into fall. After reaching the mouth of the Yellowstone by keelboat, they had traveled up that river to the mouth of Tongue River to meet a group of trappers employed by Andrew Henry. They had met at a large Crow Indian village containing two clans called the Whistling Water and the Greasy Mouths. These clans had separated from the main body of Crows farther upriver and there was talk of clan feuding. Eli commented to Thane that, in Cheyenne and Sioux country, it might prove fatal to the Crow.

It was Thane's first look at the nomadic Indian life in the West. He had seen the Mandan and Hidatsa villages along the Missouri below the mouth of the Yellowstone, and although they hunted buffalo from horseback, their lodges were earthen and permanent. They had gardens and hoed corn and other vegetables. The Crow people were related to the Hidatsas but, unlike their cousins, were always on the move, following game and the berry crops. During the summer they were never in one place very long. They lived in teepees, lodges with hide stretched over tree poles, made for quick takedown.

The Crow men were a majestic breed, inclined to personal showmanship and independence. Thane had never seen hair so long on men before, often trailing from their horses to the ground. They rode on saddles made of buffalo or antelope or mountain-lion skin, and painted their horses in brightly colored designs. Beads and weaponry, also painted and marked, clung to each of them. They indicated they were glad to have their white brothers come to visit, and showed their horsemanship by performing tricks and acrobatics, their long hair streaming in black ribbons as they rode.

Their village was large and filled with the barks of dogs and the yells of naked Crow children as they ran about, skirting in and out of the lodges and around the women, who worked steadily at cutting wood and drying volumes of buffalo meat. The men talked and watched the trappers become accustomed to surroundings far different than any they had ever seen.

The men on the expedition were a varied lot. Many were young and inexperienced in the wild, runaways from bondage or some other degrading form of life. They came in all sizes and attitudes. There were those who after a few weeks out had deserted, and others who had come nearly to the mountains before deciding this life was not for them. Those who now remained were happy with their decision and, with their first trapping season, were eager to learn the art of hunting beaver. Eli had made the trip well. He had carved himself another diamond willow cane and put it in continual jeapordy by striking it against trees and other hard objects while damning the Blackfeet. All he could talk about was the Blackfeet. He'd show them a thing or two.

While in the Crow village, Thane had watched while the warriors in turn talked and made sign with their hands and swished knives and war clubs through the air, as if they were angry. Thane was learning sign language from Eli and a few of the other trappers who knew it, and picked up parts of each warrior's talk—of how they had run an enemy down on their pony and struck him with a bow or a lance, yelling in his face. "They'll talk till the sun rises," Eli had told Thane. "Makin' palaver over their war deeds. They keep them stories greased up good, they do. They like to talk."

It was Thane's introduction to the cultural act of war stories: endless recountings of past battles and brave deeds. When Thane's turn to talk had come, he could think only of his homeland. So he talked of killing his first bear as a child, allowing Eli to help him with the sign as he went. There were nods and grunts of approval from the men, while the women brought boiled buffalo without end.

The Crows were Thane's first real look at a warring tribe. The trip out had brought little activity in the form of Indian encounters: once past the Omahas and the other friendly groups close to the white settlements, there had been a short standoff with a war party of Sioux out of Fort Atkinson; and a similar encounter with Assiniboins near the mouth of the Yellowstone. But in both instances the party of trappers was too large for even a skirmish and the Indians had retreated. And when Thane, during his first talk of war deeds with the Crow, had talked about Eries and Delawares and other eastern tribes, the Crow men had merely made faces and shook their heads. They had no knowledge of these people.

Thane wondered now as he traveled with the brigade how long it would be until he had a good story to tell at some campfire, one that held blood and thunder. This being Blackfoot land meant there was a chance for encounter at any time. But fighting the Blackfeet was not the priority. With the snows coming before long, it was the season to find trapping grounds. For the past week Eli had told Thane he was going to get a look at some Blackfeet soon. They were traveling the upper Missouri River country now, home to the Blackfeet, and the best beaver grounds in the mountains.

The Yellowstone River and the Crow village now lay to the south. The brigade moved at a good pace, led by Eli, who had a territory in mind for this first fall and winter hunt. Having been out in this same wilderness with Major Henry over a decade ago made Eli the natural choice to lead one of the brigades. Eli knew the territory and what to expect. And he was passing it on to Thane, though Eli was finding out that what Thane had said during their first meeting about not being a greenhorn was proving to be true. Thane Thompson was fast becoming seasoned to the mountains.

As he rode, Thane listened to the conversation of a trapper riding in front of him and one behind as they argued back and forth whether or not trade whiskey ruined your sex life. The one in front was convinced drink went straight to his groin as sort of a punishment, while the other maintained *his* punishment often showed up a few days later.

Their names were Blair and Hopkins, two who seemed to find time for every diversion. During the keelboat trip upriver these two had gone off by themselves to investigate a burial ground. They had returned shortly with a war party of Sioux close behind.

This was one of Thane's first encounters with warring Indians, and it had proved to be a lucky day for Blair and Hopkins.

The breeze, as usual, was from the west, and carried a cold bite. On both sides of him, Blair and Hopkins continued their discussion about their groins while the column wound its way through a maze of badlands ever closer to mountains the Indians called the Highwoods. As he rode, Thane worked at a soreness in his left arm, rubbing a large bruise that the cold morning had brought throbbing pain to. He had fallen from his horse a few days before while chasing a buffalo, landing on his left forearm before tumbling to a stop.

"You popped like a cork from a bottle!" Eli had told him, doubled over with laughter. "If you expect to hunt buffler, you'd best get back on that pony and learn to stick."

Thane had taken Eli's advice and spent the rest of the day, despite the pain in his arm and throughout his body, working the horse alongside running buffalo. The pony had been acquired from the Crows in trade and was trained, as all buffalo ponies were, to turn at the touch of a knee. He had more than once watched Crow horsemen run down buffalo and send them tumbling into the grass with the thrust of a lance or the expert placement of arrows. Thane felt he would need a lot of time to learn to ride like these Indians could, but he could now stay with a pony on the hunt.

As they neared the Highwoods, Thane marveled at a towering, flat-topped butte that stood by itself next to a smaller, round one. It was a landmark and was used by the Indians of the region to look out across the country below for enemies and game. The brigade would climb this butte to look for good trapping grounds.

The brigade wound its way out of the badlands and onto a large benchland that ran like a sea of autumn grass toward the rising humps of the Highwoods.

Behind Thane, Blair and Hopkins were still talking about whiskey and sex. Blair said he was glad for whiskey in the winter, as it kept his balls from freezing. Hopkins said he had been so cold the past winter that neither whiskey nor anything else had kept his balls from freezing. He added that it hadn't really bothered him, as he'd had no use for them at the time anyway.

A herd of pronghorns—the fleet creatures called antelope—stopped their grazing and turned their heads to watch the brigade pass by. There was a large buck near the middle of the herd that was nearly pure white. Blair and Hopkins stopped talking and Blair said, "Let's get that white buck. I'll find a good Crow woman with that hide." Hopkins nodded his approval and insisted he get to share the woman if he helped down the antelope.

Blair and Hopkins broke off from the brigade and the antelope turned and ran over a hill. Blair and Hopkins split then, to opposite sides of the hill, hoping one might scare the herd toward the other. The brigade continued ahead, paying the two little mind. Eli turned back on his horse and Thane heard him say to the trapper just behind him, "Them two will lose their hair if'n they don't get their brains sorted out."

The brigade moved on and Blair and Hopkins were forgotten. Once there was the distant sound of a flintlock rifle, but no one commented. The Highwoods were close now and just ahead, like a massive sentinel, was Square Butte. Thane watched eagles on their morning hunt circle across its face, their screams high and piercing. The huge butte was nothing more than an enormous pile of jumbled granite clad with evergreens. Ridges of towering spiral rock formed long walls that pushed their way up toward the sky in every direction. It was a mountain unto itself, apart from the main chain of the Highwoods, a block of trees and stone.

Eli led the brigade up a trail along the southeast

corner that twisted across the steep face. The horses
labored, their breath flaring in clouds of steam, the
saddles and gear creaking against their bulging muscles. Underfoot, rocks slipped from the trail and
bounced downward, cracking like hammers against
evergreen trunks. Partway up, the men got down from
their horses and walked. By mid-morning they had
reached the top and Thane looked out across the
largest expanse of land he had ever seen in his life.
Clearly visible were seven small mountains ranges,
and far to the west, through the clear air, was the east
face of the Rocky Mountains, what the Indians called
the Backbone-of-the-World. A small stream known as
Arrow Creek, with headwaters here, twisted out and
around the butte to stretch on northward through the
badlands. Good beaver grounds.

The top of the butte was nearly flat and mostly
covered with evergreens. Eli said it hadn't changed
since he had been up here close to twenty years before.
There were places where the trees had been cleared
and wood-framed dwellings built, war lodges used by
wandering groups of warriors when they came up to
look for enemies.

Nearby were the Highwoods, jagged humps of pine
and rock that glinted blue-green in the sun. Thane
wondered if he were standing in a dream. He looked
out from the top of the mountain, and his breath
caught in his throat. The distance was so deep and
vast that the eye could not reach it entirely, and vision
merely passed out into the far reaches like water into
mist. The horizon seemed to be at earth's end, to fall
out into another world. The sky bowed overhead like
polished sapphire, mixed with the puffy cotton of
autumn clouds. Far below, the landscape fell from
high grassy benches into the deep and varied form of
the badlands, a sea of slate gray and chocolate that
Thane saw from this height as a panorama of essentially grassless gullies and bottoms bisected by high

clay ridges that reached out like endless twisted fingers.

"Look out there," Eli said, with a weathered finger pointed out over the badlands. "They'll be all day coming up outta there."

They were a great distance out, trailing up from the Missouri River bottom and out onto an expanse of grassland. Buffalo. A herd so large that Thane realized numbers could not describe it. At first they seemed to be part of the landscape, brown and black and stretched out like a veil of autumn grass, but they moved like a swarm, slowly. Then, crossing the river, they spread out into smaller groups to graze.

"Sometimes a herd that size will take days to cross," Eli told Thane. "They wallow in the water and roll around and you'd think they was a bunch of kids at a swimmin' hole." He stood silent for a moment and watched them through his spyglass. "There's nary a man on this earth can see a sight like that without shakin' his head. No siree, that be something out there."

One of the men yelled at Eli and he put the spyglass down. The trapper had his arm extended down from the butte at a column of riders that had appeared suddenly from the deep coulees of the badlands. Eli looked through the spyglass and grunted.

"Injuns, for sure. They be Blackfeet too, or I'm a gut-shot buffler."

Eli studied them more through his spyglass and announced with a quick nod they were Piegans, who called themselves the *Pikuni*, one of the three divisions of the Blackfoot nation.

"Will they be trouble?" Thane asked.

Eli studied the Indians through the spyglass for a time longer and shrugged. "Have to wait and see. Looks to be a village on the move."

The Indians were now just below the butte, strung out over a good distance, the warriors riding in front and back and along both sides, while the women and children remained within this circle of protection. There was no doubt the band had been warned about the presence of the trappers in the area, for nearly every warrior had his eyes trained on the top of the butte. Then, from some draw, two warriors rode full speed toward the others, yelling and waving something in their hands above their heads. There was then a chorus of loud cheers from the other warriors, who gathered and circled the two. Then all raised bows and lances toward the top of the butte, screaming war cries.

The trappers began to talk among themselves and Thane asked Eli what was happening.

Eli answered while he looked through the spyglass. "I'd lay odds Blair and Hopkins lost their hair. By God, I'd say those two Blackfeet put Blair and Hopkins under."

"Jesus!" Thane stared down at the milling Piegans. "You mean they're waving scalps."

"Yeah, by God, and they're drippin' blood."

Thane shook his head.

"I told you about Blair and Hopkins," Eli continued. "Over some damned antelope. Now neither one's got any reason to worry any longer about his balls."

Eli then handed the spyglass to Thane and pointed down to the warriors. "See that Injun warrior right smack in the middle down there? Am I possessed of visions, or does his medicine shield have a red hawk painted on the front?"

Thane nodded. "Plain as day, kind of like a thunderbird. Now he's holding up both scalps."

Eli became uncomfortable. "Damn the luck, anyway! If I didn't know better, I'd think I was two years back in time right now. It was back on the Judith that I saw that same Injun for the first time. He had that same red hawk on his shield, leading a war party. We hightailed it upriver in a canoe and three days later they found us up close to the Great Falls and came at us screamin' blood. Next thing I knew I was packin' an arrow in my knee."

Thane looked at Eli. "You mean *he's* the one who shot the arrow into your knee?"

Eli was frowning. "As sure as St. Nick comes at Christmas."

This was the Small Robes band, Eli went on, whose main war chief was Rising Hawk, named in honor of his medicine—the red-tailed hawk. Thane remembered that the Crows spoke about this warrior often and how he liked to fight and count coup against his enemies. Now Thane watched as the warriors dispersed and began once again to move. Rising Hawk took his place at the head with other prominent warriors. He had secured the two scalps to his lance and was waving them proudly in the air.

The Small Robes band was a large one, with many pack animals and travois for transporting their belongings. Hide bundles of all sizes and shapes were carried by horses and dogs both. Eli's guess was they had come from a summer Sun Dance encampment somewhere to the north and were headed for the fall buffalo hunt somewhere in the area.

"Being they've got women and children with them," Eli said, "they'll likely travel on without a fight. But I'd venture that later they'll pound the drums and be back for our hair."

There was another trapper among them who had a spyglass of his own. Thane had tried to stay clear of him as much as possible. They called him Wild Jack Cutter behind his back and no one spoke much at all to his face. No one knew much about him, other than he had the look of an animal. His face was streaked along the right side with little scars, crosshatched— some said from Kiowa Indians to the south.

Implanted in the worn and scarred face was a set of marble eyes that appeared to have no feeling in them, just the appearance of sterile glass. Globs of gray-streaked dark hair protruded from under his otterskin cap, and when his mouth came open, there was revealed the absence of many teeth on the upper left side of his mouth. As he looked out with his spyglass at the group of traveling Indians, he said casually, "What say we do right by Blair and Hopkins and rub out some Blackfeet today?"

No one spoke. Finally Eli looked at him and frowned. "We came for beaver, Cutter, not to get ourselves in a scrape with no Blackfeet."

Cutter's mouth was twisted when he turned to Eli. "What's the matter, old-timer? No guts left? They all drain out of that hole in your knee?" He laughed.

Thane watched Eli think the remark over. The old trapper was too smart to get into any kind of confrontation when it was obvious there was real danger nearby. It would be better to test Cutter's sense of self-control in front of the other men.

"It appears to me," Eli told Cutter, "that your guts are where your brains ought to be. Just like Blair and Hopkins. Do you figure it's smart to jump Blackfeet when they've got their women and children along? Why don't you go down and try to get close to them and then see what they do to you."

Cutter grunted and put his spyglass back on the Indians.

"Go on down there if you want," Eli added. "Do as you please, if you have a mind to. Just don't figure on any help."

Thane watched while Cutter tried to ignore the fact that Eli had gotten the best of him. Cutter reached into a saddlebag and took a big bite off a strip of dried buffalo meat.

Thane had always wondered about this man, Wild Jack Cutter. He had wandered into the post at the mouth of the Yellowstone just before the brigade left for the Crow village. He never talked about himself, but some of the other trappers said that he had come out the year before when Major Andrew Henry and his men had met hostility from the Arikara Indians, and that he had disappeared during the fight. It was rumored he had killed a lot of Indians and trappers alike but that he had rarely ever been wounded, and then only slightly. Part ghost, is what they said, and too mean to die.

Thane watched Cutter while he eyed the Piegans through his spyglass and smirked. Then Cutter lowered the spyglass and looked around at the other trappers. "What do the rest of you say? Ain't this a pretty day for a fight?"

One other man spoke up. "I'll go, if'n you want me to, Jack."

This man wore a faded British tricorn hat that was so filthy it seemed it would soon rot into fragments and fall from his greasy hair. His eyes were dull and his mouth moved most of the time as if he were talking to himself. He had an eager look in his dull eyes and toyed with a reveille bugle, which he carried around his neck at the end of a rawhide thong. He now put it to his lips and blew an odd assortment of notes.

"Don't blow too hard, Toots," Eli commented, "or what little chunk of brain you got will like as not drain out the end of that horn."

Toots took the horn from his lips and looked at Cutter, who grunted again while he chewed on the meat.

"No sense in blowing that horn," Eli added. "Unless you and Cutter are fixin' to charge them Blackfeet."

Toots was the only man who wanted anything to do with Cutter. Toots had gotten upriver and into the mountains more by blind luck than by any wilderness skills he might have possessed. Twice during the journey he had fallen off the keelboat into the boiling Missouri, only to be saved by one of the French *voyageurs* who manned the boat. Just above the Mandan villages he was chased from the brush by a

she-grizzly protecting her cubs, and escaped death
only because he fell from a cliff in his blind panic. The
bear had been too smart to jump the ten feet down
after him and had left Toots at the bottom with only
some deep bruises and a badly sprained ankle.

His real name was Gerald Leggate. He was called
Toots from the fact that he carried the reveille bugle
around his neck and had an irritating habit of blowing
it at unusual moments, usually when everyone else
was trying to eat or sleep. During the journey upriver
into the mountains, a few of the trappers had become
so irritated at various times they had taken to pounding him with fists and sticks and the like. However, it
never seemed to faze Toots all that much. He would
just heal up and blow the horn again at some other
inappropriate time, and then cringe and wait for the
blows to come.

Toots had taken to hanging around Cutter ever
since Cutter had come into the post on the Yellowstone. Cutter needed someone to fetch his moccasins
for him and Toots worked out fine. Cutter then took to
working on Toots's head, so that his control over the
half-wit might become total and unquestioned. Toots
was afraid of the dark and Cutter quickly made use of
it by telling him stories of warring Blackfeet Indians
and how they cut their enemies to small pieces while
they were still alive. Toots's eyes would get wide and
he would have trouble sleeping. Cutter made him
understand he always had protection, just as long as
he did what he was told. Toots gladly accepted the
conditions. There were others who had come up the
river on this expedition who would not fit well at a
social gathering; it just happened that Cutter and
Toots were, respectively, at the two extremes of mean-
ness and idiocy.

When it became apparent to Cutter that he and
Toots were alone on the matter of fighting the Indians,
Cutter leaned forward across his horse and scowled,

looking down at the Piegans. He sulked that way for a time while the others watched. Toots began to toy with the bugle while his eyes remained on Cutter's back.

Thane took the eyeglass from Eli and swept the entire band before he stopped to look at a woman riding in the middle of the column. She was strikingly beautiful, with hair that trailed far down her back and a face that held a small nose and mouth. She looked up at the butte often, unaware that she was the object of Thane's fascination. She led what appeared to be a yearling colt behind her, upon which was a small girl not over three years of age. Like her mother, the small girl rode with a certain confidence; her tiny knees were dug into the colt's ribs and her heels frequently kicked the colt into a trot, at which time her mother would lift the lead rope to slow the colt down.

"You've had that glass long enough," Eli told Thane. "Let me see what kind of a woman it is that took your breath like that."

Thane heard Eli whistle and remark that if he were Thane, he would have never given up the spyglass. Some woman, is what he said, and no doubt with a mind of her own. She rode her pony with a great deal of confidence and dignity, and seemed not to show the alarm of the other women at knowing the danger of the Long Knife trappers nearby. She would be a strong one in the face of danger, Eli predicted, and a real fighter.

The Piegan band passed by and became lost in the gray hills and badlands along Arrow Creek. With them went the memories of Blair and Hopkins, now two pieces of dripping hair at the top of Rising Hawk's war lance. The Piegans felt they had won the day and were leaving in satisfaction. Their large horse herd, taken out a ways from the butte by the young men learning the trade of warriors, made dust much farther ahead. Eli joked that it would be nice to have that medicine shield with the red hawk painted on it, so that he could burn it and break the spell it seemed to have on him. While Thane laughed with the others, he noticed that Eli had taken his own comment very seriously.

"We'll nigh likely have Blackfeet on our tail most of the winter," Eli said to the group as a whole. "Those who want to break off and hunt south had best talk now."

No one spoke and Eli nodded. It was settled: it was important the matter be cleared up now, for time was of the essence. Now was the time of year to find the most productive beaver streams and prepare for the late fall trapping. Winter would slow them down and when spring arrived, there would be an intense hunt to garnish as many furs as possible and prepare them for shipment back downriver to St. Louis. Of all the areas in the Rocky Mountains, the headwaters of the Missouri River were the richest in fur. There were other areas that were filled with beaver, but they were not nearly as large. To find an area this size with consistently good beaver habitats was unusual. It was heaven for those who wished to harvest fur with a minimum of moving around. But it had its drawbacks: warring Blackfeet Indians and a history of dead trappers. Once again the area was going to be challenged by Thane and Eli and the trappers in the brigade, and this was heavy on their minds as they rode their horses back down off Square Butte and toward the streams owned by the Blackfeet.

The *shaman*'s daily visits to the lodge of Long Hand and Morning Swan were long past and it was decided that Long Hand would be permanently crippled, that the spirits had thought it fit to punish him for some reason. It was now Long Hand's concern and there was nothing anyone could do. Long Hand's war party against the Crow had come to a bad end and only Long Hand and the spirits knew the reason why. This was bad for Long Hand as it meant few would ever again follow him to fight the enemy.

Since his injury, Morning Swan had taken up Long Hand's bow and trade rifle to bring food into the lodge. Sometimes she rode with other warriors who were out hunting, and oftentimes she went alone. It always seemed to her that the men felt her out of place among them, and though only a few were rude enough to make comments to her, Morning Swan did not want to bring bad luck to those who did not want her among them. But it did not matter to Morning Swan what the villagers thought; she realized it was important to maintain the lodge and she was happy to hunt and do the work of a woman as well.

Most in the village understood her feelings, but there were those who thought it would be wise if Long Hand's older brother, Rising Hawk, provided for his brother's family. Rising Hawk had great influence among the young war chiefs of the band. He had been given his father's name and his father's medicine, the red-tailed hawk, for courage in battle. He was looked up to by all and had already become a leader to many. It would give him additional honor to care for his injured brother and the strong woman named Morning Swan. But Morning Swan would hear of no such thing and would not even tolerate the thought. Her hope was that Long Hand would someday recover. Then he could once again ride to war and to the hunt; he could again be called a contributing warrior of the people.

Aside from wanting Long Hand to save face among the people, Morning Swan knew that Rising Hawk was after the prize pony Long Hand had raised and trained from a colt. The brown pinto named Whirlwind was the fastest horse by far in the village, and the best buffalo pony as well. A source of great pride to whoever might own him. Rising Hawk had tried often to trade for the pony, and each time Long Hand had refused. Now that Long Hand's injury prevented him from participating in war and hunting, Rising Hawk reasoned his brother should now trade the horse to him. Morning Swan hoped she could someday accompany Long Hand to stand in front of Rising Hawk and announce that he would challenge him to a horse race. Rising Hawk would have to accept the challenge, knowing there was no pony among his large herd that could even stay close to Whirlwind. A day like that would bring honor back to Long Hand.

But Morning Swan and Long Hand both knew the wound would someday take his life. He had been right in worrying about chipped and broken bones in his hip region. The wound had never healed completely. It kept him up nights and drained bloody fluids onto their sleeping robes. He became more frustrated as time went on. There was nothing he could do, though he had prayed often to Sun, the Supreme Power, and to others of the spirit world, including the animal of his medicine, the black bear. He had been made to know that his wound would be with him until he performed some brave deed.

In a few days the fall hunt would begin and the warriors would travel to where a large herd of buffalo had been sighted. All were eager to gather a great supply of meat for the coming of the cold moons. After the hunt the drums of war would sound and the warriors would take their medicine ponies against the Long Knives, the white men who were coming into their lands to take the beaver from the streams. Just four suns past they had passed under the Great Butte that stands beside the Highwoods and there were a number of Long Knives watching from atop the Butte. Rising Hawk and another warrior named Runs-at-Night had been told of two Long Knives hunting antelope by a scout. Rising Hawk and Runs-at-Night had gone out to find the two Long Knives and Rising Hawk himself had killed them both. The drums of war would then have sounded against the Long Knives on

the butte as well had there not been women and
children among the men.

Now the sun had crossed the sky four times since
the day of the Long Knives on the Great Butte. The
Small Robes band was now encamped along the Big
Muddy River, the Missouri, and the camp was silent
in the dead of night. In the lodge of Long Hand and
Morning Swan the embers of their fire in the central
pit glowed and provided warmth against the chilly air.
Suspended from poles were parfleche pouches of food
and meat: pemmican, seeds, dried plants for making
broths and stews, as well as dried buffalo and elk and
deer for boiling. Morning Swan kept her cooking
implements to the left of the door and toward the
back, out of the way when visitors entered and sat
around the firepit. Long Hand's weapons were displayed in a prominent place, yet close enough to
where he slept that he might reach them easily in case
of an attack.

Rosebud lay sleeping in her small bundle of robes,
clutching a puppy that slept with her. Morning Swan
and Long Hand lay together nearby in their robes. She
could not sleep because of his moaning. She felt him
move suddenly and his body became rigid. Then he
yelled and rose from sleep.

"What is it?" Morning Swan asked.

Long Hand blinked in the dim light of the embers.
"I have had a dream," he said. "I think it is good. Do
you remember the large group of Long Knives who
watched us from the top of the Great Butte four suns
past?"

"Yes, I remember. You spoke of counting coup
against them."

"I should have gone up after them," Long Hand
said. "I have seen the face of a Long Knife in my
dream this night. Maybe he was among them."

"You would have been foolish to go alone," Morning Swan said. He talked often these days about
appeasing the spirits so that his wound might heal.

Many of his suggestions had been farfetched, but Morning Swan never once told him he was going crazy.

"The time for my honor must be soon," Long Hand told Morning Swan, his voice bordering on panic. "I am certain this dream will be the beginning of my return to honor."

"You were smart not to leave us while we were traveling," Morning Swan reassured him. "No one would have thought it wise to leave the group to fight the Long Knives. Your time of honor will come soon."

"I can sleep no longer," Long Hand said as he rose from the robes. "It is time that I found out what the dream means."

"But it is not yet light."

"Darkness is not bad for me. I must go to the mountains of the Bear Paw. I will take my finest horse. I know where the fasting place of my father is. I must regain my medicine. I do not want to leave this life now. Not when Rosebud is so young. What will you tell her?"

Morning Swan was on her feet putting wood onto the fire so that the light flared up into the lodge. It was all so sudden and she had not yet fully realized the importance of this dream. But she now understood that he would rather be dead than just half a man. She put her arms around Long Hand. "Please do not speak with a voice that is already not of this life. I cannot bear to hear it."

"I will again talk with the spirits," Long Hand said. "I will find the place of my father's dreams, beyond the river, in the mountains of the Bear Paw. I must learn what awaits me."

"Why don't you let your hip rest a while longer? You have not yet regained your strength from the journey to reach this camp."

"I do not have the time," Long Hand said. "I cannot go on the hunt the way I am. I cannot fight if war comes to our people. I am no good this way. I must go now, so that I might regain my honor soon."

Morning Swan watched him duck out of the lodge into the darkness. Rosebud came awake and asked where her father was going. "He is going away to talk to the spirits, so they will help him," she answered. Morning Swan lay awake in her robes and thought about Long Hand, while little Rosebud slept in her arms. The fire dwindled to but a few glowing coals that cast faintly dancing shadows against the walls. Outside, the wind came up and whipped and moaned; Morning Swan began to feel very empty inside. She hugged Rosebud close to her side and while the child slept soundly, fought away tears.

Long Hand was gone seven full days. While he was gone the hunt got underway and soon many of the women were out butchering and laying meat to dry for the upcoming cold season. There was now a daily run for buffalo in which warriors mounted on their best ponies would ride out in groups and herd the buffalo into circles, making it easier to confuse the animals and thus ride up and drive arrows through the thick hide and into the heart and lung region. Each day while this went on Morning Swan looked earnestly in the direction of the Bear Paw Mountains, just across the river, hoping to see Long Hand riding his swift pony into the village. Each day she became more concerned for, since receiving his wound, this was the longest he had ever been gone. Rising Hawk had told her that perhaps Long Hand had taken it upon himself to end the misery he now suffered in this life. Maybe he had journeyed into enemy lands to die a proud death. A warrior of Long Hand's previous stature could not find it within himself to exist in his condition through old age, even if the wound eventually healed.

Morning Swan saw the possibility that Rising Hawk was merely speaking his hopes, that he did not really believe Long Hand would venture into enemy lands alone. There would be no one to sing his praise to the villagers should he die with no others to see it. No, it seemed more likely that Rising Hawk was telling her that she should prepare to become his wife. And there was little doubt that Morning Swan was destined to become Rising Hawk's wife, once Long Hand passed from this earth. Tradition dictated that a brother should care for a lost brother's family in these cases. This was something Morning Swan did not want to think about. She knew she could expect pressure from her friends. There would be honor in becoming a wife to Rising Hawk, for he was certainly the most influential of all the young war chiefs within the band. He had raided for scalps and horses many times and his name struck fear in the hearts of his enemies. All of his wives wore fine skin dresses and adorned them lavishly with elk teeth from Rising Hawk's many hunts as well as many types of shells and ornaments from his frequent trade journeys.

But Morning Star had come to love Long Hand a great deal, and as his wife had come to enjoy their somewhat unique relationship. Long Hand supported her well and gave her many fine gifts, but he was not nearly as driven to honor and glory as Rising Hawk. Where Rising Hawk had to work hard for his honors, Long Hand seemed to come by them naturally. Morning Swan was well aware of the jealousy Rising Hawk had had for his brother before Long Hand's injury. Before the fight with the Crow beyond the Highwoods, Long Hand had been rising in power and influence within the Small Robes band. It was expected that soon he would count as many coup as Rising Hawk.

Now, with Long Hand gone, it was up to Morning Swan to decide how to secure meat for their lodge. This would likely be the best and only opportunity to accumulate enough dried meat to take them through the cold moons and keep their bellies full when the winds blew the snow through the village. She refused to accept offerings from anyone, especially Rising Hawk, and thanked them all for their thoughtfulness while maintaining that Long Hand would provide for his family when he returned.

As the eighth day of Long Hand's absence approached, Morning Swan got from her bed to add wood to the fire and contemplated what her life would be like in Rising Hawk's lodge. She knew with a great deal of certainty that Rising Hawk would not allow her the freedom she had come to enjoy as wife to Long Hand. There would be no more hunting and traveling from the village to work the horses, pastimes she had come to enjoy. Long Hand had gladly watched Rosebud while she was gone, something Rising Hawk would do only in times of injury or sickness. Under Rising Hawk, she would be restricted to gathering berries and wood with the other women. Her trips outside the village and her hunting excursions would end. She would do only the work of an ordinary woman.

The fire came to life again and Rosebud sat up and rubbed her eyes. "Is it morning already?" she asked.

"No, my little flower, go back to sleep. I'm just making it warm in here."

Instead of lying back down, Rosebud crawled over the robes and joined her mother at the fire.

"When is Father coming home?"

"Soon, child."

"Is he going to still be hurt when he comes back?"

Morning Swan took Rosebud in her arms and rubbed warmth into her small hands and feet. "We have to understand that Father was hurt very badly and only the One Above, the Good Father, can make him better. We have to remember that the Good Father has talked to your Father and that He might want your Father to come up and be with Him."

Rosebud looked into the fire for a moment. "Why

does the Good Father want my father to come up with him?"

"It is hard for us to understand," Morning Swan answered. "We can only know that the Good Father needs your father to be with Him."

Rosebud looked up into Morning Swan's eyes with tears running down her small cheeks. "But, Mommy, does the Good Father need him more than we do?"

Morning Swan held Rosebud tightly and rubbed the tears from the child's eyes. "The Good Father shows us many mysteries, my daughter. As you become older, you will see more and more of these mysteries for yourself. Through Sun and the forces of Thunder and the spirits, we can see His powers. He can be angry and He can be happy. We must believe that the Good Father does only that which is best for us."

Morning Swan made Rosebud some buffalo stew and they ate together before going back to bed. Sleep was fitful for both of them and the wind seemed to rise and tear at the lodge ever harder. Finally light came to the land and the wind settled into a soft breeze.

After gathering wood and water, Morning Swan began to fill a pot with the hump of a freshly killed buffalo. She had killed a buffalo two days before and now cooked this way each morning, in hopes it would bring Long Hand back to the village. She also set out a newly made pair of moccasins she had finished the day before. She placed the moccasins at the entrance to their lodge so that when he arrived, they would be the first things he would see.

Now Morning Swan sang her songs of prayer to Sun as He rose. Her greatest hope was to once again see her husband. Then, near mid-morning, a song could suddenly be heard coming from a hill just outside the village. Morning Swan rushed from the lodge with Rosebud in her arms. Sitting atop his swift pony and with his arms outstretched to the sky was Long Hand. He sang for a time before coming down the hill and getting off the pony. With a smile he kissed Morning Swan and took little Rosebud into his arms.

Though it was apparent he had neither eaten nor slept since his leaving, his eyes seemed to contain a measure of confidence that had not been there when he left. Morning Swan took it as a good omen. The villagers crowded around him, expressing their happiness that he had come back. Finally Rising Hawk appeared and greeted Long Hand, saying, "I hope the spirits have looked upon you with favor. Did the spirits of our mother and father speak to you?"

Long Hand shook his head. "Why do you ask me that? You know I did not seek to speak with the spirits of our parents."

Morning Swan knew that Rising Hawk was looking for the possibility that Long Hand had received a word or a sign from the next life indicating his death was near.

"When I have fully understood my message," Long Hand said to Rising Hawk, "I will then gladly share it with you."

Though direct eye contact was not polite, Morning Swan stared hard at Rising Hawk, hoping he understood her feelings about his remarks. She could see no kindness in the way he was acting. It was as if he wanted Long Hand to hurry up and die so that he would not have to be bothered with thinking about it any more.

"The council has been meeting for many days," Rising Hawk then said to Long Hand. "It has been decided that when the hunt is finished, the Long Knives that watched us from the Great Butte will be driven from our lands. I will lead the war party and there will be much honor for those who ride with me. Maybe, though, you are not able to come."

"I know how I will gain honor," Long Hand said to Rising Hawk, showing no signs of irritation at what Rising Hawk had just said. "I am able to ride. But

riding with you against the Long Knives is not the way
I intend to gain my own honor. That I will plan for
myself. I wish you great success against the Long
Knives."

Rising Hawk studied his brother and the beautiful
woman he had taken as his wife. Morning Swan was
proud of her husband and there seemed little reality in
thinking that she would ever want to be Rising Hawk's
wife, even when Long Hand eventually died from his
hip wound. It did not matter: when Long Hand passed
from this life, Morning Swan would have no choice
but to come to his lodge.

Morning Swan followed Long Hand to their lodge
and Rosebud hugged her father tightly as he carried
her inside. The child had missed him a great deal and
it seemed as if she intended to hold him so that he
couldn't go away and leave them again. But on her
father's face was an odd expression of mixed puzzlement and concern. "It is hard for me to understand
the dream I have had," she heard him tell her mother
after they were seated inside the lodge. "All I could
feel was wind against my face, as if I were moving very
fast. And again I saw the face of a Long Knife. It
seemed as though he was close to our age, with hair
that glinted red in the sun. His hair also blew in the
wind, as did mine, as if he too were traveling very
fast."

"Were you falling?" Morning Swan asked.

"I do not think so. I did not have the terrible feeling
of falling. It was more as if I were moving just above
the ground, very fast."

"How is your wound?"

"It feels better. There is still pain, but not as severe.
I know I can go out on the hunt with the others.
Things will be good for us."

"Yes, things will be good for us." Morning Swan
smiled. "But now you must eat. Your face is sunken
from fasting and your hands tremble from weakness.

Gain your strength back and we will talk more about what you have learned while in the Bear Paw Mountains."

Two

THE BRIGADE REMAINED *EN FORCE* SO THAT THE STRENGTH of the Blackfeet would not be a deterrent to the success of the hunt. More plews could be taken if the group split up into smaller units but their ability to hold off attacks would diminish in turn. The vision of the Blackfeet war chief, Rising Hawk, holding up the trophies of their two dead comrades remained in each man's mind.

The streams were literally alive with beaver and Thane grew more certain that the fall and following spring would bring a good hunt. They would work the area until the streams froze over and then return to the Crow village. Once the ice melted the following spring, the plan was to return and harvest beaver pelts once again.

The fall work began in earnest, though the thought of warring Blackfeet never left campfire discussions. Thane took part in keeping watch with the other trappers and, like everyone else, kept his weapons ready for use. During his spare time he set to molding a generous supply of lead balls for his rifle. Thane was one of the few carrying a new Hawken, but those who shot it were impressed and there was little doubt this gun would gain wide popularity among men who came out here to trap. There were still a great number of different custom-made rifles and many men had their own particular favorites. The reasons for their preferences varied from size and length of barrel and handling ability to construction of the firing mechanisms, among other things. Despite the vast array of rifles, there appeared to be one singular type that stood out: those with short, heavy barrels. These had shown themselves to be more portable, especially on horseback.

Thane realized that Eli's prediction of a rifle for the mountains was coming to pass. Based on the early Harper's Ferry models built for military use, the Hawken Brothers were bringing out rifles that fit the bear and buffalo hunter. Despite the drawbacks their rifles had, the gunsmiths who meant to compete with the Hawken Brothers in St. Louis were going to have to make guns which men could use to put down large game and still carry easily on a horse.

Thane spent the first week with Eli. They found the headwaters of a stream at the southern base of the Highwoods and there were beaver ponds everywhere. Eli and Thane both had a trapsack and they began to work. Thane watched Eli wade out into the shallows of a pond and place a trap into the water. He secured the trap by pushing a stout piece of branch through the ring and into the mud. The beaver would not be able to drag the trap into deep water.

Eli then uncorked a small bottle of castoreum, the beaver's own glandular secretion, and dipped a twig into the bottle. He placed the twig above the trap so that the beaver would be drawn to it and become caught in the trap. He stoppered the bottle up again and made a face.

"It takes a good mother to love a son who smells like that."

With each new day Thane gained confidence in his ability to work the streams. He traded days working with Eli and other trappers, carrying his own trapsack and setting his own lines. As the days ran deeper into fall the beaver catch grew with each successive cold night. The pelts were heavier and of good texture and the men were in good spirits. They had yet to see any sign of Blackfeet. They were likely on the fall hunt, killing buffalo for the upcoming winter months. War was a main priority, but it was important first to have a supply of meat that would last if the snow lingered.

Each night Thane would bring from his pack a small book he had picked up in St. Louis. *The Pilgrim's Progress* was a narrative that he had begun in Virginia and had never finished. Eli would watch him read at times and frown.

"I wish you'd let me teach you some words," Thane would insist.

"Wagh!" Eli would growl. "If'n I need you to learn me, I'll let you know."

Thane immersed himself in the book whenever possible and for the most part avoided the fires where the men told stories and gambled their furs away to one another. Eli, after a time, had to keep the gambling down, as it caused fighting among the men.

The trapping was even more successful than Eli had believed it could be. Nothing seemed to go wrong as day in and day out the men returned from their trap lines and stretched pelt after pelt across the circled willow hoops they used for drying. But on a clear morning Thane noticed a certain uneasiness in Eli.

"I'll wager you five pounds of beaver that we see Blackfeet in three days time or less," Eli said to Thane as they carried their traps up a stream. "I can smell trouble in the wind."

"I swear, Eli," Thane told him, "you've got those Blackfeet eating out your brain."

"Things have been too good," Eli said. "A man

shouldn't be able to just go about trappin' like this and not raise his rifle."

"Maybe we'll get lucky," Thane said. They stopped at the edge of a large beaver pond. "Maybe we'll get our fur and get out of here without trouble."

"Not likely," Eli said. He was opening a bottle of castoreum to scent a twig above a trap he had placed. He replaced the cork and pointed to a line of riders coming across the distance. He brought his spyglass up and told Thane they were carrying a Union Jack. He took the spyglass down and looked at Thane. "British," he said with a grunt. "Might as well be Blackfeet, as far as I'm concerned."

Thane watched them come down the slope and cross the river. They were a brigade from the Hudson's Bay Company, the competition. Hudson's Bay had brigades working throughout the area, and as this region was still jointly occupied territory, with no settlement as of yet between the American and British governments as to ownership, it was open trapping ground.

The brigade leader was dressed entirely in skins, with the exception of a military tricorn hat. He introduced himself as Fry and said the brigade had come out from Flathead House, a Hudson's Bay post on the other side of the Continental Divide. His men were a varied combination of Canadians and French-Cree, as well as Iroquois, Abanakee, and representatives of a number of Salishan tribes who worked for the Hudson's Bay Company. Many of them had their families with them and Thane knew, as Eli had told him earlier when they had discussed warfare etiquette in the mountains, that women and children meant they were traveling in peace and kept the fighting down when they ran into hostile Indians.

"I see you and your mates are pounding the bloody beaver," the Hudson's Bay leader said to Eli.

"Aim to keep it up too," Eli said. "We lay claim to hereabouts now."

"Ah," Fry said with a smile, "I wouldn't be so sure, mate. The land's open, you know. Only problem is the natives—the Blackfeet, you know."

Thane watched Eli study Fry closely. Maybe it was a warning. The Hudson's Bay Company was well established in Canada and had been for many years. They traded frequently with the Blackfeet. Hudson's Bay had intended to extend its territory south but was running into the American competition. As of yet the Hudson's Bay trappers had not been caught inciting the Blackfeet against the American trappers, but there were those, including Eli, who suspected it. And there was little doubt Hudson's Bay would do anything to encourage such hostilities.

"Why do you seem so sure of yourself in this country?" Eli asked Fry. "The Blackfeet like British hair as well as any."

"The Blackfeet are used to us," Fry said with a crooked smile. "They have a distinct dislike for you."

"We'll just go ahead and trap here," Eli finally said to Fry. "It figures to be a good year, Blackfeet or not."

"Could you use two more men, good men?" came a voice from behind Thane. Wild Jack Cutter elbowed his way between a pair of trappers and stood in front of Fry's horse.

Fry nodded. "Good, aye, we'd be needing the likes of as many good men as we can get. We would at that."

"I can do you good too," Toots spoke up quickly, moving to Cutter's side like a child. Cutter pushed him away and asked Fry if they had a couple of horses to spare. Two were brought forward and both Cutter and Toots mounted.

No one said a word. This was unusual. Americans rarely deserted to the Hudson's Bay Company, since the prices they paid their *engagés* were far lower by comparison. Usually it was the other way around, with Hudson's Bay people deserting to the Americans. Thane realized that Cutter just wanted no more of this brigade. The chances were good he wouldn't stay with the Hudson's Bay Company for long. This was just his chance to get out of this area and not be riding with just Toots for security.

Cutter and Toots melted into the Hudson's Bay brigade as Fry led his men back up the slope and away. Shortly they were out of sight and Eli was smiling.

"Can't say as I'll miss that orn'ry bastard none."

"No one will," Thane agreed. "And Toots is a walking disaster. He belongs with Cutter."

It was less than a week later when five riders who had been with Fry's Hudson's Bay brigade rode into camp and jumped down from their horses. Four of them were Canadians and one was Iroquois. They all spoke French fluently and the Iroquois could make himself understood in English.

"We want to be with you," the Iroquois said. "No longer good with Fry."

"Did you come back to spy on us?" Eli asked him straight out.

"No spy," the Iroquois said. "Just want work. I am Antoine Lavelle. I can work. I do not like Fry and I do not like the big man called Cutter who joined us. He killed one of my people but two days past."

"We can't do nothing about that," Eli said.

"No, I will have my own vengeance when the day is good," Lavelle said. "Work is all now. Just work. Do not have woman with me. Will not have one ever. So, no women troubles. Just work."

"Did you bring any traps and other goods with you?" Eli asked. "We've got none to spare."

Lavelle smiled. "They not want us to leave with even our guns. Then I and another go back under darkness. Yes, we have traps. Can we work?"

"If you pull one stunt," Eli warned, "you're all bait for the Blackfeet."

"No stunts," Lavelle said. "No women. Come to work. That's all."

* * *

The days began to pass like so many of the leaves that gently slipped from the trees onto the cool surface of the beaver ponds, settling like giant yellow snowflakes. Along the shores the thick patches of current, gooseberry, and wild rose took on various hues of orange and scarlet. The draws and uplands in turn displayed their seasonal coats of color as chokecherry and sarvice berry burned red in contrast with the gray, stickery shrubs they called buffalo berry.

The days grew shorter. In the evenings huge flocks of brown birds that followed the buffalo would descend into the trees amidst an uproar of their buzzlike calls, there to roost, and when dawn came began their insane noise. They swooped through the sky in formations that held tight through turns and landings, their beating wings at times blocking out the light of the sun.

"Bull birds," Eli would grumble. "Goddamnedest noisiest birds this side of a magpie. They'll hang this way until heavy snow and they'll be gone. Nary a sound in the air when they leave. A man would think he'd taken deaf. But it sure ain't that way now."

Thane was learning about this vast land, so much in contrast with the Piedmont and his memories of the Blue Ridge country. Back there the rounded hills would be rolling with the colors of autumn, solid and deep. It was different out here: with much less rain each year, thick vegetation grew only in the draws and along the stream banks. The open grasslands had only the cover of bunchgrass and sage, mixed in the salty bottoms with the off-green of greasewood. The color where the trees stood thick was striking in the clear air, especially in the morning when the early sun bathed the land in a crisp gold. Thane would look into the distance and see where the colors of red and gold melted with the green of the pines and junipers in the foothills, then stretched on to the base of the mountains and onward to timberline. And the mountains here were so big and high! Not rounded and old like back home, but jagged and strong, scraping the bottom of heaven.

It was on a day like this when Thane heard the sounds of rifles from a beaver pond just a ways ahead of him. Eli set down his traps and looked at Thane.

"What do you imagine they're shooting at?" Thane asked.

"I don't figure it to be Blackfeet," Eli said. "They would have made a show first."

Thane and Eli picked up their rifles and hurried to where a group of men were gathering at the base of a draw. There a trapper was shielding his face and head while a grizzly bear tore chunks of flesh from his back and legs. It was Antoine Lavelle. The bear had pulled Lavelle into a clump of brush and those who fired on the bear were only driving balls into his back and hind legs, making him angrier.

Thane went around and worked his way to where he could see the grizzly's head. The bear was a huge male, nearly black with tips of white and silver along his back and legs. He shook Lavelle in his jaws like a lifeless doll while Lavelle's eyes rolled wild in his head. All the while Lavelle had not said a word.

Thane moved into the brush and began to part the branches of a chokecherry for a clear shot. The grizzly saw Thane and lunged forward like a streak of black shadow. Thane fired, then dropped his Hawken and ran. He caught his buckskins on low-hanging chokecherry branches and went to his knees, ripped himself away, and began to run. The grizzly roared behind him and came through the brush as if none of it were there, spreading a wake of branches in its path that popped and flew like matchsticks.

Thane reached the base of a large tree and gripped the lower branches. Before he could pull himself up Thane felt a blow like a giant hammer knock him sideways and off his feet. His side went instantly numb and he curled into a ball as the bear sunk his teeth into his upper back. Thane heard men yelling and rifles firing, and felt the teeth grate against the bones in his shoulder.

Then the grizzly let go and turned toward the other men. Thane uncovered his face and saw the bear rise onto its hind legs, like a towering black cliff above him, and then slump forward. Thane found his legs and scrambled sideways as the bear fell in a heap to the ground where he had been lying.

The shouts of the men were slurrs and the vision of them was like morning haze. Thane lay on his back and saw the blue sky swirl overhead, a twisting blue that melted in and out of the tree branches. His shoulder was on fire and he couldn't move his arm. Eli's face came into the space in front of his eyes.

"Fightin' bears these days, are you?" Eli said, tearing away Thane's buckskin shirt to get at the wounds. "Damn, you don't figure to keep this up, I'd hope."

"How bad am I?" Thane asked.

"Can't rightly say just yet." He was sopping up blood with a poultice of grass and mud. "Do you figure anything's broke?"

Thane tried to sit up, but black spots swirled before his eyes and Eli helped him lie back down.

"Give it a little time," Eli said. "That bear cuffed you up some, he did. That white feather you got sure didn't bring you much luck this time. But you saved Lavelle's life."

Then Lavelle was there. He had crawled over and was now kneeling beside Eli, seemingly oblivious to the pain he must be feeling. The backs of both legs were torn badly and the side of his face and one arm were all blood. Thane looked at him and Lavelle was smiling through the gore.

"You give me life again," Lavelle said. He was breathing shallow and fighting for air as he spoke. "I saw the Other Side, but you brought me back."

Thane forced himself to his elbows. Here was

Lavelle, who had just been raised from the ground in the jaws of the huge grizzly, kneeling here talking. Thane stared at him. Why wasn't Lavelle closer to dead than that? Thane asked himself. Why am I lying here with a few holes in my shoulder and Lavelle is smiling with his arm half torn off? Thane forced himself to his feet, pushing Eli's hands away. The blood pounded in his head and he fought to make the black spots go away. His shoulder and left side ached badly. He stood and watched Lavelle look up at him and then saw Lavelle fall sideways, unconscious. He leaned over to help Lavelle and found himself falling as the black spots became darkness.

Morning Swan came down from the tree and stood holding her breath, waiting to see that the grizzly and her two cubs were gone. When she saw them in the distance working through a patch of *Pukkeep*, choke-cherries, she finally began to relax. The enraged grizzly sow had held her up in the tree for some time while her two cubs tore her berry bag to pieces and devoured in a short time what had taken her the entire day to gather.

She should have considered bears, especially the huge yellow rulers of the land, that they would be down in the bottoms this time of year. Morning Swan shook her head at her own stupidity for straying so far from the village and the other women. Maybe she shouldn't be quite so independent in the future, not if she meant to be successful at gathering berries in a year of shortage when bears were prowling everywhere.

Her bag had been full to overflowing. She could have used the berries to make pemmican, the rich mixture of berries and meat that was good throughout the winter and could be kept for long periods of time through the warm part of the year. Both the choke-cherry and *Okunokin*, the sarvice berry, would have been good food. Now she would have to go out tomorrow for more and take care not to meet any more bears.

And there were Long Knives to worry about as well. She remembered them at the Great Butte when the village was on the move. Rising Hawk and another warrior had killed two who'd foolishly left the main group. These men with white skin did not behave like traditional Indian enemies, such as the Crow people, who would come warring and stealing horses and looking for a fight out in the open. These Long Knives at times seemed to be without honor, shooting mostly when they had the advantage. They were unpredictable in nature, and if they discovered a lone woman there was little doubt they would take advantage of it.

There was little left of the berry bag and Morning Swan threw the pieces into a dry wash where the berries grew. She then reconsidered and decided she could possibly make use of the bottom of the pack and just sew new pieces onto it. As she picked it up from the dried stream bed an odd-shaped rock caught her eye. It was just smaller than her hand, mostly polished white and developed in three separate parts: a small front, large middle, and slightly smaller back. It was rounded across the top, the larger section, as if it were humped, and small points of dark brown, like horns, were mottled across the top of the smallest part, like a head. And the head had been pointed south, toward the Great Falls of the Big Muddy River.

Morning Swan turned the rock over and over in her hand. The longer she studied it the more fascinated she became. Could it possibly be what she was thinking it was? Was it a buffalo stone? Did it mean she had met with great favor this day? Yes, it could be nothing else! What a great and wonderful find! Her people would be glad, for it could mean that one of the village *shamans* might pray and receive a message. It could mean finding a great heard of buffalo, *Natapi Waksin*, the real food of the people. It could mean a good fall hunt.

Morning Swan hurried back to the village. It was nearly dark now and she realized how long she had been gone and how long the she-grizzly had kept her treed. She went into her lodge and found Long Hand feeding Rosebud.

"Where have you been?" Long Hand demanded.

"It has been a great day," Morning Swan said. "Look, I have found a buffalo stone!"

"Did it take you all day? And where are the berries?"

"Just look at the stone and don't worry about the berries."

Long Hand looked at the stone for a time and shrugged. "Yes, it could be. But you cannot tell for sure."

"I will take it to the *shaman* Horse-at-Night. He will know."

Morning Swan hurriedly left the lodge and found Horse-at-Night conversing with a group of warriors near a fire. One of them was telling a hunting story when Morning Swan held up the stone. They all looked closely and Horse-at-Night's eyes grew wide.

"Where did you find it?"

"In the dry wash north of the village."

Horse-at-Night looked at Morning Swan. "It is possible you have been looked upon with favor. Do you want me to take the stone and pray?"

"I do," Morning Swan answered. "I want you to see the buffalo."

"Can you tell me which way the head was pointed?"

"It was pointed south, toward the Great Falls of the Big Muddy."

That night Horse-at-Night kept the buffalo stone and when dawn came a camp crier announced that three scouts would depart at once for the Great Falls. In the passing of three suns the scouts returned and

reported that a great herd of buffalo was grazing at the
Great Falls. They were so many that the plains were
black. This was followed by a feast and Morning Swan
was singled out by Horse-at-Night for special honor.
The people danced around her and the Buffalo Dancers prayed for a successful hunt and gave thanks to
Sun that He had guided Morning Swan to the buffalo
stone. The village would move closer to the Great
Falls and there would be a great hunt.

Long Hand limped around the village watching the
dancing, and when his hip began to hurt him too
badly, he would sit down for a time. Rising Hawk
watched him from time to time and thought to
himself that his brother was having more and more
trouble. It would soon be over; Long Hand would
fester out from inside and his body would die. It
would be better for him if he would go to war and die a
proud death, if death was going to come anyway.

The villagers moved and set up camp less than a
day's journey from the Great Falls. Scouts were sent
out at regular intervals to keep watch and report of the
herd's movement. The entire village was in good
spirits, all except Long Hand, who knew he was in no
condition to ride on the hunt.

It was clear and cool the day of the hunt. The sun
rose and blanketed the land so that the buffalo stood
out like countless small black specks in the distance.
Morning Swan gathered Long Hand's bow and quiver
of arrows and got set to leave the lodge. She had spent
the early dawn hours on a hill just outside camp,
praying that the hunt might be successful and that the
buffalo would forgive the hunters for taking their
lives. She must now catch and saddle her husband's
horse and ride out with the warriors of the village.
Long Hand would remain in their lodge to care for
Rosebud while Morning Swan rode to the hunt.

Long Hand rose and grabbed Morning Swan's arm
as she prepared to leave. "I cannot bear the shame. I
cannot speak to you again, nor face my brother and

the other warriors. I would rather die in a fall from my horse than have this happen."

"You speak with little wisdom," Morning Swan said. "Your hip is getting better and yet you wish to make it bad again. In time you will be able to hunt and go to war as you did once. For now be patient and let me bring us meat for the cold moons."

Rosebud was sitting on a pile of robes fitting a tiny braided horsehair dress on a wooden doll carved from the soft trunk of a cottonwood. She rose to show her mother how well the dress fit and to thank her for making it. Morning Swan took her daughter in her arms and gave her a handful of *Sikapischis*, the white prairie aster that blooms in the fall.

"I will be gone until the sun sets," she told Rosebud. "Dress your babies with these flowers and keep your father company while I am gone."

"Are you going to get us buffalo meat?" Rosebud asked. "Even though Father doesn't want you to?"

"You don't want to go hungry this winter, do you?"

Rosebud toyed with the flowers, placing them into her doll's hair. "No," she said, "I don't want to be hungry."

"Then stay here with your father and I will return. We will have hump ribs tonight and there will be dancing."

Rosebud got down from her Morning Swan's arms and went back to the robes she had been sitting on. She found another doll and began to dress it. Then she looked up at her mother.

"You won't fall off, will you?"

"I won't fall off, Rosebud. I will be back later."

The village was a swarm of activity, with men, women, and young horse tenders scurrying about to make ready for the hunt. There was not the usual combing of hair and preparation of war shirts and moccasins. Instead, the women were dressed shabbily and, despite the frosty air, the men were nearly naked. This was not a day for fine clothes, but rather old

coverings that could be thrown away after the blood
and slime of the butchering soaked through them.

Morning Swan straightened her worn deerskin
dress as one of the horse tenders brought Whirlwind
to her, along with another horse, a dappled gray mare
Long Hand called Muddy. Morning Swan began to
saddle Whirlwind with a pad saddle of antelope hide
stuffed with grass, light and durable, a saddle that
Long Hand used solely for the hunt. Across Muddy
were tied a number of large parfleche bags and horsehair rope for tying and binding. Muddy was a good
packhorse and Morning Swan would use the small
mare to transport the meat and hide from the downed
buffalo.

With everything in place, Morning Swan made sure
that the long rawhide rope she had attached around
Whirlwind's neck was loose, yet fastened securely.
Morning Swan did not want to think of accidents, but
should she fall from Whirlwind during the hunt, this
long rope could save her life. She would grab it as she
fell and Whirlwind, as all ponies were trained to do
when they felt the pull of the rope, would stop and
allow her to mount once more.

Morning Swan, now mounted on Muddy, led
Whirlwind behind and went to where all the hunters
gathered into a long line, ready to begin the hunt.
Behind the hunters the horse tenders and women rode
and led packhorses for bringing in the meat. One of
the men's societies, the Brave Dogs, was in charge and
it was their duty to police the activities, to make sure
all who participated did their part and did nothing to
jeopardize the success of the hunt. Rising Hawk was a
distinguished member of this society and it was his
duty to give the signal for the hunt to begin. All those
on the hunt were to obey the commands of the Brave
Dogs without question. The importance of gathering a
great quantity of food did not have to be stressed, and
should a young warrior become too eager to gain
honor and scare away the herd, he could be punished

with banishment from the Small Robes band—or possibly even death.

Morning Swan took her place in the column of hunters as they all rode out from the village toward the herd. She rode Muddy and lead Whirlwind so that all his strength might be saved for the chase. The herd was yet a distance away and it was important to approach from downwind so as not to scare them. They followed the river bottom of the Big Muddy, trailing along its course, its waters now rising again with the autumn rains and early snows in the mountains. Her heart beat rapidly as she rode, for she had never been part of a large, organized hunt such as this. Always before she had gone off by herself to find small groups of buffalo and take one at a time. This day she would need to ride well and shoot her best.

They rode at a good pace. The light from the eastern sky was whole now and the land was drinking the warmth of a new day. Against the brown grass in the draws above the river the berries of the *Meenixen*, the buffalo berry, shone scarlet against their silver leaves and branches. *Mainstonita*, the blazing star, still bloomed among the cured stems of grass. It was the right time for the hunt, for the tops of *Okutsee*, the speargrass, were spread wide. It was the time of year when the cow buffalo were fattest; their meat was now the choicest. The bulls would not be killed, for spring was when their meat was prime.

Rising Hawk could be seen riding proudly with the other warriors in the Brave Dogs, moving up and down the line of warriors, reassuring them that the day would be a success and that the upcoming winter would be free of hunger. Morning Swan rode quietly, intent on her duty, and when Rising Hawk rode up beside her, she knew immediately what he was going to say.

"Why would you take your life in your hands like this?" he asked her. "These hunts are dangerous."

"I am gathering meat for our lodge, you know that."

"But you don't have to. You can—"

"You know I can ride, Rising Hawk," Morning Swan said. "And Whirlwind is the best buffalo pony among all those in the Small Robes band. I will kill many buffalo today. I have no fear."

"Why don't you just let me give you some of the buffalo I kill? I will gladly, you know."

"You are to be respected for your generosity, Rising Hawk, so why don't you offer it to someone who truly needs it."

Rising Hawk kicked his horse into a gallop and went to join the other warriors. They were approaching the herd now and turned off from the river bottom to follow a stream concealed by hills. Morning Swan had listened while the hunt was planned and she knew that even though the herd would graze all day and return to the river in late evening to drink, there was still the danger that a portion of the herd might have strung itself down into the river bottom. If one segment of the herd began to run, there was a chance they would all go.

Morning Swan's anticipation of the hunt increased as scouts dressed in buffalo hides and headdresses worked ahead of the hunters and reported on what they saw. A ways up the small stream the signal was given by Rising Hawk to begin preparation for the hunt.

Morning Swan did as the other hunters and made herself ready. She got down off Muddy and gave the reins to a nearby horse tender while she mounted Whirlwind. The pony began to prance eagerly, knowing full well what was ahead. Other warriors, Rising Hawk among them, looked on with envy as Morning Swan fitted an arrow to her bow and took her place with the other hunters.

Together, in a long, moving line, the hunters began to ascend the hill on their ponies, reining them strongly against their urge to burst forward into a run. The Brave Dogs mixed themselves into the line, encouraging the men to ride their best and bring meat in for the people. Rising Hawk once again came in alongside Morning Swan. There was a look of determination on his face.

"It is still not too late to give this up," he said.

"I have no intention of doing anything like that."

"I could stop the advance right now and have you sent back with the other women," Rising Hawk said. "I would not be accused falsely in thinking that your riding in the hunt could bring danger to the other warriors."

Morning Swan looked directly at Rising Hawk. "If you want I will raise my hand right now and when everyone stops, I will have you tell them why I am not going to hunt. Do you want me to do that? I will do it right now."

Morning Swan was ready to stop her pony and raise her hand. Rising Hawk said quickly, "No, do not do that. We are already too close to the top of the hill." He then dropped his pony back out of line and found another place among the hunters, away from Morning Swan.

As they neared the top of the hill, Morning Swan felt her heart pounding against her worn deerskin dress. She fought to keep the arrow from trembling beneath her finger, where she held it in place against the bow. She arranged the badger-hide quiver across her back so that the feathered end of the arrows would be within easy reach, yet not fall out during the run. It was very important to be well prepared for the mechanics of the hunt, and for the mental test of strength as well.

In Morning Swan's mind, she pictured herself atop an eagle with wings that would soon soar down upon its prey. She could already imagine the air tearing across her face and the ground rushing by beneath her at a blurring speed. She could see the black, shaggy bulk of the running buffalo beside her, the heavy grunting of the animal as it ran so powerfully at her

side. She could already feel it and she knew now it had
come, for the top of the hill was upon them. She let
her heart race but smiled with confidence. She saw
Rising Hawk's hand rise into the air, then fall. Then
she felt the incredible power of the horse, Whirlwind,
suddenly burst forward beneath her into a dead run.

The buffalo were a vast and scattered formation
that covered the rolling hills and flats between the
river and the Highwoods to the east. The edge of the
herd was just below them and as the wild line of
hunters surged down the hill, the buffalo lifted their
heads from grazing in unison and, with their tails
raised high in the air, bolted like black hulks of
lightning. Their speed was astounding, and it was easy
to see why the ponies best suited for the hunt must be
fast and have incredible stamina.

Morning Swan leaned forward on Whirlwind as the
pony stretched powerful legs into blinding speed,
making the blurred autumn grass beneath his feet a
haze of light brown. Her knees held tight against
muscles that bulged and worked to bring Morning
Swan into the midst of the raging black that was the
herd. The dust rose like thick brown mist and Morning Swan urged Whirlwind ahead, past the calves and
then the bulls and finally to the cows, who always ran
the fastest.

Whirlwind sped up alongside a large cow almost
pure black in color, and then slowed enough to keep
pace. The cow pressed forward, eyes rolling and
tongue hanging from its mouth like a pink rag. Morning Swan pulled back her bow and released an arrow
as the cow's front leg was forward in stride, allowing
the arrow to penetrate between the ribs and into the
heart and lung region. Whirlwind, quick and experienced, swerved out from the cow as it faltered in
stride. But the cow did not fall and it took another
arrow to drop the animal.

Morning Swan aimed her arrow under the shoulder,

to where she now knew the heart to be, and two cows in succession went down, tumbling forward and rolling in heaps of dust and thrashing legs. Both fell with but a single arrow. Morning Swan felt elated. All was going well and but for the blinding dust that formed a muddy film against her skin, the hunt was successful. She decided to go for a fourth and final cow, one colored a deep yellow, so that she could make some new clothes for Long Hand. The prized yellow hide would also be good as a part of a new lodge covering. Once again Whirlwind's mobility allowed her a close and easy shot and as her arrow was released, she shouted for joy as the yellow cow's feet gave way. She would now have plenty of meat for their lodge during the upcoming cold moons, plus extra to give away.

A ways in back of her, Morning Swan noticed Rising Hawk on his pony as he neared a large cow at the head of a group coming up from behind. His pony was closing fast on the cow and he didn't notice another group of buffalo closing in on him from the other side. Morning Swan urged Whirlwind ahead faster to get out of the way. Then she saw Rising Hawk's pony stumble.

Morning Swan turned Whirlwind out at an angle across in front of the herd, waving her arms wildly. The group of buffalo that had been coming up on Rising Hawk turned to one side and ran in another direction. Morning Swan then spun Whirlwind around in the blinding dust to try to find Rising Hawk.

The flat was a dense maze of brown air and churning buffalo. Finally, Morning Swan saw Rising Hawk running. She urged Whirlwind forward and gave Rising Hawk her hand. He pulled himself up onto Whirlwind in back of her as suddenly another group of running buffalo were upon them.

Whirlwind cut in front of the mass of buffalo and nearly made it across before being bumped hard by a bull which went out of its way to try to gore the pony. Rising Hawk was thrown clear as Whirlwind skittered, then rolled to one side. Morning Swan had nearly cleared her leg but her ankle was caught as Whirlwind's side crashed into the ground.

Morning Swan lay on her back, the sky blotted out by rising dust. The air was gone from her lungs and her right ankle felt as though it had been severed. The pain pulled her sideways and into a ball, her hand going to the injured ankle. The buffaloes' hooves pounded the earth like heavy thunder, and though she was nearly insane with the pain in her ankle, she waited for the herd to trample her. But she was far enough out from the main stream of the herd that their turning motion toward the distant flats away from the river drew them farther away from her. When the last of them had passed, Rising Hawk found her moaning and trying to regain her feet.

"You are a strong and a brave woman," Rising Hawk told her. "I owe you my life."

Rising Hawk was turning his arm in a circle to loosen the shoulder he had fallen upon. Aside from scrapes and bruises, he appeared to be unhurt. Morning Swan stood and found it impossible to put weight on her ankle. Some of the other hunters were gathering to see what had happened and Morning Swan asked that one of them bring Whirlwind to her.

She rode to the river and got off. She landed on her good foot but the movement caused considerable pain in her injured ankle. She hobbled over to the water and immersed her ankle into a deep and cool hole against a small bank. Shortly, the current numbed the pain.

Long Hand came and looked down. Rosebud jumped down from his arms and ran to her mother.

"Word reached the village that you had been killed," Long Hand said. "I told you this hunt was not a good idea."

Morning Swan looked up at him and shielded her eyes from the sun. "Then how would you have us eat when the snows come?"

"There are plenty of hunters. There are plenty of downed buffalo. We could have accepted some from someone." He then looked over to where Whirlwind stood grazing nearby. "Is my horse injured at all?"

"No," Morning Swan answered. "He's not."

"You were lucky. Why did you insist on hunting?"

Morning Swan shook her head in frustration. "You and your brother. Rising Hawk said he would hunt for us. Is that what you wish, that we receive meat from a brother that already thinks you are less than a man?"

"There are other hunters who would have gladly given us meat," Long Hand argued. "Do you think it is worth your life?"

"Well," Morning Swan said as she rose to her feet, "I have killed four buffalo and I must get them butchered before nightfall."

Long Hand took Rosebud back while Morning Swan started out toward the flats on foot.

"Aren't you going to take Whirlwind?" Long Hand asked.

Morning Swan turned for a moment. "I don't want you to worry about him, Long Hand. You take him back and have a horse tender rub him down if you want. I've got work to do."

The brigade had moved. South, through a gap in the mountains they called the Judith Crossing and onto the waters of the Musselshell. It was getting close to winter now, when the snows would come and remain until the following March or April. It had snowed twice now, wet and heavy, and had melted off the following day. The brigade had trapped a lot of beaver near the Highwoods and were harvesting a lot of fur here as well. But it was time to leave while their luck was holding out. Reports had come in that the Piegans were hunting buffalo not far away, at the Great Falls of the Missouri. When their hunt was over they would go to war. There was no use in risking lives now, not with all the furs they had taken already.

They would leave for the Yellowstone the following morning, there to meet with other brigades and likely spend the winter in the Crow village. The men were all in high spirits. Their thoughts were now on Crow women and warm nights in lodges where the wind was held back by the warmth of a smoldering fire. Winter, Eli said, was a time of leisure and storytelling. A time to be looked forward to after a hard fall of trapping.

It was now late night and Thane awoke with a start. The wind had risen and it gusted through camp, bringing a roar to the fire and a sudden surge in the flames. He wiped sweat from his face and lay back down on his good shoulder. His right one, though healing well, still ached from the holes left in it, tooth-mark souvenirs of the huge male grizzly. Beside him on the ground was the necklace Antoine Lavelle had made for him, a string of claws that meant its wearer was brave and strong.

Within minutes of going back to sleep, Thane began screaming and thrashing in his robes. Eli awoke and summoned help from the other trappers to get him calmed down. All had their rifles ready to fire, peering out into the night for Blackfeet. Soon they realized there were no Blackfeet, just Thane Thompson yelling in his sleep again.

"You have more of them damn bear dreams," Eli said. "When do you figure to get cured of them?"

Thane settled back against a tree to wipe beads of sweat from his forehead. "I just keep seeing him come at me. All teeth and frothing at the mouth. I can't shake it, Eli."

"Well, don't fret it none. It'll take some time, I'm thinkin'."

Thane got to his feet and walked away from camp

into the night. He found a small hill above the river
that broke down into a meadow below. It was up a
ways from the bottom, where the pines knit themselves into the rocks and formed a passageway of
green toward the high country above him. A herd of
elk nearby watched him for a time, and when they saw
he was going to sit still on the slope, they paid him no
more mind and went back to grazing.

Thane sat and drank in the night. The wind was
cool and whipped across the surrounding hills and
through the trees along the river. Overhead, clouds
ran past the moon like dark, billowing ghosts, and the
howling of wolves broke through the churning air like
sharp calls from the dead.

The dream about the grizzly was all Thane could
think about, and he couldn't shake the vision from his
head. He wanted to scream again. Ever since the
mauling his sleep was frequented by the nightmares, a
huge shaggy head of teeth and froth coming straight at
him. The dream was always the same: he couldn't
move or get to his feet. There was no escape. The jaws
would find him and they would lift him into the air.

Thane worked his shoulder to get some of the
stiffness out. It still ached and the cold ground always
brought a dull throbbing until the sun came once
again and warmed him up. There would be scars, a
number of them, including a long gash Eli had sewn
shut with a porcupine quill and deer sinew. Eli had
worked on Antoine Lavelle as well, closing cuts along
his neck, face, and the entire length of his left arm.
Lavelle had only partial use of the arm and was able to
raise it only partway. The last two fingers on his left
hand were without feeling, and the top muscles on his
arm seemed to twitch continually.

Compared to Lavelle's injuries, Thane considered
himself fortunate. But Lavelle smiled every day.
Lavelle had made the bear claw necklace for Thane as
a present for saving his life. Lavelle, despite the

severity of his wounds, seemed to be recovering faster
than Thane. "It's the Injun blood in him," Eli kept
telling Thane, to make him feel better. "They got
something in them that knits them up faster. You'll be
good as new once we get into the Crow camp."

The wind worked through the tops of the pines,
swaying them and bringing creaks and groans from
their trunks and branches. The clouds continued to
boil and shift in the sky, like puffs of heavy black
smoke saturated with moonlight. The wolves' calls
filtered through the wind, sounding like lost souls on
the black sea of darkness. They were thick out on the
flats, Eli said, rousing one another over the meager
scraps left them from the buffalo hunt. The Piegans
took everything, according to Eli, including the
hooves. The wolves were lucky to get the threads of
flesh on a few small bones.

Thane looked downslope and watched Eli now as he
climbed up toward him. He reached Thane finally and
puffed for a while.

"Thane, you've got to get some rest. It's a long trek
down to the Yellowstone."

A person would think the old trapper was a born
nursemaid. He had sat up many a night with Thane,
listening while Thane told him what the dreams were
like, offering advice. But there wasn't any help for a
man tortured by something in his head.

"I know the others talk when I have these spells,"
Thane said to Eli. "I just can't help it."

"Pay 'em no mind," Eli said. "You've got more
sense than any ten of 'em. No call to fret." Eli sat
down next to him and looked out into the night sky.

Thane felt himself tightening up once more. With
the bear dreams, Thane now had to face other fears
that he thought he had discarded upon getting into the
mountains. The terror of the dreams seemed to open
his mind up to the other worries that had followed
him out from the Piedmont region of Virginia. His

murdered father and his uncle, William Chapman, had come back into his mind and Thane found himself shifting his thoughts between the visions of the huge grizzly and the dark jail cell he had escaped.

Eli had proved to be a close and understanding friend. At first it had been hard for Thane to open up, but Eli would nod and point out how a man's past can sometimes haunt him endlessly. Now, as the stars shot through the rolling clouds overhead, Eli was starting to talk to him once again.

"A man's got to tell it to somebody," Eli was saying, "even if it's a tree. You know, there's a big old lonesome pine down south of here on Wind River that I came across way back when I first saw this country. That pine is so big a man can't begin to put his arms around it. That tree's seen a lot in his day, and when I had nights like this I took to sortin' things out with him. Figured nobody else was of a mind to listen and that tree was all ears."

Thane thought at first that Eli wanted him to talk to him again about his father and William Chapman and the grizzly, or whatever else, and have him get whatever it was out of his system, so that he could get on with the business of trapping. But tonight Thane was in for a surprise. Though Eli had alluded to a troubled childhood before, he had never really spoken about it. Tonight he began, and Thane realized his own past was mild by comparison. Eli talked about dreams he himself had had at one time in his younger life. Dreams about fire.

"For a long time," Eli said, "I wanted to scream whenever I saw flames jumping. Any sudden burst of fire took me back to a bad time, a real bad time."

Eli then spoke of a horrible night during his childhood when their small cabin was destroyed by flames. Eli was nine at the time and trying to recover from the news his father had given him less than a week before: he was leaving, to find work, somewhere. He would be gone a long time, but would someday return for him. Eli had awakened to flames in the cabin and had run out the door. Then came his mother close behind, carrying his little sister, Elizabeth, a little ball of fire in her arms.

Eli had been unable to move. He could not get his feet to lift from the ground. His mother was screaming as she ran with the child, and then became engulfed in flames also, like a torch in the night. They fell into the river, the two figures swirling in fire, and finally Eli ran to find them.

But the river had taken them and the night clouds had hidden the moon. He couldn't see anything and his calls had gone unanswered. They were gone and only the rush of the river had answered him. Then Eli had remembered his older brother, Joseph. Eli found Joseph just outside the burning cabin, dazed, lying back flat on the ground, his eyes staring into the night sky. Joseph was babbling, telling his mother that little Elizabeth wanted a story read to her and that he didn't mean to leave the books so close to the lantern.

"It took me a long time to get over the feelin' that I couldn't move when I saw my ma and little sis on fire like that," Eli said. "I saw them every night for a long spell. Well, clean through the years until I come across that old tree I told you about down on Wind River. He seemed to understand."

Eli went on to tell how, after the fire had destroyed their cabin, he had wanted to run somewhere, anywhere, to find his father. But his brother Joseph didn't want to go. He just wanted to loiter around the charred remains and look out across the river, as if he expected their mother and little Elizabeth to come walking out of the water.

Joseph hadn't even remembered the burial. He hadn't remembered the neighbor, with tears in his eyes, leading the two of them to the grave for the final rites. Eli had tried to get Joseph back to normal, but

Joseph never got back to normal. Finally, they were
sent to an orphanage. Only boys were allowed there, at
the edge of the woods where the trail ended. Neither
Joseph nor Eli had picked up a book since the fire and
there the teacher's instructions were enforced with a
stick and a lash. He was a small, thin man with eyes
set deep in his head over bushy eyebrows and lips that
curled inward. When a student didn't read fast
enough to suit him, he would bend his stick over his
back. Many of the students, including Eli, began to
stutter when they read. Finally, there came the day in
that place when Eli was struck with the stick and he
began to yell at the top of his lungs. The teacher had
taken his lash to quiet Eli, but Eli continued to yell.
He yelled and yelled, but not so much from the pain.
Eli told Thane that he realized now that he was
releasing some of what had been pent up within him
for so long.

The teacher, Eli continued, wouldn't stop striking
him. It was if the yelling just drove the teacher to
further madness. The other children, including Joseph, just hid their eyes. It was on that day that Eli
made his break from civilization. He struck the
teacher. He pulled the lash from the teacher's hand
and with a quick sweep of his arm, knocked out the
teacher's eye. When the other children uncovered
their eyes, they saw the teacher standing before Joseph, his hands held over his eye, blood and matter
sliding through his fingers. Then he roared at Eli, this
thin little man for whom Eli now had only contempt,
and rushed at him. Again Eli struck him in the face, in
the other eye, and Joseph had to pull him off from
beating the man to death with a chair.

"From then on it was one day after another of just
runnin'," Eli said. "Just me and Joseph, runnin' all
the time. One settlement and then another, beggin' for
food and clothes. Then we lost ourselves in the deep
woods. Kentucky it was. That's when I learned to fend

for myself. I could kill squirrels and such. We got by, me and Joseph. And then old Carmen Brown took us in. I'd tell you about her if you've a mind to listen."

Thane nodded. He was learning more this night about Eli than he had ever known previously.

"She was a good old lady, she was. Black as they come. All by herself, on the run from some whites who owned her. She gave me and Joseph a lot of good meals. She got me to read again. For a long time all I could think of when I looked at a page was that thin, little man who beat us all the time. It was none too pleasant. Then she got me over that."

"Why didn't you tell me you could read?" Thane asked.

Eli shrugged. "I can't read like you. Not many of us out here can. I learned some new readin' with Carmen Brown, but after she died I took to the road and that little man who beat us was always lookin' over my shoulder again. She used to say, 'Read for me now, y'hear! That man ain't here! No sir, I fix him good. Read now!'"

Eli explained how Carmen Brown insisted he read from the Bible each night and Eli would bargain with her: if she told him about her husband, who was a worker in the Northwest Territories during the opening of the fur trade, he would read from the Bible.

"You see," Eli explained, "it was from her I got interested in trappin'. But she sure hated that business. Old Carmen had lost her husband up in the woods and she never got over it. She must have loved that man a lot. Her face would pinch up tight when she talked about the two of them in their younger days, then how they took him away to work. He came back and told her about how he'd liked it up there. Then he went back and got himself killed by Injuns. It always made me want to leave and search my pay out. But she always said I'd be crazy to go into savage country like that and end up like her Jesse did."

Old Carmen had been a tremendous source of knowledge to both Eli and Joseph. They had learned to read and write well, in addition to gaining knowledge of numbers and charts. This had kept Eli and Joseph together. After old Carmen died, the two brothers had lost their closeness.

"Joseph read the Bible when he wasn't behind a plow," Eli recounted. "Facin' the ass of a mule and maybe preaching someday were the only two things he cared about."

Within a couple of weeks Eli had found his way to a tavern, and had returned to the farm hardly able to stand. Eli told Thane that he and Joseph then had their first real fight, and Joseph had held a Bible up to ward off Eli's fists. Taverns and women became the norm for Eli, while Joseph read the Bible and tended the farm. Eli wanted to earn enough money to get him to St. Louis, where he heard men were headed west into the wilderness. He hired out to a wealthy landlord, whom he beat severely after being cheated on wages. He then found himself in chains on a work farm.

Eli then realized he was wasting his life. On a dark night and with no money, he escaped from the work farm and set out for St. Louis without even saying goodbye to Joseph.

"Do you figure Joseph ever thinks of me?" Eli asked Thane.

"I imagine," Thane answered. "You're of the same blood."

"I got myself to St. Louis, I did," Eli said. "It's been a passel of years since I first come out to this country. I worked for a little Spaniard named Manuel Lisa. He was bound to rule this country, to take it over and wring the fur right out of it. Had a lot of dreams, he did. There were those of us who'd never seen the likes of country like this and, well, the Blackfeet done a proper job of showin' us the door out."

Thane watched Eli look through the trees into the black distance. "You going to start reading again?" Thane asked him.

"I'll let you know, young hoss, when I'm good and ready." Eli then chuckled. "We'll see. But I don't want you bein' no schoolmarm around the others. You hear?"

Thane nodded and took a breath of the wind that was still whisking through the trees. "I don't see any more bears," he told Eli. "Maybe I can sleep now."

Eli gave him a clap on the back and they returned to camp. All but those on sentry duty had gone back to sleep and, while Eli settled into his robes, Thane sat back against a tree and watched the fire lick up toward the night sky. As he always did after one of his bad dreams, he tried to put the incident with the grizzly behind him and forget it altogether. This could not happen, though, and as he so often had before, he wished that he could somehow open his head and cut out the charred fragments of this memory that brought such horrible visions to his sleep.

Since coming up the river into this wilderness, Thane had already learned a great deal about the mountains. Now that he was here, Thane knew they would hold him always. He knew there would be those times when he would ask himself why he hadn't stayed in Virginia and fought back against William Chapman, but in the end he would realize there was little to gain in owning a plantation he actually cared little about. His father had known this and, though it hadn't upset him, Thane knew he had wished, as every father does, that his son would take over.

William Chapman had ended all of that, no matter how it might have eventually turned out. Thane would always wonder if his father would have sold the land, and whether Chapman's obsession with murdering him hadn't come about because Chapman knew he would. There may never be an answer, Thane thought to himself, and just as well, for there was no reason to ever see Virginia again.

When finally he began to doze off, Thane lowered himself into his robes and looked into a windswept sky where stars blinked from holes in the racing clouds. Thane closed his eyes and thought again of the giant butte near the Highwoods and thought about the following spring, when he would return with Eli and the brigade and they would once again climb that giant rock and see all this big country.

Three

THE SUN AS IT FELL WAS A DANCING GLEAM OF GOLD OFF THE
Yellowstone, the Elk River, as the Crows called the
major flow of water that marked their homelands. The
French term was *La Roche Jaune*; and though the rock
bluffs here looked more white than yellow, Eli said the
name fit proper high up at the headwaters where the
name Colter's Hell had come to have meaning as well.

The river twisted on through the bottom of the
Yellowstone, past cottonwoods and the thick growth
of wild rose, current, gooseberry, and snowberry that
mottled the bottom with brown, gold, and fiery red.
Thane felt the land was showing its last vivid glow of
life before winter as the brigade formed a long line
that trailed down through the opening in the steep
sandstone rock cliffs that walled the valley. They rode
toward a large number of lodges that nearly filled the
bottom. From a distance fires glowed like large red
trinkets, sending smoke into the sky that held on the
evening air like low clouds.

From a high limb on a lone cottonwood, a fish hawk
scanned the river below. Thane watched the fish hawk
rise in the air, circle once, and dive like a rock toward

the water. The fish hawk rose from the river's rippling surface, a large fish twisting in its talons, and swooped back up into the cottonwood.

The Crow people had gathered to greet the coming of their white hunter brothers. They rose on their tiptoes in their excitement and began to shout and wave their arms. In the village a drummer was pounding in time to an evening song and the horses had been brought in close to the village by the young horse tenders. Crow scouts—Wolves, as they called themselves—who had come out to meet the brigade the night before and escort them into the village, were now yelling as well and waving bows and lances in the air, riding down into the village to greet their kinsmen. Eli winked and Thane watched him rub his hands together as he had the previous evening when he told Thane that, come the next night when they got to the Yellowstone, he was going to snuggle up to a sure enough warm woman.

Though Thane did not discuss it as often nor in terms as clinical as most of the other trappers, he thought about women and their absence out in this wilderness. Eli said it was just like eating: feast or famine. There would be months spent away from villages and encampments, but when the Crow women welcomed white trappers, it was with the most generous of hospitalities.

The Crow people looked every bit as colorful as the autumn vegetation along the river. All were dressed in finery and had prepared themselves for a great celebration. The word was circulating among the men of the brigade that the *Absaroka*, the Crow people, the People of the Raven—the Large-Beaked Bird—had much to celebrate about. Joined here in this camp were two bands, Where-the-Many-Lodges-Are and the Kicked-in-Their-Bellies, which had come together for the fall hunt, and the hunt had been good. Downriver, along the tributary called the Bighorn, there had been a large herd of buffalo and a great many elk, and now meat was plentiful for the upcoming cold season.

As they rode into the village, Thane was reminded of holiday festivals in Virginia, except that these people were far more highly dressed. The men, whose long hair had been combed to a deep sheen daubed on top with white clay, often with horsehair bristles and feathers implanted as well, carried decorated weaponry and were dressed in brightly painted antelope and deerskin war shirts. From their war shields hung scalps and bells and animal tails, among other ornaments. Many held buffalo robes painted with symbols of war deeds and decorated with ermine skins and tails, beads, porcupine quills, and fox tails. They wore wolf and otterskin anklets to which were attached various bells and animal tails, which dragged along the ground behind them.

The women, many with faces painted red and a streak of red through the part in the middle of their hair, wore dresses made of elk, deer, antelope, and bighorn sheep skin. Their robes were highly decorated with beads and quills, but lacked the paint decorations of the men. The young boys ran naked and wild in their own celebration, mongrel dogs of every size and color yapping at their heels, while the small girls, often dressed to imitate their mothers, preferred to stay near their parents.

The elders and prominent warriors were the first to extend formal greetings. A warrior who had gained a large following among the Where-the-Many-Lodges-Are band, called Rotten Belly, extended greetings on behalf of all his people. Rotten Belly was a main leader and, though the Kicked-in-Their-Bellies spent most of the time in the Wind River country, they were pleased to now welcome their white brothers.

Young warriors took the trappers' horses to be cared for and put out to graze. Some of the men were a bit on edge about it, as the Crows had a reputation for expert thievery. Eli finally convinced them that the festive nature of the event would be enough to deter them from stealing. A lot of compliments were given by the Crow warriors on the great many fine beaver pelts taken in the land of their enemies—the *Pikuni* Blackfeet. Some of the warriors whooped and showed scalps on their lances and war shields. The night would certainly run until dawn with stories of war deeds against the Blackfeet.

Antoine Lavelle, since his recovery from the grizzly mauling, had seemed to be Thane's own shadow. He had insisted on trapping with Thane and Eli, and often with Thane by himself. He had told Thane daily that he, Antoine, was Thane's slave to do with what he wished. Thane had avoided being alone with Antoine for there were times when Antoine would get very close to Thane and ask Thane to look at him. Thane would push him away whenever he tried to put his arms around him. Thane had tried hard to convince Antoine that he would have acted the same in stepping in to help, no matter who it was the grizzly was mauling.

There'd been times when Thane became angered and the hurt would show in Antoine's eyes. But within a matter of hours the emotional pain would be healed and he would be right back at Thane's side. Even with his handicapped arm, Antoine could work nearly as fast and as well as the other trappers, and he would often point this out to Thane and ask if he wasn't good for trapping. Thane would nod and tell Antoine over and over that he was indeed valuable to the brigade.

Thane had wanted to give the bear claw necklace back to Antoine, so there would be no question that Thane wished contact with Antoine on any other than a friendly basis. But Antoine had refused to take it back, and pointed out that the necklace meant only that Thane was a great warrior and nothing else. After a period of time, Thane had finally made Antoine

realize he wanted no more to do with him. Antoine
had still remained in the general vicinity of Thane,
but at a greater distance.

Eli had been amused. He would scowl if Antoine got
within ten feet of him, but he found it interesting that
the Iroquois trapper reacted the way he did toward
Thane. "You won't need no woman from here on," Eli
would say with a laugh. "Just think, no troubles and
fret, like with a woman. Might as well count your
blessings."

Tonight, here in the Crow village, Antoine left
Thane's side to join in the festivities. Thane saw him
with two figures dressed as women and decorated in
lavish jewelry.

"Ah!" Eli said to Thane. "Your night has been
spoiled. Antoine's found his own kind." Eli pointed to
where Antoine stood and talked, seemingly happier
now than he had ever been since joining the brigade.
The two Crows, men dressed as women, touched
Antoine's arm as he discussed the bear attack.
"*Berdaches*, they call them," Eli continued. "Men-
women, in the Crow tongue. Guess you'll just have to
find a good Crow gal now."

While Eli was still laughing at Thane, he was
greeted by a Crow warrior nearing middle age who
laughed himself with glee and hugged Eli tightly. Eli
spoke to him in Crow and introduced Thane. The
warrior immediately noticed and admired Thane's
bear claw necklace.

"You must be a strong and good warrior," the
warrior said to Thane in sign, "for my friend, The
Swimmer, knows only the finest of men."

The warrior's name was Bear-Walks-at-Night,
prominent among the Kicked-in-Their-Bellies band.
Eli explained that many years ago, when the warrior
was a young boy and Eli had been working for Manuel
Lisa, Eli had saved this man from drowning in the
Wind River. Bear-Walks-at-Night was forever grateful

to Eli and now wanted him to stay in his lodge. It would be good, Bear-Walks-at-Night made sign to Eli, if he could allow his young friend to stay also.

Thane followed Eli and Bear-Walks-at-Night to where a group of men were gathering to smoke and tell stories. They were a society called the Kit-Foxes, a distinguished group of warriors within the tribe. Thane and Eli had been given the honor of being asked to join them this night. Bear-Walks-at-Night, one of the senior members of the Foxes, as they called themselves, was to host the gathering outside his lodge. He was costumed in a war shirt made from the robe of a grizzly bear, fringed with teeth and claws, and attached to the top of his head was the hair from two white horse tails, which trailed at least two feet behind him on the ground.

While Bear-Walks-at-Night and the other men prepared for the gathering, Thane watched some of the other activities in the village. He noted with interest, in the light of the many fires around the large village, that various men's and women's societies were already dancing and playing games. To them the coming of fur brigades into the mountains was a good thing—more fighting men with whom to join against their traditional enemies: the Blackfeet, Sioux, and Cheyenne nations. As Thane had learned for himself, the Crow people were closely related to the sedentary tribes of the upper Missouri, the Hidatsa, and often visited and traded with the Hidatsa as well as the neighboring Mandans. The Crows had come to believe the encroaching white men could be of benefit to their way of life.

In many ways the Crows already showed European influence, mainly in the use of cooking utensils and toiletries in their day-to-day lives. Trade cloth, axes, kettles, awls, glass beads, iron tools, and implements of many descriptions had already become a part of their existence. It was much easier to cook in an iron kettle than boil food with hot stones placed into heavy leather pouches. Women and men alike considered themselves far more important once decorated with metal earrings and jewelry. And, Thane realized, the importance of trade rifles, iron arrowheads, and other war implements could not be overstated.

The warriors of the Kit-Fox Society took their places, seated cross-legged, in a circle, with Eli to the right of Bear-Walks-at-Night and Thane next to Eli. The pipe was passed from left to right and each man in turn, before smoking, gave homage first to the Sky, then to the Earth, and then to the four directions. When each man had smoked, Bear-Walks-at-Night turned to Eli and asked if Thane would tell them his bear story.

"Just tell it the way it happened," Eli said to Thane. "I'll come in at times and tell what I saw. And take off your shirt."

"I don't know," Thane said. "I don't know if I can do this."

"Yes, you can," Eli insisted. "Make it good. Put some power into it." Eli had his fist clenched.

Thane started to take off his shirt and hesitated. Eli jumped up and growled, "Hell's fire, there. Show them your battle scars. Big medicine. You'll be big medicine here."

Eli turned Thane so his back was to the fire. The jagged scars showed like deep black trails. The warriors voiced their approval and many got up to touch the wounds, in hopes of possibly receiving some of the power from where the bear had placed its teeth. Thane was uneasy from the beginning, asking Eli if this was all necessary. Eli continued to growl and point out to Thane how important it was to be respected among these people, so that trade relations would be at their best.

When the warriors were satisfied with their inspection of Thane's wounds and were once again seated,

Thane began to tell his story in sign language. He told how he had heard the gunfire and then went running to find Antoine Lavelle in the jaws of the grizzly. The Crow warriors were nodding and rumbling in their chests. Good stories about brave men and their battles with the grizzly were fine entertainment. Their faces glowed with the fire and smoke from the pipe swirled above their heads like thin summer clouds.

Thane went on to say how he had gone into the thick brush to fire upon the bear. Thane hesitated here, seeing the face of the grizzly as he had that day, when it rose from Antoine Lavelle to face him, its jaws all froth and blood. The small, enraged eyes were before him again, burning with hate. Thane now began to tremble. Fear gripped him as if he were staring once more at a nightmare. Things around him became a blur and he began to lose sight of Eli and the Crow warriors, whose faces showed they were now waiting for the best part of the story.

Thane put his hands to his head. He lost control as his fingers came together into fists and he slumped to his knees. His shoulders hunched up and he began to yell, low at first, then rising to a crescendo. The Crow warriors at first thought he was acting the part of the bear, whose life was ending with the balls fired from the trappers' rifles. But Eli knew it wasn't an act and came to Thane's side.

"What is it? Thane, boy, you losin' your head on me?"

Thane was rocking back and forth, his fists still clenching his hair. He had stopped yelling but was slurring his breath through his teeth in a ragged pattern. Sweat ran off his body as if he had just emerged from the river. The Crow warriors were now pointing and talking among themselves.

Eli took Thane to Bear-Walks-at-Night's lodge. There he drank a mixture of herbal brews that relaxed him and made him drowsy. He slept throughout the night and arose the next morning to find the villagers staring at him wherever he went. Eli said the Crows thought he had the bear inside of him and that they were afraid he might attack them. Throughout a number of days they watched him, and when they learned he yelled in his sleep, they were certain Thane held the grizzly within him. They began to call him Bear-Man.

That week another fur brigade came into the Crow village on the Yellowstone and with them were a number of newcomers to the mountains. The brigade was led by a Tennessean named Jethro Tipson, who gave the appearance of two men stacked one upon the other. Thane had gotten to know this man quite well during the trip upriver. He was somewhere in his mid-thirties, with experience in the mountains just after the War of 1812. He had a broad and pleasing smile that seemed to always lurk at the corners of his mouth.

Had this man been dark-complected instead of fair, his presence would have been ominous. The Crows, upon first seeing him late that summer, had bestowed upon him a long name that translated into "Tall-Laughing-Man-Stretched-to-the-Sky." So the trappers all shortened it to simply "Stretch." Stretch Tipson was well-liked as a leader and his size was enough to keep men in line. It was not his way to burden people with his philosophy of harvesting beaver, but to allow each man to pick his own style and speed.

Stretch took life as it came, and most of the time that was easy. He was remarkably even-tempered. Nothing seemed to bother him, not even alarms over bears or hostile Indians in the middle of the night. He laughed a lot and found life in general to be a pure delight. During the trip upriver, the expedition had gotten into some bad water near the mouth of White Clay Creek and the men had suffered from temporary dysentery. Jethro had commented that their condition did have its advantages: after all, there wasn't a hostile Indian anywhere who could take any honor in killing an enemy with the runs.

Stretch had brought his men into the Crow village from the upper Tongue River country, which lay south in a body of mountains the Crows called the Bighorns, named for the mountain sheep that frequented the slopes. The brigade was to have reached the village about same time as Eli's, but had been detained by an enormous herd of buffalo that were crossing the river.

Stretch had brought a note from Major Henry. Eli didn't bother to read it, but handed the note to Thane. The Major, as everyone had taken to calling him, was going to retire from the mountains. General William Ashley, his partner, was going to need the help of all the experienced trappers under his command. He wanted to try and organize everyone as much as possible for the following spring's hunt.

"I figure it to bring on a change," Stretch told Thane and Eli. "It will mean there will have to be some leaders come to the front among these men. Otherwise there won't be an organization for very long."

Eli was looking around at the hunters who had come in with Stretch in the new brigade. Most of them were young, twenty and under. They had likely never been far from home until now.

"Can any of them youngsters shoot?" Eli asked Stretch.

Stretch laughed. "Hell, most of them have a hard time with their horses. You can't expect everything."

Eli grunted and watched the young trappers as they mingled among the Crow people, sticking together, their eyes wide. They were learning, in a new land where all the rules had changed.

"I'm glad it's you who's got them kids and not me," Eli told Stretch.

Stretch shook his head, trying to hide a smile. "No, the Major told me that I was to turn them over to you as soon as we got here. I guess he figures you're a better nursemaid than me."

Eli wasn't laughing. "In a pig's ass!" Eli growled. "I'm just fool enough to be around a bunch of milk-faces is all." He shoved both Thane and Jethro. "No call to laugh, neither of you. There's nary a gray hair between the two of you neither."

"We've come to know Blackfeet sign from Sioux, though," Stretch said. "But I've got one that come up the river late with a few others who'll set you to wondering, I'll tell you."

Stretch pointed out to them a man who stood out from the others. He was a slightly built English actor from the East whose stage life had grown routine to him. The actor was dressed in skins, as were the other men, but on his head was an English cap of the type worn by Robin Hood, from under which dark hair streamed and twisted, like tangles of fine thread. His dark, flashing eyes took in everything, turning the information over within his head to be written down later in the journals that Stretch said he kept always close at hand. He had absolutely no interest in trapping beaver but instead wished for new adventures in theater and characters to portray. He knew he would certainly find them within the ranks of the fur hunters in the Rocky Mountains.

Thane noticed a white owl feather in his cap and realized it was from the tail of a snowy owl. Thane then met Sir John Preston. The two men decided to compare feathers and agreed that they were indeed identical.

"It's not often a man runs into someone else with the same lucky feather," Thane said.

Sir John smiled. "I'd say not. And I'd say as well that I've come to learn I'll not need the luck against the bloody Indians, I doubt. These men, well, they're a rowdy lot. If their horses don't put them off, then, by God, they'll shoot themselves in the foot or someone else by accident. I need armor, is what I need, not a bloody owl feather."

Thane introduced him to Eli, who studied him carefully and shook his head. The title of Sir was from nobility, John explained, though Eli scoffed and casually remarked that "Sirs" would likely lose their noble asses to the Blackfeet. John was not offended, but laughed and wrote it into his journal. He had already written a great deal since coming out.

Thane considered Sir John to be an acutely adaptable individual to be able to jump at once from starched stage costuming and fine wines to the wilderness, apparently without losing a step. His laugh was contagious and the Crows took an immediate liking to him when, during his first night in the village, he mesmerized them with selected dialogue from his favorite Shakespearean plays. Sir John worked his lean and supple body as he spoke, throwing his hands out and lifting his head to the sky, the words careful and expressive. The Crows began to pound their drums while Sir John used the middle of their village as his stage. He moved from one dramatic pose to another, reciting lines that were met with the same hushed silence that he might have expected in New York. But here it was the way he presented himself and not the words that held the Crows—the deft and sure movement, the knowledge of body language. A trade blanket served as a toga and a buffalo-horn war hat as a crown. Julius Caesar was never so interesting as here along the swift flow of the Yellowstone River.

After his coming to the village, Sir John was asked to perform every night. He graciously accepted and had more fun than any member of his audience. Before long he had taught various tribesmen how they could participate, though most of them would just nod their heads when their turn to speak came. Thane even agreed to learn various parts from selected plays, more to assist Sir John than anything else. Sir John felt he must work at his profession from time to time lest he lose his touch, and he needed someone who was willing to take the work seriously.

The work seemed to fit Thane well. The Crows were habitually calling Thane Bear-Man now and they anxiously awaited the time when Thane would grow claws from his fingers and fangs would spring from his mouth. His light complexion already reminded him of the lighter-coated great bears, and while the Crows watched him perform with Sir John they held their hands flat on the ground underneath them, ready to spring should Thane become a grizzly.

Sir John found the Crows worthy of many pages in his notebook. He wrote continuously on their appearance and daily manner. He went around the village and jotted down scenes he witnessed, and spent a lot of time around a pet raven tethered in front of a lodge. The bird was named Joker, and whenever Sir John approached he would raise the feathers on the back of his head and caw some garbled Crow words he had been taught. Thane was told that the words meant, "Cover your ugly face," something he had been taught by a young boy, the bird's owner. Sir John would lean forward and whistle shrilly at the bird, causing him to turn his head sideways and stare. These rituals were nearly as entertaining as the evening theatrical performances.

When the moon changed, the Kicked-in-Their-Bellies band announced it was time to return to the Wind River for the winter. A feast was planned, with games and dancing, so that the mountain segment of the Crow nation might go on its way in happiness. It had been a good visit.

For three full days there was constant activity. Each society presented its dances and the fall ceremonies were concluded. Horse races between the men were a frequent occurrence and the betting was heavy. Warriors also gathered to show their skill with weapons, and

competitions with bow and arrow, lance, and rifle
were held.

It was the rifle competition that drew the most
attention. Since the Crows were far more adept with
bow and arrow, they conceded the skills of rifle
marksmanship to their white brothers. Eli took charge
of the contest and measured off twenty full rods for
the contest. Trappers and some Crows in turn took
aim at small patches of bright-colored cloth mounted
on tree trunks. The entrants were quickly pruned
down to five of the best shots. Among them were Eli
and Thane.

Thane stood in line and held his Hawken in the
crook of his arm. Since coming upriver and reaching
the West, the men had all taken to naming their
pieces, and Thane decided he would call his rifle
Gulliver, for the traveler made famous by the writer
Jonathan Swift. Gulliver seemed like a fair name, as
Thane had covered a number of miles already, seeing
distant and different places, and considered himself to
be in the company of Yahoos.

When his turn came, Thane touched off and drove a
ball into a small circle of blue cloth.

"Clean as you please," Eli said upon inspection of
the shot. "But likely a lucky blink of the eye."

Eli took his turn and a small dark hole appeared
where the ball from his rifle hit. He winked at Thane.
The contest continued, and the other three men
eventually fell out of the competition as the patches of
cloth became ever smaller. At last, when Thane and
Eli remained alone, Eli moved to a fallen log and
propped a tomahawk, blade forward, against it. He
then placed two small saucers on either side of the
blade.

"You shoot first," Eli told Thane. He placed his
thumb on the edge of the tomahawk as he spoke.
"You've got to split your ball against here, so that the
two halves break the plates on each side."

The onlookers nodded and murmured their approval. It was a good test of skill, especially at twenty paces. The trappers and the Crow warriors began to place bets. Eli looked at Thane and asked, "What do you plan to put up?"

"I've got the pelts of thirty good beaver," Thane said quickly. "Will you see that bet?"

Eli rolled his eyes. "Cocky young buck, I'd say. Ah, but this old hoss has the steadier hand. Done!"

Thane took a breath and steadied his arm as he held Gulliver in line with the tomahawk, placing the front sight tight along the blade. He squeezed off and heard cheers arise. Through the smoke he saw the two shattered plates. He grinned at Eli.

Eli grumbled and took aim. His grizzled jaw was set tight and his wrinkled hands held the stock of his rifle as if they had been carved from the wood itself. The blast sounded and the two plates fell away into pieces. More cheering arose.

"What say we step back five paces?" Eli challenged.

Thane nodded. "Make it easy on yourself."

Thane fired and this time heard moans from the onlookers. The ball had hit the edge of the tomahawk, but not enough to break both plates. One was in pieces and the other still intact. Thane stepped aside and watched Eli calmly lower the barrel of his rifle and shatter both plates. Cheering arose and Eli turned to Thane.

"Young buck, you're now shy of thirty beaver plews."

Thane put his rifle into the crook of his arm and fidgeted with embarrassment. The eyes of the onlookers were upon him and most were silent, waiting to see what he would do. Finally Thane looked at Eli and made a proposition.

"This doesn't appear to be my day to shoot," he said, "but I'll make another wager with you. Double or nothing against what you have just won from me."

"What might that be?" Eli asked.

"I propose," Thane said, "to go north to the Great Falls of the Missouri River and come back with that hawk medicine shield. The one that belongs to that Piegan Rising Hawk."

Murmurs of excitement and approval for Thane's courage rose among the onlookers. Eli studied Thane.

"You figure to go up to the Piegans and get Rising Hawk's medicine shield?" he asked. "And bring it back down here?"

Thane nodded. "Then it is yours to do with what you wish."

"Ah! You don't aim to do that. Them Piegan will butcher you."

"Not if they don't see me."

Eli looked at the men who were now crowding close to hear what was being said. Many were shouting words of encouragement and all wanted Eli to take the bet. Thane knew Eli could hardly refuse.

"I don't want to think I'll see your hair on a Piegan coup stick," Eli said to Thane. "I'd feel powerful bad to think I'd caused that."

Thane refused to back down. "You aren't causing anything, Eli. It was I who made the offer. I'm just betting I'll get the medicine shield and sixty plews of your beaver to boot. If I fail, you've got my whole catch. What do you say?"

Eli thought it over while the men urged him to take the bet. Finally he nodded.

"I'll go the bet with you," he said. "But don't expect tears from me if'n you don't make it back."

Square Butte, the large flat-topped mountain the Indians called the Great Butte, was behind them now. Three days out of the Crow village, Thane sat in the early light of dawn with the war party, preparing for the raid on the Piegan village. The warriors were all nearly naked and carried bows and knives; a few were

armed with trade rifles. The thundersticks, brought by
the white traders, were still not preferred over traditional weaponry.

Thane watched them prepare for war, the thirty-
odd warriors and just under a dozen younger horse
tenders learning the ways of battle away from home. It
would be a raid and not an all-out challenge against
the Piegan camp. The Piegans were too many and too
strong for direct confrontation. Instead, this would be
a test of stealth and bravery, of the ability of each
warrior to obtain horses and enemy scalps by surprise.
The most dangerous part of the mission would be to
escape with the stolen horses.

While Thane waited for the warriors to get ready to
depart, he worked his shoulder with his left hand, as
he did almost every morning and sometimes during
the day, trying to ease the dull, throbbing ache that
was now a routine part of his day. The warriors
watched him squeezing the muscles and rotating his
arm, talking among themselves. Thane knew they felt
he was invoking the power of the grizzly that had
attacked him, which was now personified within him
as a result of the scars on his shoulder. But for Thane
it was a source of discomfort. When would it ever
heal? He wondered if there were still infection deep
inside somewhere. There was little good in dwelling
on it now; the Piegans were encamped down along the
river and the raid against them would soon commence.

Daybreak had arrived and soon it would be time to
make the silent advance upon the village. Crow scouts
had already taken note that there seemed to be an
absence of Piegan scouts in the hills. Perhaps they felt
that since the village was so large, there was little need
to worry about an attack.

The light continued to grow from the east and
brought with it a light wind. It was an odd wind, for it
was warm. Light and warm and unexplainable except

that it was there and could be felt. The Crow warriors put their hands into the air to feel the breeze and looked at one another. Thane, not yet knowing the usual weather in this country, saw little to be alarmed about.

Now, in the west, a strange thing was occurring. The light in the sky had reached the mountains and an odd sight was revealed. The Crow warriors watched it and held their hands over their mouths. Thane watched it and grew fascinated. Lightning. In late fall. Streaks came down from the sky, through dark clouds, and the rumble of distant thunder broke the quiet.

Bear-Walks-at-Night, the leading war chief and pipe carrier, looked up from his hand-held mirror. He had been painting his face for war. He looked into the west with the other warriors and his face grew solemn. From somewhere deep in the badlands came the howls of wolves. Some of the warriors began to chant, looking into the sky.

"The warriors talk to their spirit helpers," Bear-Walks-at-Night explained to Thane. "The storm is a bad omen. We will turn back and leave the Piegan lands now."

"But I must have Rising Hawk's medicine shield," Thane said.

Bear-Walks-at-Night pointed to the west. "The sky is black. Our medicine is bad. We must go back."

Thane noted the serious intent in Bear-Walks-at-Night's voice. Thoughts of horse stealing and possibly gaining scalps were now out of his mind. He seemingly had forgotten everything he had told Thane during their journey up here, including that a small daughter of his had been taken during the raid by the Piegans in the past. The little girl would surely be a woman now, Bear-Walks-at-Night had said. Her name had been Morning Swan.

"My medicine is good," Thane said. "I do not fear the storm."

Bear-Walks-at-Night shook his head. "There is no power greater than the storm. You are foolish to think that."

The warriors began to dress themselves, still chanting to their spirit helpers. They had come to fight alongside Thane and gain honor by taking scalps and horses. They had not expected the spirits to be angry. It could mean the loss of many warriors if they went ahead with their plan.

Thane did not want to think about going back without the medicine shield. Not only would the other trappers laugh at him for not even trying, but he would loose a number of hard-earned beaver plews to Eli. Though his shoulder was throbbing, Thane decided he would complete the mission he had started.

"Don't go all the way back to the Yellowstone," Thane said to Bear-Walks-at-Night. "Wait for me. I am going into the village."

"You are foolish," Bear-Walks-at-Night told Thane. "It is not important to show courage when you know your life will be ended."

"I need that medicine shield," Thane explained. "I will sneak into the village and take the shield. Then I will rejoin you."

"We cannot take the chance of being spotted if they send out scouts," Bear-Walks-at-Night said. "We must go back."

"Travel to where we cross the waters of the Musselshell," Thane said. He held up a finger. "Give me one day. If I do not meet you there by this time tomorrow, you can all leave and consider me foolish for what I have done."

Bear-Walks-at-Night conferred with some of the other warriors. He finally returned to Thane and nodded. "One sun's passing. If you do not meet us down on the waters of the Musselshell by then, we will paint our faces black and sing the song of the dead for you."

Thane left Gulliver, his rifle, with Bear-Walks-at-

Night. It would do him little good if he were to fail in his quest for the shield and be captured by the Piegans. And it would only slow him down. He would need only his knife and one good horse. He would also need an incredible amount of luck, he decided, as he would be alone and there would be no other source of diversion for him while he sought out Rising Hawk's medicine shield. He would have to work quickly and it would have to happen today, this morning, or he would be lucky to get away with his life.

Facing the storm that pushed over the mountains and down toward the river, Thane set out for the Piegan village. Behind him the Crow warriors put their war articles away in the bags they had brought them in and mounted, losing themselves in the gray and brown of the Missouri River bottomland. Thane did not turn to see them leave, nor did he watch them disappear from view, leaving him alone. Had he looked after them, even for a second, he might have turned back to join them. He might have felt a great understanding of their fear of the storm.

It was spitting rain now, little drops spread by the wind that crossed the valley and were whisked into nothingness. They were cool and soft and refreshing, not unlike the first storm of spring, which now served only to confuse the senses and deceive the mind into thinking that nothing in this country ever followed a pattern. Nothing could ever be considered final here, except perhaps the way in which the Crows made their decisions. Nothing was more important than the well-being of the group as a whole and the warriors, to preserve themselves for a better day for war, had left thinking him a fool whose scalp would be taken before the sun was very old.

The storm crossed quickly and the rain served only to moisten the air and bring a soothing dampness to the late fall grass. The lightning was gone, a freak of the early day, and nothing more would come of it. Thane watched the dark clouds part and go their own

way, leaving the sky open and clear to a distance no
man could fatham. The sudden warm wind remained,
now a calm breeze that carried a broad V of geese
across the sky above the river. Farther out in the sky
two more flocks winged through, honking and waver-
ing in and out of formation as if they were on an
unseen string.

The storm left the land fresh and alive. The heavy
musk of sage and juniper filled every draw, and when
he left his horse tied in the brush along the river, the
sweetness of decaying fall leaves arose from the damp,
wooded floor. A meadowlark hopped through linger-
ing blades of cured grass and took flight, yellow breast
flashing with a glint of sunshine. Thane smiled. Eli
had said to watch that bird in the late fall. The
meadowlark knew when the real cold was coming to
stay. He could handle the early snows, huddled under
a sage or under the trunk of a fallen tree, but when the
real storms reached the horizon, the meadowlark took
wing and was gone. Gone to the south, where he
would wait until the soft snows of late spring brought
him back to sing in the summer.

Thane opened a vial of dog urine and covered his
face and hands. His buckskins already smelled of
wood and food and grease and now there was no
worry that the camp dogs would detect him. Next he
covered his exposed skin with black earth, mixing it
with grease as Eli had shown him. He worked his way
along the bottom, staying low within the dense stands
of willow and young cottonwood that had colonized
themselves in thick groups. It was a wide bottom that
sprouted life from every square foot of black earth.
Most of the cottonwoods were as big around as his
arms and never any larger than his legs, though they
reached up high in places. They were all young trees,
much the same as Thane had noticed along all the
water courses. Except for areas frequented by Indians,
such as the Crow encampment down along the Yellowstone, there were never any large old trees. Eli said

it was the beaver chewing them down and the buffalo
rubbing them that kept the trees out here from
reaching maturity.

The sounds of the waking village were strong in
Thane's ears as he took position in a heavy stand of
willows and peered out. Women in scattered groups
were making their way to the river for water. Others
carried loads of firewood. A short distance away three
warriors were in the river bathing. Smoke was rising
from cooking fires and the Piegans for the most part
were enjoying an early meal.

Thane crept closer to the edge of the village. He
looked at the lodges, clustered in groups all along the
edge of the river. He moved slowly and with great
caution, prostrating himself in the cover of the dense
growth whenever groups of women or men, or yelling
children and barking dogs, passed along the trails to
and from the water.

Toward the center of the village Thane saw a lodge
painted with the forms of running buffalo. Tethered in
front of the lodge was a large brown pinto. A war
shield hung suspended from a pole near the door flap.
Rising Hawk's war shield, Thane knew, because of the
bright red thunderhawk on its front. He stayed low
while the three men who had been bathing in the river
went past. One of them limped badly and the other
two walked ahead of him, speaking and waving their
arms around. The limping warrior stopped for a time
to rest. His breathing was labored with the strain of
pain and he worked his hands on his hip, in much the
same fashion Thane worked his injured shoulder.

Thane held his breath. If he moved even an inch the
warrior would spot him. Shortly the warrior moved
on, limping and talking to himself. Thane took a deep
breath to steady his nerves. He worked his way
through the willows to their edge, where he planned to
jump and rush for the horse. He took his knife from
his belt and coiled himself.

He was ready to spring when a small girl walked

seemingly out of nowhere with a bowl of stew in her hand. She was eating while she walked, spooning broth into her mouth and spilling it down her front. Again Thane tried to still himself but the small girl caught his movement and her little black eyes stared at him.

Thane looked back at the little girl, and though he wanted to rise and run the other way, he didn't move. The little girl, her face smeared with broth, began to laugh. A hiding game, she must have thought. Thane remained still while the little girl laughed more and came toward him. She reached in her bowl of broth with the spoon and offered it to Thane, who opened his mouth while the little girl pushed the spoon in.

Thane swallowed and the little girl laughed. She filled another spoon and fed Thane once again. From somewhere behind came the sound of a woman's voice and the little girl turned and said something. Thane slid back down into the willows as the woman, the long-haired beauty Thane had seen through the spyglass from the top of the butte, came over and took the little girl by the hand. She seemed to be favoring one leg slightly, as if she had injured an ankle. The little girl held back and pointed with her spoon, laughing. The beautiful Indian woman, her long black hair spilling down across her back, stopped and looked into the willows.

Thane crouched as low as possible. He could see her eyes as the woman peered into the willows. She spoke to the little girl and the little girl kept pointing, pulling her mother's hand to come nearer the willows. But the woman held the little girl back. She finally picked the little girl up in her arms and turned back toward the lodges, looking over her shoulder. Thane could not tell whether or not she had detected him, but the little girl was struggling to get free from her arms, unhappy that the game had ended.

There was no time to waste, Thane realized, and jumped immediately from his position in the willows and sprinted toward the tethered pony. He took the war shield from the pole and with his knife quickly cut the tether and jumped on the pony's back, while women and men alike stared and held their hands over their mouths.

The beautiful woman with the little girl in her arms was a blur now as Thane rushed past on the pony, running full speed through a maze of barking dogs and yelling people, including warriors who were gathering their weapons and running for their own horses. He kicked the pony into a dead run across the flats above the river, toward the Highwood Mountains that jutted sharply into the morning sky.

Four

THE PONY WAS SWIFT AND CARRIED HIM OUT AND BEYOND the village. The war shield bounced against his leg as the distance widened and the mountains loomed ever closer. Thane was sure he had outdistanced the Piegan horses when there appeared one paint pony that came up from behind like the wind. Its rider was the limping warrior that Thane had watched catch his breath earlier. There was little Thane could do but kick his pony harder and watch the Piegan behind him ride low over his horse as the distance between them was gradually churned down to nothing.

Thane used his knee to turn his pony and swung out from the pursuing horse and rider. But the warrior's horse turned even more sharply and soon the warrior was fitting an arrow to his bow as his pony started to pull alongside. Thane pulled at the war shield tied to the saddle until it finally loosened and came free. The warrior was nearly beside him, so confident of his own pony that he was waiting for a clean shot.

Again Thane turned his pony and again the warrior's horse stuck with them, holding fast to its speed so that its rider might shoot the bow. In desperation,

Thane put his horse through a series of maneuvers to try to shake his pursuer, but there was nothing he could make his horse do that the other pony couldn't do better. They were two riders on two ponies nearly abreast, zigzagging across the grasslands at high speed, the ponies surging forward with their legs churning the autumn ground like heavy hammers.

The warrior shot an arrow and Thane felt it slam into the war shield with the power of a large stone. The arrow hit a glancing blow and shot off into the air. His arm went numb but he held onto the shield and turned his pony as the second arrow came and sliced through the upper part of his thigh. Blood spurted like splashed water and a fire welled up that brought a dizziness to him. He felt his pony slow down as he nearly lost control and fell, waiting for the final, fatal arrow to come.

But the warrior had fallen from his pony and lay twisted on the ground, writhing and holding his hip. He was chanting in a loud voice, a high call that sounded not unlike a keening for the dead. His pony, the swift pinto, stood beside him, its sides heaving for air. In the near distance a cloud of dust signaled the coming of other Piegan warriors. Thane turned his pony, holding tight to keep from falling, and rode for the bottomland along a nearby creek.

As he rode into the bottom, Thane realized he knew this creek. The wide-open bottom, filled with beaver dams and lodged with young aspens, was where he had spent the early fall trapping with Eli and the rest of the brigade. Just a ways up from where he had been mauled by the grizzly. He knew he was getting weaker with each moment from loss of blood and would not be able to stay on the horse much longer. It would be better to abandon the horse and take his chances hiding.

Thane lowered himself from the pony and grimaced at the pain in his leg. He held fast to the medicine shield and gave the pony a swat on the rump. The horse trotted out of the bottom and on toward where Thane could hear oncoming warriors. They would be over the brow of the hill in little time, and Thane knew he must now depend solely on his ability to endure cold water.

Beaver slapped their tales against the still ponds and dove under as Thane waded out from shore toward a heavy clump of red willow. The grove was on the edge of deep water and would afford him a tight and secure hiding place. The water was freezing cold and numbed him immediately as he waded to the willows, took a breath, and submerged himself.

He came up through the tangled willow grove and hung his arms over the lower trunks, securing the medicine shield next to him. The growth was so thick and tight that it was impossible to see out. The Piegan warriors were in the bottom now, shouting to one another from various locations while they searched for him. He heard dogs. They barked and howled and made any number of noises, but they would never sense him with the mask of water.

Though he ached all over now from the freezing cold that threatened to make him chatter his teeth from his head, Thane knew that to move could mean death. If he tried to raise up or lower himself, either one, the rustle of the willows would give him away. The warriors continued to search in earnest now as the afternoon wore on. They were persistent, for they knew Thane was somewhere in the bottom. He was good at hiding. Perhaps if they gave him enough time, he would make a mistake.

Finally, when Thane felt he could stand it no longer, he rearranged his position. It was late in the afternoon and the sun was down behind the brow of the hills above the bottom. He listened and waited. It had been some time since he had heard the warriors' voices but that didn't mean they were gone. One or two might have remained behind to watch. But Thane could hear no sound now but birds cawing and jostling one another in the branches of the trees for roosting position. It was a good sign: they were not disturbed. It meant no one was in the immediate area.

Thane took the medicine shield and lowered himself out of the willows through the cold water and found his way to the bank. His instinct was to build a fire and warm himself but he knew such a notion was ludicrous and dismissed it quickly. He would have to suffer at least through this first night, until he got far away from the village.

The air was crisp now that the sun was going down and his buckskins began to stiffen immediately. He realized he could never make it to the Mussellshell before Bear-Walks-at-Night and the other Crow warriors gave him up for dead. If he made it back to the Yellowstone now it would be on his own. The birds settling to roost in the trees broke into a loud chorus and rose in a swarm, circling the bottom and finding their way to other trees nearby. Thane crouched and waited some time for the appearance of Blackfeet. When he was sure there was no one there, he started out of the bottom and began his trip back to the Yellowstone.

Morning Swan laid her left hand, palm down, upon the rock. Holding the knife in her right hand, she then placed the blade against the last joint on the little finger of her left hand and pressed down. The knife cut through and ground against the rock. The tip of Morning Swan's finger slid away from the knife's edge and a pool of shining red appeared.

Long Hand had been brought in across his horse. No one really knew how he had met death, for there were no marks upon him except for a few bruises suffered in falling from his pony. He had not been shot nor stabbed. Rising Hawk suggested he had fallen while chasing the Long Knife and this, along with his badly degraded hip, had been enough to kill him.

Earlier, Morning Swan had cut her hair short and taken the claws of an owl to carve deep gashes in both of her forearms. She was dressed in plain clothes for mourning and they were now covered with blood.

She was now alone along the river, where the Great Falls cascaded down and foamed against the rocks at the bottom of the falls. Morning Swan and Long Hand had come here often. He'd sat with her and played a song on his flute. This place harbored good memories for her. Now that Long Hand was gone from this life, the Great Falls could no longer hold joy.

Morning Swan remained there until long after dark, singing mourning songs and praying for Long Hand's delivery to happiness in the next life. His last days had been filled with so much pain. It was good that if he must die, then it was in the way of a warrior protecting his family.

When Morning Swan returned to the village, she saw Long Hand's sister and two other women preparing Long Hand's body for the trip to the next life. They had dressed him in his finest war clothes and were painting his face. When the sun came again to the land, he would be placed in one of the trees along the river. Then they would kill Whirlwind, the fast and strong war pony, so that Long Hand would have a good horse in the next life.

Earlier in the day, just after Long Hand had been brought back to camp, Rising Hawk had told her the news. He had told her that her husband had died a proud death, though it was not clear whether or not he had counted coup against the Long Knife trader. Rising Hawk had stayed out to look for the Long Knife longer than the others, for he was now worried that his medicine was broken. The Long Knife had stolen his pony and his medicine shield. He had found his pony but not the shield.

Morning Swan knew she faced a grave decision. With Long Hand no longer alive, she was destined to become one of Rising Hawk's wives. She did not want to live in his lodge and she knew it would be impossible for her to adjust to life under his rule. There was no choice but to leave the village. Her ankle was still sore from the fall while hunting buffalo, but she could not think about that; though it had improved greatly, she knew re-injuring it during an attempt to escape would cause her to fail.

It was late and this was in her favor. Whirlwind was tethered in front of the lodge while inside one of Long Hand's wives, a girl named Flower Catcher, watched Rosebud as she slept. An older woman, an aunt to Long Hand, had been there earlier, but when Morning Swan entered the lodge, she noticed the older woman was gone. The girl told her the older woman would be back and that there was broth made for her. Morning Swan thanked her and told her she could go.

Morning Swan knew she must move quickly, for the older woman would surely insist on staying with her to ease her grief, and would likely be back shortly. Packing what belongings she could easily carry, Morning Swan prepared to leave the Piegan people forever. She would not witness the burial of her husband, nor could she say goodbye to her many friends. She must be gone in but a few moments or risk losing the chance to escape.

With Long Hand's bow and quiver of arrows slung over her back, Morning Swan untied Whirlwind and led him into the shadows behind the lodge. There were but a few campfires remaining, mostly old men smoking and telling stories. Long Hand's mother was deceased but the female members of her clan, mostly aunts and cousins to Long Hand and Rising Hawk, could be heard keening in their lodges, mourning the passing of their relative. Mist filled Morning Swan's eyes and she fought the impulse to visit the body of her fallen husband. She could not. In time she would feel glad that she hadn't, for she wished to preserve his memory as a warrior alive and strong and well.

Morning Swan climbed upon Whirlwind and stead-

ied the jumpy horse. Rosebud was asleep, strapped to
her breast. The child would likely remain asleep as
long as things remained peaceful. She was used to
sleeping on horseback, during times of traveling and
when Morning Swan would take her for long rides in
the evenings. It could be that way this evening,
peaceful and quiet, but it could be a chase if something went wrong. They would certainly be spotted by
Wolves, the watchers stationed out from the village to
sound alarm if enemies came. But the Wolves would
likely think she was merely out mourning the loss of
Long Hand and would think nothing of it.

Whirlwind snorted and Morning Swan rode him to
the edge of the village. A ways out, she began a song of
mourning for the dead. Again she thought of leaving
her husband forever and her voice wavered and she
wailed in long, sustained notes. Before she had gotten
far she was stopped by one of the watchers. He took
hold of Whirlwind's bridle.

"You are out late," he said to her. "It is not good to
travel out from the village now."

"I fear no harm," Morning Swan said.

"You have many belongings with you," the watcher
said.

"I wish to have my husbands things close to me one
last time. That is why I am riding his horse."

The watcher nodded but said, "I will help you get
back to the village. Rising Hawk warned all of us on
watch tonight to be sure and not let you go too far."

Morning Swan acted instinctively, kicking the
watcher's hand loose from the bridle and urging
Whirlwind forward. The watcher fell to the ground
with a shout as Whirlwind surged into a run, carrying
Morning Swan and her child into the darkness.

The watcher shouted an alarm, but Morning Swan
knew there would be few who would answer it once
they learned she was away from the village and riding
Whirlwind. There was not a pony in the village, at an
even start, that could remain within a stone's throw of

this horse. With a good head start, Morning Swan knew there was no chance of anyone reaching them.

She allowed Whirlwind to run three-quarter speed across the flats toward the Highwoods and then, when the village was lost, settled him into a fast walk along the river. Rising Hawk would be angry by now and might come out after them himself; but he would think better of it when he realized how foolish he would appear trying to catch up with Whirlwind. Morning Swan thought about Long Hand as she rode, wondering if they weren't riding over the same ground that he had taken to try to kill the Long Knife earlier that day. Her eyes flooded with tears and she wished him a happy journey to the Other Side.

The night was cold and the light of the half-moon shone like thin snow on the ground. She rode along the edge of a small herd of buffalo that rested for the night, their backs like a sea of humps in the moonlight. When she got downwind of them, they rose almost together and thundered off into the night, the sounds of their hooves echoing across the still benchland below the mountains. Rosebud was wide awake. She was laughing; she thought it was a game. "Are we going to win?" she asked her mother. Morning Swan smiled and hugged her daughter. "Yes, Rosebud," she answered, "we have already won."

Thane made his way through the Musselshell bottom, limping badly and feeling light-headed. The Great Falls seemed a lifetime behind him. He wanted to stop and lie down but would allow himself only brief intervals of rest. He could rest all he wished when he reached the Crow village.

In the three days since his feat in the Piegan village, he had managed to live on berries, rose hips, and the smooth meat of a sharptail grouse. He had killed the grouse more by luck than skill, finding a small flock fighting among themselves for roosting spots in a lone cottonwood. His rock had glanced off the trunk but

struck a young grouse lower in the tree on the re-
bound. It was a meal he had devoured in a short time.
It frustrated him to see so much game and yet not be
able to get to any of it. Though he had seen buffalo,
deer, elk, and antelope, he had nothing to kill them
with and could only watch them from a distance while
they studied him. It made him respect the Indians and
how they had adapted themselves to this land.

Though his shoulder still troubled him, Thane
cared little about it now. This new and ragged wound
across his upper thigh occupied the pain center in his
head and the ache in his shoulder seemed insubstan-
tial in comparison with the constant burning sensation in his leg. It was red and inflamed now and the
wound had become swollen so that it appeared open
and raw, like a gash through an undercooked roast.

He had plastered mud on it but that didn't seem to
help. So he worked it with his hands until he nearly
fainted from the pain. He knew it was important to
maintain circulation and keep infection from entering, though he knew it had to a great degree. He knew
it was good to allow the wound to drain blood but he
worried about losing too much and becoming too
weakened. It was important now to maintain his
strength and keep moving. What he needed most was
solid food. He was at least three days from the Crow
village and if he didn't succeed in getting some more
substantial food into his system, his chances of making it were slim.

The wound slowed him considerably and Thane
worried not only about hunger, but bears as well.
Grizzlies were common in the bottoms now. They
were getting ready to go to their dens and were in a
feeding frenzy, searching out berries and roots and
whatever meat they could find or kill. Though Thane
had yet to see his first spring in this country, Eli had
told him that these big bears were scavengers as much
as anything and could be seen every spring feeding on

drowned buffalo that had fallen through the winter ice.

But fall was different and the grizzlies had less carrion to pick from. It was now that they ate more vegetation and tore large rocks from their places in hillsides to look for marmots and gophers. And they were everywhere. Twice Thane had found himself hiding from grizzlies that were in the vicinity, traveling the trails or busying themselves in berry bushes. They were usually a distance from him, as Thane knew enough not to frequent the heavily used trails in thick cover for fear of surprising one of them. He wanted no more of those bears. He was not dreaming of them as much now and he wanted it to remain that way.

Sleeping was easy for him now and his body craved it. Though he was able to fight it and stay on his feet, it worried him. The first night after hiding from the Blackfeet he had walked nearly until daylight before collapsing. The cold had kept him awake and his chilled and water-soaked buckskins had worn raw sores on the back of his knees and under his arms. Now, with the approach of the third evening, Thane felt the need to stop or fall forward from exhaustion. His eyes were watering and his nose was running badly. Since the first night, he had been sneezing and coughing. In his misery Thane thought to himself that an afternoon in the ice-cold water of a pond, hiding from Blackfeet, will do wonders for your health.

He found a place to rest against the side of a hill, the smell of sage enfolding him where he sat. A meadowlark rose from beside him, startling him, and flew off down the bottom. Thane smiled; perhaps the story about the meadowlark knowing when the real cold was coming was true and since they were still around, at least the days would remain warm for a time and hold off the snow.

It was indeed warm where he sat, and when he

studied the medicine shield he realized how it gave
him strength. He had kept himself going with the
thought of Eli's face once he reached the Crow village.
Surprise would round the old trapper's eyes and his
mouth would open with a loud curse, though he would
be happy to see Thane's return. The other trappers
would laugh and collect their bets from one another
and they would talk about him all winter around the
campfires. He would have his furs back, plus Eli's, and
when spring arrived, he would catch more beaver and
be the richest man in the mountains.

Thane looked across the bottom, his mind filled
with the thought of his glory in reaching the Crow
village, when a buffalo ran down the slope from
behind him. He watched it come, a large cow, grunting and panting, its tongue hanging, swinging back
and forth from its mouth as it came to a slow trot. The
cow buffalo stood for a moment on wobbly legs,
drooling bloody foam, then slumped over onto its side
and kicked limply for a moment.

Thane quickly slid down into the brush along the
bottom and lowered himself until he was sure nobody
could see him. He peered out through the tangle of
willows and wild rose to watch the area. Piegan
hunters would surely be arriving any moment and,
though the thought of fresh meat was driving him
wild, Thane worked to keep his sense of self-
preservation intact.

He watched for a while longer, his mind swimming
with thoughts of fresh meat and feeling his stomach
react to the smell of the buffalo. Finally, it drove him
to sneak through the brush closer to where the buffalo
lay still, like a hump of black-brown in the grass and
sagebrush. Perhaps he could hurry out before the
hunters arrived and cut out the tongue. That would do
him. That would help him recoup his strength. As he
drew closer he thought maybe the buffalo had been
running for some time and maybe the hunters did not
know where it had run to. That was it, Thane told

himself. None of the hunters knew that the buffalo was here. It would take them time to decide where to look for the buffalo. He told himself this over and over. And while they were confused, he could use the time to his advantage. He could go out and feast on the buffalo and regain his strength.

With his hunger now in full control Thane stumbled out of the brush, knife drawn, and dropped to his knees beside the head of the fallen cow. He pulled on the tongue that lolled out of the mouth and cut at it, his hands trembling as he worked. Part of it came loose in a tangle of saliva and blood and Thane raised it to his mouth. He tore at it but with little success. It was leathery and slippery, and his teeth could not easily rip through the tough outer layer. He put the tongue on the ground and cut a small strip off and stuffed it into his mouth. He chewed momentarily and swallowed. He had forgotten completely that Piegan hunters might be coming at any moment. He went farther back on the animal to the hump, caring little how exact he might be in the butchering, and began to just cut. He first slit the hide that lay over the hump and pulled it back, then ripped into the meat itself. His hand trembled as he stuffed raw stringy lengths into his mouth and swallowed them.

He felt a presence behind him and turned to see an Indian woman watching him, an arrow fitted to her bow. With her was a small child, the very child who had fed him while he had hid in the bushes at the edge of the Piegan village. Behind the woman and the small girl was the same pinto horse that had run his horse down so easily. The woman stood a short ways off, well out of his reach yet close enough to easily drive an arrow through him. The meat came back up from his stomach and into his mouth and he fell forward onto his hands and knees, wretching.

Morning Swan knew who he was the moment she had watched him rise from the brush and go toward the buffalo: it was the Long Knife who had rushed into the village to steal Rising Hawk's horse. It was the same Long Knife who had then killed Long Hand. Rising Hawk's stolen medicine shield dangled from his left arm. She wanted to pull the arrow back and watch it take the life from his body but Rosebud was tugging at her arm and pointing at him.

"Eat," she said. "He was hiding from me. I gave him food to eat and he laughed."

Morning Swan wondered at what Rosebud was telling her. Then it came to her: she had wondered that day what Rosebud was talking about when she had picked her up to carry her back to the lodge. She had seen Rosebud pointing into the brush when she came to get her. At the time Morning Swan had thought her daughter had seen a fox or perhaps discovered a snake or some other small animal. There had been no time to look and see what it was, for the morning meal was boiling over and Long Hand had already returned from his bath in the river with the other men. Later, after the Long Knife had stolen Rising Hawk's horse, Rosebud had kept saying that that was her river friend, someone whom she had played with close to the river. He had been hiding there and Rosebud had found him. Now Rosebud wanted to play again with him. What sort of man would play with a child while he waited to steal a prize horse?

Thane sat back on his knees and watched the Indian woman. She had chopped off the long black hair that had trailed down her back the previous day and he saw long lines of dried, blood-marked gashes up and down her arms. Thane cared little now that his own face was all blood from the buffalo meat and that the front of his buckskins was stained from his wretching. His only concern was what this beautiful Indian woman would do with him. Her eyes were cold and it appeared she wanted badly to kill him. Instead, she came forward slowly with her small child. Now it occurred to Thane that it was odd she was out here with her little girl, and that they were alone.

Thane made sign. "I mean no harm. I am hungry and want only to eat."

Morning Swan stood and stared at Thane for a time. Her thumb and fingers still held the arrow firmly in place and it was all she could do to keep from pulling back and releasing. Rosebud started to walk over beside him but Morning Swan called her back. The little girl turned to her mother and insisted; she was not the least bit afraid of Thane and this more than anything troubled Morning Swan the most. It was hard to allow that her little daughter was intrigued by the Long Knife.

"I do not understand why you hunt alone so far from your people," Thane finally said. He caught himself speaking the word for hunting in Crow while he made sign. He was sure this would make the woman even angrier, knowing how the Piegan and the Crow were bitter enemies.

"I see you have been living among the Crow people," Morning Swan said. She was speaking in the Crow tongue. Not fluently but certainly understandably. "You are lucky my daughter likes you and that I am returning to the Crow people myself or I would surely kill you."

Thane was taken aback. It amazed him that she spoke Crow. But as he thought he wondered if she had not learned it as a child, if she were not really Crow. He listened while the woman spoke again.

"It was you who killed my husband. He was the warrior who chased you on that horse." She pointed to where Whirlwind grazed nearby. She placed her hand back on the arrow where its notch fit onto the bowstring and began to pull back slightly.

"I did not kill him," Thane made sign. "He fell from his horse. I don't understand why he fell, but he fell and I left before the other warriors caught up."

Morning Swan thought about what he had said. It was true, there were no marks on Long Hand other than a few bumps and bruises from the fall. He had not been shot or struck with anything. Perhaps it was true: his hip had given out and he could not stay on the horse. Maybe the Long Knife had done nothing more than try to get away.

"I'm trying to get back to the Crow camp on the Yellowstone," Thane said. "If I understood you right, you just said you were going there also. Have you been living with the Piegans since being stolen as a child, and have you somehow escaped them? Is it possible that you are the daughter of Bear-Walks-at-Night who was named Morning Swan?"

Morning Swan was astonished. "Yes. How did you know? Are my mother and father still alive and among the Crow people?"

Thane nodded. "I know them both very well. Your father is well respected and he told me about you."

Morning Swan removed the arrow from the bow. She walked over toward Thane and watched while Rosebud took a handful of grass and wiped at the blood that clung to his lips and mouth.

"What is your name?" Morning Swan asked him.

"Thane." He repeated it twice again while Morning Swan worked to pronounce it.

When she was finally comfortable with the name she said, "Yes, Morning Swan is what I am called. I was named that by my people and the *Pikuni*, the Piegan people, did not change it."

Thane nodded. "I was not aware that this was your kill." He motioned toward the buffalo. "As I told you before, I have had little to eat since the day I was in your village and I am very hungry."

"It is no longer my village," Morning Swan said as she sat beside Thane. "Do not say that the village is mine. It is not. I am no longer of the Piegan people. The warrior who owns that medicine shield was to be

my new husband. I did not want that. I have left with
my daughter and can never go back."

"I'm sorry about your husband," Thane told her.
"But I speak the truth when I say I had nothing to do
with his death. If he hadn't fallen from his horse, he
would have killed me for sure." Thane pointed to the
gash across his buckskins and the top of his thigh. "He
did that with an arrow. I'm lucky to be alive."

Morning Swan took a deep breath. She began to tell
Thane about Long Hand and the injury to his hip and
how he had always wanted to regain the glory he had
lost when the hip kept getting worse and how he
couldn't even bring meat in for his own family. It all
came out at once, as if it had been pent up for him to
hear. Morning Swan now realized that this Long
Knife whose name was Thane was the same one in
Long Hand's dreams. Long Hand had always felt that
killing this Long Knife would return his glory to him.
But it was not to be and now Long Hand was dead and
this Long Knife, weakened and hurt, was alive.

"My husband saw you in a vision," Morning Swan
told Thane. "He saw you when he went to the Bear
Paw Mountains to talk to his spirit helper. He told me
he prayed and fasted and saw a Long Knife, and that
he thought this meant honor for him. Then his
brother, Rising Hawk, said he thought it meant death
for him. I can never forgive Rising Hawk for that and I
will never become his wife."

"I haven't lived among your people long enough to
understand all you are saying," Thane told her, "but I
can understand your sorrow and I can only say I'm
sorry it happened. I only wanted this shield to win a
bet with another man, an old trapper who waits for
me down in the Crow village."

"Well, I guess you have won your bet with him,"
Morning Swan said. "You were very brave to do what
you did. There are not many men who would risk
going into the middle of a large enemy village for the

horse and medicine shield of a powerful warrior. Now it is time to take some meat from the buffalo before the great bears come and chase us away. Then we can all three eat and gain strength."

Thane allowed Morning Swan to do the butchering and watched while she first spoke prayers over the animal's body. Thane knew it was meant to ask the buffalo's forgiveness for taking its life, so that she and the others who ate the meat might themselves have life. When she was finished with the prayer, she cut into the animal's midsection, reached in, and took out the liver. She sliced pieces off the organ and gave them to Rosebud, who began to eagerly devour them. She then gave pieces of liver to Thane and he found himself stuffing his mouth. Rosebud then put one of her liver pieces into his mouth and giggled. She was ready to play once more.

Thane noticed the last joint of the little finger on Morning Swan's left hand was missing. The skin and flesh were dried around the end of the bone and a scab was forming. Thane had seen many women in the Crow village with similar mutilations and Eli had said it was a sign they had lost a loved one, usually in battle. Some of the women were minus a number of joints on both fingers. He let Rosebud feed him some more liver while Morning Swan finished taking the meat she needed.

"We will cook some of the hump meat when darkness comes," Morning Swan told Thane. "It is not good to allow smoke into the air when you do not know who might be close by."

With her knife, Morning Swan then opened the buffalo along the back and took out a piece of tendon that ran along the backbone. She looked at Thane's leg and pointed to the wound.

"That will need to be treated and then closed, or the leg will become rotten and you will die."

Thane blinked. "It's just a little red. It will go away."

"The arrowhead has cut deeper than you think."

"Do you know what to do for it?" Thane asked.

Morning Swan nodded. "First we will take enough meat from the buffalo to eat well until we reach the Yellowstone. Then we must move far from this place before darkness comes or the great bears and the wolves will keep us awake with their fighting all night."

Thane and Morning Swan cut meat from the hump section and along the back where the tenderloin lay. Morning Swan had a large skin bag that she filled and placed on the back of her horse. She told Thane Whirlwind was the fastest horse in all the mountains and that he had been her husband's prize buffalo pony. He would have died at the foot of Long Hand's burial scaffold.

They moved down the Musselshell and found a good place to camp among a stand of older trees. Old beaver dams that had been washed out were scattered through the area and Morning Swan explained that for some reason the beaver had not made their homes here for some time. She pointed to where a section of hill had slid down from the slope and into the bottom. Thane would not have noticed but Morning Swan showed him how the huge cut in the hillside grew a different kind of grass. Then it was easy to see.

"It is likely the beaver left because the hill fell and changed the flow of the river," Morning Swan said. "Then the water began to run through here very fast, destroying their homes each spring. They have no doubt moved down the river to make many new dams and that will slow the water down up here in time. It will be many winters though before they come back here to stay."

They settled into camp and Thane helped Morning Swan gather firewood. She looked at him with an odd expression and asked him why he was doing women's work. Thane shrugged and sat down under a tree and let Rosebud show him how to correctly dress a doll.

When there was enough wood, Morning Swan searched through one of her bags and found a small tool for digging. She explained to Thane that she wanted to make a poultice of plant material for his leg but that it was too late in the year to find any growing plants that could be used to draw out the inflammation. She said she had decided instead to dig some roots and boil them that night when she cooked the meat. She would then plaster the paste on his wound and allow it to work throughout the night. The following morning, when the swelling was down and the inflammation drawn out, she would sew the cut together for him.

Thane watched Morning Swan dig while Rosebud played beside her, pretending she too was skilled and knew which dried plant tops would have the roots beneath them that she needed. One by one she dug and gathered various roots of different sizes from different plants. Thane had no idea what they were but was fascinated by the way Morning Swan would walk slowly through the bottom and find them, pointing others out to Rosebud so the girl would begin digging for her.

When the sun fell, Morning Swan had collected a number of roots and was selecting the ones she wanted. She put the others in one of her bags for later use and set to building a fire. Thane had meanwhile cut chunks of the hump meat from the buffalo and put sticks through it to roast. The pieces of liver he had eaten earlier had given him strength and the smell of the fresh meat made him ravenously hungry.

"Eat until you are full," Morning Swan said. "If you are very tired, the roots will work better on your leg. I must sew your leg together before we leave tomorrow."

The three of them ate from the hump meat and soon Rosebud was wrapped in a small doeskin robe, fast asleep. The small girl was not the least disturbed by the distant sounds of the night, the wolves that howled over the fallen buffalo. Morning Swan remarked the bears had taken their fill and the wolves were signaling that it was their turn.

Morning Swan carried Rosebud, wrapped in the doeskin, to a buffalo robe she had arranged to sleep in. Under the robe she had placed a thick blanket of leaves; the cold ground would not get to either of them. She rummaged in one of her bags and gave Thane an elkskin dress to wrap up in. He smiled when she told him she knew he didn't need it, for he had surely been sleeping on the open ground before they met.

Thane and Morning Swan built up the fire while they talked about Rising Hawk and his prowess as a warrior among the Piegans.

"He will not like losing his medicine shield," Morning Swan said. "And he will look for you always."

"What if I was to destroy it?" Thane asked. "Burn it or something?"

Morning Swan shook her head. "That would not be a good idea. The spirits were with you that day when you ran into the village and stole Rising Hawk's horse and war shield. If you destroyed the medicine shield after taking it, the spirits would likely become angry and you would suffer. You might even die."

"It's just a piece of painted buffalo hide," Thane told her.

Morning Swan did not say anything for a time. She did not look at Thane either. She tended to the coals in the fire, getting them hotter so that she could place more rocks in them. Finally she said, "It is certain you do not understand the natural powers. You do not respect that which you can plainly see is very strong. How do you Long Knives remain alive without giving homage to the Great Powers of Earth?"

"We have God, a Creator to whom we pray and give our respect. He is the power we worship."

"Does your God control the powers that exist everywhere: the storms, sun that gives life from above, the unseen noises of the darkness?"

"Yes, He does," Thane answered. "But I don't know what that has to do with a piece of painted buffalo hide."

"The medicine shield is protection," Morning Swan explained. "It is very special to its owner, for it contains the strength of his spirit helpers."

"How can that be?" Thane asked.

"It is something you must believe in very deeply. Otherwise there is no power."

Thane was looking at the shield. It was clear to Morning Swan that he had no idea what she was talking about. She thought she might get him to understand by equating it to the powers that ruled Thane's life.

"Do you Long Knives pray to your God to look with favor upon you, to give you food and forgive you for the wrongs you do in this life?"

Thane nodded. "Well, we pray so that we might have what we want."

"We pray for what we *need*," Morning Swan said, "and if we are special in the eyes of the Great Powers then we might get what we want. A medicine shield is the main part of a warrior's life. If he has pleased the Good Spirits and the One Above, then he becomes a warrior and he is given strength. This strength is a part of him and it is contained in his medicine shield and his medicine bundle."

"His medicine bundle?" Thane said.

"That is his main source of power." She was watching Thane's confused expression as she spoke. She realized he could never understand it with just a short explanation. It was possible he would never understand it fully at all. "It is not important for you now," she told him. "Some day you may understand what I am telling you. But first you have to watch and listen carefully whenever you are around ceremonies and dancing. You cannot understand power without first respecting it."

Morning Swan began to deftly carve roots into small pieces, letting them fall into the bottom of a cooking bag of thick skin. She then pounded them to a pulp and added water. She lifted a number of hot stones from the fire with two sticks and dropped them into the bag, and began to stir the mixture while the water hissed and spat inside.

Thane thought about what she had said and looked at the medicine shield where he had left it against a nearby tree. He had noticed over the course of the afternoon that Morning Swan avoided it and would not even look at it.

"Is there some reason you do not like to be around the shield?" Thane asked her.

Morning Swan continued to mix the roots as the water came to a boil. "I told you, the shield has power. I do not want to become mixed up in that power. It is not my power and I am already afraid of Rising Hawk and what he will do to me if he ever catches me."

Thane watched the pulpy mass of roots ooze out onto a piece of skin wrapping Morning Swan had placed near his leg. She now cut off his buckskin pants above the wound and, after allowing the roots to cool down some, mixed them with dried grass and placed the poultice on his wound.

The feeling was warm and refreshing. Thane had expected pain but the effect of the poultice was comforting. He knew within his mind that this mixture was going to help him, and after Morning Swan had tied the skin wrapping in place around his leg, he thanked her.

"Why don't you leave the medicine shield where it sits and not take it down to the Yellowstone?" she said.

Thane looked at her with surprise. "I told you, I

made a bet that I would bring it back. If I don't bring
it back I will lose the bet and a whole fall's worth of
beaver plews."

"Please don't ask me to handle it," she said.

"I won't."

"Not ever."

"I won't, not ever."

Morning Swan then gave Thane a cup filled with a
thick tea made from the roots. It was bitter and his
mouth tried to reject it, but he swallowed it when he
saw Morning Swan watching him closely. It went
down hard and he shook his head.

"What is that stuff?"

"It will help you and you will sleep better."

Morning Swan went to her robes and joined her
daughter. Soon she was asleep and Thane settled into
the elkskin dress she had given him, wrapping it
around his upper body as best he could. He lay on his
side with his arm as a pillow and stared into the fire,
which was now down to a few dancing flickers of flame
and white embers. He looked past the fire to where the
medicine shield rested against the trunk of the tree,
the red hawk on its front looking like a strange dark
bird with its huge beak gaping open in the faint light
outside the fire.

Thane found he couldn't close his eyes without
seeing the shield. Each time he tried, the thunderbird
would be there, and when he opened them, the
thunderbird would still be there. He couldn't decide
which seemed more vivid, the real thing leaning
against the tree or the distorted, huge-beaked thing he
saw when he closed his eyes.

He decided to keep his eyes open for a time. The
medicine shield stood still against the tree but Thane
thought he could see the eyes of the hawk growing
wider. Thane quickly turned his back to the shield
and readjusted his elkskin cover. He closed his eyes
and forced himself to keep them closed. He felt
himself getting drowsy from the effects of the root tea

Morning Swan had given him. It was good he was relaxed, he thought, but he wished the vision of the thunderbird would leave his mind.

When the sun came, Thane rose to find Morning Swan waiting for him. He bit down heavily on the stick Morning Swan gave him while she stitched the wound in his leg. The prick of the quill she used for a needle filled his eyes with water and caused his nose to run steadily. Though the herb poultice she had plastered onto his leg the night before had done its job, the wound still retained a good deal of inflammation and before she was finished he felt like screaming.

"The wound will be sore for some time to come," Morning Swan told him, "but it now looks much better than it did and it will heal itself."

Thane once again downed some of the thick, bitter tea-like fluid Morning Swan brewed. She told him this would not make him drowsy like the mixture the night before, but would serve to help heal his wound from within. Then they ate leftover buffalo cooked the night before and started out for the Yellowstone.

Thane felt awkward riding the pinto with Rosebud while Morning Swan walked. She found it odd that he would ride only for short intervals and have her ride most of the time. He wanted her to pay his leg no mind; it was healing and the pain was easing out with the swelling, he insisted. But they made much better time when she walked and he held Rosebud on Whirlwind. That way she could break into a slow jog and allow the horse to trot.

Morning Swan found Thane to be embarrassed about his situation and there were times he said that it might be better if they went on ahead and left him. He could make it now easily. His strength was returning and there remained but one long day of travel to the Crow village. Morning Swan argued that Rosebud would never forgive her if the two of them went on ahead; she had grown fond of Thane for some reason that escaped both of them. Though Thane was not used to children, he found Rosebud to be a very likeable child. In fact, he found himself growing more fond of her all the time. She seemed to be as confident on the horse as if she were an adult, and most often, when she rode with Thane, she would insist on riding in front and holding the reins herself. Then she would have Thane put his hands around her, as if holding onto her for support, and she would laugh and remark about her riding abilities.

As they traveled, Thane grew more interested in the country and in learning about it from Morning Swan. She had learned many things from both the Crow and Blackfeet cultures and was eager to share her knowledge. She could remember as a child hearing Creation stories from the Crow elders and wondering at the feats of Old Man Coyote, who never ceased to be up to something. Among the Blackfeet, she was treated as any other child might be so that she would grow up to be a woman who cared about the Piegan people and would bear strong sons for battle. Morning Swan had heard stories from Piegan elders that resembled the Crow Creation stories, but among the Blackfeet it was *Napi*, Old Man, who was responsible for the world and the creatures in it.

"It is important that all people learn how to live on Earth, the Mother," Morning Swan said. "Though we see things through different eyes, our source of origin is the same, the One Above, and it is important to learn that we all need the same things to live."

Thane wondered what made Morning Swan's mind work. She had resolved herself to know her own being and how she fit into the mold of daily life. She had gone beyond that to teach herself how those things around her reacted to natural occurrences: how different areas might react to the same rainstorm, or why buffalo preferred grazing in one location over another. She showed Thane how these animals ate certain kinds of grass and left others until the best grass was gone. She pointed out areas near the river that had been grazed so hard for so long that there was little left but small grasses and stickery plants that the buffalo would not graze.

"The soil is life and it is the way of all that is natural to protect the soil," Morning Swan explained to Thane. "Buffalo take their life from the soil by eating what grows, mainly grass. They are like everyone else and are lazy. They do not go far from water to graze. So they eat up the grass along the rivers and streams. When the good grasses that keep the soil strong and healthy are eaten for a long period of time, they die out. They cannot live when their leaves are chewed off all the time.

"When they are gone smaller grasses come in to take their place; and when these are finally gone, bushy and stickery plants come in to cover the soil. These plants are not eaten by the buffalo because they taste bad and have stickers. The soil is then protected by these plants and over time the good grasses will come back again if the buffalo stay away and let them grow. So you can see that it is important to understand that the soil is life and that we must respect that life."

Thane enjoyed listening to her while they traveled. She seemed anxious to show her astonishing knowledge, pointing out the different tree and grassland areas as they passed through them, explaining the different kinds of rocks to be found and how that meant the various soils there were also different. Where the soils changed, Morning Swan showed how the types of flowers and grasses changed as well. Some grasses grew only in sand and nothing else; others grew only where the soil was heavy and gummy when wet. Different kinds of plants grew on different slopes of the hill; some on the north side would not grow in the sunshine of a south slope and some plants could not grow where there was much sunshine at all. She laughed and called them "shadow plants," which liked to hide. Some trees and flowers, she said, would only grow if a fire came over and heated the soil so that their seeds would burst and allow growth.

Morning Swan had also learned how to use plants to save herself. Besides knowing a vast number of edible plants, Morning Swan had learned how to tell north from the growth of moss on trees. In areas where there were no trees she had learned as a small child that there were flowers that followed the sun, and if you were lost and the sky was cloudy, those flowers would still know where the sun was. Then you could set your course on east or west, wherever the flower was pointing during that time of day. The flower told you how to travel.

Thane was amazed at how much Morning Swan had taught herself from the basic knowledge she had gained as a child. She had taken the things she had learned and carried them many steps farther in order to learn the reasoning behind each principle. She had learned in effect how to read the land and, like some sort of physician from Thane's world, diagnose subtle illness, a change in vegetation, or the hint of drying on evergreen needles. She could tell where fires had burned many years past by looking at the kinds of forest trees and grasses; and after a rain, she knew by how well the soil had absorbed the moisture whether or not there were problems.

Now it occurred to Thane that it was not so astonishing that she had a great deal of insight into how the beavers utilized the valleys for the good of her people and the land in general. She had spent a lot of time studying her surroundings and what made things work.

Otherwise, she was like all the Indians he had come to know out here: somehow close to the land, so very close, and attuned to every nerve and fiber of their own being. They seemed to know each other and themselves so well that it presented them with a pathway down which each one could travel. He or she would decide in early age what their lot in life was and others would accept that and say nothing to them, except that maybe there could be more in store if they really wanted it.

It had not been the same for him in Virginia, Thane remembered, nor for others. You grew up learning what others wanted you to know and striving to be somebody that oftentimes you weren't fit to be, then suffered the humiliation of not succeeding in being just like everyone else. Among these Indians there might be the will to become strong in war and thereby rich in material things, owning a great number of horses and other possessions, but if all that didn't come to pass you could just be who you wanted to be. If it wasn't in you to be a great warrior, then you could even dress like the women.

Thane remembered the *berdaches* he had seen the first night upon coming into the Crow village and how Antoine Lavelle had found himself with them, had somehow relaxed and fallen into his niche in life. After that he didn't feel he needed to spend as much time around Thane; he was content, and even though some of the trappers continued to make fun of him, he paid them no attention. Among the Indians everything was reduced to a natural level, and things ran more smoothly when you were of the opinion that you weren't going to beat nature anyway, so it was better to just go by nature's laws.

What law, Thane wondered, had allowed him to make his way to the Piegan village and make away with the medicine shield? What had spared his life at the hands of a warrior who would surely have killed him if he had not already had a festering wound deep in his hip? And to meet this warrior's wife, herself trying to escape the village and begin a new life! It was difficult to put into perspective and it made him ask himself why he was still alive.

Back in Virginia, he had escaped a gallows noose, something that had been constructed especially for him and had stood there waiting for him. Since coming out to the mountains, bears and Blackfeet Indians had somehow created within him an odd affinity for death. They were on his mind constantly and would no doubt remain there as long as he trapped in this region. Now he was learning from this strong Indian woman that living in the shadow of death was natural in this country: if grizzly bears and enemies were not nearby, then there was the risk of injury or starvation. The land was so vast and demanding, and after just a few days with Morning Swan, Thane realized there was so very much he had to learn.

Five

WHEN THANE AND MORNING SWAN RODE INTO THE CROW village on the Yellowstone, they found the inhabitants staring wide-eyed, their hands covering their mouths. Was Thane a ghost, the people wondered, who had found a woman to take as his own? Bear-Walks-at-Night had said that this man was surely dead.

But they were glad to see Thane and learn that Morning Swan was the daughter of Bear-Walks-at-Night, who had taken the Kicked-in-Their-Bellies to winter on Wind River. Morning Swan was disappointed that her parents had departed, but knew she would see them before long. First there would be a feast and celebration.

The dancing went on throughout the night. The circle of warriors surrounded the medicine shield Thane had brought from the Piegans, hanging on a pole placed in the center of the village. Bear-Man, the one who had the grizzly inside him, was indeed a strong warrior. He had been wounded in battle but had come back from enemy lands with a great prize. They jumped and shouted and yelled war cries while older men sat cross-legged, nodding and smoking while they watched the ceremonies.

Thane found as always that it was interesting to watch the dancing and the warriors dressed in full battle regalia while they waved weapons and showed scalps and war booty from past triumphs, but much of it was lost on him without Eli and the other trappers. They had left some days ago to winter with the Kicked-in-Their-Bellies band on Wind River. When Bear-Walks-at-Night and the other warriors had returned without him, Eli had spent the night by himself and announced the following morning they would leave and winter farther south, closer to the other brigades that were preparing for the spring trapping season. They had assumed there was little hope they would ever see Thane again.

Morning Swan was happy. Though she had wanted in the worst way to see her father and mother again, she had found a distant relative among this band of Crows and was catching up on what had happened over the many years since her capture by the Piegans. No one had ever thought Morning Swan was still alive, and she was welcomed as someone who had been gone but for a few weeks. She told them how she had lost the man she had been married to and that was her reason for cutting her hair and taking the end of her finger. Though many of them had never heard her name, they knew her mother's clan and that made her one of them. That she had spent many years among the Piegans meant nothing; she was home now.

Thane regained his strength and let his leg heal up to a greater degree while Morning Swan and little Rosebud enjoyed themselves with their relatives. But after a couple of weeks Thane was anxious to rejoin Eli and the others and Morning Swan was equally as anxious to be reunited with her mother and father. The Crows gave them horses and food and wished them a good trip.

Within a few days they were traveling the fork of the

Yellowstone River named for Lieutenant William Clark of the Lewis and Clark expedition. It was a narrow, twisting river that took them south through a valley shadowed by high mountains that wound far back, Morning Swan said, into the country of the fire waters. High up in those mountains, she told Thane, smelling waters bubbled and hissed from the ground. Though the snows fell deep there, the ground was warm and bare where the waters came up to the surface.

They were soon crossing a broad valley between the Wind River Mountains and the Bighorn range to the east. The sky was filled with low, dense clouds and the wind was coming in sharp gusts. Though the nights had been cold and an occasional small storm had brewed, the weather had been good. But now, in all its force, winter was coming down on them.

"The waters of the Bighorn are just over that hill." Morning Swan pointed. "We had better find shelter before the night comes."

She then kicked Whirlwind into a gallop. Rosebud laughed with glee and told Thane to kick his horse. Rosebud had taken to riding with Thane more than her mother. She bragged that Thane needed someone to help him ride, that he wasn't all that used to horses. Thane wouldn't argue: he had noticed even the small children among the Crows were incredible riders.

They made camp in a dense stand of cottonwoods along the river and built a lean-to of young willow branches covered with creeping juniper boughs and then with buffalo hides. They built the lean-to against the side of a hill, an undercut that served them well. The cottonwoods that surrounded their location would break the wind and the lean-to would keep the snow off them.

"You left your lands to live in the snow like this," Morning Swan told Thane with a laugh. "The beaver must be very important to you."

"Not to me," Thane said, "to the people who want felt hats."

"What is a felt hat?"

"There are a lot of kinds of felt hats," Thane explained, telling her what he had learned from Eli, "and the underfur of the beaver makes the best kind. It's soft and thick. Men where I come from wear them on a daily basis, the way the Indian men out here wear various animal headdresses."

Morning Swan nodded. "You do not wear such a hat. Why do you care about trapping the beaver?"

"That is how I earn my living," Thane said. "In the land of the white man, goods and materials are not always traded. Usually money is exchanged."

Morning Swan was not used to the term, as it was unheard of among the Indians peoples. But she had seen the Long Knife traders giving it back and forth to one another when betting and games were taking place. She was not really concerned about that, but there was one thing she wanted to know.

"Are there a lot of men in your lands who want these hats?" she asked Thane.

Thane nodded. "They'll take as many beaver as we can trap from these mountains."

"Does that mean you are going to trap them all?" Morning Swan asked.

Thane laughed. "No, I don't think that's possible."

The storm came in strong at first. The wind brought in a blizzard and the air was a mass of swirling white flakes. All was white, a glaring white that faded only with the setting of the sun. The horses were huddled together among the trees, their heads bowed and their backs to the wind. Morning Swan had built a fire and, with water from the river, boiled meat for them. The back of the lean-to reflected both the light and the warmth of the fire and the inside was comfortable. When the light left totally and darkness blotted out the snow, Rosebud yawned and snuggled up in a pile of robes.

Thane began to rub his shoulder. The stiffness and the deep pain, he had finally realized, would likely never go away. Not for an appreciable time anyway. It was just a fact of life he was going to have to contend with, something like eating or changing clothes.

But living with the pain was something Thane had yet to get used to. He could not block it from his mind, for it was mind-consuming in the manner it worked on him. It would come and haunt him for no apparent reason: it might be warm or cold or in between when the pain started. It didn't come on predictable occasions like a change in weather. It was there always, rising up when it felt like it, and it drove him crazy.

But Thane realized frustration would not make it go away, and when the pain mounted, he focused his attention on other things.

"That's quite a daughter you have there," Thane commented to Morning Swan.

Morning Swan handed Thane a bowl of meat. She had noticed ever since first meeting Thane that his shoulder was troubling him. He had told her about having been mauled by one of the big yellow bears, but he would never go into the details. Morning Swan saw that as not unusual. She had known a warrior among the Piegans who had been mauled also, only much worse. He had lost an arm and part of his lower leg. This warrior had said often that he wished the bear had killed him, for now he could not be a whole man and could not go into battle and fight like other warriors. If he was going to die in battle, he wanted to be a whole man when he died and not just a part of a man who was expected to lose his life because he wasn't whole.

That warrior had eventually decided to search out another bear to kill him. He had finally found a male grizzly marking a tree with its claws. The warrior had then himself reached up on a nearby tree and, after watching the bear, had imitated its movements by marking the tree himself. The bear had attacked and ripped his head off.

Morning Swan did not like to think about it, for it reminded her of Long Hand. In his quest for wholeness, Long Hand had essentially taken his own life as well. He had to have known better than to run Whirlwind as fast as he could with the bad hip. It was certain in Morning Swan's mind that Long Hand had wanted to gain glory or die trying.

Morning Swan watched Thane eat and look at her little daughter. She dished herself up some stew and thanked Thane for his compliment.

"I am glad you think highly of Rosebud," Morning Swan said. "She thinks you are her new father. She knows that when fathers die or are killed in battle, soon there is a new father to love them and care for them. So she thinks you are her new father."

Thane was silent for a moment. He watched the small girl as she slept in the bundle of robes, her thick black hair shining in the firelight. Then he turned to Morning Swan. "It's good to see your hair is growing out some again. When I first saw you from the top of that butte, I thought to myself what pretty long hair that was." Then Thane turned and looked out into the night, feeling awkward for the remark. He knew she hadn't cut it because she'd wanted to.

"It has taken me some time to understand that Long Hand is no longer in my life," Morning Swan finally said. "For some women, they can never realize their man is gone. But for a long time Long Hand and I lived with the knowledge that the wound in his hip would kill him. I look at you and think I should hate you because it was the ball from a Long Knife thunderstick that struck him and ruined his hip. But I cannot hate you. You are a Long Knife and a friend of my true people, the *Absaroka*, the Crow, but I loved my husband when I was a Piegan. Somehow I cannot understand all this. But now Long Hand is dead and I know his spirit rests. I do not feel he is angry with me for traveling with you. I think he is pleased."

"Why do you think he is pleased?"

"I know he is glad I am not with his brother, Rising Hawk," Morning Swan answered. "And I am sure he is glad Rosebud is happy. Maybe my daughter sees some of him in you."

Thane finished his bowl of meat. Morning Swan was watching him and he felt more awkward than ever. Outside, the storm was letting up some and the wind was dying down. It lifted their spirits to know they would not have to travel the next day in bad weather. Now the storm had settled into a steady snowfall without the wind. Thane decided to get up and go check the horses.

The snow was light and fluffed up around his feet as he walked through it in the darkness. He talked low to the horses as he approached them, so they would know him. He piled more cottonwood bark for them to eat and watched while they chewed contentedly. They seemed comfortable, and after he left them, he walked to the river for a drink of water.

He rubbed his shoulder for a while, standing by the water where the ripples absorbed the snow as it fell. Light steam was rising and it made the shadows blurring and indistinct. He was beginning to kneel down at the water's edge when he heard one of the horses snort. He stood up, but all was still. The snow was falling silently and the river murmured as it ran past. He knelt down then and leaned forward on his stomach.

The water was cold on his lips and he drank deeply. As he stood up he saw something move among the trees nearby. It seemed to him to be large and bulky. He cursed his luck. He hadn't even brought his rifle. He waited for the bulk to stand up on its hind legs, he waited for the roar. The snow kept falling, thick and soft, and the bulky shadow remained motionless. Or

was it motionless? Thane was sure it moved. Then one
of the horses snorted again.

Thane turned and ran. He tripped and fell forward
into the snow, catching himself with his hands. The
snow puffed up and spread across his face and slid
down his neck. He got up and ran again, the wet snow
turning to water that stung his face and neck. When he
reached the lean-to he grabbed his rifle. Morning
Swan stared and asked him what was wrong.

"I think maybe there's a bear out there and I came
for my gun."

Morning Swan looked at him. "A bear? No, I think
not. They are in their dens sleeping."

Thane took a deep breath. He felt foolish. Of course
there was no bear. She was right, they were in their
dens and wouldn't likely be out until spring. Now he
didn't know what he had seen. He told himself it
could have been a deer or an elk, or anything. What
made him feel worse was that after a moment when he
had caught his breath, he realized that the bulky
shadow was likely nothing at all; nothing but a clump
of bushes or a snow-covered hump of driftwood. He
wanted to think the mist rising from the river had
been playing tricks on him. He wanted to think there
was some reason for his mistake, other than the fact
he was still mentally unstable from the mauling by the
grizzly. He laid his rifle back down and took a seat
near the fire.

Morning Swan studied Thane for a time, watching
his eyes while they darted back and forth from the
darkness to the light of the fire. He would not look at
her. His foolish shame was too deep. She wanted to
tell him that it was not a bad thing to have fear, to be
unsure of what is around and unseen. The darkness
holds many secrets and there is no one who can
explain them all.

There were other things about this man she could
not understand: what made him so unpredictable,
showing courage that most men could never gather

together in an entire lifetime in order to take a medicine shield and win a bet, and then suddenly jumping at his own shadow? Surely someone who took it upon himself to risk his life for a medicine shield, mainly just to save face among those he worked and traveled with, could handle the smaller problems life brought forth with ease.

But it was not that simple with this man, Thane, whom Rosebud was adopting as her next father. No, this man was driven by more complex things than just the desire to be part of the open country, like the other Long Knives who had come out to trap the beaver from the streams. Morning Swan had heard him say more than once that what brought most men out here was not the trapping itself, but the end of that trapping—the freedom that allowed them their own time. He had tried to explain to her that life where he had come from, far to the east, was vastly different. His race, the white men, lived as the Indians in groups. But that was where the similarities ended. Among the Indians, individual freedom was prized, while among the whites it was merely a fantasy everyone desired but could not live. There were mindless laws for everyone to follow so that the population was bound in their thinking and the way they lived their daily lives. They were told what was right and wrong by men in power who stood to gain by oppressing those beneath them.

Morning Swan could not understand all that Thane had tried to tell her about his own people, but after listening to him, she was certain that these white men like Thane, who were now Long Knives, had come from a different society than she had ever known. These Long Knives had lived their lives among their own people with great difficulty and had come out here to escape that life. It was understandable to her that they would want to escape essentially being held captive by their own people. The way Thane explained it to her it was as if everyone wanted to rule

the others and have total control over their lives.
Morning Swan could not understand such an attitude,
and had asked Thane during their discussions if his
people weren't always struggling within themselves to
be different from the others around them, while at the
same time pretending to be content in doing the same
things.

Maybe this was the answer to some of the mystery
that dwelt within this Long Knife named Thane.
Merely by watching him Morning Swan knew things
had happened in his past that were like the bear,
kicking and scratching and biting inside him. This
made him look off into the distance for long periods of
time without speaking. He was not watching the geese
fly for that long, she knew, nor was he simply admiring the country. His mind was someplace else, back in
the land where he came from, and it was bothering
him.

And the bear itself was inside of him, one of the
huge yellow bears that ruled the land. When he
rubbed his shoulder the bear appeared on his face; it
colored his features dark with fear and strain, as if the
bear would appear at any moment and once again
grab him with its gaping mouth. Tonight he had seen a
shadow along the river and the bear had once again
come to him; it had come out of his mind and had
built itself into fear that came out through the misty
darkness along the river. It was a bad thing to have a
bear inside you.

Morning Swan reasoned within herself that she
could like this man. Rosebud was always good at
understanding character and she liked him a lot. This
meant the man was good-hearted, at least, and was
likely honest in his daily life. But he would lose
something if he did not eventually get rid of the bear
and the other bad things in his head. Maybe she could
help him in time.

Thane lay back in his robes and allowed the crackling fire to put him to sleep. Soon his mind was

swooning in an uncontrolled state, a dream again lowering itself from somewhere into his mind. He swam in the open air along the river, through the mist that rose from the water. He found himself lost there, unable to find his way out, not knowing where he was or how he got there. He saw the eyes first, the narrow yellow eyes that were hot with rage. Then the huge head with mouth open and huge teeth gleaming came at him, the froth dripping and the tongue red as fresh blood.

The sweat poured from him as he jumped up in his robes. Morning Swan was holding him, trying to quiet him. Rosebud was awake, standing before him with her little black eyes wide with concern. She put one little hand on each side of his face and held him, as if she alone could steady his shaking. She looked into his face and her small black eyes were filled with worry.

"Mommy is here," she said. "You don't have to be afraid."

Thane managed to smile. "I won't be afraid. You can go back to sleep."

"Lie with me," Rosebud said.

Thane crawled over to the small bundle of robes and helped her get herself snuggled down into them once more. He lay beside her and Rosebud put a small arm around him and smiled. She closed her eyes and was soon asleep again.

"This will help you," Morning Swan said.

She was holding out a small bowl of herb tea that she had made while Rosebud went back to sleep. Thane went over beside her and took the bowl. He looked into it for a moment.

"Go ahead and drink it," Morning Swan said. "It will help you sleep."

Thane set the bowl down and moved closer to Morning Swan. At first her eyes showed confusion, but when he leaned over and touched her lips with his own, she smiled.

Morning Swan felt herself letting go while Thane

began to kiss her softly along her neck and shoulders. She allowed him to touch her, his strong hands gently caressing her, finding her breasts and molding them until she found herself overwhelmed.

He took off her clothes and then removed his own. He was strong and lean in the light of the fire and in his eyes was a deep admiration for what he saw. He laid her down in the robes and gently moved atop her. Morning Swan felt her breath go as he entered her. He was strong yet controlled in movement. Morning Swan lost herself in the pleasure it brought her. It had been so long since she had had a strong man, since before Long Hand had injured his hip.

Now she was bothered. Long Hand had been her only man for so long and it was hard to realize she was suddenly with someone different.

"Please stop," Morning Swan said to Thane. "Please." She fought tears. The memory of Long Hand was there and she still loved him, though he would never come back.

"What is the matter?" Thane asked.

Morning Swan shook her head, the tears running down her face. "I'm sorry," she said. "I guess it is too soon to be with you in this way."

Thane lay beside her and took a deep breath. "I didn't mean to make you feel bad."

"It is no fault of yours. I just need more time."

Morning Swan lay still for a time. There was silence in the lean-to and the fire crackled. She thought about Thane and how he had not become mad at her for stopping him. His passion was reaching its greatest point when she had told him to quit. She looked at him and he was lying still, looking up at the shadows the fire made on the roof of the lean-to.

"Are you angry?" Morning Swan asked.

He shook his head. "I wouldn't have started if I knew."

Morning Swan lay back down and looked at the ceiling of the lean-to herself for a time. Long Hand was gone now, happy where he was, she was sure. She could feel that he was. She could feel that he was no longer in pain and now wanted her to be happy in this life. Maybe she was making a mistake by feeling guilty about being with Thane.

Morning Swan sat up and leaned over Thane's chest. She saw his eyes look questioningly into hers and knew that her breasts pushing into him were arousing him once more. She began to rub his chest with her fingers, moving through the soft, thick hair. His muscles were hard and he was very well built, and now he was warm to the touch. Morning Swan felt her desire rising again and she leaned down to kiss him.

"I didn't want to make you stop," she said. "It's just that I began to feel bad."

"I'm sorry," Thane said. "Maybe it is better this way. I don't want to cause you any pain, or make you remember things you would just as soon forget."

"I think I am better now," she said. "I think the unhappy feelings are past and gone. Gone now for good."

Thane looked up at her and pulled her lips to his. She reached down and he groaned with pleasure while she brought him back to full erection. He once again began to make love to her and she lost herself in his motion. She heard herself cry out and heard his voice as well. Then they lay together while the fire dwindled down to coals.

"I don't aim to pay you extra for the woman."

Eli had a sparkle in his eye. He had quit hoping Thane would somehow return from the Piegan country with his life and, though he had told himself often to accept Thane's loss, had spent every night thinking of the young trapper. Somehow, in this crazy and unpredictable world, Thane Thompson had made it out of Piegan country, and with Rising Hawk's medicine shield to boot.

Thane had just recovered his breath from the long

and tight hug Eli had given him. The old trapper was wiping his nose and he was smiling from ear to ear. Besides being dumbfounded at seeing Thane alive, he was equally startled at the sight of Morning Swan.

"You don't stop till you get everything you want." Eli laughed.

Morning Swan was now with her father and mother. There was excitement in the village, for no one would have ever suspected she would return or that she might even be alive after all this time. Bear-Walks-at-Night had ordered nine of his best horses to be given to Thane as a present for returning his daughter. Bear-Man was a great warrior.

Stretch Tipson was there, as was Sir John Preston. They were both glad to see Thane and made it a point to get his whole story, from beginning to end, in every detail. Sir John took notes like mad and shook his head in disbelief at the tale. Thane added more details each time he retold the story while sitting around campfires smoking with the warriors or lolling in the hot springs at the edge of the village. A favorite gathering place during dull winter days, the hot springs were usually filled with bathers, unless Sir John was there.

It was a far better stage than he could have found anywhere in the East and Sir John considered the rising steam a fit background for Shakespearean ghosts and witches. It was common to see his eyes roll and his voice lift to the sky, sending Crow villagers scurrying for fear he would rouse spirits that might harm them.

Stretch Tipson spent as much time as anyone in the hot pools and looked like some huge crane wading through the shallows. Eli spent a lot of time soaking his knee and allowing Thane to suggest he soak his head as well. The old trapper was not worried about Thane getting the best of him for, whenever Thane would start in, Eli would wink and bring up Morning Swan.

"I ain't figured yet whether you went up after that medicine shield or the woman," he told Thane. "Seems to me you saw winter comin' on and saw fit to warm your bedroll some."

"Just the same," Thane commented, "you're light a good sum of beaver plews. Maybe I'll retire."

Eli snorted. "Maybe we'll have another shootin' match before the spring hunt."

Thane wasn't going to take any chances with his winnings. Over the winter Eli goaded him often and Thane had to keep himself alert to be able to come back with remarks. Usually he told Eli he would shoot against him again only if Eli would concede to using his cane as a target. Eli came back with the remark that Thane would do the whittling on the new one. Besides, this cane was special.

Eli seemed to feel it had a certain magic attached to it, for many times he would have fallen and injured himself if it weren't for that diamond willow cane. The cane had withstood many a stiff jolt, including a test in which Eli had slammed himself onto it while tumbling down an icy bank, falling upon it chest first while the cane was lodged against a tree. Instead of cracking and breaking, the cane had simply bowed and snapped back.

Between Eli's cane, Sir John's entertaining antics, and Stretch's birdlike baths in the hot springs, the winter was shaping up to be a pleasant and entertaining one. Morning Swan was happy, and Rosebud made it a standard practice to show him any new dolls she might have acquired and any other things of interest she thought he should know about. Often she would ask Thane when he was going to move into the lodge with her mother. All Thane could think of to do was smile and tell her he didn't know.

Thane had thought to himself many times that he was beginning to develop a special feeling for Morning Swan, and though he tried to fight it, the feeling grew stronger. This was a hard thing to accept, for he wasn't sure of Morning Swan's feelings. He caught himself watching her as she worked or visited with the women of the village. He found excuses to talk to her, though he was having trouble finding new things to talk about. He told himself finally that he was going to have to modify his behavior or he would find himself drifting farther into emotional involvement.

Morning Swan was gradually thinking less of her past among the Piegans and more of her present happiness and what lay ahead for her. She was no longer seeing visions of Long Hand or thinking about where he was in the next life; this was something that happened to everyone in time, and when a person was gone, you didn't speak their name or dwell on their passing. This allowed her time to think about what she wanted to do now. She was back with her true people and was enjoying more contentment now than she had ever known before.

Thane was on her mind a lot now and she enjoyed his company. But she wanted to control her own feelings and did not want at the same time to lead him on in any way. Her sexual experience with him during the storm on the Bighorn River had brought about occasional times together in his lodge. She enjoyed them but did not want to have him depending on her for fulfillment. She realized that each intimate moment with him brought deeper feelings for him and for now she did not want to commit herself to a man for a while.

In watching Morning Swan, Thane realized her newfound independence was growing on her by the day. She was free now of her responsibilities toward the Piegan husband he had never known, except from the back of a horse during mortal combat. She was no longer burdened with worry for this man and he could see in her eyes the sparkle of freedom and contentment. When he talked with her she was polite, but he found himself carrying the conversations for the most part. It was if she were telling him she would never be rude to him but that she wished he would put some distance between them.

This tore at him from two directions. As the days went by he found he could not help growing more attached to her, not just because she had saved his life but because of the woman she was. She was not one to ask her man what to do or how to do it; in fact, it occurred to Thane that she normally did things to suit herself and having a man to consider would necessarily mean limiting that mobility. For that reason she was not going out of her way to show that she wanted a man again, Thane realized. That was the reason she was gradually beginning to avoid him if possible.

And he was trying to maintain his own independence. He didn't want to think that she was something special, a fact he could not dismiss no matter how hard he tried. He didn't want to think that he might be so lucky as to have her for his own when the thought of committing himself to any woman at all had never occurred to him before meeting her. She was someone who could manage her own destiny with ease, and unlike most of the other Crow women in the village, she did not think that white traders were something special.

Now there were many trappers moving in and out of the area. Whenever the weather let up they would come into the village for a while, some to stay the remainder of the winter and others just to visit before heading out toward distant camping areas. In her mind they were all busy making friends with the Crow people so that regional trapping and trading would go smoothly. They asked her people continually where the best beaver streams were, and they always had an eye for the women. She was not impressed with the combs and mirrors and other trinkets that were passed out regularly. It was on her mind that men were useful only to those women who could not fend for themselves and needed protection and someone to provide for them. This was not the case with Morning Swan.

Thane noticed her attitude toward him becoming gradually cooler. She had told him she did not wish to make love for a while, as she was not sure of her feelings. Thane decided finally that he should risk setting himself up for a fall. He found Morning Swan outside camp, where she was cutting down a dead tree for firewood.

"I need to know what you really think of me," he said to her outright.

Morning Swan stood up from where she was cutting branches from the tree.

"I think you know the answer," she said. "I think you are strong and brave. I think you are kind. But there are those things in both of us that neither of us knows yet. And I am not ready for commitment."

"Don't you think a warrior in the village will ask you to become his wife?"

"That does not mean I must accept. My father is well off, and even if he weren't, he wouldn't give my hand away for any reason. I am free to make my own decisions."

Thane watched her work on the dead tree, piling the branches neatly into stacks that she would carry back to the village. Nearby a white weasel, an ermine, scurried across the snow in front of them. If it weren't for his black nose, ears, and the tip of his tail, the ermine would have been completely invisible in the snow. When the animal stopped, Thane had to blink to find him.

Soon the ermine grew curious and jerked in rapid movements toward Thane, rising on hind feet with a busy nose to study him. When Thane moved to sit down on a nearby log, the ermine dove into a hole in the snow.

"I am going to be leaving for the spring trapping

season before very much longer," Thane told Morning Swan. "It's going to seem odd traveling without you."

"You could stay here in the village," Morning Swan suggested. "You don't have to leave."

"But I do have to," Thane told her. "I came out here to trap beaver. What would everyone say if I just decided to live with the Crows and do nothing?"

Morning Swan stopped her working and turned to him. "Why do you worry about what everyone will say? Are you not your own man?"

"Well, yes."

"Don't you have Rising Hawk's medicine shield to prove your power is great and that you are brave?"

"That doesn't mean I want to give up what I came out here to do."

"Then you have your answer," Morning Swan said. "You trap the beaver and I will live with the Crow people. Besides, I am not sure I like what you are doing."

"What do you mean?" Thane asked. "You don't like the trapping?"

Morning Swan nodded. "I don't think I like the idea of trapping the beaver. How many are you going to trap?"

Thane was still puzzled. "I don't know. As many as possible, I imagine."

"That is what worries me," Morning Swan explained. "There are lots of beaver now, but if you trap as many as you can each year, there will soon be few and then the land will be in trouble."

Morning Swan saw that Thane was completely perplexed and this frustrated her. She had spent time talking to him about the land during their trip from the Blackfeet lands down to the Yellowstone and it seemed now that he had heard little of it.

"Can you remember the first night I met you, when we camped on the waters of the Musselshell?" she asked him. "When we saw the old beaver dams where the hill had fallen into the river? Do you remember that?"

Thane nodded. "What are you telling me?"

"Did you not see how the banks of the river were cut back where the beaver dams had been washed away? The beaver stops the strong waters in the spring from washing out the bottoms. If you trap all the beaver, the bottoms will become fast-rushing water and the land will be ruined."

Thane shook his head. "We can never trap out all the beaver. There are too many of them."

"Do you think there are more beaver than there are Long Knives in your lands to the east?" Morning Swan asked.

"Well, I don't know," Thane said.

"I don't either," Morning Swan continued. "But if every one of them wants a hat, don't you think that will cost the lives of all the beaver?"

Thane looked down at the snow where the ermine was poking his head out of the hole. She had a point. She had a mind that looked far ahead, Thane realized. However, he couldn't imagine her being right about trapping all the beaver.

Morning Swan picked up a load of wood to carry back to the village. Her face was pinched with anger.

"I care about my people's lands," she finally told Thane. "And I know it is far easier to destroy things than to care for them. I have seen that among my own people. There are times when far more buffalo are killed than are ever butchered, but no one worries because there are so many.

"I just want you to know," Morning Swan continued after catching her breath, "that any man I will have as my husband, white or Indian, has to care more about other things than he does for himself. I do not think I will ever find such a man."

Thane watched Morning Swan leave with the wood. She moved fast and she was as angry as he had ever seen her, even more so than when she had wanted to shoot him with an arrow at their first meeting. This was the first he had heard of her concern for the beaver population. He should have realized this the night they talked about beaver hats. With so many beaver in the streams, though, it was hard for Thane to imagine her passion. But it was real, and he concluded she would maintain her attitude.

He turned his attention to the ermine, who was again out of his hole and moving, stopping on occasion to look at him. The ermine stopped beside a fallen log and was motionless for a long moment, then dug rapidly under the log, and moved like a flash into the hole. The ermine popped back out with a struggling mouse in its mouth, turned to Thane, and then was lost among the thick brush and fallen branches along the river bottom, leaving behind only tiny specks of tracks and little droplets of red in the white snow.

Part Two

1825–1833

Six

THANE STUDIED THE COUNTRY FROM THE TOP OF A LOW hill. The Siskadee, the Prairie Hen River, wound south across the sweeping plain toward the endless distance. Snow was banked in the draws and across the rolling valley. Only the ridges were swept completely clear by wind. Hints of green were showing where the sun had touched bare ground for more than a few days and the south slopes were blanketed with tiny yellow flowers.

General William Ashley himself was with them. During the late winter he had come into the Crow village with more men, and now that spring was approaching, they had all left to cross the mountains for the trapping grounds along the Siskadee. They had found their way here through South Pass, where Eli said he had come into this country from the north with Major Andrew Henry nearly fifteen years before. Since this last surge into the mountains, a group led by Jedediah Smith had rediscovered it the previous March and were claiming recognition.

Antoine Lavelle was with them, still limping and enduring his handicaps from the vicious mauling he had received at the hands of the grizzly. Thane realized that Antoine would always consider him a special friend for saving his life from the bear and that the Iroquois would always be somewhat of a nuisance because of it, but now Antoine was nearly always with another *berdache* and he troubled Thane no more in that way.

Sir John, always taking notes, was finding the life out here more demanding than he had expected, and was having trouble relating to the people. In his mind everyone out here learned to exist, in his words, "on a level just above the wild animals." While watching a ceremonial dance late one evening to rid the village of evil spirits, Sir John had said, "If it weren't for hand-to-eye contact among these people, they would be on all fours either grazing or eating carrion." The remark had seemed exceedingly patronizing to Thane and he'd reminded Sir John that these wilderness tribes had their own way of life and that their code of honor was far more rigid than in any colonized region of America.

"Do you find yourself getting used to these people?" Sir John had then asked Thane.

Thane had nodded. "Yes, I do."

Sir John had then left the ceremony, remarking, "If you are not careful, you will soon be one of them."

With the snow and cold winds it had been a hard journey, but Thane felt good to be in a new place, new country. He was riding a fine blue roan named Whistler for the sound that came from his nose when he ran. Whistler and eight other fine horses had been a present to Thane from Bear-Walks-at-Night for returning his daughter, Morning Swan, to him. Thane had grown very fond of the pony, though he felt he might never again see Bear-Walks-at-Night or Morning Swan.

For that reason, Thane felt that getting out on the trail again was good. He had grown bored in the Crow village, especially after deciding things between

Morning Swan and himself were finished. But now he often looked behind them as they traveled, hoping to see Morning Swan and Rosebud hurrying along to catch up, though he knew Morning Swan would not do that even if she wanted to. Every now and then some speck in the distance behind them would make him stop his horse and get out his spyglass, only to see a mountain sheep or an elk standing or walking along a distant trail. Thane told himself to look ahead and not back; he had grown disappointed too often searching and hoping she would show up.

The Siskadee was big country. Ashley divided the men into groups and Thane was again with Eli and part of their old brigade, midway down on the river. There were others who took some of the men with them to other reaches of the valley. Ashley specified that they all meet after the trapping season at a designated place along the river. He would mark the trees so they could locate the spot.

The Spanish had come to call this the Green River, Eli said, and likely that name would stick in time. They would begin the spring beaver hunt here as soon as the ice began to thaw in the streams. That wasn't far off and the men were anxious. The snow was leaving, but the occasional squalls and stinging winds made the camps wet and sleeping out on the open ground, be it dry or damp, made Thane's shoulder ache miserably. Now his leg added additional pain. It had healed itself, but there was still a lot of scar tissue and cold weather hampered his circulation.

Wintering with the Crows in their warm lodges had softened him physically, Thane realized, but his parting with Morning Swan had calloused him emotionally. He missed her more than he had ever dreamed, and no matter what he set his mind to thinking, she would push her way back in. In an effort to forget her he had finally gotten himself to quit looking back with his spyglass, and he had given Rising Hawk's medicine shield to Eli in hopes it would put an end to his memories of how he acquired it and his first meeting Morning Swan. But Eli proudly displayed the shield on his saddle for all to see and the memories only grew more distinct in Thane's mind.

Thane worked at himself a lot now, until he got it into his mind that he would likely never see Morning Swan again, and if he did, that he would not remain in the same camp. Thane reasoned that her decision was the best for both of them: she certainly didn't want to go off with him and leave her family once again, not after being gone from them most all of her life, and Thane wasn't ready to follow the Crow village from camp to camp.

These Indians had a certain ritual to their lives, and though they went off on war raids often during the summer months, the Crows found little reason to venture out way beyond their homelands. There was a lot of country out here, Thane said to himself each time he looked to the far horizons, and the more of it he saw, the more he wanted to see. Exploring had gotten into his blood.

Thane reminded himself he had done little while in the Crow village to soften their parting. After Morning Swan had told him she wanted to remain unattached for a while Thane had taken to other women in the village, more out of spite, he reasoned, than anything else he could think of. It had surely hurt her, though she'd hidden it well, and Thane knew she'd expected him to seek out other women once she told him she was no longer sexually available to him.

There were plenty of women in the village who thought he was special, and since he had not awakened from sleep yelling for some time, there was not much talk about the bear inside him now. He was strong and a good warrior; he would be good to be with. Maybe, they thought, he would even consider taking one of them as a wife. Morning Swan had made her choice and that was the way of things: be available for the man that wanted you or see him find someone else.

Now Thane had the guilt to contend with as well. Though his aristocratic upbringing had been rife with hypocrisy and essentially meaningless norms, the lessons drummed into him about remaining true to the one woman you care for echoed through his mind. Since he had never really cared for a woman like this before, he had never worried about casual relationships with the few women he had come upon in his young life who would accommodate him. In Virginia, the men set about pursuing sexual goals with the thought that it was expected, if not totally accepted, but the women kept their fantasies intensely private, and only the most discreet among them could enjoy abandoned relationships without being branded a harlot.

Out here the norms were different: Thane had often witnessed a couple adjourn to a lodge filled with children; usually some if not all of the children soon came out of the lodge on their own accord, not because they had been dismissed but rather because of boredom. Sex was something they had witnessed through all phases of their childhood and there was nothing secret about it. Watching adults cavort was a waste of time.

Since first learning of this, most of the other trappers had already fallen into a series of gleeful sexual escapades with numerous Crow women. Thane wanted to reason that Morning Swan had cast him off and in doing so had told him that she didn't care what he did, but Thane knew that was not the case. She'd watched him constantly, pretending not to, and Thane knew, the few times they had talked since their discussion beside the river, she had wanted to ask him again if he wouldn't reconsider leaving the fur brigade for her.

Seeing less of Morning Swan had diverted Thane

toward his only other interest to fill the void of long
winter nights: reading. He found while in the Crow
village that he had tired of the endless stories told by
the warriors, who often remained awake all night,
many of these tales repeated over and over *ad
nauseam* until he found it more rewarding to turn
again toward the pleasures offered from the printed
page. But he soon found himself with the same
problem.

Thane had only the works of Jonathan Swift he had
brought out from St. Louis with him, dog-eared and
stained with speckles of dirt and camp grease. He had
read them over and over by the light of fires, using
pine needles as bookmarks. He knew all these characters like members of the family and at times, when he
looked at his rifle, he would say, "Hello, Gulliver,"
and then expect the weapon to answer back. He often
thought maybe the rifle had gotten tired of its name
and needed a new one.

Sir John had readily noticed Thane's predicament
and had offered to loan Thane some of the books he
had with him, including some of his Shakespearean
works, on the condition that Thane learn various
parts by heart to assist him when called upon. Sir
John was continually worried he was losing his touch
on stage, a lament generally scoffed at by those who
watched him perform, and needed someone to play
scenes with him. To this Thane readily agreed, as it
was invigorating to have access to new reading material.

Thane viewed Sir John as someone entirely out of
place who would never be able to adjust. He seemed
like a man somehow lost among people he did not
know or could not communicate with. He paid little
attention to the trappers and had taken all the notes
he thought he could use regarding the Crow Indians.
He had taken to asking Thane what peculiarities he
might have noticed while in the Piegan village. Thane
would always point out that the Piegans had had no

particular use for him, so he hadn't stayed in their village long enough to concern himself with details.

Sir John had come to see Thane as one of the few men who concerned himself with things of the mind as well as the body. Sir John saw Thane's interest in the theater as surprising since most all of the other men had never even set foot inside such a place. Thane, though, was a man who enjoyed learning things and hearing what other men had to say, if he didn't have to listen to it time and again. Sir John appreciated this, as he was a man easily bored himself.

"I have the inclination to think," Sir John said to Thane one evening, "that you would prefer the printed word to the traps and the skinning had you the choice."

"You can only trap beaver so long before you start seeing them in your sleep," Thane said. "It's the country out here that makes me want to go as far as I can and see what there is to see. It boggles the mind how open it is out here."

"Yes," Sir John agreed, "the country is immeasurably immense. I cannot formulate within my mind why you don't worry, my good man, about becoming lost in this endless sea of wilderness."

"I came out here to get lost and, now that I am, I can't get enough of it," Thane told Sir John. "If you've got books enough, I'll take you all over this country and read them while you stick close so you don't get lost."

At that Sir John had to laugh. "I deem myself a miserable woodsman indeed, but I have the utmost trust I could talk myself out of anything or from anywhere, perhaps to the point where the trees would deliver me up, if needed."

Eli, who always seemed to show himself whenever Sir John talked about his abilities with the spoken word, asked Sir John, "Do you think if you said 'please' to the Blackfeet, they would spare your ass?"

"You might find my manner a bit pretentious to suit

you, Mr. Kleinen," Sir John said, "but I assure you the last word has yet to be written concerning unexpected events and their equally unexpected outcomes, if you would so consider."

"I know there's things to be learned from books," Eli said. "But the Blackfeet, they don't read."

Sir John nodded. "I imagine that to be true; and that, my good man, can be used to an advantage."

"If you don't know these hills," Eli argued, "you ain't about to have no advantage."

Sir John pointed to Thane. "He is my escort through this country, and I, in turn, have books for his reading pleasure."

"And yours, Eli," Thane said, remembering how Eli could read but had given it up because of the painful memories it brought forth.

"Don't start on that again," Eli said. "I told you I'd let you know when the time was right, and that's that. You just go ahead and take your actor friend off on Sunday picnics. As for me, I'll save my hair if it's all the same to you."

Thane was as sure of his woodsman abilities as Sir John was of his communication skills. And it was good to know that Sir John was charitable enough to share his prize book collection without question. But that in itself was not going to allow Thane to begin anew without Morning Swan.

Now even the reading was not keeping Thane from thinking about her. In the Crow village he could read nights knowing Morning Swan was just a few lodges away and that he could at least view her during the day. Now, across the Wind River Mountains from her, reading would only bring back memories of her and make him wonder if he really wanted to remain with the brigade or go back to be with her.

Stretch Tipson, who had also brought his brigade into the middle part of the Siskadee, sat near a fire with Eli and Thane one evening while Thane brooded.

The men were casting lead balls for their rifles and Thane thought about the day he had returned to the Crow village with Morning Swan and Eli's great pleasure and amazement at seeing them and Rising Hawk's medicine shield.

In a pot set over hot coals lead melted, and Thane lowered a small dipper into it. He ladled the molten lead into his mold and watched the ball form and solidify.

"Maybe I should have just come back with the Crow warriors and forgotten about that damned shield," Thane commented. "You'd have the beaver pelts I won from you now and I'd have a good leg instead of a sore one to go with my sore shoulder."

Eli grinned slightly. "And one less Injun woman to think about to boot. Don't you figure there's nary another black-haired woman in this mountains? I ain't figured you on that yet, Thane."

"I'm not concerned about no woman," Thane growled. He burned the tip of his finger in the molten lead and drew it back, shaking it and cursing.

"There's a lot you've got to learn about these mountains and the women in them," Eli told him. "You ain't seen half this country nor who's in it yet. Quit scowlin' about one who's got her own ways. There's a plenty more just a-waitin' for a young trapper to bring them a pretty necklace."

"She's worth more than a damn necklace," Thane said. "She saved my life. I can't just let that pass."

"Hell, I'd have saved your life, had I come along," Eli commented dryly. "But I wouldn't have figured you to bed me down for it."

Stretch Tipson, wanting in on the conversation, nodded and said, "I think my size makes them women consider me some kind of special warrior. There's too many of them around for me to get to liking one in particular. Besides, why would you want to let one woman direct your life?"

"These Indian women aren't like the white women," Thane argued. "They don't try to control you. They let you stay free."

Stretch took a round ball from the cast and studied it. He was smiling at Thane. "Are you going to tell me that in the long run a woman ain't a woman, wherever you find her?"

Based on what he was hearing, Thane decided Morning Swan could have her own way and he could have his. There was little reason he should let himself become attached to this particular Indian woman when the mountains were full of them. And Morning Swan was so different from the others: she had no intention of becoming an underling to a man who would do the hunting while she did menial tasks in and around the lodge. She was more than willing to cook and make clothes like the other women, Thane observed, but she would never allow herself to act as subservient.

The last thing Thane wanted to do now was leave what he had come out here for. Trapping had become a part of him, and with the other men, it was becoming an institution. They were the first to really get themselves established for many years and he could see many good years ahead. Thane reasoned that Morning Swan's concern for the beaver population and the good of the riverbeds was well founded to a degree; but beaver multiplied rapidly and there seemed little chance that these animals could ever really decline in numbers.

They were soon joined by Sir John Preston, who for a time carefully watched them molding rifle balls, turning up his nose at the odor. He had come, Thane knew, to find out whether Thane had been learning parts from *Macbeth*, as he'd promised he would.

But Thane's mind was now far from cultural notions as they related to practical life. He was trying to come up with a way to get over Morning Swan. He was now thinking about Stretch's notion regarding good women and how they own you in the end. That was certainly true: ordinary women filled a sexual void but were not much for drawing on the emotions; then a good woman would come along and she was harder to tempt sexually, and the harder it was to reach her sexually the more you wanted her until she finally gave in. By then you were trapped by her and she could lead you anywhere.

Thane took a deep breath, frustrated in his thoughts, when Sir John asked him if he had mastered any of the scenes from *Macbeth* yet.

"Christ!" Thane told him. "Do you expect a man to spend his life doing your bidding?"

Sir John raised his eyebrows. "Well, I must say you bloody well have the spirit, my good man, but I fear you've taken it all a bit out of context."

Thane looked at Sir John. "I didn't mean to be harsh. I've had other things on my mind, I guess."

"Pay it no mind," Sir John said. "Might I suggest you direct your grievances toward an acting career? You could bloody well land a good following in no time. I do believe you're cut out for the stages back there."

"I don't ever intend to go back east again," Thane said. "I've had enough of that life. I intend to stay out here for the rest of my life."

"The rest of your life? My good man, this country is too empty to remain here forever."

"That's the way I like it," Thane said. "I've had my fill of crowds and laws and people getting pushed around by the wealthy."

At that Sir John laughed. "You are far smarter than your last statement," he said to Thane. "That is, unless you don't believe the men who financed this operation you are now taking part in are not among the wealthy and influential."

"Most certainly they are," Thane said. "William Ashley is lieutenant governor of Missouri and I'm sure he knows a lot of influential people. And I understand Major Henry did quite well in mining outside of St. Louis."

"There you have it," Sir John pointed out. "Do you think those men, or any other men who have or might come into power in this fur-trading business, are going to share their profits with the men who work for them if they can possibly help it?"

Thane thought for a moment. He realized he and the other men who had gotten trapping equipment from Major Henry were certainly under obligation to repay their debts, which would be taken out of their beaver catch this year. It would then be necessary to equip themselves once again for the upcoming hunt. What Sir John was saying was that the trappers could easily get caught up in a situation where they were essentially working for nothing.

Stretch Tipson then broke in. "Who's to say we have to sell our furs to just one company? I hear tell there's bound to be plenty more come into these mountains."

"Ah, yes, the second-hand entrepreneur," Sir John said, pacing about the fire as if on stage, "the enlightened one who, upon seeing that others have become successful in a venture, seeks to establish himself in that same line of trade. Certainly there will be those sorts who gad about and offer themselves as businessmen, but do you think for a moment they will be as well capitalized as the larger, more established companies? Do you think they will give you a fair amount for your labors? They, more than anyone, will be happy to rob you blind."

Now Thane and Stretch and Eli all were watching Sir John. There was more to this man than merely a performer. Sir John knew people well, and though it seemed at times that he regarded individuals in terms of characters he knew from the theater, there was a certainty in the way he looked at someone. It was as if he put those he met into categories; and if someone were hard to fit into a category, he sought to learn more about that person.

"I fear you will see, gentlemen," Sir John continued, "that the fur business was meant to make a few lords and a great many peasants."

"Maybe there's those who don't give a hoot in hell for profit, just so there's beaver and buffler hump to feed on," Eli said to Sir John after a moment. "There'll be plenty who come out here lookin' to get rich, but there's a sight more of us who like the open spaces."

"Granted," Sir John acknowledged with a nod. "But mere simplicity does not suit everyone." He looked then to Thane. "Am I correct?"

Thane was putting newly molded rifle balls into a leather pouch. "I don't find it simple out here," Thane finally said to him. "I don't think I ever will find it simple out here. A man can do with his life what he wants and never be bored, here or in the East. Or a man can be bored to death, in the East as well."

Sir John nodded. "I see, but you might someday reconsider. And if that day comes I would like to have you with me, to show the people back there that a man of the mountains can act Shakespeare on an Eastern stage."

"I don't care to see that country again," Thane told him once more.

"Don't you ever think about your youth and where you grew up back there?" Sir John asked. "Don't you ever think about seeing the people or the country some time in the future?"

Eli and Stretch Tipson both looked at Sir John. They didn't say anything, but Sir John was close to violating the cardinal rule of association out here: you never ask a man where he's from or why he came out. If he volunteers the information, fine, but to press him could cause problems.

Thane realized Sir John liked him and was merely curious as to why he had even come out here in the first place. Sir John had never asked anyone that question before, essentially because he took no real interest in the others, aside from possibly Eli. So Thane did nothing in answer to Sir John's question but shrug.

The plantation and the death of his father hadn't crossed Thane's mind for some time, and now that Sir John had mentioned home, there arose a certain curiosity within Thane. It seemed a lifetime ago now that he had met Eli and had left two dead men in his burning trading post outside St. Louis to journey out to this fabled land. Thane now thought of Eli and his past, the terrible fire that had consumed most of his family, things he had had to live with for so long. Then he wondered about Jethro Tipson before he had come out here and was given the name Stretch. And what about Sir John? Why was he really here? Had acting in the East actually bored him all that much so that he needed to find new characters to revive his stage presence? It seemed to Thane that a man could run as far as he wanted, but his past was stuck like glue inside his brain.

"It sounds like you've grown bored with this country already," Thane said to Sir John. "And you've hardly more than got out here."

Sir John looked out to where the sun was dropping in the west, leaving a skyline that bore the color of flaming coals. His breath rose in the cold from his lips like soft haze and he watched small birds bustling for roosting space in the naked branches of a cottonwood.

"What makes you feel so alone out here?" Thane asked him. "There are a lot of men here, yet you walk around as if there's nobody here but you and you can't find the way out."

"I don't know anything about this land," Sir John finally said. "It is indeed a terrible thing that I cannot feel comfortable out here; but you see, I was not born in the woods nor can I become accustomed to a place that is wild and uncontrolled. This land cannot be tamed, and I am a master at controlling the environment I work in. I can make crowds laugh and cry at will, even run from their seats in fear. But there is nothing I can do out here. The Indians, though they take delight in them, do not understand the plays. And the other men, well, they might as well have no eyes to see with, for all that their brains will acknowledge for them. Liquor, women, and food are their sole concerns in life. But I will persist out here, that I will. Perhaps I will stay until I either have satisfaction or death."

Sir John walked over to the river's edge and watched a family of otters slide down the opposite bank and out onto the ice. They romped and squealed and rubbed one another with their noses, and dove under the ice whenever the mood would strike them. Thane, now finished bagging his lead shot, got up with Stretch Tipson and talked about cutting some meat from an elk's hind quarters. Eli, satisfied he now had enough balls molded for himself, poured two skin pouches full and tied them tightly.

"For Blackfeet and buffler," he laughed, "whichever gets into my sights first."

As the days passed and the ice turned to slush, the beaver catch grew in multiples. They came up from their stick and mud homes in droves and each trapper had more than he could do to harvest and care for his catch each day.

As the evenings grew longer Thane took to practicing with Gulliver. The Hawken rifle was now like an appendage without which he could not function. He had become a marksman of more than passing merit and he seemed at times obsessed with conquering targets smaller and smaller at longer and longer distances.

Eli commented that he thought Thane was getting ready to someday go back into Blackfeet lands and see if he couldn't rouse them again. Sir John had been watching Thane over the days and had come to understand Thane's attitude differently. It came to him suddenly, while watching Thane shoot one evening, that Thane wasn't shooting necessarily at the target, but at something it represented.

"You appear, my good man, to be ridding yourself of something from the past," Sir John said, coming up behind him.

Thane had been shooting at the skull of a beaver, some forty rods distant. It was placed on a rotting tree trunk facing forward, so that the eye sockets stared forward, with the two huge front teeth protruding like short, curved daggers. Part of one lower jawbone had been blasted away and a chip had been taken from the very top of the skull. There were numerous holes and slices in the trunk near the skull; at that distance Thane wasn't hitting it often, but often enough.

He placed a patch in the barrel, then rammed a ball down and seated it against a fresh charge of powder. Sir John watched him pull back the hammer and drop black granules of powder into the pan. Thane had not spoken the whole time and Sir John was now certain he had struck a soft spot.

"Is that a bloody beaver's skull you'd be a blowing to bits, my man," Sir John pressed, "or would it be another's skull you seek to shatter?"

Thane raised Gulliver and spoke as he sighted. "You're plenty direct enough, aren't you, John?" The rifle boomed and a small black hole appeared in the trunk just below the skull.

"I'll learn to load this thing for distance or go crazy trying," Thane commented.

"What did you think of *Macbeth*?" Sir John asked.

"Everybody has ghosts they've got to face," Thane said. "And yes, you're right, I prefer to shoot mine."

"You're better off out here, a man like you, than back where ye'd be for getting yourself into deep trouble," Sir John observed. "These men, oafs for the most part, can't help it. But you—I'd say you were once aristocracy. Might I be right?"

Thane reloaded Gulliver. "I was never really cut out for that kind of life," he said. "I'm happy for the education and the knowledge I might never have otherwise gained, but the life is truly boring."

"Ah, yes." Sir John straightened his hat. "Might I try a go at your target?"

Thane handed him the Hawken. "I know you've shot before. Just hold it steady."

Sir John sighted down the barrel and fired. Smoke rose around his face and he coughed and blew at it. "Such a dreadful piece of machinery," he commented. "I much think the Indians have a sensible notion in sticking to their bows and arrows."

Thane looked at the target. There seemed to be no new damage to the skull.

"I couldn't see where you hit," Thane told Sir John.

Sir John pointed into the trees. "I believe I may have struck a tree trunk some distance back, certainly not anywhere near the skull, you understand. My aim was slightly awry, I must say. But at all costs, I must learn to shoot one of these. Someday my life will certainly depend upon it, if I stay in this bloody outland."

"Tell me," Thane asked while he reloaded the rifle, "did you come out here to just write plays, or was there another reason?"

"I grew up in the theater," Sir John said, taking Gulliver from Thane. "Thus, I became well accustomed to the lives of actors and found myself, in adulthood, being an actor off the stage as well as on. I had hoped coming out here might give me new insight into life."

Sir John touched off and this time a hole appeared in the trunk, though far below and to the left of the beaver skull.

"So have you found things refreshing out here?" Thane asked.

"This is a much broader theater," Sir John said.

"Many of the whites out here, mainly those who are in charge, are the same as when they began their journey. They have found no reason to 'live and let live,' as it were. Nothing has changed, they have just brought their greed and prejudice with them.

"The savages, I find, are truly free in their lives. They are able to do whatever they wish whenever they wish and do not suffer from circumspection. That, my good man, will be the downfall of our own race."

Thane realized Sir John had more bitterness within him than anyone else out here, no matter their background. He had been raised in a grand environment, with everything he could hope for and the attention of the reigning classes. Yet he had become confused with life as he wished to perceive it.

"Maybe people don't learn from the writings in books and plays," Thane said. "And you think they should."

"It is not only that," Sir John confessed. Thane had reloaded the rifle and Sir John was now taking it from Thane. "But it seems not even *I* can learn from them. *I*, who have read countless literary masterpieces and have studied theater all my life, cannot control my own destiny, not when I know it is upon me."

"You mean you really didn't want to come out here?" Thane asked.

"I don't know what I wanted," Sir John said. "I was madly in love with a woman who acted with me on several occasions. She ran off with a river pirate, a filthy *pirate*, mind you. I felt I could come out here and perhaps win her back once I had mastered the guise of buckskins and running horses. Now that I am out here, I don't want the woman or the buckskins."

Sir John started toward the beaver skull. He walked, with Thane behind him, until he had come within point-blank range of the skull. Sir John then pulled the hammer back on the rifle and started to raise it to his shoulder.

"No, my good man," he said, "I find that I am like all the others. I know that there are many pitfalls in life and I become ever more aware of them when I study the plays I have learned to recite over the years. What is so bloody maddening is that I fall into the traps anyway."

"You are liked here and you will be missed," Thane said, "but you should go back if you don't want to stay."

Sir John lowered the rifle. "What is that you say? You say I am *liked*?"

"Sure," Thane said. "I, for one, would hate to see you go. And so would Eli, though he seems gruff to you. These men out here might not know anything, but when someone like you is among them and can sleep on the ground, he is accepted and he is liked. Besides, you can do a lot of things they can't, and they admire that even though it might appear they don't care about it or like you for it."

Sir John turned and studied Thane for a moment. Finally he lowered the rifle. "Well," he said, "if you aren't speaking in jest, maybe I will reconsider my circumstances."

Sir John went back to camp that night feeling as good as he ever had since coming into the country. He had a new feeling of worth and camaraderie, and considered himself a true member of the fur brigade. Early the next morning a group of mounted Indians were sighted on the skyline. The men gathered together and checked their rifles.

"Shoshones," Eli said, looking through his spyglass. "And I'd say they're riled up some. They know we come from Crow country."

Thane knew from what Eli had been saying all the way into the Siskadee that the Shoshones could go either way and at any time. This was country they fought continually for and it seemed to them at times that they had no allies. They had always been known to be friendly most of the time, but they could be indignant on a moment's notice, depending on how they were supplied with trade articles.

"Do you think they'll fight us?" Thane asked.

"They'll parlay with us first to see if we meet their standards, then they'll settle down."

Eli signaled in sign that the hearts of the Long Knives were good and that the Shoshone people were their brothers. The warriors talked some among themselves and came down off the rim of hills to the east, where they had taken position with the sun at their back.

The Shoshones, in Thane's view, were different in many respects from the Crows. They did not dress as fancily nor did they put as much emphasis on friendly relations. Upon first coming into camp they were indignant about the trapping going on in their lands, and made remarks about whether or not they liked the Crows and if they liked people who associated with the Crows. Though allied against the Blackfeet and Sioux nations, the Shoshone and Crow peoples quarreled over hunting rights to the Wind River country and there had been killings resulting from this friction.

The main Shoshone leader was an older warrior named Bird Rattle. In his hair was embedded the skull of a ground owl, its round eye sockets each filled with a piece of trade mirror painted red. In his hair were three eagle feathers tipped with horsehair and marked to show that he had counted coup in battle and was well respected. He was telling Eli how it was in their lands.

"This is our country," Bird Rattle was saying in sign and Shoshone tongue to Eli, "and we do not know if the Long Knives who come here are brothers or enemies. Just as we never know if the Crows are brothers or enemies. We will fight all those who take from us and give nothing in return."

Sir John appeared. He was carrying the medicine

shield Thane had brought back from the Piegan village.

"Well, my good man," Sir John said to Thane, "don't you think this is the time to tell of your brave deeds?"

"Good idea," Thane nodded. Eli was standing nearby with his eyebrows raised and Sir John winked at him.

Thane made sign to Bird Rattle and to the other Shoshone warriors. He pointed to the medicine shield he had taken from Rising Hawk.

"We have come as brothers to the Shoshone. I have the medicine shield of the strong Piegan warrior Rising Hawk, which I took from its stand outside his lodge."

There was silence among the Shoshone warriors and Thane held the medicine shield up for the warriors to view. The Shoshones put their hands over their mouths and stared at Thane while he continued.

"I am glad to know the Shoshone people are bitter enemies with the Piegans and the other Blackfeet tribes, for I have wounds from fighting them."

Thane told them about the arrow scar along his upper leg and how he had nearly died escaping from the Piegans. The Shoshones, particularly Bird Rattle, were impressed. They forgot about their anger and decided to smoke and make friends with these Long Knives, one of whom was a great warrior. Eli chuckled and clapped Sir John on the back while Thane led the Shoshones into camp. The day was then consumed in establishing friendly relations with the Shoshones.

During the talks, Eli came from where he had been skinning beaver and placed a pile of tails upon the ground in front of Bird Rattle and told him there would be a great many of these for their cookfires. Bird Rattle smiled and made sign that he and his warriors would feast tonight. Thane learned from Eli that the Shoshone considered beaver tails a delicacy. This seemed hard for Thane to imagine at first, as

buffalo meat was far better. Eli remarked that the
Shoshone had their reasons and it was important only
to take advantage of this and save trouble.

The Shoshones spent the better part of a week there,
telling stories and collecting beaver tails for their
people. They were put to work making hoops from
willows on which the beaver hides were stretched to
dry. They, like the Crows, were amazed at the many
different things these Long Knives had to offer in
trade and were soon loyal workers and allies.

Sir John took the opportunity to show the Shoshones something they had never before seen, and he
enlisted Thane's help. For entire evenings, Sir John
and Thane would act their parts and bring responses
from their Shoshone audience. Thane found himself
upstaged continually by Sir John and watched while
the warriors' eyes widened and they whispered among
themselves. Just as the Crows had been, they were
amazed at Sir John's stage abilities and many of them
wanted him to show them how he made some of the
faces he did while talking, and who the evil people he
impersonated were and where they lived.

Bird Rattle, however, remained most impressed by
Thane. He watched Thane continually and asked
repeatedly to hear the story about Rising Hawk's
medicine shield again. After a time he indicated to
Thane that he wanted Rising Hawk's medicine shield.
Thane told him the medicine in the shield would
become bad should anyone else own the relic. Bird
Rattle did not argue, but accepted this and told Thane
with a grin that he had a young daughter who had
come of marrying age. He wanted his daughter to
belong to a strong warrior like Thane.

Thane did not want to insult Bird Rattle, so he told
him he had a wife among the Crows. When Bird
Rattle asked him why his wife was not with him,
Thane managed to convince him that she was visiting
her family and would join him later in the season.

As the trapping continued in earnest a day didn't

pass that Morning Swan did not cross Thane's mind. She was there wherever he went, and her voice began to make itself heard inside his head, the voice that had denounced the trapping of the beaver from the streams. Whatever he told himself about the great numbers of beaver here and how easily they would survive this onslaught, each one he took from his traps brought Morning Swan's angry face into view. It was as if she stood back in invisible form, with her arms crossed, glaring at him for deciding his own ideas were worth more than she was.

She would be there while he skinned each beaver and stretched the pelt across a willow hoop for drying, then took the tail to camp for the Shoshones, leaving the rest for the wolves and coyotes that were ever present. Her invisible presence would then follow him to camp, and during the night he would wonder where she was or if she had forgotten him completely by now.

Likely she had, he reasoned, for she was strong in spirit and her family was now uppermost in her mind. Soon the trapping season would be over and they would head for the rendezvous location somewhere in this valley. Thane told himself that he would then sell his furs and would travel into different country to get more furs for the following year. In time, he reasoned, Morning Swan would dissipate from his mind like spent powder from a Hawken rifle.

Seven

IN THE CROW VILLAGE, THE CHANGE OF SEASONS MEANT moving the lodges to the summer camping grounds. For Morning Swan it meant starting her life over again with her own true people.

Little Bird, wife to Bear-Walks-at-Night, watched Morning Swan build a fire and prepare food for her daughter, Rosebud. Little Bird had come to think a great deal of Morning Swan. To Little Bird, Morning Swan seemed like her own blood rather than her adopted daughter. Ever since Morning Swan's first day in the lodge, a new happiness had settled in that Little Bird hoped would remain forever. She had watched Morning Swan appear on that snowy day, riding a flashy brown pinto pony she called Whirlwind. No one had known at first who she might be and since she had been dressed at the time as a Piegan, there had been talk she was lost somehow.

Little Bird remembered that day vividly. Morning Swan was with the young Long Knife they called Bear-Man, the white warrior Bear-Walks-at-Night and the other Crow warriors on the raiding party had left up in the Blackfeet lands during the storm. Bear-

Walks-at-Night had felt bad about leaving Bear-Man and, upon seeing his return, was overjoyed. The coming of his daughter back into his life was cause for even more happiness.

For Little Bird it had been good to see Bear-Walks-at-Night so delighted and to also gain a new daughter. Her only daughter had died in infancy and she had had three sons from another husband, two of whom had been killed in a raid by the Sioux. Then she had watched helplessly while her husband was gored to death by a mad buffalo.

Morning Swan would necessarily fill a void in her life that had been there for many winters. Since Morning Swan's coming, that void had been filled nicely, even if Morning Swan was a hard woman to understand. And though she thought a great deal of her, only now, after the passing of nearly six moons, did Little Bird think she was beginning to really get to know Morning Swan.

Morning Swan had accepted Little Bird immediately and they'd become friends from the beginning. When Morning Swan had decided to learn quillwork and beadwork, she'd told Little Bird she wanted to learn it from her, and then given her presents of tobacco and other things, including a supply of elk teeth for sewing on dress. Little Bird had then taught her a special design for decorating dresses and moccasins for dancing and wearing to ceremonies. This had sealed a lasting friendship and a special bond.

But Little Bird was entirely traditional in the way she looked at life. Too traditional in some ways to suit Morning Swan. Little Bird reminded Morning Swan that being a woman meant certain responsibilities and an established place among the people, a place subservient to the men. Though a good woman was well respected among the men, she was still thought to be forged for the production of strong warriors. Individuals, male or female, were encouraged to form their own personalities, but it was the will of the men that prevailed.

Morning Swan realized this and understood that she would never be recognized in council, nor would she be regarded as anything but a strong woman with a strong will who could do the things men do if she wished. She would never be regarded as an equal. Morning Swan did not wish to gain a lot of honors and become noted for anything; she just wanted to be accepted and respected for her views.

It seemed to Little Bird that Morning Swan should have been born male. If that had been the case, she would no doubt be a member of the council by now and would have already counted coup in battle. But she was a woman and Little Bird thought that she should now begin—no matter what she had had to do in her past life to survive—to think and act more like a woman. There were things about Morning Swan that Little Bird wished she could change: her lack of concern over remarrying, for instance. It was almost unheard of for a woman to remain by herself, especially with a small child to care for. And there were many young warriors in the band willing to be husband and provider for her.

But Little Bird had realized quickly that Morning Swan was her own woman and as independent as any of the men. She was certainly as capable a hunter, as she demonstrated one evening by stalking and bringing down a large bull elk. Little Bird felt concern in a way but did not interfere. Bear-Walks-at-Night certainly showed no real concern, so Little Bird felt it right to just be content herself with the way things were and not try to mother Morning Swan in any way—she was certainly beyond that.

There are things, though, that a woman can sense within another woman and Little Bird sensed love-sickness within Morning Swan. Somewhere in the middle of the cold moons Morning Swan and the

young trapper, Bear-Man, had grown apart. Morning
Swan had been affected by this and was trying in her
own way to relieve herself of his memory. Little Bird
saw this clearly and thought that it might be good to
try to help Morning Swan through this time in her life.

The days had turned warm in the valleys, and
though the snows still came on occasion, it was time
to move the village to summer camping areas. They
would again travel to the Elk River to be with their
relatives within the clans of the Many-Lodges band,
and travel up into the higher ground amidst a small
range of mountains where the Medicine Rock was
located, along the waters of Arrow Creek. It was time
for the warm moons ceremonies and the villagers
were happy. Now, while they prepared to move, Little
Bird thought it appropriate to talk to Morning Swan.

Morning Swan had built herself a travois and was
stacking her belongings on it when Little Bird approached. Little Bird gave Rosebud—whose wide
black eyes danced whenever she saw Little Bird—a
small doll and asked her to dress it for the journey
down to Elk River. Rosebud bounced away with pride
at being able to dress a doll for Little Bird.

"Do you hope Bear-Man, when he is finished with
trapping the beaver, will come down to the Elk River
to see you?" Little Bird asked Morning Swan.

Morning Swan looked up from her work. "I think it
would be better if he didn't. It would be best if we did
not see one another again."

"Maybe in time you will feel differently. Either that
or time will heal your sorrow."

"Bear-Man has made his choice," Morning Swan
said, "and I see no reason to chase him around. I do
not care to live among the other trappers. I want to be
with you and my father, and the rest of my people."

"Maybe Bear-Man will some day want to live with
us," Little Bird said. "Our people all like him. He is a
great warrior. He is blessed with great honor."

"That is the problem," Morning Swan commented.
"He knows he is blessed with honor. Though he does
not fully understand yet, he realizes the spirits look
upon him with favor. So he thinks I will want him so
badly I will do whatever he wishes."

"You two are very much alike in many ways," Little
Bird said. "I do not want to tell you what to do, but if
you want to remain as independent as you are now
and still have a husband, there are not many men to
choose from who will allow you that freedom. Bear-
Man is the only one I can think of who would let you
hunt for the lodge as you do now."

Morning Swan shrugged. "I suppose you are right.
But why do I need a husband?"

Morning Swan was glad Little Bird had spoken to
her about Thane and what she intended to do about
him. What she intended to do was nothing. The more
she thought about Thane and the past winter, the
more she considered how different they were. She had
noticed how Thane seemed continually restless and
had become bored staying in the village all winter. She
saw how he had taken to looking at lines of figures in
what he called books, while hearing things in his head,
which he had told her he called reading.

This was not an activity Morning Swan understood
at all; among her people, all stories were told orally
and passed down from generation to generation.
Winter counts were painted on buffalo robes in the
form of pictures, which told a story. But there was no
way she could understand what he saw in these books
of his. When they had stopped seeing each other to
make love he would point into a book and tell her how
she was acting the same way as women in his lands
and that there was no reason for it. Morning Swan had
always asked him if the women in his lands enjoyed
having men want them only for their bodies.

Morning Swan was sure within herself that she
could not be happy living Thane's life. He wanted to

spend his time exploring the country and she wanted to remain with her people and have the one thing she had finally gotten for the first time in her entire life: stability.

But in the back of her mind, Morning Swan realized that the times she wanted ahead for herself and Rosebud might not come to pass so easily. She realized more than anything else that the coming of the Long Knives into the mountains meant great change. Though some of the Long Knives wanted merely to live day to day and cared little about anything else, many others of these white men were not like the Indian peoples in any way. They put up flags and other markings in places and said that now these locations belonged to them.

What these white men had yet to learn was that the land was there to use for life-support and not for ownership. Morning Swan worried that they would never learn this. In getting to know Thane she realized there were traditions he had come to know as a child that would always be with him. One of these was that he was somehow superior to her people and could therefore have them do his bidding. It was in his mind, as if he had been born with it, and this attitude was reflected among most all the trappers, whether or not they were chiefs among their people. Many of the trappers were French or French and Indian mixed and it was easier to relate to them, for their attitudes were different. But the men like Thane, with the pure and pale white skin, were lordly in their manner and Morning Swan didn't care for it.

Morning Swan wanted to believe that in time Thane might possibly change to a degree. In traveling with him from the Piegan lands to the Elk River, Morning Swan had noticed his admiration for her ability to coexist with the land for survival. This was something he wanted to develop within himself. Morning Swan could see that he now held much more respect for the rivers and the grasslands, for the winds and the storms that could come at any time, something that anyone who is not a fool develops when near death, as Thane had been. In the back of her mind, Morning Swan then began to hope that he might be one of the few who decided finally that this land might be tamed, but it could never be conquered.

During the warm moons, the Kicked-in-Their-Bellies moved camp all over Crow country. They remained for a time on Arrow Creek, where Morning Swan took part in the tobacco planting ceremony, as well as the dance to bring the buffalo. With others who had been successful in past hunts, she lined up and shot her arrows toward the sacred Medicine Rock, the huge rock of unusual power that could bring the buffalo. She left offerings of beads and other presents at the base of the Medicine Rock, where it was said the ancestral powers rested and where the Little People made their home.

It was the Little People who owned these mountains, and all the other mountains. The elders in the village spoke of them often, and there were those who knew their power and told of how they had come to be the protectors of the Crow people. It was said the Little People possessed a certain strong medicine and that, though very small in stature, they were very powerful, each with the strength of ten men. It was said the Little People had often helped in battle against the Striped-Feathers-Arrow people, the Cheyenne, a traditional enemy; and also the Lacotah, whom others called the Sioux.

Whenever an enemy came into Crow country—and sometimes this was the Arapaho to the south, and at times the Shoshone and the Salish and the Nez Perce—there were stories of the Little People driving these enemies away by hiding in the forest and then leaping out to tear the hearts out of their horses.

Though Morning Swan had never seen any of the Little People, she knew well of their power and left all communication with them in the hands of those who knew their medicine.

The spring hunt went well and Morning Swan killed enough to bring in a lot of meat and also have new hides for covering her lodge. Throughout the warm moons, the village moved to be sure there was enough grass for the horses and enough wood and good water for the fires. They camped on the waters of the Tongue and then on the Little Bighorn, at the place of Many-Ash-Trees, and also on Lodge Grass Creek. While there, twelve young warriors went on a raid against the Lacotah. Two of the young men were killed, and when the mothers and other relatives of the young men went into the hills to mourn, Rosebud said to her mother, "No one would have died if Bear-Man had been here to carry the pipe."

But as the warm moons came and went, and another season of cold then passed as well, Morning Swan saw nothing of Thane. He did not come, though some of the men spoke of seeing him to the south, in the lands of the Shoshone, the Snake people. It was said he had taken one of their women and she was traveling with him. Morning Swan overheard this while they discussed the white traders and the strong one among them they had named Bear-Man.

Somehow Morning Swan had thought Thane might still return to the Kicked-in-Their-Bellies and remain with her, but she now realized that was no longer likely. They were in a favorite camping place, along the waters of the Rotten-Sun-Dance-Lodge, when she decided one night after Rosebud was asleep to go off by herself and wait for her spirit helper—her medicine, the white swan—to come to her in the morning. She would go to a special place where there were a number of beaver ponds that backed the water up into large pools filled with fish. Upon a hill above the ponds was a special grove of aspen trees. It was a place that seemed to her to be a dream, a meadow fed by waters that backed up underground from the beaver dams, filled with small birds and animals and an abundance of wildflowers that filled the bogs with color.

Morning Swan began her walk through a warm evening in which the moon was round and soft and the stars had come down so that they might be touched. For the passing of nearly four full seasons now she had held her tears. She had fought against the true feeling she had for Thane, the feelings that had remained with her though her mind had told her they were not meant to live together. This night her tears came and she let them flow as she made her way up into the large patch of aspens which grew on the side of a hill.

She knew this place well. She called it the Place-of-the-Swan-Trees. She had learned of this place when still a young girl, before the Piegan raid. This was where she had first received her medicine, after falling down a hill and hitting her head. She had awakened to see a beautiful white swan looking at her. The swan had led her to the beaver dams and to a pond of water, where the swan got in and began to swim. Then it had told her that this place was special and to come here to talk whenever times were bad. The swan had told her to always think of the water and to protect it, for it was the most necessary part of life. As she looked around now, it was easy to understand what the white swan had been telling her. The many dams the beaver had built stopped the water and held it in place for the many speckled fish that jumped and splashed; and then it backed up far underground to supply moisture for the wildflowers and the big grove of aspens that grew up on the hill.

The words of the swan had remained with Morning Swan, and though she had not seen the swan each time she came, she knew the aspens, which were always there, were friends of the swan and would help her any way they could.

Throughout her early life, before she was taken away, she had come to the beaver ponds and then up to the aspens in times of happiness as well as sadness, and as before when her heart was heavy, the trees, their leaves whispering in the night breeze, had comforted her and relaxed her with their soft embrace. They spoke to her now, as they always did when she looked to them for help. It is hard, the aspens told her, when someone's soul touches yours yet there is disharmony. But a person must be how they are inside, and if being with another creates tension within, then it is not good to remain that way.

Lying back against the ground, looking at the stars through the tops of the trees, Morning Swan felt sure she had been hoping against her better judgment that Thane would forget about his wandering urges to be with her. But she knew that he was also not one to be trapped by another's demands, nor harbored against his will. He was like some sort of wild creature who had escaped a leash and was running from that leash, which he felt was somehow stalking him.

In her mind, Morning Swan could not fully understand what it was deep in Thane's mind that made him seem distant. She had never been able to reach into him and have him totally relax around her. She had never witnessed him come to total relaxation around anybody, not even the old Long Knife named Eli, who was his closest friend. Perhaps, Morning Swan thought, the bear was still within him and he could not relax until the bear was finally gone.

The night broke to day and the leaves of the aspens took on the colors of light to deep green as the growing light touched them, round and lightly toothed. Each one hung delicately on wire-thin petioles, shimmering like opal-green silk. In the draw below, the soft cooing of mourning doves echoed through the dawn, and their wings sang overhead as they flew to water and back.

Morning Swan remained within the aspen grove and watched the sun rise into full view. She watched below, where the beaver dams held the ponds of water, and saw a single white swan moving effortlessly across the surface of the still water. But as soon as she stood up to go down and listen to the swan, she saw the bird disappear behind some trees, and it never reappeared.

Morning Swan wondered then why the swan had decided to leave. She looked down into the village and saw a small figure begin to make its way toward the aspens. Soon Rosebud was seated beside her.

"Why didn't you wait for me, Mother?"

"I came up late last night," she told Rosebud.

"Why didn't you bring me? You always feel better when I am with you."

Morning Swan was continually amazed at how fast Rosebud was developing, growing physically as well as mentally. She couldn't remember being as smart as Rosebud was at the same age. Dolls had now given way to learning to cook and sew real clothes. Her black eyes were always confident, and lately she had taken to looking after her mother in a way.

"You like these trees, don't you, Mother?" Rosebud said.

"From the time I was your age, and before, I have liked this place," Morning Swan said. "I hope you will come to love these trees as I have."

"Are these trees very important to you, Mother?"

"They offer me a kind of peace that is hard to explain. They allow me to think and understand better."

"Could you get over it if somehow they were lost, by fire or something?" Rosebud asked.

Morning Swan looked at her daughter. "I guess I

would have to, wouldn't I? We all have to accept loss, even if it is a favorite patch of trees."

Rosebud smiled. "When we leave this camp, the trees must stay behind. But I will be with you."

Morning Swan hugged her daughter. "You are a wise child. Yes, I love you far more than the trees and I always will. You and I are one. We can help each other."

So it was within Morning Swan now to rationalize that a life with Thane, at least at this point, was not possible. She knew she would never fully dispel him from her mind. She could try, but she would likely not be able to. But for now, she would think as little of him as she could.

Rosebud wasn't talking about him much any more and that was good; she had grown accustomed to his absence and in time would likely forget him completely. He was better suited to moving whenever he wanted to and seeing all he could out here. He wanted to reach far mountains and rivers in distant lands in all directions that meant nothing to her, as her people were here in these mountains and the only real traveling they did was to trade fairs among the other clans along the lower Yellowstone and along the Platte River. Sometimes they traveled a distance east to visit and trade with their distant relatives, the Dirt Lodge People, along the Big Muddy River where they lived near the Mandans. There were also times, when relations were good and there had been no recent warfare, that the pipe of peace would be carried to the Shoshone and the Nez Perce lands to trade. But now Morning Swan did not want to think of Shoshone lands. If Bear-Man had taken a Shoshone woman to travel with him, then that was the way it must be.

It was time to look ahead and not back, Morning Swan decided. They had a new life to live now with her people, all throughout the Crow country, enjoying the warm weather that was coming upon them. It was good to be alive and free and capable of providing for oneself. The land was good.

With two years of trapping now behind him, Thane was learning the mountains. Since the first rendezvous a year past on a fork of the Siskadee named after Major Andrew Henry, he had been in the Bear River country, through the Snake River canyon, and then up into the country west of the great peaks the French called the Tetons. They had trapped there along the river and up to a big lake before moving back down into the Siskadee, which everyone was calling the Green River more and more.

The spring hunt on the Green River had again been a good one and Thane was getting more and more of a reputation in the mountains. By now most everyone had heard of his encounter with the grizzly his first season out and his excursion into Blackfoot country for Rising Hawk's medicine shield, which he displayed proudly to all who cared to see it. The scars on his shoulder and leg were now white and jagged, grim reminders of his near misses with death. Thane had come to use them as a symbol of his strength.

He had worked to strengthen and bolster his upper body, to improve the blood circulation and thereby lessen the agony of his shoulder on cold mornings and during a change of weather. Antoine Lavelle had told him that exercising the injured areas had helped him a lot, running on the injured leg and overworking the torn arm, producing more mobility and strength. It had helped Antoine considerably, though nothing would enable him to regain full use of his arm.

Thane had taken a lesson from Antoine and had begun doing regular workouts with his shoulders and arms, chinups from the limbs of trees and pushups off the ground. He stayed with his program each day, whether or not he was motivated at the time. At first his shoulder had ached from the excessive work, but before long his shoulder was reacting well and the muscles on his shoulders, arms, and chest were bulky and iron-hard.

Thane was not, however, completely healed mentally. The occasions were rare but the nights still would come when he would arise in his sleep and grab Gulliver, his rifle, only to find the grizzly did not really exist. He was concerned that this problem might never go away, as grizzlies were common and he would see them in great numbers during the fall months when they roamed the valley bottoms in search of berries, and then again in the spring when they congregated along the major rivers to feast on buffalo that had fallen through winter ice and drowned.

Old Ephraim, as the trappers had all come to call the grizzly, was the true lord of the land and it seemed ironic to Thane that he had met the most terrible beast in all this country his first month trapping. In his mind, Thane felt the mountains had served him up to their most formidable hunter, as if to test him to see if he could take the worst from the very beginning.

After the grizzly and the taking of Rising Hawk's medicine shield, Thane found himself looked up to by most everyone trapping in the mountains. The Indians believed his medicine to be strong and good and were honored to be in his presence. Thane found it sometimes amusing and most often boring. He saw himself as no different than any of them, just luckier. In either case, with the grizzly or the medicine shield, he would surely have been killed if someone hadn't come to his aid. The grizzly had died at the hands of the other trappers, and after leaving the Piegan village, he had been saved by Morning Swan.

There was nothing, Thane had finally come to realize, that was going to rid his memory of her. Though he had told the Shoshone war chief, Bird Rattle, he could not have his daughter because of a Crow wife, he had later gone into the village and had told Bird Rattle he would take his daughter after all.

He had accepted her as his wife, but only for a time. Leaf-on-a-Bush, though only twelve years of age, had catered to his every need, which in itself had come to annoy him. He didn't want a woman who was always at his side, begging to do something for him. He didn't want a woman who looked to him for protection every time a new day came when they were traveling enemy lands.

Finally, the young Shoshone woman had confided in Thane that her heart really belonged to a young Shoshone warrior named Elk Heart, whom she had cared for since being a young girl. Elk Heart had been greatly disappointed when Bird Rattle had announced to the Shoshone people that his daughter would be the wife of the strong Long Knife warrior with the medicine shield.

Thane had then traded Leaf-on-a-Bush to Elk Heart for a dozen good horses and a number of beaver pelts. Elk Heart and Leaf-on-a-Bush were happy, and when Thane had then given the horses to Bird Rattle and explained to him that he would likely someday be going to the north into Blackfeet lands to trap, Bird Rattle had also been happy. Bird Rattle was sure that Thane had already united his male member with his daughter many times and that his power had been thrust into her so that her babies, no matter who the father now might be, would become strong warriors.

"It must be a blessing to have such a special tool," Eli said to Thane. "You got lightning in it or something?"

"Your knee don't seem to keep you from dropping your britches on occasion," Thane told Eli, reminding him of this most recent visit to the Shoshones. "You had a warm robe to curl up in most every night."

"But it was the same robe," Eli complained. "I cain't even count the different beds you been in lately."

Now, with another rendezvous not far away, Thane

was again traveling with Eli. The brigade was under Thane's command now for the most part, Eli having given way to the younger man with respect and gratitude. It was easier for Thane to shoulder the burdens of watching over inexperienced men; he had more patience. Besides, Eli figured, it was time Thane lived up to his reputation.

Spring had arrived and Thane rode at the head of the brigade, with Eli right behind. They were going toward the Bear River country, south to the Cache Valley, near the Great Salt Lake. Midway down Green River they struck a small tributary stream where a party of Shoshone were camped, on their way to the white trappers' rendezvous. The Shoshones reported seeing a war party of Atsina, often called Gros Ventres, who were passing through the area. The Shoshones welcomed the brigade with open arms and said it was good they had come. Now the two parties would be too strong for the Gros Ventres and could travel together the rest of the way to rendezvous.

Eli and Thane, along with three other trappers, went on a side trip up into the Popo Agie country. Eli wanted to reunite with his longtime friend, the giant pine tree, while the other three trappers were interested in adding to their supply of beaver plews. In the higher country, where the air was still cool and the snow still settled in shadowed areas and banked along the north slopes, the beaver had not yet begun to shed their fur and the three trappers, named Lettle, Cashmore, and Whitson, were anxious to work the streams.

There seemed to be little concern among them for the Gros Ventre war party, as Eli believed they had passed on through and were likely a good ways north by now, headed back to their homeland near the Blackfeet. As allies of the Blackfeet, the Gros Ventre were in the minds of many just another division of the tribe so feared by all in the mountains. Eli, who knew

all the tribes out here, said he knew for a fact the Gros
Ventre were kin to the Arapahoes and had gone north
years past. They traveled back south regularly to visit
the Arapahoes. But to most trappers Gros Ventre and
Blackfeet were one and the same word.

Thane and Eli left the three trappers to hunt the
upper streams above South Pass while they went
around the edge of the mountains to the Popo Agie.
They moved along the river, past an area called the
Sinks, where the water disappeared underground, and
then further up until Eli finally stopped his horse and
dismounted.

"I wanted you to finally meet this big feller, while
we're in the country," Eli said to Thane.

Thane watched Eli walk reverently toward a huge
pine that stood by itself. Thane then dismounted and
joined Eli, who stood at the base of the tree talking.

The pine was gigantic, as if it had been alive since
the beginning of the world itself. It was hard to really
know how high it had once been, as the top had died
out and the winds had whipped it back. Around it
were younger trees and Thane noticed they had a
different form of needle. Eli explained that this old
tree had survived a long-ago fire and was now one of
the only trees of its kind in the forest here.

Thane marveled at the grandeur of the tree itself,
the personality it seemed to emit, like an ancient man
who never spoke but merely communicated with his
mind. Its branches spread out in all directions like
huge gnarled arms, and clusters of needles took form
only along the ends of little boughs that reached out
and grew wherever they could find light enough
through the mass of growth.

Thane wondered at it for a time, watching birds fly
zigzag courses from it to other trees and back. The
pine was a landmark for all living things: strong and
alone, a descendent from another time and place, the
last of a breed which might never be seen again.

"Don't you think this old man could tell some stories?" Eli laughed.

"I've never seen anything like it," Thane said to Eli. "There are a lot of old, old trees back in the Blue Ridge country, but I've never been so impressed by anything in my life. I'll bet Sir John and Stretch Tipson would like to see this."

"Stretch would check to see if he wasn't just as tall," Eli said, "and that Englishman would start to talkin' gibberish. They ain't ready for this yet, not like you are."

Eli realized that after the mauling by the bear and his close call with the Blackfeet, Thane had never taken life in these mountains for granted. Stretch had yet to realize he wasn't bigger than the whole country and Sir John needed to appreciate it more. There were more and more men coming into the mountains now and Eli figured there would be a great many who would come out just to see what was here. Some might stay, and a lot would go back where they came from, and a good many, Eli predicted, would go under. He saw this country as a future graveyard for greenhorns whose bones would come to be scattered by the wolves and then settle into the mud of the rivers and streams.

Eli took Thane to the base of the tree and motioned with a bony finger up into the branches. Among the branches were pieces of tattered skin robes that hung loosely and remnants of arrows, war clubs, and other weaponry.

"A burial tree?" Thane asked.

"At some time," Eli said. "I told you there was a good many tales hidden under the bark of this here tree."

That evening they made camp just off from the big tree near a sweetwater spring and Thane set a cut of buffalo hump ribs to roasting. The wood was damp and smoked for a time until it dried and began to take on a deep red. A breeze toyed with the flames and now and then sent swirls of sparks into the air, rising like fireflies into the night. When they had eaten, Thane settled back to watch the coals glow and listen to Eli while the old trapper rubbed the stiffness out of his knee.

"I've come to get up in years," Eli was saying, while he worked on his knee, "and there's nothing to say I'll get by tomorrow, or even tonight. But as long as I keep breathin', I aim to look across these mountains. I might've lost my hair long ago, but I should never have gone back to those crazy white diggin's."

"You're out here for good now," Thane told Eli. "There's no better place for you than here. No better place for anybody, for that matter."

"There'll be plenty who see it that way before long," Eli lamented. "Plenty. God, but it's a crime what happens when folks cram together someplace."

"This country's too big," Thane said. "And the Blackfeet won't let people cram into their country."

Eli continued to rub his knee, but looked up at Thane. "What do you figure, that the Blackfeet got more people than hell does? Christ, what happens if just a few of the folk back east get a whiff of what's out here? They'll be out to settle quicker than a bull can fart. And there'll come a damn sight of people along behind. The Blackfeet, they'll take a lot of hair, you can figure; but there ain't enough of them that they won't sooner or later get wiped out themselves."

"What would bring folks out here?" Thane asked. "This isn't where anyone would take up farming."

"Not here, but farther west," Eli said. "It rains more the farther over you get. They'll come to see and they'll cross this country like bees to honey."

Eli finished rubbing his knee and was getting ready to roll into his robes. Thane pulled a worn and frazzled book from one of his packs. It was a copy of *Gulliver's Travels*.

"Don't turn in just yet," Thane said, placing the book on Eli's lap. "Read some of this to me."

Eli looked hard at Thane. "I thought I told you I'd commence to readin' when I was good and ready."

"You'll never be good and ready," Thane said. "You'll never read another word in your life if someone doesn't build a fire under you."

Eli raised an eyebrow. "And you figure to raise a fire under me?"

"I know you've wanted to get into a book again for some time," Thane said. "I noticed it when I was reading, how you'd watch me like you wanted to come over at times and ask for the book. Go ahead now and read."

Eli picked up the book and opened it. "Ahh! I don't know about this."

"Read," Thane insisted. "Go ahead and read."

Eli took the book in one hand and gripped his cane tightly with the other. He began to struggle with the words. Thane urged him on and he continued to struggle, clenching the cane and beating it against the ground beside him. Thane moved over and held the cane down.

"Just read," Thane said. "Nobody is going to hit you if you can't pronounce the words. Just relax."

"What are you talkin' about?" Eli said to Thane. His eyes remained on the pages of the book.

Thane realized Eli would never admit to having problems reading because of the emotional trauma in his early life, so Thane just once again asked him to read.

Eli looked up from the book to Thane and his lips began to tremble. Thane took him and held him and Eli put his head against Thane's shoulder and the tears came. He held Eli for a time longer and then Eli wiped his eyes and began to grumble.

"Don't worry about anything," Thane said again. "Just read."

Eli started in on *Gulliver's Travels*, slowly and methodically, working to pronounce each word. After a time it came more smoothly and Thane could see

that Eli could have been a good reader throughout his
life, had he not gone through the torture as a child.
But there was a lot of time left for him to read, in the
Crow village and anywhere they might happen to be.
Eli was laughing a bit now as he looked up at Thane,
happy to be getting the words better. Eli had just
reopened a new world of wonder.

Eight

WILD JACK CUTTER SCANNED THE COUNTRY WITH HIS STER-
ile, glassy eyes as he rode south through the mountains. Toots was behind, wearing his filthy tricorn hat
and with his bugle around his neck, leading the pack
string. The passes were open now and in a couple of
days they would cross the top of the mountains on the
Pacific side of the Divide, at the head of the Columbia
River, and make their way on down into the Siskadee.

Their ultimate destination was the rendezvous in
Cache Valley. The two had few pelts to show for the
spring hunt and it was on Cutter's mind to remedy
that. They wanted to make a good impression on
General Ashley at their first rendezvous with the
Americans since deserting old Eli Kleinen's brigade
up near the Great Falls. That would mean showing
that their trapping skills warranted attention by arriving fully loaded with beaver.

Cutter, never one for straining himself when he
could capitalize on someone else's work, had the
notion to be patient and wait for the right opportunity
to get the furs they needed without doing any trapping
themselves. Besides, it was too late in the year to

consider harvesting this year's fur. Cutter was not worried. There were trappers they had seen along the way whose luck had been good; it was just a matter of catching a few of them off by themselves.

Now that the fur trade was firmly established in the mountains, Cutter wanted to get back in the good graces of the American companies. Those whose allegiance had leaned toward the British were not highly thought of. He and Toots might possibly have made a mistake by joining the Hudson's Bay Company when sides were being drawn for the fur competition in the mountains. They should have quit Fry and his Hudson's Bay brigade a year back, Cutter was thinking to himself. The Americans were clearly going to eventually dominate the fur trade in the mountains and it was time to make the jump.

As it was there were few fond memories of the Hudson's Bay Company in Cutter's mind. The pay had been small and the stay boring. Fry and his men put more emphasis on establishing trade networks and developing points where they could meet regularly with the tribes of the Blackfeet and those Indians on the Pacific side of the mountains who were willing. Cutter's idea was to trap and get the beaver, no matter if the Indians liked it or not. What was the use in wasting time with talk and gimmickry? There wasn't nothing to rubbing out an Indian.

Toots had remained with Cutter all this time and he had no intention of leaving him. Cutter meant safety, security, and entertainment, an odd sort of entertainment that Toots appreciated. Toots liked to see Cutter cause blood to flow, which seemed to be something Cutter had to initiate at least once a month to keep himself happy. Toots loved to watch and gain satisfaction for all the years he had been bullied and tormented, from school days through his adult life.

It didn't matter to Toots what Cutter did to his victims, as long as they suffered. Toots had watched with glee while, during the first week with the

Hudson's Bay Company, Cutter had killed an Iroquois with red paint around his eyes who had been smiling at him. It had been gratifying to Toots to see the Iroquois's face when Cutter's knife ripped open his belly, to see the Iroquois stare at his own entrails as they fell out onto the ground. Toots had reached a strange ecstasy within himself at seeing the dying light in the Iroquois's eyes as he slumped to his knees, his mortal life hanging in long coils that draped through his fingers.

Fry had become angered, but Cutter had told him he didn't want no man-woman sort of being looking at him that way and Toots had said the Iroquois had been reaching for Cutter's crotch. That had settled the matter. Cutter had then led Toots into the brush on the outskirts of camp and allowed Toots to fondle him and ultimately gratify himself with oral application to his genitals.

It suited Cutter just fine: kill someone and then have Toots suck him off. Cutter liked to kill and Toots liked to watch and then thank Cutter in his odd sexual way for pleasing him. Cutter saw it as a means of getting pleasure two ways.

But after a time it became a maddening sort of thing for him. He liked to kill and have Toots respond, but afterward there was a strange depression which set in over him. And it couldn't be remedied by having Toots service him again, for even though Toots wouldn't object, the pleasure was not as gratifying as when Toots had seen blood and was sexually excited himself.

So Cutter found himself wanting to kill more and more, especially as this strange sexual need grew on him. He was becoming obsessed with Toot's response to death and dying. With Fry's brigade, he had almost gone too far, and it was good that they had decided to leave the Hudson's Bay Company.

That first week with the Hudson's Bay Company, Cutter would have killed another Iroquois too, if he hadn't left right away. The Iroquois's name was Antoine Lavelle, Cutter remembered, and his smile had been the same. The man had been lucky.

Since butchering the Iroquois, Cutter had found the opportunity to kill more Hudson's Bay men and get away with it. It wasn't uncommon to lose personal articles and maybe a prize horse to someone who was intending to desert anyway. Cutter had gotten good at seeing this intention in the eyes of the men, and Fry had eventually seen it as a means of keeping the men in his brigade from deserting. Cutter and Toots would catch them deserting and kill them, then show off personal articles of theirs the men would have made off with.

It was only when Fry suspected Cutter of selecting deserters that he had told Cutter there would be no more police work in his brigade. Two men had been killed who, according to the others in the brigade, had had no intention of deserting. It was then that Cutter and Toots had made up their minds to return to the Americans.

Cutter and Toots crossed the Yellowstone Plateau and worked their way south into the Siskadee. Most all of the trappers had already left the area for rendezvous and Cutter knew it would be hard to catch up to them now—unless there were a few who had remained behind.

Now Cutter stopped and rubbed the beard on his scarred face. It grew patchy through the crosshatched knife marks on his right cheek, something the Kiowas had done to him years back. He pulled his spyglass from his saddle pack as Toots rode up alongside.

"What you see, Jack?"

"Shut up," Cutter answered. "I'll tell you when the time comes."

A large party of riders had come over the hill in front of them and were reining their horses.

"Gros Ventres." Cutter lowered his spyglass. "Reach into that bag on the second mule and get them scalps for me. Hurry!"

Toots dismounted and stumbled on stiff legs back to the second mule. He rustled in a skin bag while Cutter growled at him to pick up the pace, as the Gros Ventres were now coming toward them. Finally Toots handed Cutter a number of scalps, the hair long and stringy, with the scalp skin dried and mounted on small circular willow hoops. Cutter selected the best trophies and smiled while he began to stroke the hair of the scalps, as if they were pets.

The Gros Ventres rode in close, their bows armed. They saw Cutter hold the scalps up into the air and begin to speak in their language.

"We come as brothers to the Gros Ventre and Blackfeet peoples," Cutter was saying. "See, we have slain our enemies, the Crows, and you may have these as presents."

The Gros Ventres began to talk among each other. Cutter continued to speak to them, telling them they had come from the north and were their brothers. Soon the Gros Ventres were nodding and they came forward, their bows lowered.

Cutter smiled at Toots, who was wide-eyed. "Now they'll see what I think of the Crows," he said.

While Toots and the Gros Ventres looked on, Cutter began to cut pieces from one of the scalps and stuff them into his mouth. He chewed grinning at them, and began to yell, his mouth filled with dried skin and hair.

The Gros Ventres put their hands over their mouths and turned their horses. They had found two Long Knives who it appeared were enemies of the Crows and brothers to the Blackfeet. But the big one was a crazy person and to even be around someone so crazy was not good. It was best to leave them alone.

When the Gros Ventres had gone back over the hill, Cutter spit out the hair and pieces of scalp. Toots was leaning against one of the mules. He was vomiting.

"What the hell, Jack?" Toots asked. "God A'mighty!"

"We ain't got the time to fiddle and smoke pipes and all that," Cutter said. "And we didn't stand a chance fightin' them. It was best just to scare 'em off."

Two days later Cutter was looking down off toward a small creek. He was watching the activity of three trappers who were hobbling horses and making camp. Cutter noticed the number of mules with them that were loaded down with beaver pelts. He lowered the spyglass and grinned.

"Well," he told Toots, "maybe we got lucky after all."

There seemed no question the three trappers were headed for rendezvous down on Green River. Cutter continued to watch them through his spyglass while they set a cut of elk meat to roasting.

The three trappers, Lettle, Cashmore, and Whitson, fed the fire with branches and sticks and talked about the upcoming rendezvous. They had a good number of furs with them, including Thane's and Eli's, and were enjoying good success here as well. Fresh beaver plews hung in multiples drying on hoops from the branches of the pines around them. But now, after two days without Thane or Eli, unrest was settling in.

"We oughtn't to be here, I'm thinkin'," Lettle said. Since arriving, his eyes had been moving all around.

"I'm tired of hearin' that," Whitson told him. "For the last time, there ain't a Gros Ventre nowhere close. They take the back trail out on account of the Shoshone."

Cashmore, who had been listening, grunted. "The Gros Ventres butcher the Shoshone regular."

"That ain't the truth," Whitson argued. "Them Gros Ventres come a visitin' this time of year. They don't hanker to war, not with women and children along."

"Just the same," Lettle put in, "we'd have been a

sight smarter to just stay down low with the bunch. I've got a bad feelin'.''

The sun had settled down over the horizon and when the night came on fully, it was Lettle who again began to complain. He asked the other two if things felt right to them. He was looking out past the edge of dim light made by the fire.

"Stand watch if you've a mind to," Whitson told him. "We'll be back down out of here tomorra, and a good sight richer in beaver too."

Cutter and Toots sat back in the shadows, on the side of a little rise, within earshot. They had come in on foot, leaving their own horses and mules hobbled back a ways. Toots was barely able to control himself, so excited was he about what Cutter had planned.

"When you aim to do them in, Jack?" Toots asked, squirming where he sat on the bank.

"Keep yourself quiet!" Cutter hissed. "If they hear you . . . Damn, I'll break your neck yet."

Cutter then broke away from Toots and moved off a ways to sit, thinking it would keep Toots silent and worried if he sat alone. Toots remained silent in the darkness while Cutter watched the three trappers sitting down by their fire. Cutter wanted more time to study the situation with the three trappers and not have Toots at his elbow, doing odd sorts of things.

Toots remained nervous and alone, with Cutter sitting a ways over and paying him no attention. He wanted to move over closer but every time he had tried that in the past, Cutter had cuffed him like a bear. Toots had always enjoyed having Cutter look out for him, but as of late, Cutter was not as pleasant as he used to be.

Cutter listened to the trappers talk a while longer. They discussed Thane and Eli and when they would be back the following day. Whitson and Cashmore finally decided to crawl into their robes, while Lettle remained awake and alert, his head turning in all directions.

Cutter moved back over to Toots. Toots began to breathe happily, until he felt Cutter's hand.

"You ready?" Cutter hissed. He had Toots by the cuff of the neck.

Toots raised his rifle partway and struggled for air. "It's here, Jack. I kin do it."

"And don't make any noise," Cutter warned him before he left.

Cutter was lost in the darkness and Toots began to fidget again. Toots didn't like it much when Cutter was out of sight; he had come to depend on Cutter as a cub bear might its mother. Toots was well aware that there were those who wouldn't mind catching him alone and extending less than cordial greetings toward him. As long as Cutter was with him, Toots had a lot less to worry about.

Toots's main downfall was lack of discretion. He often played his horn just to aggravate people so that he might enjoy himself at their expense. It was doubly rewarding to see them become angry and then back down when they saw Cutter approaching. Though Cutter would often become annoyed by Toots and his displays of idiocy, he was content with Toots. Toots was like a woman in a lot of ways and it was convenient to have him for everything he needed and not have to contend with female problems.

Toots tried to look forward to the blood tonight as much as always, but it was not possible. He felt more on edge than ever before, as Cutter usually did all the work and Toots stood by gleefully and watched. Tonight was the first time Cutter was involving him directly in the killing process. Cutter had told him that it wasn't smart to try to jump three men, even if they were all asleep. And with one awake, it would be foolhardy. But Cutter was intent on getting the rich supply of furs from them and Toots knew he was depending on him for help. Toots wasn't at all sure if he wanted the responsibility.

Lettle sat with his back against a tree and looked out

into the darkness around camp, his nerves tingling and his muscles taut like bound cord. He wasn't big and he wasn't that strong and he had known for a number of days that everyone was going crazy over all the beaver. Why had they come up here? Why did he think he had to have more pelts, like the others? And there had been Gros Ventres sighted in the area. How crazy could a man be?

And where were Thane Thompson and old Eli Kleinen? They should be down here by now and they should all be camping together down at the bottom of the stream near the pass. This was crazy being up here like this. Thompson should be here at least. God, nobody went after him. That man was something, the way he could fight and get himself out of scrapes. The Injuns all called him Bear-Man, big medicine in the mountains, and they made signs of strength when they talked about him. Without his shirt, he looked like a man torn apart and remolded, sewn into a block of bone and muscle. Nobody was apt to challenge him, not if they had any sense.

Lettle stood and stretched and went over to the fire and squatted. The licks of red flame worked at the wood and in them he saw Thane Thompson, riding with that medicine shield tied on the back of his saddle, everybody from everywhere asking about it. That first rendezvous back down on the Henry's Fork—God, how they had looked at Thompson and wondered at how he had gone after that Piegan's prized war article. They had all asked Eli how he felt when he watched Thane sell the furs Thompson had won, and Eli had smiled and answered, "There's nary a bet I was happier to lose."

Lettle was thinking about being Thane Thompson himself when from the corner of his eye he saw something fall into the fire. It startled him and held him staring. His eyes widened as the fire suddenly exploded in his face. He screamed and was blown backward.

Whitson and Cashmore both flew from their robes toward their rifles. Whitson was met by Cutter, whose rifle went off in his face and parted one eye from its socket. Toots stood in front of Cashmore with his fingers frozen on his rifle, while Cashmore stumbled for his own gun. Toots began to whine like a frightened dog, unable to pull the trigger on his rifle. Cashmore cursed at Toots and swung the barrel of his own rifle around.

Toots dropped to the ground and covered his head with his hands. He was curled in a ball, whining louder than ever, unaware that Cashmore had fired just as Toots had fallen, missing him, and that Cutter had pulled one of his pistols and Cashmore was now lying still on the ground with a ball lodged near his spine.

Cutter noticed that Lettle was blinded and burned badly from the scrotum of gunpowder he had thrown into the fire. He watched while the dazed Lettle came to his knees, groping to find a tree and pull himself to his feet, his face a mass of blood and gunpowder stains.

Whitson lay still, the one eye hanging down on his face and the back of his head mushy, while Cashmore lay moaning, paralyzed by the ball in his back. Cutter went over to where Toots still lay cringing.

"Get up!"

Cutter slammed the butt end of his rifle into Toots's ribs.

"Get up, you worthless cur." Cutter pounded Toots once again and Toots crawled away on his hands and knees.

At length Toots got to his knees and came toward Cutter, tears staining his cheeks, his hands held up like a child's.

"I'm sorry, Jack. I was scare't to move, I really was." He stopped and slumped back down when he saw Cutter's hand raised to strike him.

"You could've got us killed," Cutter slurred. "I

ought to knock your brains out, whatever there is of 'em."

Cutter paced back and forth for a time, working to release his anger. He walked over to where Cashmore lay and rolled him over on his back. Cashmore's mouth was open as if to speak, but it remained open with no sound, his eyes wide with fright.

"He cain't say nothin'," Cutter told Toots matter-of-factly. "No use to have him that way."

Cutter placed the muzzle of his second pistol against Cashmore's forehead and pulled the trigger. Cashmore's head bounced off the ground from the concussion like a melon falling to earth and he lay still, blood pouring from a fist-sized hole at the base of his neck, with only the whites of his eyes showing.

Toots pointed to Lettle, who had found the trunk of a tree and was propped against it, holding his badly burned face. Cutter had reloaded his rifle and cocked the hammer back. Toots began to yell.

"Don't shoot him, Jack. Don't. Use your knife. Do it slow. Please."

Cutter reconsidered and uncocked the rifle. "We got to make it look like them Gros Ventre done it anyway," he said. "Might as well start with him."

Toots rubbed the tears from his eyes and began to smile. He moved toward the blind Lettle, confident now that Cutter was no longer angry but filled with blood lust. Toots's excitement mounted as he watched Cutter pull his knife and walk slowly toward Lettle, who was now lying back against the tree. When Cutter got to the tree he began to talk to Lettle softly.

"It's over now," Cutter said in a soothing tone. "Everything is going to be all right."

Lettle, who was nearly insane with pain, became confused. He had no idea whose voice he was hearing. He held out his hands and asked, "What happened? Is it over?" He had no idea who he was talking to or what, really, was going on.

Cutter took Lettle's hands and supported him while Lettle got to his feet.

"It's over," Cutter repeated. "We drove them Injuns off."

Lettle was still disoriented and barely aware of what was happening. But he knew something wasn't right and he knew the voice he was hearing belonged neither to Cashmore nor Whitson. He struggled through the pain to make his brain work. He heard Cutter say something about Gros Ventres again and how they had driven them off. He felt his buckskin shirt being opened in front and tried to jerk away.

"What are you doin' to me?" Lettle asked. "Who are you?"

It was cold and sharp and quick, and the feeling spread clear across his lower stomach. Instinctively, Lettle put his hand down and massive amounts of blood, followed by his intestines, gushed out over his hands. Lettle dropped to his knees as the pain and shock overwhelmed him. Toots stood nearby and said repeatedly, "That's good. That's good."

Lettle was dead in less than a minute. In a way Toots felt robbed, as men he had seen gutted before oftentimes took longer to die and often did strange things while in the throes of death. Lettle, whose eyes were but charred flesh, could not show the wide white eyes and the look of utter pain and horror that Toots had been hoping for. He died puking and kicking, but his face was otherwise a black, burned mass of expressionless flesh.

Nevertheless, Toots was excited and he lowered himself on Cutter. Cutter backed away and cuffed Toots alongside the head with the back of his hand.

"You ain't getting your pleasure this time," Cutter said. "I could be dead as stone now 'cause of you. Lucky thing Cashmore saw fit to aim at you instead of me. Like as not we'd both be dead, you lyin' on the ground like some ball of shit or something."

Toots again came toward Cutter on his knees and

Cutter cuffed him again, hard enough to daze Toots badly.

"I said no. Now get back."

Toots rolled on his side for a time, then got to his knees and crawled to a tree. He sat back and watched while Cutter began mutilating the bodies of the three trappers, to make it appear as if Gros Ventres had committed the atrocities. He cut them into pieces, dismembering the torsos of arms, legs, and head, scattering the parts all around the camp, fuming all the while about his near miss with possible death at the hands of Cashmore, and all because of Toots.

Toots evaded Cutter's glare as much as possible. For the first time he felt an anger growing within him. Cutter had never acted this way before, not after exciting him like that. It wasn't fair to excite him and then allow him to remain frustrated and unsatisfied. Toots thought it over while Cutter continued to strew the camp with human heads and limbs, as casually as if he were tossing rocks and sticks. Toots didn't like the way Cutter blamed him for failing; Cutter should have known better than to ask him to help in the first place. It hadn't been a good idea and he had told Cutter that in the beginning. But Cutter had said it was time he did his part for a change.

Toots said nothing to Cutter while they caught the mules and horses belonging to the three men and loaded them with the furs. They rode out then, and as they left Toots thought to himself that Cutter had better not frustrate him ever again.

The sun crossed overhead and through the haze a formation of geese passed honking, headed north for the summer. Eli talked about the old tree throughout the morning and it seemed to Thane that somehow Eli wished he could stay up there with it. The trip to the Popo Agie had been more like a family reunion than a trip to scout for beaver.

It was planned they would head back up there after

rendezvous and trap during the fall, winter over, and trap again the following spring. There was plenty of beaver and it was good country to boot. The grass was thick and there was both elk and occasional buffalo for meat. The thought of it made Eli a happy man.

The morning progressed and they wound their way back down and toward the little valley where they had left their three friends. Thane and Eli both commented about the number of ravens and magpies that were flying in and out of the camp down below in the trees. They yelled down but got no answer. And it seemed odd someone would not be out checking traps.

The closer they got to the camp, the more Thane and Eli both sensed something was wrong. Then Eli pointed out dark shadows along the opposite hill, wolves loping through the timber away from them. There were a number of them and the last one stopped to look at Thane and Eli. In his mouth was a human arm.

Thane was speechless. Then Eli said, "By God in heaven, what's gone on here?"

Both Thane and Eli had trouble making themselves go into the camp. They left the horses a ways out and walked in slowly. Thane worked to keep his stomach from acting up and he also fought an incredible weakness and feeling of helplessness that flooded over him. More ravens rose cawing and squawking from the camp, carrying strips of meat in their bills. What Thane and Eli found left of the three trappers had been badly ravaged already. Men who had been their friends and companions were now nothing but strewn pieces upon which swarmed masses of flies.

"Do you suppose the Gros Ventres found them?" Thane asked, realizing that they mutilated their victims as the other tribes did.

Eli seemed puzzled. "I got to study this some before I know. It ain't pretty, but I aim to figure it out."

Thane watched Eli work through the camp, studying the parts of the three men. Their heads were in one location, which seemed odd to Eli. The eye sockets had all been picked clean and the facial tissue was a mass of holes picked by birds. He studied Lettle's head and what remained of the men's torsos and limbs, then commented to Thane that he didn't figure it was Indians.

"I don't see a single arrer anywheres around," Eli said. "Like as not their bellies and backs would be poked full of 'em, so they'd take 'em into the next life."

"It seems hard to imagine who would do this kind of thing then," Thane said.

"Some will go to callin' up hell for a pack of beaver," Eli said. "Looks like we might have seen the like here."

Thane and Eli buried the remains of the three and started back down for the main brigade. It was a quiet, solemn trip. Thane reflected on brighter moments, when the brigade had first crossed South Pass two years before, and the rousing cheers that had echoed then across snow-blown hills. So many men so happy to finally reach their destination to set traps in place and sit around open fires for the rest of their lives. It occurred to Thane there were a lot of ways to die in these mountains.

Finally, as they neared the main camp down on Green River, Thane told Eli he wanted to go ahead and see if he couldn't catch up with whoever had killed their three friends and made off with their beaver catch.

"Won't likely do you no good to run off ahead," Eli said. "Whoever it was has been travelin' day and night to put distance ahead of us and them, and they're likely close to rendezvous right now."

"I'd like to catch them before they sell our furs," Thane said.

Eli took a deep breath. He was as angry as Thane but had come to realize his age was a factor in what he

could accomplish. He relied more and more on the
cane and it grew more difficult for him to even mount
a horse. Though Eli was only in his mid-fifties, his life
fighting weather and Indians had made him an old
man.

Despite the loss of three of their companions, the
brigade retained its carefree feeling and the men
continued to laugh and joke through the remainder of
the journey down to Cache Valley. This rendezvous,
General Ashley had promised, would be a time they
would remember. It would be far more than just a
meeting, as had taken place the previous summer.
This time Ashley would be there to procure their furs
with merchandise from St. Louis, including new traps,
rifles, riding tack, and other provisions necessary to
undertake another year of trapping in the mountains,
as well as all sorts of trade articles the trappers could
purchase and in turn trade for the favors of the Indian
women present.

And there would be whiskey, Ashley had promised.
That, even as much as the Indian women, was what
the men looked forward to. This would give them a
chance to catch up on their drinking and storytelling
with other trappers in the mountains they had not
seen for some time. It was in Ashley's mind that this
second rendezvous would put him into financial security for the rest of his life, enabling him to retire from
the trade.

From the first night of Ashley's arrival there occurred continuous, unrestrained carousing and gambling. Day in and day out trappers arrived from
various regions of the mountains, whooping and
yelling and extending vibrant greetings to one another. They sold their furs to Ashley, whose clerks and
bookkeepers tallied numbers and gave some men
notes for value received less the cost of supplies for the
upcoming year. As the rendezvous went on and the
whiskey was passed around, most of the trappers

returned to Ashley's trade tent and turned in their notes for more whiskey and trade articles for the Indian women.

The Shoshones had come, as well as bands from the Bannock, Flathead, and Nez Perce tribes to the north and west. It was a good thing to come and visit with their white Long Knife brothers who were also enemies of the Blackfeet and Atsina peoples. These Long Knives brought many good tools for work and for war with them, including metal arrowheads and lance points. They had also brought with them the fusils, the trade rifles. Many of the Indians were learning to use them fairly well, and though these guns were still not as good in quick, close fighting as a bow and arrows, they gave them an edge in distance skirmishes. It was good these Long Knives had come into the mountains.

After a few days the rendezvous camp had taken on the tone of a giant festive occasion. Thane, however, could not settle into the spirit of the occasion. The first day in rendezvous he had spotted Toots and Wild Jack Cutter. And he had learned from Ashley that these two men had been among the first arrivals, bringing with them a great number of beaver plews. Thane felt reasonably sure that it had been Toots and Cutter who had found their three friends and had somehow gotten the jump on them. It sickened him to think these two could do something like that and then march into rendezvous as bold as you please.

He found Cutter near a fire eating, with Toots sitting close to him like a dirty child.

"That was the wrong thing to do," Thane told him, "killing those three trappers."

Cutter grunted. Meat filled the left side of his mouth, as the right side was devoid of teeth.

"Word around here is the Gros Ventre done it," he said, his glasslike eyes squinted.

"There are some of us who know better," Thane told him.

"It ain't likely you can prove that, now is it?" Cutter said with a sneer. "Why, you see, me and Toots here, we sold our furs already, didn't we, Toots?"

Toots nodded like a puppet. "Sure did, Jack. Sure enough did."

"Word is you came in with a lot of pack animals," Thane said. "Mind if I take a look at them?"

"They're not ours no more," Cutter said, still sneering. "No, you see, we traded off our horses to some Injuns for buffalo robes. We did that way before you ever got to camp."

Thane watched Cutter while he ripped more meat off the hump ribs and chewed noisily. Now and then Cutter would glance over at his rifle, but he knew Thane would beat him to it.

"You won't get away with it, Cutter," Thane said. "There's plenty of time."

Cutter laughed. "What are you goin' to do, Thompson, get me with your big medicine? Yeah, I heard those stories about you and that medicine shield. Hell, I don't believe you ever stole it from the Piegans. Likely you found it somewheres and just aim to take the credit."

Toots laughed, then picked up his horn and blew a loud blast on it. He laughed again.

"We'll settle this some other time," Thane told the two of them. "You two had better be watching your backtrail from now on."

Thane walked away. He felt Cutter's eyes glaring into his back as he left. Thane was aware that Cutter would kill him any time he could get a chance, but that he would have to make it look, in his awkward way, like Indians, or possibly catch him alone and shoot him from behind. The more Thane thought about it, the more he realized that Cutter did not want merely to kill him, but to do some awful thing to him before he died. Deep within Cutter's eyes was a madness Thane had never encountered before, and it made him wonder how a man could be so lethal and yet so composed.

Thane remembered Antoine talking about how Cutter had killed his Iroquois friend while with the Hudson's Bay Company brigade. Someone who would disembowel another man for sport was beneath the lowest ranks of humanity.

While he was thinking, a trapper came up to him and said, "I hear tell you and the Englishman put on quite a show."

"A show?" Thane asked him.

"You know, stage actin', or somethin' of the sort. We'd like to see it."

Thane studied the trapper for a moment. "Tell you what," Thane said. "You and your friends who want to watch put up twenty plew of beaver and you'll see a show like none other you've ever seen."

The trapper raised his eyebrows. "Twenty plew of beaver?" he said.

Thane nodded. "Good stage plays aren't cheap."

"How 'bout a good jug of whiskey?" the trapper asked.

"Twenty plew of beaver," Thane repeated. "You'll have more than that come to watch, then you charge them a plew a head to get in."

The trapper thought a moment and his eyes lit up. "I figure to take you up on that." He pointed to where a group of trappers and Indians were gambling near a large fire. "Be over there in a short time and I'll have your plews."

Thane found Sir John talking with a group of Nez Perce Indians, making use of the sign language he had learned and taking notes. He smiled when he saw Thane.

"These are bloody interesting chaps," Sir John said of the Nez Perce. "They have developed their own breed of horse. How quaint, wouldn't you say?"

"We're lined up for a show," Thane told Sir John.

"And we're getting paid. Where in New York could you get beaver plews for a stage performance?"

"Beaver plews?" Sir John said. "Gad sakes, man, I thought you were ridding yourselves of them. Now you want more."

"We'll sell them, John," Thane said. "To William Ashley."

"What a precious thought," Sir John remarked, following Thane toward the campfire where the trappers were waiting.

Soon a wide circle of trappers and Indians developed and Thane got ready to take center stage with Sir John, who was already warming the crowd up with antics and verses. Some of the Shoshones, who had watched Thane and Sir John act earlier on the way to rendezvous, began to clap as they had once seen the trappers doing. They clapped and clapped until a trapper finally told them to wait until the show was over. But they just nodded and continued to clap until finally someone offered them a jug of whiskey to cease the noise.

Eli and Stretch Tipson, upon hearing from Thane that he and Sir John were receiving beaver in payment, began to laugh.

"That Englishman might be worth it," Eli said to Thane, "but for as good as you are, it better be old beaver."

It was dark and a summer thunderstorm was brewing. In the distant west, lightning streaked the sky and low rumbles worked their way closer and closer to the encampment. Sir John smiled broadly as he began his lines, realizing that the storm was adding to the atmosphere. In fact, some of the Indians were backing away. Sir John's odd voice as he spoke and the way he moved his hands made them wonder if he were not bringing storm spirits into the camp.

Thane had just started his lines when there came a loud blast from nearby, a blast from a horn. Everyone looked to see Toots, drunk and laughing, push his way through the onlookers and into the center where Sir John and Thane stood. A few drops of rain started to fall, heavy drops but far apart so that they splattered when they hit. Toots made his way over to Thane and tooted on the horn and laughed. When he again raised the mouthpiece to his lips, Thane smashed the heel of his hand into the end of the horn.

Toots staggered back and rolled his eyes. He began to spit blood from his smashed lips. He looked around while the trappers began to laugh and the big drops of rain splattered against his face.

"Jack!" Toots began to yell. "Jack! Help me."

"Cutter can't help you," Thane said. He grabbed Toots by the collar and held him with one hand while he ripped the horn loose from his neck with the other.

Toots expected to be hit and covered his face with his hands. Thane dropped the horn to the ground and began to smash it with his heel. The trappers began to laugh and Sir John stared, wondering what would come of all this. Cutter stood nearby and watched Toots's horn become crumpled metal. His glassy eyes were slits that burned like the firelight around him. He knew he would be a fool to try to challenge Thane Thompson.

When he was finished with the horn, Thane picked it up and threw it at Cutter's feet. There was no laughing now and the rumble overhead seemed to echo from Cutter's heart.

"Fix it for him, Cutter," Thane said. "And then go back to the Hudson's Bay Company where you belong."

Toots was still cringing and he started to yell when Thane grabbed him by the collar and tossed him at Cutter's feet. He fell in a heap and looked up at Cutter like a beaten dog. Rain was dripping from the brim of his filthy tricorn hat and the trappers began to laugh again.

"Ain't you goin' to do something, Jack?" Toots asked in a whining tone.

Cutter didn't answer but turned away and was gone. The laughter picked up while Toots wrapped his fingers around his beaten horn and stumbled after Cutter, yelling for him to wait. Soon the trappers began to disperse to other areas and resume their drinking and gambling and looking for Indian women.

"So much for the play," Sir John said to Thane.

Thane shrugged and took a deep breath to dispel his anger. "It's just as well. I hate to act in the rain."

Eli walked up to Thane and said, "You'd best sleep with an eye open from here on out."

But Cutter and Toots were gone. They had caught their horses even as the storm continued and had left the rendezvous. Cutter knew he would not be able to endure the anger that was boiling within him if he remained. Seeing Thane Thompson would perpetuate the emotion and he would not stand a chance against the man head-on. Cutter preferred to win his advantage by surprise and there was little chance of that now. That could come in time.

Thane divided the beaver plews with Sir John, and added twenty he had harvested during the spring hunt to trade with a Nez Perce war chief for six fine horses. Appaloosas, which he would take back up into Crow lands and present to Bear-Walks-at-Night, who would smile and inspect them and take them each for a ride. Thane knew them to be excellent buffalo ponies, and this would please Bear-Walks-at-Night all the more. Prized possessions, showing that Thane indeed thought a great deal of his daughter, Morning Swan.

The more he thought about it, the more Thane realized he could have no peace within himself until he saw Morning Swan again. She might not want anything to do with him, but at least then he would have it settled for good. He was already becoming disillusioned with trapping beaver, not necessarily the traveling and exploring associated with it, but the mundane, day-to-day task of skinning and stretching plews. And the loss of three men and the big catch of furs to Cutter and Toots made it seem to him that there was never any assurance that you were going to be rewarded for your work, unless you considered death a reward.

"I'm going up north again," Thane told Eli as rendezvous ended.

"What?" Eli said. "Back to Blackfeet lands?"

"No. Crow country."

"There's bound to be a passel go up there," Eli said. "Can't see how there'll be enough beaver for everyone. And I don't figure you for the type who likes to trap elbow to elbow."

"I'm not thinking of trapping all that much," Thane said. "I thought we might take some time off and just live with the Crows."

Eli laughed. "Well, I'll be. Still got that woman on your mind, I see. I guess I figured as much when I saw you with the beads and the necklace the other day— and those horses you got from the Nez Perce. They weren't exactly no pack mules, I'd say. No, I'd venture old Bear-Walks-at-Night will be grinnin' from ear to ear."

"So you'll come along?" Thane asked.

"This old knee won't take much more cold water," Eli said with a laugh. "You figure to ask the actor along?"

Thane laughed. Eli and Sir John had come to consider one another friendly adversaries. When things got dull for one he would seek the other out for an argument of sorts, which would usually be over the same topics and end up with no resolution. Still, it was a pastime for both of them and it kept their wits sharp.

"Maybe we can take a trip up on the Popo Agie," Eli said to Thane. "I hanker for that old tree again."

"We'll have a lot of time to spend," Thane said. "We'll see a lot."

They left with a brigade Stretch Tipson was taking

up into the Flathead country. Thane was anxious to see the headwaters of the Yellowstone, the country called Colter's Hell, where John Colter had walked some twenty years before during the very early fur trade. Stretch was now working for three trappers, Jedediah Smith, David Jackson, and Bill Sublette, who had just bought out General Ashley, who had decided to retire from the mountains. Stretch intended to reach the trapping grounds higher up and thus avoid the many other brigades that were flooding the Green River and Great Salt Lake region.

Thane found himself anxious to reach the Crow village and see Morning Swan again. Trapping and beaver plews were now far back in his mind and he didn't care where anyone else was this upcoming winter; he wanted to be with the strong Crow woman who had found him cutting up a fallen buffalo. Her dark eyes had been filled with anger then, and he hoped this time they would be filled with joy.

Nine

THANE AND ELI RODE THROUGH THE MOUNTAINS WITH
Stretch Tipson, seeing a land in its prime. The brigade
followed the Snake River past the Tetons and then
north, up onto the high Yellowstone plateau. It was a
vast mountain wilderness where timber grew in thick
patches and then opened into sweeping meadows
filled with springs and bogs. It was summer range for
elk and moose, and bighorn sheep were common
where the rocky hillsides broke up from the rolling
bottoms.

Scattered along the various streams were geyser
basins brimming with steaming cauldrons of sulphur
and hot water. Here the land was plastered white with
minerals and the pools were colored deep blue. Thane
found it easy to understand why the land held such
fascination for whoever viewed it. High spewing foun-
tains of steaming water rose up into the sky and
produced rainbows through the trees. Streams gushed
from the rocks and long steep cliffs, tumbling waterfalls nourished gardens of bright colored flowers below.

They made camp along a river they called Firehole

and the night was spent telling yarns about fights with
Blackfeet. The next morning they were greeted by a
war party of Crows, returning from the Three Forks to
their village with horses and scalps, which they proudly displayed. They were Kicked-in-Their-Bellies and
Thane recognized a number of them. They rode up to
the brigade to tell proudly of their war deeds. They
had fought with a mixed group of Piegans and
Kainah, the Bloods. The warrior who carried the pipe
was named Runs-in-Water and he was proud of having led a victorious raid.

Tied on their horses were two wounded Piegan
warriors the Crows had taken captive. One had an
arrow still imbedded in his thigh and the other was
bleeding from a rifle wound to the shoulder. They
were taunted endlessly by the Crow warriors, and each
also suffered from a sharp skewer that had been driven
through both cheeks, so that their mouths could not
open. The wounds had caused their faces to swell and
become distorted. Runs-in-Water invited Thane to
kill one of them if he wished.

"I do not feel like killing today," Thane told the
warrior.

Runs-in-Water nodded. "Maybe another day," he
said. He studied Thane. "We still talk of you in our
village, and because of you, Morning Swan will not
take a husband."

"It is my intention to go to your village and ask
Bear-Walks-at-Night for Morning Swan's hand,"
Thane told him. "That is where I am going now."

Runs-in-Water seemed disappointed and Thane decided it would be good to change the subject.

"It is good to see that you have gained a victory
against the Blackfeet people," he told Runs-in-Water.
"You bring honor to yourself and your people."

Runs-in-Water nodded and turned his horse away.
He rode over to the Piegan warrior with the arrow in
his leg and pulled his head back by the hair. With a
quick jerk of his hand, he drew his knife across the

Piegan's throat and blood spewed all over the warrior and the horse.

The Piegan slid sideways on the horse, which began to jump around from the smell of fresh blood. Runs-in-Water held the horse while he cut the dying Piegan loose and let him slide to the ground. He gave the pony to another warrior and got down from his own horse. All the Crows were yelling war cries and Runs-in-Water, yelling his own war cry, took the Piegan's scalp for all to see. He went over to the other captive Piegan and rubbed the bloody scalp in the face of the captive, who tried unsuccessfully to turn away. He then turned to Thane.

"I will kill many more of the Blackfeet. And I will kill the strong one, Rising Hawk, and show that my medicine is stronger than even yours, Bear-Man."

That night there was more celebration by the Crow warriors. They tied the remaining Piegan to a tree and danced in a circle around him, darting in at times to burn him with flaming sticks. The Piegan never moved, but stood defiantly with his eyes wide and wild in his bloody and distorted face, his muscles rigid. He seemed to be looking but not seeing, having placed himself in a trance. The burns produced glaring red marks all across his chest and abdomen, and in places along his arms and legs. Soon many of these red marks were blisters filled with water, which the Crow warriors delighted in bursting with hot knives.

The next morning the Piegan warrior, fighting shock, was tied to his pony and hot coals were placed on his wounds to revive him. Sir John had been taking notes throughout the previous night and continued again as they prepared to depart.

"You seem to have taken a fancy to that torture session last night," Eli said to Sir John. "Don't they do that sort of thing in your plays?"

"Only when it appears in the script," Sir John answered.

Eli grunted. "I ain't figured you out yet, I'll say that for sure."

Stretch Tipson came over to where Thane was tightening the cinch on Whistler before they departed.

"I want to be the first to congratulate you, Thane," Stretch said. "That woman, Morning Swan, is the best in these mountains. You can't go wrong by her."

"I thought you told me some time back," Thane said, "that I was foolish to care about one woman. Remember that?"

Stretch grinned. "I remember that. I thought you might find another one somewhere and she might then take a shine to me. But I found out she's only got eyes for you."

"Why, you scoundrel." Thane laughed. "Fine way to treat a friend."

Stretch pulled a rawhide sack from his saddlebag and handed it to Thane. "Give these to your first child. I know you like to read and I got these back at rendezvous from a Flathead. Don't ask me where he got them."

Thane opened the sack and found three small primers suitable for teaching children to read. They were stories about sailors coming home from the sea.

"Well, I greatly appreciate this," Thane said. "Why didn't you keep them?"

Stretch shrugged. "I don't know. I just had the feeling that I should give them to someone who'll use them before I get the chance to. I don't know if I figure to marry or what. Maybe some years from now you can give them back to me, if I haven't gone under by then."

"Ahh!" Thane said. "I'll get the chance to give them back. It'll be a long time before you go under."

They followed the course of the Yellowstone from its headwaters near a big lake. The river took them to the edge of a huge canyon. There two waterfalls cascaded down over hundreds of feet and into the narrow bottom, where the water foamed and splashed its way down and out of the monstrous, yellow-rocked gorge. Everyone got down from their horses for a rest and a chance to look over the edge and see the magnificent canyon.

"That's a sight," Eli said.

"If I were an artist," Sir John added, "I would spend a good deal of time here with brush and paint." He was writing in his journal as he talked, filling two or more pages.

Suddenly there was a shout from some of the men. One of the trappers had lost his footing and was yelling as he fell through the air into the deep canyon. It was Stretch Tipson, and Thane could only watch helplessly as the big man waved his arms and legs frantically, then slammed off the wall of the canyon far below and disappeared into the churning waters.

The Crow warriors immediately began chanting to their spirit helpers. Thane was looking over the edge of the canyon, unable to believe it. Eli was beside him, shaking his head, asking some of the others how it had happened. No one could say for sure, except that he had simply lost his balance while looking over the edge.

Sir John was staring down into the foamy water far below. He spoke to no one in particular, in almost a whisper. "My God, but this land can be sudden. It can take your breath away and the next instant take your life away as well."

Then two of the Crow warriors rushed over to the remaining Piegan captive and quickly tied a piece of cloth over his horse's eyes. For the first time, the Piegan began to make noise, trying to cry out through his swollen mouth, struggling all the while to break loose from his bonds. Once the horse was blindfolded, the warriors turned it toward the canyon and slapped its rump. The horse bolted and being unable to see, ran over the edge of the canyon. Both the horse and the Piegan captive also sailed far down and into the frothy current.

None of the trappers spoke. Thane stared at Runs-in-Water, who was chanting to his spirit helper, oblivious to much else around him. Thane looked at Eli, and he said he could only suspect that the Crows had offered the Piegan as a sacrifice to the canyon so that the spirits would no longer be angry and take another life.

But the Crows remained restless and they were prepared to leave the place immediately. The canyon was bad medicine on this day. Other days might be good, but today it was important to leave. Thane talked to a trapper named Desconne, who would now be the brigade leader, about recovering Stretch's body and also that of the Piegan. Desconne told Thane they would follow the river out and locate them both, then bury them decently. Thane bid the brigade good luck, as did Eli and Sir John. Then Thane took one last look at Yellowstone Canyon and got on Whistler.

Rosebud bent down with the forked stick and pushed it into the soft, sandy earth. She worked it down until she felt the base of the root and then pushed upward, careful not to put too much pressure on the stick and break it. She worked with the tool, loosening the soil around the root and around the plant itself. Then, with a broad smile, Rosebud finally extracted a huge breadroot, the top of which she promptly weaved into place with the other roots in her collection.

The day was fresh and still, and the sky held a deep and resonant blue that washed over the valley, strong and pure. Rosebud was with her mother and a number of other women and girls on the slopes out from the village. They had been out on the hillsides and along the bottoms since early morning, working with their digging tools and weaving strings of vegetable roots. There were wild onions and licorice roots among others, and of course the prized breadroot.

There had come a soft rain during the night and the soil was just moist enough to allow for working the roots out without difficulty. Rosebud was happy to be with her mother, learning the plants and their uses. No one was ever too young to learn how to survive. She had already collected a lot of roots, but she did not want to go over to where her mother worked until she had weaved a string of roots into a circle twice as long as she was.

Rosebud was proud to know so many plants already, and this morning was a particularly good time to be out, as the blue blossoms of the breadroot plant were wide open and easy to spot. If these plants in particular were not harvested soon, the stems would dry up and break off at the ground. Then it would be impossible to find the big white roots for another year.

As she continued to harvest the roots, Rosebud collected a few of the biggest clusters of flowers, each bright blue, nestled in a sheath covered with fine, hairlike growth. Rosebud remembered back to when the white trapper named Bear-Man, on their way down from the Blackfeet lands, had shared one of these roots with her after digging with his knife and accidently finding it. Since it had been just before the coming of the snows, the plants had all been dried up and finding roots to boil and treat his leg wound had been difficult. Rosebud remembered how he had been excited upon finding the root, and when her mother had informed him it was good to eat, he had peeled some first for Rosebud.

As Rosebud continued to dig, the breadroot plants reminded her more of this big Long Knife, gentle and yet with a wild look in his eyes. He had come from a faraway land so filled with those of his kind that they lived in huge villages. Rosebud could remember his stories and she knew her mother had come to like him a great deal. Rosebud too missed him, though she never said anything to her mother.

Rosebud thought often of that day back in the "village of the other people," as she now called it, when she had fed the Long Knife, thinking he had been playing a game with her. She knew her mother continued to miss him as well, but for some reason did not want to be with him. Rosebud could not understand the reasons Bear-Man had left the village now two winters past and had never returned. Though Rosebud could see in her mother's eyes that she wished he would return, her mother always said that it was best if he remained with the other Long Knives. Rosebud knew her mother did not mean those words; it was hard to understand the ways of adults.

Morning Swan went about her own work and watched her daughter, just up the hill from her. Rosebud was no longer a small child, but a rapidly growing young girl now, capable of formulating her own ideas about what she saw and heard. Even though she had yet to see even seven winters, Rosebud was smart and attentive. Morning Swan thought often to herself how much a small child can comprehend, though adults treated small children as ignorant and unable to understand issues. Rosebud often saw things clearly, whereas the older youths and adults made them into complex issues. Just this morning, upon hearing the women discuss the best places to go to dig roots, Rosebud had suggested they just start digging and not waste the day arguing.

Now Morning Swan looked up to see Rosebud waving down at her. Rosebud had found a particularly large breadroot and she was holding it up and pointing at it for all the girls and women on the slope to see. There was some nodding and shouts of approval—along with some laughing, as the root was bigger than Rosebud's hand—and they all went back to work.

This was a good year for roots; the winter snows had been heavy and the spring rains soft and slow. Now there was an endless sea of color—various shades of red, blue, and gold—that washed down from the mountains and out onto the plains. The little roots the Long Knives said looked like white carrots had been profuse and they made the meat stews tastier. There were a great number of onions, their clusters of white and sometimes rose-colored flowers nodding in the breeze. In the draws and the bottoms, the wild plums and chokecherries were finished showing their blossoms, making berries for late summer and fall, and the gray and prickly buffalo berry bushes were filled with young, squawking magpies.

Now that the middle of the warm moons had come, there were many other plants ready to harvest that grew in the mountains and along the slopes where the cold lasted longer. With these plants blooming it was time to move higher to get them. After today, they would move the village to the higher streams and creeks above the Elk River valley, and the days up there would be spent as they had been here in the valley, weaving plant tops together for use as food and medicine.

Rosebud started over toward her mother. She had woven a long string of roots together and was telling another small girl who had joined her not to step on them. Occasionally someone would offer to pick the string of roots up and help her carry them, but Rosebud she would shoo her away and tell her she could manage. When she finally reached her mother, she was out of breath and puffing, pulling the string of roots into a pile.

"Did I do good?" she asked her mother.

Morning Swan stopped her digging and gave her daughter a hug. "You did very well. How are you going to eat all those?"

"Do I have to eat all of them myself?" she asked.

Morning Swan laughed. "I think there will be a lot of people who will want to eat your special roots, especially your grandfather and grandmother. They will be very proud of you."

Then Morning Swan and Rosebud looked across the hill as the other women began to point and to run down toward the village, many of them leaving their roots behind in their excitement. Nearly a full moon

past a number of warriors had gone into the Three
Forks country to hunt and raid against the Blackfeet
peoples. They were returning, many of them yelling
and running their horses up and down the hills
outside the village, waving scalps and showing off
stolen horses. With them were three Long Knife
traders, including the one the Crow people called
Bear-Man.

Rosebud's eyes widened. "He is back! Do you see
him, Mother? Aren't you happy? Yes, he can help us
eat all the roots."

Rosebud took her mother by the hand and they
hurried back to the village to join the celebration.
There would be a feast tonight and there would be
dancing. The warriors had returned victorious and no
one had even been wounded.

From the moment he entered the village, Thane
looked for Morning Swan. He finally saw her coming
down from a hill above the village with Rosebud
tugging at her hand to make her hurry faster. Rosebud
had grown so much it was hard to believe. She was
going to be very attractive, like her mother. Thane
watched Rosebud as she finally let loose of her mother's hand. As she ran, her long strands of black hair
glistened in the sun like polished coal. Thane then
realized just how much he had missed these two.

Without hesitation, Rosebud ran up to Thane's
horse and demanded to know why he had been gone
so long. She did not even wait for an answer, but told
him he now had to stay. Thane got down and Rosebud
jumped into his arms. Her eyes widened.

"Your muscles got bigger," she told him. "Really
bigger. What did you do?"

"I've been working to make myself strong," Thane
told her. "It looks to me like you haven't exactly been
staying small."

"No, I'm digging roots now," Rosebud stated
proudly. "I want you to come out and I'll show you."

"In a little while," Thane told her. He took a small

mirror from a saddlebag and handed it to her. "This is for you, so you can look at yourself while you comb your hair."

Rosebud's eyes widened again and her mouth dropped. Morning Swan walked up and Rosebud was jumping up and down as she showed off the mirror.

"Does this show that I'm getting bigger?" she asked.

Morning Swan smiled. "If you look close, maybe you can tell. Why don't you go and let your friends see it."

Rosebud skipped off and Morning Swan looked up at Thane. Her eyes held a lot of questions, but before she could ask them, he pulled a gleaming seashell necklace from one of the saddlebags and placed it around her neck.

Morning Swan's breath escaped her and she stared at the necklace. It was a series of polished white shells interwoven with bright red and deep blue glass beads, set off by a silver pendant that hung between her breasts. Thane then produced a matching set of silver earrings that were miniatures of the larger pendant on the necklace.

"The necklace and earrings are for you," Thane told her. "I thought you might like them."

Morning Swan continued to look at Thane and finger the necklace, unable to speak, while Thane moved close to her and took her in his arms.

"I've never stopped thinking about you," he said. "I know I'm not doing all this right, but I can't play a flute very well so I can't spend a lot of time calling for you in the evenings. I'll just say it. I want you to be my wife."

"I still want to remain with my people," Morning Swan said. "I don't want to travel all over to trap beaver."

"We will remain with your people," Thane said. "I've had enough of beaver trapping. Being with you and Rosebud is what's important to me."

Rosebud came running up behind them. She was

whooping and shouting. She nudged her way in between Thane and her mother and said, "I want in on
this."

Thane picked her up and the three of them em-
braced, while the village looked on and cheered.

Morning Swan wore her necklace often, and with
pride. Her wedding to Bear-Man had been a celebration which lasted three days and nights. Bear-Walks-
at-Night proudly displayed the Appaloosa horses
Thane had given him, and in the eyes of the Crow
people he grew in stature. It was good to have a
son-in-law who was a good man and a strong warrior,
but to have the Long Knife they called Bear-Man was
a feat of extraordinary measure.

Little Bird was extremely happy for both Morning
Swan and Bear-Man. They were both very happy and
she hoped their love was strong enough to endure the
differences between them and the trials these differences would certainly bring in the future. These were
two strong people whose minds were not easily
changed and neither of whom would back down very
far from an issue.

It was not hard for Little Bird to come to like Thane
a great deal, though by custom she was not allowed to
speak to him. His first day in the village Thane had
made it a point to have Bear-Walks-at-Night tell Little
Bird he was glad to see her. He had even brought
presents for her, a necklace of smaller seashells, as
well as beads and mirrors, and a big pot for cooking.
Since he could not present them to her himself, or
speak to her in person, she received them from
Bear-Walks-at-Night, who told her they had come
from Bear-Man to her.

Bear-Walks-at-Night was delighted to see that Eli
had come also and was pleased to welcome him into
his lodge. He extended the invitation to Sir John as
well. Had Eli been interested in housing half the fur
brigades in the mountains, Bear-Walks-at-Night

would have been only too willing. He often recalled the story of how Eli had saved him from drowning and preferred to call Eli by the name Swimmer whenever he spoke about him.

Everyone mourned the passing of Stretch Tipson and for some time Thane wondered at his sudden death. As time passed the thought of losing Stretch would recede, until Thane would go to his collection of books for something to read and see the three small primers. Thane decided he would keep those primers always, and some day he would have a son whom he would name Jethro, after the big man, and this boy would learn to read from these books, as Stretch had hoped.

Morning Swan helped Thane get through his mourning by reminding him that Stretch was in a happy place and that it was best if he became happy as well. Thane realized this was the case, and soon found himself realizing that life would go on. Among the Crow and the other Indian tribes, death was a necessary part of the order of things. When a death occurred the people would mourn in drastic ways, often cutting themselves up over many parts of their bodies; but when the mourning was over, there was once again a great deal of happiness.

Sir John fell back into his old role as constant entertainer. He was given the name Crazy Arms, for the way he moved his arms and shoulders while performing scenes from various plays. He took to acting once again whenever he could find an audience, but soon the villagers showed less and less interest in his performances. Thane told him he couldn't expect to have a continuous audience and that he would do well to learn horseback tricks or some other hobby to fill in his time.

But Sir John performed. He told Thane he would perform alone if need be, but he must perform. He could be seen in the evenings and often late at night, setting a stage for himself and working on his gestures while he spoke lines to no one in particular. Some of the villagers on occasion would watch him for a time, but soon the adults dwindled away almost entirely and all that were left were children. And when they became bored, they would sneak up behind him and pinch him or disturb him in various other ways. Rather than suffer additional ridicule, Sir John ended his performances.

As time passed and Sir John learned more of the Crow language, he came to realize that stories of war meant a lot to these people, but they tired of hearing about themes they could not relate to. Roman Caesars, kings, and foreign lands were people and places they had no concept of and could therefore not understand nor care much about. And speaking about what others had accomplished was not impressive. They wanted to hear what *he,* Sir John, had done. They wanted to know about *his* war exploits. Eli warned him against telling any tales that had not happened, as lying about warfare was forbidden. So when Sir John confessed that he had never stolen a horse or counted coup or killed an enemy, or even made off with a gun or knife, the people quit listening to him.

"This is an odd lot you've come to live with," Sir John remarked to Thane one evening. "First they like my acting and now even the children are derisive."

Thane was oiling Gulliver and polishing the barrel. "They just don't understand what you're doing," Thane said. "When you first came into the village a couple of years ago, it was something new for them. Maybe they thought you were one of the characters you talked about. Now they've heard it before and they want to hear about what you've done to their enemies, the Blackfeet and the Sioux. You can't blame them. They have no concept of a genuine stage performance."

"They learn very quickly," Sir John said. "It would seem to me that they should forget about their bloody tribal wars for a time and set into something a bit more healthy. Don't you think?"

"They don't live for anything else," Thane said. "And if you can't live without an audience, I suggest you go on a raid against the Blackfeet or the Sioux and then write a play about it."

"Preposterous!" Sir John waved his hand toward Thane and walked away, shaking his head.

Sir John continued to grow restless and, before much more time had passed, he decided to gather an audience he believed would be captive. An audience of one, tethered to a perch by a leather thong.

Sir John had by now learned some sign language and could speak some of the Crow language, enough certainly to get by. He remembered the boy with the pet raven from his first trip to the Crow village and learned his name was Turtle. Sir John wandered through the village asking where he might find Turtle and his raven. When he found them, Turtle was teasing the raven by holding pieces of fat just above his bill. Joker, Sir John concluded, was in fine form and as vociferous as ever.

"Turtle," Sir John said, approaching the boy, "I would like to purchase your raven from you."

Turtle, who was used to jokes concerning his bird, smiled. "Why does Crazy Arms want my bird?"

"I would enjoy teaching him to act," Sir John answered.

"You can have him when I get eight good horses, which I will pick out," Turtle said, dropping a piece of fat, which the raven caught on the way down.

"Horses?" Sir John frowned. "What do you mean, horses?"

Turtle then thought a moment. "That's right. You're a poor, funny man with a funny hat. You are not rich in horses. I guess I will not sell my bird then."

"I will get you horses," Sir John said. "I'll get them from the strong trapper, Bear-Man. He will lend them to me."

Turtle fed the raven another slice of fat. "Does Bear-Man know your plan?"

"He will soon enough," Sir John said. "But eight horses is too many."

"Then make it six," Turtle said.

"Four."

Turtle thought a moment. Finally he nodded. "But be good to this bird. And if he doesn't want to flap his wings, don't beat him."

"What?" Sir John asked.

"He doesn't mind well," Turtle explained. "I like to see him flap his wings, but he won't do it unless I'm not looking."

"So you beat him?" Sir John asked.

"He needs it," Turtle said, "but I haven't the heart for it. So don't you do it."

"How do you beat a large black bird?"

"With a stick, I would imagine."

Sir John frowned. "You wait here and I shall return in a brief moment."

Sir John found Thane preparing for a hunt with some of the warriors. Thane was saddling Whistler and could sense that Sir John was nervous for some reason.

"Is there something you wanted to tell me?" Thane asked Sir John.

Sir John ground his foot into the loose earth. "Well, I might as well come out with it. I am in need of four good horses. Perchance, would you give them to me?"

"Four good horses?" Thane smiled. "Are you getting married? Who is she? I had no idea."

"No, no, it's nothing like that, I can assure you," Sir John said quickly. "It is merely my intent to purchase Turtle's pet, the big black raven."

Thane laughed. "I won't even ask you what you want that bird for, but *four horses?* Wouldn't he settle for a stick of hard candy?"

"Horses is what he wants," Sir John said. "He

demanded six, but I talked him down. I was assured within myself that you could be of help."

Thane thought a moment. "Tell you what. You go back to Turtle with three horses and tell him I will bring him back a mountain lion and he can make a quiver for his arrows from the pelt."

Thane then picked out three good ponies and Sir John led them back to the village. He returned to Turtle with the ponies and the news about Thane's offer and stood back while Turtle jumped with glee.

"Bear-Man is to bring me the skin of a mountain lion? It will surely be good medicine. That is far better than another horse. Joker is yours."

Sir John returned to Bear-Walks-at-Night's lodge with the raven on his arm. He perched the bird on the limb of a cottonwood and looked into the bird's eyes. Joker did not appear very attentive, for his eyelids were drooping. It was midday and he was filled with cuttings of fat.

"Pay attention," Sir John said. "I am going to teach you some lines from Shakespeare. How does that suit you?"

Joker continued to sit with droopy eyelids. While Sir John talked, they closed. This was not a good way to begin an acting lesson. The pupil must be totally alert and observant, and not have droopy eyelids. Sir John's first decision was that Joker would receive less to eat so that he might be better able to remain awake and pay attention.

"Snap to! Snap to!" Sir John admonished the bird. "You want to be the first raven to learn Shakespeare, don't you?"

Joker's eyes opened momentarily. Sir John began the lesson, but Joker merely cawed once and let his eyelids droop once more. Soon the lids were entirely closed.

"Very well," Sir John said to the bird, "but I want you to know that one of these bloody days someone is going to acknowledge me for my contribution to this world. Yes, that very damn well will happen, you wait and see!"

The warm moons progressed and when the cold moons came, Thane settled into life with Morning Swan and the Kicked-in-Their-Bellies band. They again made their winter camp on Wind River and Thane spent much of his time hunting or with Eli in the warm mineral waters at the edge of the village. The snow fell heavily and the warmth of the village was a safe haven from the bitter winter. Thane learned how to tell stories in the Crow fashion and entertained the people often with his tales of the Siskadee and the country to the south around Bear River and the Great Salt Lake. He often told the story again of his encounter with the great grizzly bear and the people never seemed to tire of hearing it.

Thane also told Turtle about how he had stalked a mountain lion and had shot it with the Hawken. Turtle prized the lionskin quiver with his arrows more than any other possession, and even though Rosebud said a number of times that he wasn't as hot as he thought he was, Turtle worshipped Thane as much as he did his own relatives, the warriors belonging to his clan. Thane talked to all the young boys on various occasions about the land where he had been born, far to the east, and the differences between the people who lived back there and the Crow people. Thane talked about the huge fields of tobacco that were planted back there and it made the boys think that the land was filled with medicine.

The various stories, though, sometimes made Thane long for the brigade and the free life. Though Eli and Sir John remained in the village also, the others were somewhere out there sharing their own stories and talking of the spring hunt, making bets on who would get the most beaver and where the rendezvous would be held. At times he thought of Stretch Tipson and his odd destiny with fate, and how fragile life truly was out here.

But the winter wore on and camp life grew to be a boring routine for him. Though he loved Morning Swan, Thane was constantly at odds with himself over his immobility. He wondered what was happening in different parts of the mountains and what lands filled with prime beaver were being discovered. Thane knew he could never find those things out here in the village. There was no talk or concern among the Crow people over the Hudson's Bay Company or new fur-trading ventures coming into the mountains. The Crows welcomed all white traders and their general philosophy was the more that came, the better the fighting odds against the Blackfeet and the Lacotah.

More trappers did come as the winter wore into spring, and Thane was able to learn a few things about what was going on. But the country was so immense that most of the newcomers knew less than Thane. They were moving around on speculation, working their way south and west into Shoshone and Flathead and Nez Perce lands. Others talked of going south and east, into the Platte River country and down onto the Laramie River. The Sioux tribes and the Cheyenne were unpredictable but they were not the Blackfeet. Trapping was reasonably safe almost anywhere away from the Blackfeet. They were killing trappers with a renewed vigor now and there was talk now that the Piegans were being joined *en force* by their brothers in the Blackfeet confederacy—the Kainah, better known as the Bloods, and the Siksika, the northern Blackfeet. Fur brigades, it was said, were commiting suicide by entering Blackfeet lands.

And with the buildup of the three Blackfeet tribes, the talk was that they were pushing out to the south and the east and the west to make war. There had always been concern about the Blackfeet and the Gros

Ventres, their allies, all over the northern Rocky Mountain region, but now there was alarm. The Blackfeet were at war with everyone.

As the fur brigades continued to come through the village on their way to the spring hunt, each one in turn tried desperately to convince Thane to join them. He was offered everything in the way of material gain from horses to a good share of the beaver catch if he would go along. Everyone in the mountains knew about the trapper the Crows called Bear-Man, who had survived a grizzly attack and had gone into a Piegan village to steal the war shield of the Piegan war chief Rising Hawk. Those just coming out for the first time were especially eager to see and meet this man, whom many called the best fighter in the mountains. Though there were a number of men who now had reputations, including Jim Bridger, Tom Fitzpatrick, the Sublette Brothers, and others, none of them possessed the assured appearance and the raw power of Thane Thompson.

Morning Swan watched all this with interest and concern. She could see that her worry about the coming of the white man was already taking shape, and much faster than she had expected. Somehow, the white people in Thane's old lands were tiring of their way of life and many of them wanted to escape. They had heard this land was open and free and there was a great deal to see out here. But they brought with them their old habits and Morning Swan was sure that in time they would just be doing the same things here they'd done in the lands they had left. Then they would again be unhappy.

Throughout the late winter and early spring, Morning Swan became ever more indignant toward the white newcomers. She became ever more aware of the differences between them and her people. She wished, in a way, that her people would drive them out, as the Blackfeet peoples were doing. But she knew that would never be a reality. She talked with her father,

Bear-Walks-at-Night, who finally remarked that he wished she would stop feeling the way she did and consider that the Long Knives were allies of the Crow people and that, after all, she was married to one.

Morning Swan could not argue that she had married a Long Knife, but she viewed Thane more as a person than a white man. She saw in him a lot of similarities to the others of his race, but there were also differences that, in her eyes, set him apart from them: he did not see these lands as a place to conquer or to stake ownership, nor did he act in a patronizing way toward her people, as many of the Long Knives did, especially those who were considered the leaders and in charge. But the one thing she was concerned about was Thane's unpredictable nature.

It seemed that for a time he was happy where he was, and then the next moment he was unsure of himself and what he wanted to do. Morning Swan was sure he loved her and Rosebud, but she was not sure what it was inside him that drove him to pace around the village and be generally discontented with himself and his situation.

But Rosebud was as happy as she had ever been and she spent a lot of time showing Thane how she could ride and tend a horse. Whirlwind had sired a foal born late the previous summer and Rosebud had named the filly Moon Eyes, for the soft cream color in her eyes. Now Rosebud could lead the yearling and could jump up on her back. The colt was too young to really be ridden to any extent, but Rosebud prided herself on having been able to get on Moon Eyes and ride a little at a time without any help.

Rosebud had watched how the older children rode their horses and how they had learned from the adults the various methods of taming and teaching a horse to stop and turn by merely using the knees and reaching out to the horse's nose. Moon Eyes was too young to train vigorously but Rosebud knew when the time was right, she would be able to do it herself.

Thane finally came to realize he was as happy here as he could be anywhere, and that it would not be right to ask Morning Swan to leave her people and risk injury or death, along with Rosebud, in enemy lands. While Rosebud kept herself busy with the colt, Thane spent a great deal of time with Morning Swan. They went many places together outside the village, and when the camp was moved to the Yellowstone valley once more, Thane went with her to her favorite place—to the aspen grove on the hillside. Once again the village was located up one of the tributaries, near a place called Rotten-Sun-Dance-Lodge-Creek.

It was late evening and the birds were singing roosting songs. On the way up the hill, Morning Swan pointed out a chickadee, the small medicine bird that spoke of the seasons. His little voice always changed when the snows left and now he was singing, "Summer's near, summer's near."

Thane listened and watched Morning Swan smile and imitate the tiny black-capped bird perfectly.

"Can you hear it?" Morning Swan asked Thane. "Can you hear him singing, 'Summer's near, summer's near'?"

Thane entered the little valley with Morning Swan and was amazed at the large beaver dams that forded water all the way up the small creek. Beaver were everywhere and they slapped their tails against the water. A small herd of mule deer bounded out of the bottom and continued up the hillside a ways before turning in unison to watch. They were not badly frightened and soon continued browsing on the tender new shoots of the shrubs along the hill.

They reached the grove of aspens, and in the late day the leaves glistened a deep green, almost shimmering as the light evening breeze touched them and made them quiver.

"These trees are my friends," Morning Swan said of the aspens as she stood among them with Thane, the setting sun glistening on her hair, her eyes framed by the light. "They have been a part of me since I was but a small child."

"This is a nice place," Thane commented. He took Morning Swan in his arms and held her close to him. "I can't imagine ever being without you and Rosebud. Ever since that first day—"

"Shhh." Morning Swan touched a finger to his lips. "There will be time for talk later."

Morning Swan took Thane by the hand and they walked deeper into the aspen grove. There she settled with him into a bed of grass and let him remove her dress. She then removed his clothes and they lay together in the twilight.

He was gentle and took time to caress her and kiss her all over. She ran her fingers over his smooth skin and bulging muscles, feeling the strength well up from within him. His lips and tongue set her flesh afire and the warmth worked deep into her. He found her breasts and her nipples tingled at his touch.

"Come to me now," she finally said, stroking him and leading him to her.

His controlled strength was something she felt she would never tire of, his ability to take her to the highest point of passion without rushing, allowing her the time to achieve the greatest pleasure she had ever known. And each time seemed even more wonderful than the last, his power going deep into her and taking the breath from her lungs.

It was again as it always was for Morning Swan, a rush of sensation that left her relaxed and fulfilled throughout her entire body. Now he lay beside her, and the shadows of the oncoming night were mixed with the soft wind that rustled the leaves of the aspens. They did not need to speak, she leaning over his chest with her breasts against him and her long hair trailing across his broad shoulders, his eyes looking into hers. Theirs was an unspoken unity at these times, two lives together at the base of the high mountains.

* * *

Toward the end of the warm moons, a crier rode through the village shouting that a large herd of buffalo grazed not far from the village. There was a great deal of excitement and Thane asked Morning Swan if she wanted to ride with him in the hunt.

Morning Swan smiled. "I would like nothing better, but it would not be good for me."

"It would not be good for you?" Thane asked.

Morning Swan smiled and placed Thane's hand on her stomach. His eyes lit up.

"Are you with child?"

Morning Swan, her smile broadening, let Thane pick her up and twirl her around.

He continued to cater to her throughout the upcoming cold season, though she told him constantly not to be so concerned, that everything was going well. After a time Thane finally consented to allow Little Bird to do whatever was needed during the pregnancy, as it was the norm for the women to care for someone in childbearing condition.

Finally, when the warm moons had again come, Morning Swan was ready. It was very late when she got up from her bed to go into the special lodge. Rosebud and Thane were sleeping soundly and on her way out she kissed them both. Then she went to the lodge of her father and awakened Little Bird. They went to the special lodge together and Morning Swan waited outside the lodge while Little Bird went inside and prepared everything for the birth.

When the special lodge was ready, Morning Swan was asked by Little Bird to enter the lodge. Four live coals had been placed on the ground at the right places, and as Morning Swan came in, these were covered with sweetgrass while Little Bird recited a prayer. Morning Swan walked over the smoldering coals in a circle, from left to right as the sun crosses the sky, and took her place at the bed. She placed herself down, knees first, on a number of buffalo robes rolled up so that the hair was on the outside, and with each hand gripped two large stakes which had been pounded into the earth, allowing her elbows to rest upon the rolled robes. Little Bird again prayed. Now Morning Swan was ready to give birth.

A boy soon emerged from the birth canal. Little Bird covered him from hips to knees with a mixture of grease, red paint, fine clay, and powdered buffalo chips. While he squealed for air, Little Bird continued her duty. She then covered him in a layer of buffalo hair taken from the head and wrapped him first in soft buckskin and finally in tanned calfskin. Then she presented him to Morning Swan.

"He is strong," Little Bird said. "You and Bear-Man can be very proud."

Little Bird went back to her lodge and Morning Swan remained to rest and nurse the baby. It was close to dawn when Thane appeared at the door.

"Ah, why didn't you tell me the time had come?" he asked.

"It was not yet time for you to know," Morning Swan answered with a smile. "Now it is time."

Thane knelt beside her and placed his fingers on the sleeping boy's tiny face. "It's truly a miracle," he whispered. He and Morning Swan had discussed the name Jethro, after Stretch Tipson, if it was a boy.

Morning Swan held him out. "Take your son out to greet the day, and hold him up for the One Above to see. Thank the One Above and then name him after your friend."

Thane took the baby, holding him gingerly, while Morning Swan smiled and told him not to be afraid of holding him. Dawn was a sheet of blaze red that broke first to pink and then to gold in the crisp air. Thane held the child to the sky and spoke.

"I guess you're one and the same to all of us," he said. "I can't thank you enough for this beautiful child. See that he does well and grant me the knowledge to raise him right."

Thane held him for a time longer while the sun rose

and the green land welcomed the light. It would be a warm day, and it would be a day of triumph in Thane's heart. Here and there camp dogs barked and the trees were filled with birds singing morning songs. Somewhere close by Thane could hear the high notes of a tiny bird, the chickadee, singing, "Summer's near, summer's near."

Ten

RISING HAWK SAT CROSSLEGGED ATOP THE BROW OF THE
hill and watched the hawk circling, calling out in its
shrill voice. It was the red-tailed hawk, the bird of his
medicine, and the sun was just rising upon the land.
Another warm moons season had come and Rising
Hawk gave thanks that he was still alive.

He might have died long before now, he realized, or
have suffered some awful punishment. Losing his
medicine shield, by whatever means, was unthinkable
and unforgivable. Since the Long Knife had come into
the village and left with it, Rising Hawk had been
waiting for the day when his fate would catch up with
him. He had gone on no war raids, nor had he even
gone on the hunt, relying instead on his clan brothers
for meat for himself and the lodges of his women. It
had been embarrassing and degrading to say the least,
but without his medicine shield he was risking the
uncertainty of bad medicine at all times. It was safer
to suffer humiliation than dishonorable death.

Five winters had passed now since the loss of his
shield and Rising Hawk still had no answer to how he
should go about getting it back. He had consulted

various of the medicine men, none of whom said they could help him. Even though he had offered them all gracious gifts in return for their services, they'd each told him that the spirits were remaining quiet about it and that he would have to be patient and wait. Sometimes these things took longer than seemed necessary, but there was no hurrying fate, whatever kind it might be.

Now, with the coming of another warm season, Rising Hawk was no more aware of what might befall him than he had been the very day after losing his medicine shield. Nothing had come to him in all that time, no matter how reverent his actions, and there appeared to be little he could do but wait.

Rising Hawk sat watching the hawk. He would watch it all day, every day, throughout the warm moons if need be. This was what he had done now during each of the warm moons since the loss of his medicine shield. While other warriors went to war and counted coup and returned with horses to dance and celebrate, he sat alone on some hill, fasting and praying and waiting for the hawk to speak to him. He was drastically down in weight and there were those in the village who were convinced he would likely die before he again received new medicine. No one could understand why this had happened to Rising Hawk: he had always been strong and honorable and a great young leader. Only Rising Hawk, within himself, knew the reasons for his misfortune.

By now Rising Hawk had gone beyond guilt, beyond the period of time he had spent wishing he had been better to his brother, Long Hand, and his brother's wife, Morning Swan. This guilt had lasted for nearly four full seasons, until he'd realized things were already said and done and that he was sorry and could now only wait to see what the spirits might do with him. There were times, though, when he wished he could see Morning Swan and tell her he would not have demanded she live with him, as he had then impressed upon her. He wished he could tell her that she need not have any relations with him at all. But she was so beautiful and at the time he had been such a powerful warrior. He could not understand a woman who did not desire a man with the respect of the entire Blackfeet nation.

And what he had come to realize since all of this was that the woman who was his first wife, his sits-beside-him-wife, loved him more than he had ever realized. Yellow Tree came to see him each and every day, no matter the weather, to bring him water and food and to sit down beside him for a time. There were times when she had fasted and prayed with him, and even gone off by herself to seek an answer in his behalf. She brought him new moccasins for his feet and robes to cover him with when the rains came. There were times when she would turn away, so that he would not see the tears that stained her cheeks.

Yellow Tree had always loved him in this way, when he was a strong warrior and even now when he was reduced to fear and insecurity. She had always stood by him, and even during that time after Long Hand's death when he had been so taken by the notion of having Morning Swan, she had cooked and sewed and cared for his needs without so much as a word, though he had been able to detect the hurt in her eyes. Still, he had been uncaring, yielding to his own selfish interests. Honor, Rising Hawk now concluded, could blind a man beyond reason.

Now Rising Hawk did not know what he must do to get his medicine shield back. He could only continue to suffer in the way he had been for these past five winters and hope the message would come to him in some form. He had given away his wealth and now owned but two horses and his bow and arrows. He had given everything to the poorer members of his clan and to young warriors wanting some article of war

that might increase their own power. Rising Hawk
had accepted no payment for these things. He wanted
now to convince the spirits that he had changed and
that he would forever remain humble. He hoped the
spirits heard him and understood what he meant by
his actions. He hoped they would help him get his
medicine shield back. But he did not know when that
might be and he could only wait.

Jethro grew rapidly and his black eyes took in everything. He watched everything from his cradleboard
and Thane held him often, whenever Rosebud would
let him, and felt the tiny hands gripping his fingers,
opening and closing and pulling to gain strength.
Thane gave him things to look at and examine, and
got in trouble once when he allowed the baby to crawl
to a pouch of lead rifle balls, three of which immediately went into his mouth. Thane got them out quickly
while Rosebud frowned and Morning Swan put the
shot pouch away where Jethro couldn't reach it.

Eli took a great deal of pleasure in carrying Jethro
around the village, bragging how he was the baby's
grandfather. Eli had even taken it upon himself to
read to the child from the primers given to Thane by
Stretch Tipson. Eli had developed a reading habit and
he now often criticized Sir John for misinterpreting
Shakespeare and for using the raven, Joker, as a witch
in Macbeth.

"Gad sakes, Eli," John would tell him, "there's no
need to be so literal, you know. After all, the bird is
coal black."

Eli would often take Jethro to watch Sir John
perform in front of the bird. Jethro had a special
liking for Eli and laughed whenever he saw him
coming. Sir John remarked often to Eli that the infant
was merely amused by being able to drool on the thick
gray beard.

When it came time for Jethro to learn what all

babies were required to learn, Thane had to again stand back and not interfere. Morning Swan and Little Bird taught him not to cry whenever a hand was put over his mouth and to lie still when placed in tall grass. It was important that infants learn these things, as crying or moving could give away a position in hiding during an enemy raid on a village.

Jethro learned also that he could not expect attention whenever he demanded it. As was often the custom, unnecessary crying usually brought a douse of water into the nostrils, after which merely the mention of water would bring silence. Rosebud had a tendency to cater to him, which no one objected to, but even Rosebud knew to follow the rules while a baby was being trained to respond to its mother in times of danger.

As a result, Jethro developed amusing ploys to get what he wanted. He realized that yelling and crying were offensive and therefore learned quickly to make cute little noises in his throat and work his mouth whenever he was hungry. He would make popping, sucking noises that indicated he was ready to nurse. Morning Swan found herself dropping her work on the spot with a laugh to feed him.

As Jethro grew older, Rosebud and Little Bird both helped with his care while Morning Swan went about her work. Jethro had outgrown his cradleboard and was difficult to watch, as he could crawl away in the flash of an eye. Rosebud now assisted him in learning to get the feel of the back of a horse, and she would place him in front of her on Moon Eyes, who was now a strong young mare. Soon Rosebud was leading the mare while Jethro rode by himself, his small legs dangling from either side, giggling with glee with his little hands entwined in the mane.

After a time Eli took a wife. Takes-a-Basket was an older aunt of Morning Swan's who had lost her third husband to the Blackfeet a number of winters past and since then had been living with her sister and her husband. She warned Eli that she had been bad luck to all three husbands, all killed by enemies in battle. She vowed that she would be a good wife but said that she must never look upon his war articles, especially the thunderstick he carried at all times.

Sir John remained single, owing more to the fact that his eccentric playacting left most of the villagers wondering about his mental condition. He spent his time either acting or writing in his journals, or off by himself on some mountain, studying rocks and their formations. He had taken a keen interest in the various colors and textures of stone throughout the Crow country and whenever the village moved, he could be found off somewhere looking at cliffs and rocks and adding notes to his writings.

Time for Thane was now like a fleeting dove among the trees. Jethro was growing fast and years were passing quickly. Rolling on the ground with his son became a constant amusement. Jethro enjoyed making his father into a horse and he was nearly impossible to throw off. Meanwhile Rosebud was learning to make robes and dress them with quillwork and beadwork. It hardly seemed possible. Already Rosebud was approaching young womanhood, and in a few more years would be ready for marriage, if she so chose. It would be up to Thane to give her away and he couldn't imagine her as someone's wife. The toddler who had seemingly only yesterday fed him from a bowl while he hid in a mass of shrubs was already talking to her mother about the strong young warriors in the village.

The more he thought about this sudden passing of time, the more concerned Thane became. He watched the Crow people raising their children and teaching them the things they had learned in the same way, according to the same customs that had been handed down over many generations. He watched young men go into the hills and come down again after a medicine dream and saw them go into battle and either die or gain honor. He saw the oldest of the young women in a family taken as the bride of a warrior, and then saw her sisters, in turn, become his wives also. He saw the winter fires spring up and the stories being told as each cold season went by and the people waited for another warm season to come. The Crow people were doing things the same way, but little by little things were changing beyond their control.

Now there were steamboats on the Missouri and, during high water, they would churn their way up the Yellowstone, spiting fire and smoke, bringing trade articles. Trading posts sprang up at the mouth of every tributary along the Elk River, the Yellowstone. At first these boats scared the Crows badly, but in time they grew to understand that this strange smoking canoe was just another example of the Long Knives' strange and powerful medicine. And they felt that the more of this activity that occurred, the better it was for them in their unending battle against the Blackfeet.

Thane was by now well known throughout Crow country as big medicine to their people. He was praised by all whenever other bands and clans came to visit, or when the Kicked-in-Their-Bellies journeyed to other parts of the mountains and plains to trade. As far down as the Laramie fork of the Platte River and then up into the Lakota country of the Black Hills and beyond, to the Big River, the Missouri, and the Dirt Lodge people to whom the Crows were related, all knew of the one they called Bear-Man. He was the one who carried the medicine shield of the strong warrior, Rising Hawk, of the Blackfeet people. It was he, Bear-Man, who had broken Rising Hawk's medicine. He was powerful medicine, this warrior, Bear-Man, and whenever he carried the pipe in battle, there was little doubt a victory would come.

* * *

Time passed in the mountains and the Crow people began to see change. The buffalo herds came and went and the hunts were generally good, though now the herds were being run from place to place by the many trappers in the mountains and the increased pressure by the various tribes to secure winter food supplies. Thane realized it would become harder and harder to secure meat. There would be more friction, even between friendly tribes, as hunting parties ventured out farther and farther from their villages, overlapping one another's hunting grounds. And with the Blackfeet killing all who came into their lands, the hunts to the north would be rushed and generally unsatisfactory.

The warm moons once again swept by like the winds that rose from beyond the mountains. Once again the colors of the hills and valleys were scarlet and gold. Then the leaves were gone and the snows came, the eternal snows, white and sullen and hard upon the land, in the season that always tests the soul. Now, no matter how much meat there was in the village, there was always hunger before the coming of the green grass and the return of the great buffalo herds. There were always a great number of these beasts killed every year, but the coming of the white brothers put additional burdens on food supplies. Now that the Long Knives were frequent visitors and feasts to welcome them were common, the food supplies dwindled ever more rapidly and it became necessary to hunt almost continuously.

Thane managed to keep himself busy during the deep winter months by bringing meat into camp. Jethro was learning to hunt, and whenever game was close to camp, Thane would take him along. Jethro had been given a bow and arrows by an uncle and he delighted in shooting rabbits with it.

But the larger game did not stay close to the village, and as Jethro was not yet old enough to go long distances, Thane often went out by himself, far out from the village to where the migration of the elk herds the fall before had ended in the scattered feeding grounds throughout the valley, or higher on the slopes where the deer and bighorn sheep spent their time. The herds were always close to the warm seeps from underground that flowed into the streams and the river, where the ice never formed and the grass was available and green the year round. Though there was concern about Blackfeet raiding parties, the snow moons were generally a time to remain near the village and prepare articles of clothing and war for the upcoming warm moons. And since the Long Knives had come into the mountains, the Blackfeet peoples were suffering ever-increasing war losses and they could ill afford to risk death due to the weather. Thane was watchful, but allowed himself the luxury of going off by himself and savoring the country.

This was an unsettled country when it came to the weather, Thane concluded. Bitter cold could be replaced in a matter of hours by warm winds from the southwest that would quickly take the snow. Just as suddenly the sky could fill with clouds and a storm could blast in from the north. Thane watched the animals to understand what was going to happen: most usually the herds would flock to the slopes and bottoms in large groups to fill up with food before a storm came in, generally intent upon their eating and disregarding anything else. They would eat continually, rarely taking the time to even lift their heads. Then they would fill up with water and take refuge in nearby cover.

It was a pattern with the herds in the valley, staying in cover during the storms and coming out when the worst was over. And all the while there was the presence of the wolves, packs of them that watched the herds day in and day out, running them and feeding on the weak that straggled behind and fell prey to their steel jaws. Thane had believed at first that the wolves would have an easy time of it. But they had a lot of difficulty running down their prey unless they could catch a herd out in the open. Wherever there was brushy cover, there was little chance the wolves would make a kill. It was too difficult to run, and in close quarters the advantage went to the animal with horns and sharp hooves.

When the snows again left and the land turned to life once more, Thane went out into the country to trap. This year he wanted to return to rendezvous and he wanted to take Morning Swan with him and show her off to the other trappers, many of whom had taken mountain brides themselves. He wanted to show them the reason for his decision to remain away from the brigades and stay with the Crows. With a number of beaver pelts he would take this spring, together with the ones he had accumulated from the fall before, he would return to his friends with pride.

Thane invited Eli, but the old trapper declined the invitation, owing to the fact that his knee now stiffened up on him at irregular times and he didn't want to be on horseback along some high trail along a cliff when that happened. Sir John had never gotten used to the weather in this country and he preferred a warm lodge to the uncertainty of sleeping out in the open.

Thane was by now used to going off by himself, and he decided to choose an area within Crow country he had not previously explored or trapped, deep in the mountains the Crows called the Beartooth. It was high and strong, this rugged mountain wilderness, and each time they had built camp at its base Thane had been eager to ride up into this high place.

"Why do you feel you have to go off to trap alone?" Morning Swan asked. "Why don't you stay here with your son?"

"I want to learn that country and take him up

there," Thane answered. "He's too small now. I'll bring him back some ermine and you can make a coat for him."

Morning Swan began to talk again as if she hadn't heard him. "I would not mind it if you were going off to pray, but you are not. You are going by yourself to take the beaver from a land that does not belong to you."

"I've never been up there," Thane said. He was saddling Whistler and was no longer paying much attention to her. "I thought it would be fun to go up and look around, and I might as well take a few beaver while I'm up there."

"That is a strange and powerful country," Morning Swan warned him. "It is foolish to go that far into that country alone."

"Ahh!" Thane turned from Whistler and gripped Morning Swan's shoulders. He squeezed them roughly. "I'm not afraid of going up there. What's the matter with you?"

Morning Swan said nothing. She twisted away from him and was gone. Thane shrugged and finished getting the pack string ready to depart. He could see Eli sitting on a stump a ways off, studying him while he leaned on his cane. Thane waved and Eli nodded. No one wanted him to go. Rosebud's goodbye earlier had been rather curt. It didn't hurt, Thane told himself, for a man to get off and enjoy himself once in a while.

The Beartooth was high and wild. Thane came to know the country, each twisting stream and alpine meadow. He found his way into high mountain passes and crossed game trails along rocky slopes that overlooked vast distances where nothing but snow-capped peaks loomed. As he worked his way deeper into the high mountains of the Beartooth—taking rich beaver from icy streams as he went—he realized how truly isolated this region was. Though the Crows journeyed into the high Yellowstone often, they did not wander far off the established trails. This country, it was said, held strange mysteries.

The days went quickly and Thane was ready to return to the village. All he cared about now was catching a few more beaver to take back. He would have some stories to tell at rendezvous, how he had spent his spring in isolation and had trod in country most men feared. He began to think of it as his land and within himself he saw this country as a place he had discovered and set boundaries around. He carved his name in trees and chipped it onto the face of rock cliffs and promontories. He marked these places down on paper and drew sketches of the landscape. In his mind he was a leader and a wilderness dignitary—until the day that would change his perceptions of things once again.

Thane was finished with his trapping and was preparing to return to the village. He rode through a bright morning to which the sun brought a deep green, scattered with the ever-present spring flowers of blue, gold, and scarlet. At the edge of a small meadow he noticed a lone pine tree and thought it fitting to leave his mark there. He was carving his name across its trunk, not noticing that on the other side of the tree, etched deep into the bark, were the claw marks of a male grizzly who had staked out his territory.

Thane was standing on top of his pony's back, balancing himself with one hand against the tree while he carved with his knife, something he had watched the Crows do themselves when etching on sandstone cliffs down in the valley. He was concentrating on cutting his name deep into the tree when his pony suddenly bolted. He fell heavily on his right shoulder. The mass of scar tissue built up inside from the grizzly mauling broke loose. He lay stunned for a moment before he grunted and got to his feet, that old flame of intense pain once again rising from deep in his back and shoulder. He found he could move his arm but with a lot of pain. Then he remembered why he had fallen. He would have to teach Whistler all over again to stand still while he was working. But his pony and the pack string of mules were running down the trail and out of the meadow. He turned and saw a huge grizzly, standing high on its hind feet, sniffing the air.

With his rifle now gone with his horse, Thane was defenseless. His right arm was growing numb, and even if a knife would protect him, he would have to use his left hand. But all of those thoughts were ridiculous, he knew. A bear of that size would never go down with a single shot, no matter how vital the organ that was hit, and a knife would do no more good than a sharp stick.

As the grizzly roared and dropped to all fours to charge, Thane scrambled up the tree. His instinct of preservation outweighed the pain in his arm and shoulder and he scrambled up the trunk as if he had been born to climb. The grizzly roared again and Thane worked himself high into the tree, fighting panic. The sound of the bear brought back memories from deep within his mind. Once again he saw the face of the grizzly that had mauled him his first year out, near the Highwood Mountains.

The grizzly tried to pull himself up into the tree after Thane but the lower branches, though large in comparison with the smaller trees around, snapped like firewood under his weight. The bear tried to clasp his arms and legs to pull himself up, but that too failed and he finally remained at the base of the tree, growling and popping his jaws.

Thane looked down through the branches at small, angry eyes that glared up at him from within a huge, dished face. The bear was a monster, even larger than the one which had mauled him near the Highwoods. Thane turned away and looked across the mountains, holding onto the branches to keep his balance, unable to cup his ears against the continuous low growling.

The bear once again tried climbing the tree. Again it

failed, and after sliding back down numerous times, it began to shake the tree, rising on its hind feet and pushing against the trunk. Thane was happy for the size of the tree. A smaller tree would have been uprooted at the base. But the bear was so powerful that even this large tree shook and Thane found himself gripping the branches and blinking pine needles out of his eyes for a long period, until the bear finally decided he would not be able to shake Thane out.

The grizzly remained throughout the day, pacing around the base of the tree, patiently waiting for Thane to come down. Thane remained in his place, shifting arms and his weight to ease the tension and the strain on his muscles. He was having considerable trouble with his right hand and arm and keeping hold of limbs was proving to be a problem.

Just before nightfall, the grizzly left. Thane worried more about coming down now than at any other time. The bear could be hiding and he would never see it until it was too late. After waiting a good portion of the night, Thane began to slowly descend the tree. The moon was now straight above, an oblong white melon that cast an eerie white glow through the trees. He looked in all directions and waited for some time in the lower branches before coming down. His right arm and shoulder went from numbness to acute pain and holding himself in the tree was becoming ever more difficult. Finally he dropped from the tree and fell to the ground.

His cramped leg muscles protested his sudden movements, but he quickly rose to his feet and began to run, seeing the grizzly emerging from behind every shadowy tree and shrub thicket. He fought to keep his composure and to keep from running blind. His worst enemy now was uncontrolled fear, the manic terror that emerged from his brain and filled him with waves of gripping horror. He ran and ran and, finally, fell exhausted near a small stream, his right arm hanging uselessly at his side.

He heard himself screaming, as if he were someone else listening but unable to stop it. Again he climbed a tree, and when he had stopped screaming, he heard only silence around him. He got down and told himself making noise would only lead the bear back to him. He began to walk through the darkness, supporting his right arm and shoulder at the elbow with his left hand. It made walking awkward but he had no choice. He told himself that he must now get down from the mountains and back to the Crow village. It was time now to forget the grizzly, he convinced himself; there were a lot of other ways to die.

Rosebud stood with Sir John and watched him talk to the raven, Joker, moving about and reciting lines while the bird cocked its head and began to caw approvingly. Rosebud giggled continuously and clapped her hands whenever the raven would hop on its perch and make noise.

Turtle also watched, anxious to see what progress Crazy Arms—whom many thought was now also crazy in the head—had made with his bird. As far as Turtle could tell, the raven was just a better squawker now than before.

Rosebud and Turtle discussed the bird and Eli, who had been pacing around the village, limping awkwardly and slamming his cane against meat racks and lodge poles ever since the departure of Bear-Man to trap the Beartooth. Eli now came over and interrupted Sir John in the middle of a line.

"Why don't you stop jabberin' at that bird and saddle a couple of horses for us?" he asked Sir John.

Sir John cleared his throat. "I must say, I cannot take any fancy whatsoever to your ardent lack of manners. Now why, might I ask, would you want me to saddle a couple of horses?"

"I've got a bad feelin' about Thane," Eli said. "He should be back down from them mountains by now. It's time we looked for him, I'm thinkin'."

It was then that a crier rode through the village announcing the return of Bear-Man's pony and pack train, but the absence of Bear-Man himself. Rosebud ran to find her mother, who was rubbing fat from the inside of a buffalo hide. She had already heard the news.

"If he is strong enough to go up there by himself," she said to Rosebud, "then he is strong enough to return by himself."

"Mother," Rosebud asked, "aren't you afraid for him? Don't you worry that he might die, or is already dead?"

Morning Swan stopped her work for a moment. She saw that Rosebud was nearly in tears. "If he is already dead," Morning Swan told her daughter, "then there is no way we can help him and it would be foolish to send more out to face danger. If he is not dead, then maybe he will learn something."

The sun rose again and Thane walked. His arm and shoulder were a mass of pain and he continued to support them, working to block out his misery. He had walked through most of the night, following the stars which seemed just beyond his fingertips in this high land. It would be at least another two days, he realized, before he could expect to reach the village. This land looked far larger now than it had from the back of a horse. The distant peaks of the Yellowstone Plateau to the south had seemed at about eye level when he had been riding; now they seemed a towering and distant land.

While he walked, Thane fought with the irony of what had happened and how once again he had been brought down by the power and brute strength of a creature that could never be conquered. He wondered if the white bears were infecting his life, as might a plague or pestilence, an infection that would never leave, but would keep him in its grasp forever. Just when he had thought the world was his for the taking, he had suddenly been reduced to struggling for survival. It was a reminder to him that what Morning Swan told him continuously was true: the land was master to all.

With only his knife to secure food, Thane found himself at the mercy of hunger and weakness. There was a lot of scattered snow still remaining on the high Beartooth and sleeping out at night with his shoulder in its present condition was totally impossible. The encounter with the grizzly had drained him and he found using his left hand was awkward and did not merit the strain and effort. Digging roots, even the starchy ones, would not provide him with much energy anyway. He was going to have to make it mainly on the reserves in his body.

The time went by as though the earth were standing still and Thane thought constantly that he was not moving, that he would never reach the edge of these mountains. More than once he squinted into the sky and checked shadows on rocks and trees to be sure he was traveling north and east, to where the Crow village lay. His mind grew hazier as he traveled with little rest and a great deal of exertion. Pain was a constant companion that continually brought him to the brink of madness. There was nothing he could do, and throwing rocks in anger with his left hand only added to his frustration.

So he finally consented to channeling his anger into a determination to walk out alive. Life teemed around him in this high paradise. He passed herds of migrating elk, but chose not to stop and look at them. It was too frustrating to see them and know he could get no meat. As he went on he passed high mountain lakes where swarms of scarlet-sided trout jumped in the

waters. Grouse rose in front of him to fly out of reach.
He saw bighorn sheep, wolves, and then late the
afternoon of the third day he saw the shaggy mountain
goats—which the mountain tribes considered to be
the sacred small white buffalo that lived high on the
rocky ledges. They were great medicine, and as Thane
watched them, he had the feeling there was a sort of
power there that he could not explain. Something, he
felt, was going to happen.

As late evening fell, Thane found himself descending the mountain. He was weak and going downhill
under control was far more strain than he had antici-
pated. He fell twice and caught himself, screaming at
the pain in his shoulder. Finally he lay down in the
shelter of a low overhang of rock to rest and regain
some strength. But his exhaustion overwhelmed him
and despite his best efforts, his head settled back
against the rock.

When the sun was gone and only twilight remained,
he suddenly awoke into a world he did not understand. They were standing around him, small and
odd-looking, and in the crimson light he could not see
them clearly. They frightened him, but he was so
numb with pain and exhaustion that he merely remained seated and watched as more of them appeared, seemingly from out of the rocks around him.
There were many of them, like dim little shadows
scooting about through the rocks. Thane shook his
head to try and clear his senses.

"Bear-Man, strong and mighty, has foolishly offered himself to death."

Thane heard the words in his head, and he knew he
had not imagined them. The small beings remained in
the shadows while one of them stepped forward and
pulled a huge stone from the earth in front of him.
Dirt and vegetation fell from it as the little being
brought it up. Thane heard the voice inside his head
once again.

"This is a land no one will ever understand. The mysteries are too ancient. Many have come and gone before and their spirits fight over what is to happen here. The bear who chases you, the big white grizzly, he is the past and the future. You must fight him again to survive."

Thane felt powerless. He tried to scoot away from the small figure in front of him, shadowed by the huge rock and the oncoming night, but his back was against the cliff wall and he couldn't move. The voice continued.

"Not even the most reverent among the people who now live here, the Crow people, know all there is. No one will ever know all there is. That is the way it must be. Let it be that way. Do not try to control what you cannot control or make things the way you wish them to be. It will only cause pain and sorrow. When the rocks begin to fall, do not be on top of them. Do not be under them. Do not be beside them. Be *in* them! Do you hear me? They are the strength of the world. You must be part of them and one with them. Only then can you be one and whole."

Then the small being turned and tossed the immense rock down the slope into the night. Thane heard it strike something below with a heavy thud. A low bellow followed and Thane cringed in fear. The little beings began to disperse and Thane found he couldn't move. The bellow had stopped but he was held fast by a strange force, not a terror or worry over injury or death, but a power he had never felt before or even knew existed that transfixed him. In this state he watched them leave, returning to where they had come from, inside the rocks around him. They went in a line, filing past him like miniature, oddly formed soldiers, disappearing into the cliff.

The last one of them came from down below, where the rock had fallen, and carried upon his back a fallen elk. It was a huge bull whose antlers spread high and wide and Thane stared, seeing the small two-legged image with an arm wrapped over the elk's massive neck, with one of the elk's shoulders positioned high on his own back, the rest of the animal dragging behind. Thane noticed that the dwarf carried the elk with little effort, and watched while the little being dropped the huge elk in front of him and disappeared with the others into the rocks.

Now it was completely dark and it was a long time before Thane could make himself move. When he did he gasped for breath. His shoulder was cold and stiff and ached from deep within. This was the only thing that told him he was sitting there, flesh and blood, and not in a dream. He stared at the elk, which lay with its neck and front shoulders at an odd, broken angle. He looked up from the elk and into the complete darkness all around him. In the sky a series of stars fell like white coals from the heavens. Thane watched to see if the sky would fall completely, and when it didn't, he made himself get up. For a time his legs were unsteady. Then, with caution, he kicked the body of the elk. It was huge and rigid.

After more time, Thane gathered some wood with his good hand, and after a lot of struggle, made a fire. He steadied his trembling hand, and with his knife he cut into the elk. The meat was real and the taste was real. He ate slowly, feeling his strength returning to him. He knew now that his body would recover and that he would not die before leaving these mountains, but Thane worried about what he had seen and that his head might never clear.

When Thane entered the village he was greeted warmly by Eli, who laughed and slapped him on the back and called him a strong young bull. His shoulder injury was obvious, but he assured everyone it was only temporary and that soon he would be fine. But Thane was somehow changed, and he acted as though he felt a certain amount of guilt for having come out of the Beartooth alive. He talked about the grizzly that had scared his horse out from under him and then treed him for hours. This he dwelt on mostly, avoiding questions as much as possible about the long walk out. When asked how he had found meat without his rifle, Thane said only that he had been lucky enough to come upon an elk that had been killed by a falling rock, and would say no more.

Morning Swan did not once make reference to his injured shoulder, nor did she offer any sympathy. Thane wanted no sympathy so this did not bother him. What did bother him was Morning Swan's attitude about his going into the Beartooth in the first place. It seemed to him that there was nothing wrong with getting out to see the country. Maybe he had been foolish to go alone, and into such a high and desolate country as the Beartooth. Had it not been for the unexplained visit from the small beings, Thane realized, he would have likely met death.

The more Thane thought back on the incident on the side of the mountain, where the little beings had come to him, the more he wondered if it had been an hallucination. Though he had been weak with fear and hunger at the time, he had gone through something that could not be explained, something that had moved him and would forever remain with him. The event from beginning to end was firmly etched into his mind, including the words that had come to him. He had taken the elk's eye teeth from the jaws and now had them with him, a set of lucky teeth to carry around. He was pondering the notion of making a special little bag for them so that he might save them as a reminder of an experience he felt he would never fully understand.

But its effect on his mind was not what it had been with the bear; no doubt, Thane surmised, because these small, human-like forms had come to his aid

rather than to kill him, as had the bear. He would have
no worries about dreaming of this incident and having
the visions awaken him in a cold sweat. This he was
sure of, and why he was so sure of it, he could not
explain to himself. He felt as though these beings had
somehow told him they would protect him if he
opened up his mind and learned to be wise instead of
merely powerful. Thane was already aware that
strength was the master of a great deal, but he was now
learning that true strength of mind and body was a gift
that came only to those who understood it and
acknowledged its source.

Thane realized this more and more, as the days
passed and he could not fully gain back the use of his
shoulder and arm. Though his shoulder would move
and he could use his arm to some extent, it was
impossible for him to rotate his shoulder fully without
excruciating pain. Nor could he shoot Gulliver without great difficulty. The impact brought fire to the
joint of his shoulder. He became more and more
troubled by it, and soon this worry turned to alarm.
He could no longer exercise the way he had, doing his
chinups on branches and the pushups. His shoulder
would not allow it. He wanted to scream in frustration. He found himself wanting to be alone more and
more, fighting the reality that the fall from Whistler
had done far more damage to the shoulder wounded
by the grizzly than he wanted to realize.

Nothing he did brought the shoulder back. Hot
baths brought temporary relief but the pain remained
and the frustration mounted. He began to wonder
what the trip into the Beartooth was going to cost him
in the end. And he began to wonder again what his
vision meant and how it fit into this drastic change in
his physical stature.

Soon the two began to eat at him simultaneously:
when his shoulder pained him, he would think about
the vision. He would hear the words about survival

and being a part of the rocks and the land. This occurred most often when he was hunting and he would miss an easy shot. Eli would squint at him in disbelief and he would have to turn away. The pain caused by shooting had begun to cause an unnatural flinch when he fired. His great shooting ability, as well as all the other things he had been able to do with authority, were going fast.

Morning Swan sensed his anxiety, and though she remained angry that Thane would not at least acknowledge he was wrong for going into the Beartooth alone, she loved this man deeply and found herself wanting to help him. At first she thought it was his physical problems that were causing his mental anguish. After all, they had before. The great white bear had caused him trouble since first coming into the mountains. The bear had left deep scars on his body, which he had used for a reason to build his muscles up and make himself look like an invincible man. Now that the bear had again caused injury to his shoulder, she thought that Thane's odd actions were the result of his loss of power.

Morning Swan knew Thane relished the place of honor he had among her people, as well as among the trappers and other Indian tribes all over the mountains. Ever since she had first met him coming down from the Piegan village, she had sensed that within him physical stature was a very important thing. This was not unusual and it was expected among all men in these lands, no matter their race. Morning Swan could sense that Thane was beginning to understand that strength and power were admired, but could be taken away just as fast as they had been acquired. Keeping power was much harder than attaining it.

Thane was now on the verge of not only losing his power, but also his physical well-being. Morning Swan was beginning to see the same pattern in his thinking that she had witnessed with Long Hand. She could see him fretting and growing ever more concerned that he would not be able to function normally, going through the days in frustration because he could not use his arm. And when the time came for them to travel to the rendezvous, she sensed his frustration reaching a peak.

A few days before they were to leave, Morning Swan overheard Thane talking to Rosebud.

"Rosebud, you know I can saddle Whistler by myself. Now, get back away from him and let me do it."

Rosebud came over to her mother and bit her lip. Morning Swan gave her a hug. "He doesn't mean everything he says, you know that."

"I just wanted to help," Rosebud said. "I know his arm isn't good."

"Don't worry," Morning Swan said. "His arm will get better and then he will be sorry he spoke to you that way. Now, go get some wood for the fire."

When Rosebud was gone Morning Swan went over to where Thane struggled to get the saddle on Whistler.

"So you don't want Rosebud around now," she said to Thane. "When did you begin to feel that way?"

Thane let the saddle fall to the ground and turned to Morning Swan.

"You know better than that. I just don't want everybody nursing me, that's all."

"Rosebud doesn't think she is nursing you."

"A man is supposed to be able to saddle his own horse."

"Yes, but even I can see that you are having trouble. And it is getting worse every day. Soon you will destroy yourself. Remember, I lived through this once before."

Thane took a deep breath. "Well, I didn't mean to upset Rosebud. I just feel helpless and I don't know what to do. Tell her I'm sorry."

"No," Morning Swan said. "You'll have to tell her that yourself. But first you must tell me about your time on the Beartooth. Something more than the bear and your fall from the horse happened up there."

"I don't know if I can talk about it," Thane said. "I don't know if you'll believe me."

Morning Swan looked at Thane in astonishment. "Why wouldn't I believe you?"

The mere suggestion that the story was unbelievable in Thane's eyes set Morning Swan to thinking. She knew then something important had happened to him and that it, in fact, might have been a vision or a medicine dream. If such was the case she did not want to hear about it if it would harm his medicine, but Thane told her he knew no reason why he shouldn't discuss the event.

Thane then finished saddling Whistler and Morning Swan caught Whirlwind. Together they rode out from the village and up the Rotten-Sun-Dance-Lodge-Creek toward the grove of aspens. During the trip Thane told her everything from the time he had fallen from Whistler's back up until the morning after the little beings had appeared to him. She nodded while he spoke, and when he was finished she looked at him and told him something very important.

"You have seen the Little People," she told him, "the protectors of my people. They have great medicine and they do not appear to very many. Therefore, you are someone special in their eyes and they have come to you for a reason. Maybe when we return to the village it would be wise for you to talk to someone about this."

Thane knew very well what she meant by "talking to someone" in the village. She was referring to one of the medicine men, a *shaman* who knew of the powers and could invoke them. Thane mostly kept away from them, more out of ignorance, he realized, than any real fear. They were everyday men, often warriors who fought with the others. But they had ties with special forces and Thane had heard stories that made his encounter with the grizzlies seem like nothing.

"For two good horses," Morning Swan continued, "you might have your dream interpreted and learn what it means."

"I would feel better just leaving well enough alone," Thane said.

"It must be your decision," Morning Swan told him.

When they reached the little valley where the aspen grove stood, Morning Swan covered her mouth in astonishment. The valley had changed and not for the better. The beaver ponds filled with jumping trout were mostly non-existent and the beaver themselves were not to be seen. The bogs where the water from the dams had backed up were no longer there and the grass and flowers were struggling to retain their green growth.

It did not take close inspection to see that the beaver dams had receded and that, in fact, most of them had washed out. The heavy trapping in the area was starting to take its toll. The beaver population was depleted markedly and the surrounding valley was suffering as a result. The constant trapping had reduced the numbers of beaver to the point that they could no longer keep the dams in repair and thus retard the rush of oncoming water during peak flows in the spring.

As they walked along the bottom there was a distinct absence of live beaver, but a lot of sign indicating that a brigade had trapped the area in the early spring. Bones and partially eaten carcasses littered the area, and the absence of wolves and coyotes indicated there had been so many beaver killed that there was too much meat. But for a few sounds of tails splashing the water here and there, it seemed the surviving beaver had deserted the area. The remaining ponds were smaller and shallower and the fish population was down as well. Those fish that remained would likely winter-kill during the next siege of thick ice.

Morning Swan had her fists clenched and she was glaring at Thane. "This land is going to die. I told you this when we left the Piegan lands. The Long Knives are going to see to it that the land is dead. Can you see how that is going to happen?"

Morning Swan pointed up and down the valley. During the spring, she explained, runoff water from melting snow and rain had come down the stream channel and washed out those dams not in repair, resulting in a great loss of ponded water. This rush of water had also taken the beaver lodges and food caches along the bank, leaving those beaver still remaining with little to eat and no homes. If the small population of beaver left stored caches of food and built homes, the dams would fall into further disrepair and this would cause further stream degradation; if the beaver built dams, they would be without food and homes and freeze or starve to death during the upcoming winter.

"I don't want this any more than you," Thane told Morning Swan, who was now beside herself with anger. "But it's not fair to blame me. I can't keep everybody out. You know that. The whole world's coming out here now."

"Everybody says, 'I can't do anything,'" Morning Swan spat bitterly. "Well, everybody *can* do something, and if they get together they can do a lot of things. What good does it do the Long Knives to take all the beaver and then have none to trap?"

Thane took a deep breath. "You know what it's like among your people as well as mine: take it while it's here, because if you don't, someone else will."

"Yes," said Morning Swan, "and when there is nothing left you will all point to one another and say, 'It wasn't me, it was him.' By then it will be too late for everybody."

"Maybe I can talk to the council," Thane suggested. "Maybe they will understand that if all the beaver are taken at once, there will be none left and the land will suffer."

"I hope the council will listen," Morning Swan said. "Because if no one cares, our land will soon be crying for life."

Eleven

THANE CAME OUT OF THE COUNCIL LODGE AND LOOKED TO the east, where the sun was just rising. The village was just becoming active and smoke drifted up from the tops of the lodges into a breeze that took it out from the village, where it was lost in an endless sky.

Throughout the night Thane had passed the pipe and talked in behalf of himself and Morning Swan, explaining their view concerning the destruction of the creeks and rivers—the overtrapping of beaver from the lands. The council had listened but it had seemed to Thane from the beginning that he was not making the impression he had hoped.

It was brought to Thane's attention at the outset that neither the Crow people nor any other people could claim ownership to the streams and rivers. The land was only used by the people, and with thanks. Shortly into the discussions Thane could also sense that their attitude about the Long Knives was steadfastly one of kinship and affection, and disturbing that relationship would be difficult. Even though some of the other Crow bands had come to make a practice of stealing trappers' horses and furs, the Kicked-in-

Their-Bellies remained loyal.

It was a fact that in one of the other bands another Long Knife, a mulatto named Jim Beckwourth, had become established and was considered to have great medicine—possibly an even more powerful medicine than Thane had once enjoyed. Thane had heard rumors that Beckwourth was next to a spirit among this particular group of Crows, owing mainly to the odd and fabricated story of another trapper concerning a long-lost chief's son, kidnapped by an enemy tribe and now returned in the person of Beckwourth himself. So it occurred to Thane that in the eyes of the Crow people the Long Knives had come to be looked upon as special individuals, and if these special individuals took all the beaver, then the spirits had dictated they were supposed to have all the beaver.

In addition, what one band decided was certainly not preordained to take effect among the other bands. To the contrary, it was often the case that clan rivalries precluded agreements between some bands on anything, no matter how beneficial the suggested practice might be. Thane had come to understand that there was enough clan friction among these people to keep seasonal ceremonial gatherings hopping, and clan police occupied night and day.

When Thane broke the news to Morning Swan she merely took a breath and nodded; she hadn't expected to get her wish. She had only hoped there would be enough foresight on the part of some of the elders to want to help conserve the beaver. This setback did not deter her, however, and she felt that possibly the other tribes in the mountains that were not so closely allied with the Long Knives might see her point. She intended to work this again through Thane, who would talk to the various tribes in council. Certainly they could now understand that their own homelands were suffering.

Before the coming of the many Long Knives there

had been so many beaver in the mountains that anyone who expressed concern about their numbers would have been looked upon as foolish and unable to understand the laws of reproduction. Beaver habitats throughout the mountains were plentiful and whenever their population suffered from predators or disease, or other natural catastrophes, they would then reproduce that many more offspring to compensate for the losses. But once the trapping began in earnest, there was no means by which the beaver population could maintain itself. It was as if a catastrophe were occurring each fall and then again each spring. The trappers took them by the thousands and those that remained could in no way replenish the stock.

Thane, in watching over the years, had noticed how the plew size had dropped markedly. In the beginning, when he was with Ashley's men on Green River, there had been a number of older, mature beaver and their pelts were large. This had been the case all over the mountains, in every stream and river. Now the pelts taken anywhere were considerably smaller, owing to the fact that the only individuals left in the population now for the most part were young and not fully grown.

There was no question that beaver were suffering, not only from a population standpoint, but from an economic one as well. Prices were down and dropping. The various groups of trappers that wandered through the mountains and invariably ended up spending time among the Crows reported on the changes in life back east. Hearing them had convinced Eli all the more that the era of the open mountains was coming to a close.

"All this will be gone in not many years, I'm thinkin'," he told Thane while he worked to replace a worn cinch on his saddle. "I hear tell the greenhorns and porkeaters damn near outnumbered those with beaver at the last rendezvous. That spells the end. The good times have done passed by."

"What's happened to beaver that it doesn't fetch the price it used to?" Thane asked him.

"They say beaver's old-fashioned in the cities now," Eli said. "That bunch that was through here a week past, they said there was not much call for beaver no more. Yep, fancy men got silk hats now, they say. They said these mountains would see the likes of a different bunch out here soon, in the likes of preachers and such, that they were comin' out strong already."

"They want to ruin it all, is what they want," Thane said.

Eli was reflecting. "Yeah, they're a-headed this way. But I don't 'spect my brother, Joseph, would figure to be among 'em. Doubt if he could stand the trip at his age. Just as well. They should all stay to home, bein' they don't know peedaddle about this country."

Eli was still wondering about his brother, after all the years, and it affected him to think that the world he had left was creeping out into the mountains now. Times would never be what they once were, and Thane realized that if Eli weren't so badly handicapped by his knee now, he would be far angrier about it than he now seemed to be.

The group that prepared to leave for rendezvous was more of a war party than a trading party. Though Rosebud and Jethro both protested at not being allowed to go, Thane convinced Morning Swan that, even though there were always a number of children present, a rendezvous could be a violent place. And, with the Blackfeet all over, the trip down could prove to be a fight all the way. It was best if Rosebud and Jethro remain with Morning Swan's parents.

The more Thane thought about it, the more he realized this would likely not be much of a pleasure trip in the end. A number of young warriors, including Runs-in-Water, were preparing themselves for travel with Thane and Morning Swan, each with their best war articles. A number of them had fasted and prayed and gone into the hills during the course of early spring to prepare for these upcoming warm moons, sure to be filled with warfare. The Blackfeet were warring continuously now and, as their war parties had spread out across the mountains, Thane knew without question they would meet up with them somewhere along the way.

Eli said he was going only because he wanted to fight Blackfeet once more while he was still able, and to see a good rendezvous again before they petered out. Sir John, who by now had accumulated what could be considered almost a complete history on what he had seen in the mountains, was anxious to meet some of these newcomers who were not trappers, but clergymen and adventurers. Sir John could boast of being the forerunner of this group of travelers and looked forward to hearing from them what changes the East had undergone since his leaving.

They were nearly sixty strong as they worked their way south, along the Bighorn River. Morning Swan pointed out to Thane the location where they had camped in the winter storm that first year, when they were traveling to reach her band. It brought back a lot of memories to Thane and made him realize a lot had occurred since then. It made him miss the children, Rosebud and Jethro, who always delighted in traveling, wherever it might be. It made him wish that he had not insisted they remain behind. Then they reached the mouth of a small stream that led to a camping site Morning Swan called the Place-of-Yellow-Willows. Along the stream were the remains of four butchered trappers.

The work of a Blackfeet war party. The various parts of the men were scattered and the remains were a feast for a number of ravens and magpies in the area, and wolves that were now slinking off with bits of bone and flesh. Thane and some of the Crow warriors got down from their ponies to inspect what was left of the trappers. The blood had not yet darkened.

The Crow Wolves sent out ahead to scout now

returned, and on their heels was a large group of Blackfeet.

"They are the Kainah, the Bloods," Morning Swan said as she pointed. "And some Piegans as well."

"Looks like I found my fight," Eli said to no one in particular.

The Blackfeet came riding across a broad plain above the river. They spread out into a long column and began to chant and yell war cries. Some of them were holding up the scalps of the fallen trappers. The Crows answered with their own war cries and began to paint themselves for battle.

It appeared that the Crows outnumbered the Blackfeet, unless there were other Blackfeet hidden nearby. But the Blackfeet, fresh from the kill of the trappers, had smelled blood and were ready to kill all their enemies in a single day. They made signs to the Crows to this effect, but when Thane rode forward and held up Rising Hawk's medicine shield, telling the Blackfeet in their own tongue that this was going to be a bad day for them, they began to talk among themselves.

Old memories of the deaths of relatives at the hands of this enemy brought a number of Crows forward in their familiar battle routine, charging independently against their enemy, intent on gaining glory for themselves. Most of the Blackfeet were Blood warriors and they too remembered the death of relatives at the hands of their Crow enemies. But Thane, the one known as Bear-Man, and the medicine shield brought a strange fear into them.

Today was not a good day for the Bloods and Piegans. But it was not Bear-Man who led the charge to count coup. Instead it was Runs-in-Water, whose medicine was strong and who immediately counted coup against the Blood war chief, driving a lance through his neck and out the base of his skull. Blackfeet arrows and balls from trade fusil rifles did not touch Runs-in-Water as he rode his pony headlong into the midst of the Blackfeet. He took the Blood war chief's scalp while the other warriors scattered.

Now the other Crow warriors gained strength and they began to chase down members of the Blackfeet war party. Five Bloods and two Piegans were soon killed. The enemy was scattered now all across the open plain above the Place-of-Yellow-Willows. One Crow warrior took an arrow in the upper arm, but it was not serious.

Eli wanted to gain his share of the glory to brag about at rendezvous and kicked his horse into a run. What Eli didn't see was a Blood warrior who had ridden his horse through the trees and who now came out from behind, screaming a war cry. He was upon Eli before he knew what was happening and Eli turned his pony just in time to avoid a direct blow on the head from a tomahawk.

The blow caught Eli along the upper arm, just behind the elbow, and cleaved through the meat to the bone. Eli yelled and grabbed his arm, then fell from his pony. The Blood warrior turned his pony to come back, but when he saw Thane bearing down on him he turned his pony away.

Thane quickly kicked Whistler into full speed to run down the warrior. The chase took him out from the main fight, and when he had finally caught the warrior, he leveled Gulliver across his left forearm and shot the warrior from behind. The Blood stayed on his pony for a distance further before tumbling off. But Thane didn't go after him as the recoil from Gulliver brought a hot and terrible pain to his shoulder. He pulled up on Whistler, holding tight with his good hand to keep from falling off.

He began to see stars and slid down from his pony and knelt down to clear his head. He cursed, frustrated. He heard a singing sound as an arrow slammed into the ground just in front of him at Whistler's feet, causing the horse to jump and run off. Thane called to Whistler but the pony had been too frightened by the arrow. Thane looked behind him to see four Blood warriors taking position to come at him.

They saw he was now afoot and Thane watched them laugh and talk to one another. They were going to make a sport of this kill. Thane tried to ignore the pain in his shoulder and began to reload Gulliver. He could hear them from a distance, talking to one another in Blackfoot. There was little chance he would be lucky enough to live through this, Thane realized, but he would get at least two of them.

The Blood warriors took their position. Thane could see that they were going to make a horse race of it: whoever had the fastest pony would count first coup. They screamed in unison and rode forward at him.

The warrior on the far left had the fastest pony, Thane could see, and he would get to him first. The warrior carried a trade fusil, as did one of the others. One had a bow he was arming and the fourth a lance. Thane's head pounded and he realized his only hope was to kill the first warrior, then catch the warrior's loose horse and outrun the other three.

Thane dropped to one knee and brought Gulliver to his shoulder. The Blood warrior quickly slid to the other side of his pony and Thane waited. The pony came ahead and the Blood warrior reappeared, a hand holding the fusil and just his head being seen under the pony's neck. Thane took a breath and steadied Gulliver, sighting down the barrel and bringing the front bead to rest on the painted face. He had to concentrate, he knew, and put out of his mind that the recoil from the rifle was going to put him in a lot of pain.

Gulliver boomed and acrid blue smoke filled the air around Thane's head. Thane dropped the Hawken and slumped to his knees, his shoulder exploding with pain. He breathed heavily, clutching his shoulder, and looked up as the warrior's pony shied to one side of him and then ran back in the other direction. Thane cursed loudly; he had missed his chance at catching the pony. The Blood warrior was lying in a patch of new grass. His arms were flopping against the ground and his head was shaking, throwing clots of blood into the air. Thane pushed himself to his feet. He had to reload Gulliver. The three remaining Bloods, thinking him wounded, were now riding down on him, the one in the middle holding the lead.

The one in the middle was upon him, thrusting a lance. Thane barely got the Gulliver up into his left hand to ward off the lance thrust, feeling its point slide along his hand as it glanced off his rifle. He was slammed sideways and to the ground from the impact. The Blood was turning his pony to finish Thane before the other warriors got there when he suddenly jerked from the impact of an arrow to his upper chest and tumbled from his horse.

Thane was to his feet. He looked behind him and saw Morning Swan on Whirlwind, screaming war cries as she fit another arrow to her bow. The other two Blood warriors were now nearly upon Thane and, seeing Morning Swan, hurried their shots. Thane heard a ball whiz past his ear and an arrow clipped the top of his right ear, sending him to the ground once more.

Morning Swan was rushing past him on Whirlwind now, yelling as she rode head-on toward the two Blood warriors. When Morning Swan loosed another arrow she was upon the two warriors, and for the one nearest her it was too late to fight. He had dropped his fusil to the ground and was arming his own bow when Morning Swan's arrow pushed clear through him, through his ribs just under his arms, taking chunks of lung tissue with it as it exited. He coughed and a fine pink mist filled the air around his head like talcum, and he fell backwards as his pony bolted.

The warrior bounced against the ground and arched his back before he died. Thane had run to get the fallen lance from the first warrior and he rushed the final warrior, who was looking back at Morning Swan, his hand over his mouth. The Blood saw him at the last instant and turned his pony just as Thane loosed the lance.

The large point cleaved a massive hole in the warrior's upper thigh and drove itself on through the pony's ribs and deep into the lung cavity. The pony jerked and kicked and screamed, launching itself into a crazed, dying frenzy, while the warrior clung to its mane with one hand and tried to remove the lance with the other.

The pony reared back and kicked and screamed and finally lost its footing and lunged sideways into a heap, drooling bloody froth and lather as it plowed the air with its hooves. The lance snapped like kindling wood and slim fragments flew like tiny daggers through the air. The warrior, trapped beneath, was crushed. Thane then reloaded Gulliver and ended the horse's life.

Morning Swan got down from Whirlwind and stood beside Thane. She looked into his eyes, where she saw a grave and helpless concern.

"I'm not much good for anything, am I?" Thane said to Morning Swan. "I might as well not have a right arm, for all it's worth."

"That will change," Morning Swan said with conviction. "You will soon be well again."

Runs-in-Water now rode up on his pony and displayed three fresh scalps. He did not look at Thane, but addressed Morning Swan.

"In time," he said, "you will want a warrior with true medicine, one who can fight and bring honor to the lodge. I will be waiting."

Thane yelled at him then. "Tell that to me, you young fool. Get down from your horse and let's see who has the medicine."

"No, that would not be good," Morning Swan said to Thane. But already Runs-in-Water had dismounted and was coming toward Thane.

The pain in Thane's shoulder was forgotten in favor of total anger and frustration. The younger Runs-in-Water did not stand a chance as Thane pounded him without mercy. Once, when Runs-in-Water tried to draw a knife, Thane took it from him and slammed the handle into Runs-in-Water's hand, breaking the bones behind the first two knuckles. Runs-in-Water finally got to his feet and wiped the blood from his nose and mouth, then climbed on his pony without a word.

Thane was breathing heavily and was now feeling the intense pain in his shoulder. The pain did not, however, discourage him. It actually made him feel more assured. He was now confident that the muscles in his back and shoulder were not the cause of his misery, but the problem lay somewhere in the bone of the shoulder. He vowed then that no matter the pain, he would again build himself back up.

Morning Swan smiled. "You are as great a warrior as you ever were. Now we must find Eli and I will sew up his arm. He too has other battles left in him."

The rendezvous of 1833 was held on Horse Creek, in the Green River Valley. It was a big one and the talk at first was mainly of the giant battle the year before in Pierre's Hole, when the whole rendezvous had joined forces against a massive part of Gros Ventres. There were stories of bravery and valor and how the battle was the biggest one in all of the mountains to date.

Eli proudly displayed his arm, swollen and discolored, and talked about the fight with the Blackfeet at the Place-of-Yellow-Willows. Morning Swan had sewed him up, and though he had been quite sick during the rest of the trip down, he was feeling good now, considering the severity of the wound. Herbal teas and poultices had in reality saved his arm. Now he sat with a group of trappers around a fire. They were drinking whiskey and there were hump ribs roasting over the fire, but they were all eating mouthfuls of raw flour and sugar. For most of them the entire year had passed without a taste of either.

While they laughed and made sticky balls of whiskey and flour, Eli told his version of his encounter with the Blood warrior.

"I took no mercy on that blood-screamin' Injun, I didn't. No siree, I lifted his hair, I did." He held up a scalp he had borrowed from Thane. "We had us one helluva horseback duel, me and that Blood, and he scratched me a bit, but when I commenced to give him my war whoop, he turned tail and run, he did. You should have seen his eyes . . ."

Thane found the rendezvous as lively as he had expected. Trappers from all over the mountains were again seeing one another perhaps for the only time during the entire year. They had a lot of bragging to do and a lot of drinking to catch up on. There were a number of newly established companies attending the rendezvous now and there was fierce competition among them, as they tried to solicit the trade of the numerous free trappers now in the mountains. Free trappers were the lifeblood of the trade and the rendezvous was their annual bath, during which time the various fur companies vied for the beaver and other fur these trappers had accumulated during the previous year.

A contingent of well-known trappers, including Jim Bridger, had formed the Rocky Mountain Fur Company a few years before, and now there was another newcomer named Bonneville, who had a fort and trading post some five miles up Horse Creek from the mouth of Green River. Much of the talk, though, centered around the American Fur Company, John Jacob Astor's giant, which was pushing its weight around the mountains with force. The Company, as it was referred to, was doing its level best to monopolize the trade and had its foot in the door, having established Fort Union at the mouth of the Yellowstone River. There was talk that the shrewd Scotsman who ran the fort, Kenneth McKenzie, was supplying the Blackfeet nation with powder and ball, hoping they would consider him their friend and those who didn't give them guns their enemies. But the Blackfeet were aiming those trade rifles at all trappers regardless of their allegiance. Thane surmised this as the reason the mixed Blood and Piegan war party they had fought on the way down had been so well armed.

There were three different main camps, each located around the tents and wagons of the parties they wished to sell their furs to. Thane and Morning Swan established themselves where the Rocky Mountain Fur Company had set up its goods for trade. Everyone mingled back and forth from camp to camp and there were times when almost everyone got together for a big horse race or some other festivity.

Morning Swan was wearing her finest antelope dress and the shell necklace Thane had given her. Whirlwind was decorated with beads and cloth and bright red ribbons. She was a sight, and in the parade of Indian wives, she stood out from all the rest. From the first day, however, Morning Swan wished they had not come.

"I wish to leave this place," Morning Swan told Thane. "These men go crazy with the medicine water and already I have had to fight two of them to make them leave me alone."

Thane was aware of this. One of the men had complained to him about Morning Swan nearly killing him with a blow from a war club. Thane had told him he was lucky the club had merely struck his upheld rifle and not his head. The trapper had thought seriously about challenging Thane, knowing he was handicapped by injury to his right arm and shoulder.

It was all over rendezvous now, the story of the fight with the Bloods and how Morning Swan had saved his life. Since their arrival, Thane had been watched by all, and there was open discussion regarding his physical condition. What they had not heard was how he had beaten the strong young warrior, Runs-in-Water, until he could barely walk. If someone wanted to fight, Thane thought, that was fine. He would oblige them and then they would no longer have doubts about his shoulder.

Thane had come to this rendezvous primarily on behalf of Morning Swan anyway, to convey her wishes and concerns over the all-out trapping of beaver throughout the mountains. This wasn't going to set well with the trappers, so Thane wasn't concerned about making new friends. He was more conscious of Morning Swan's concern about the rivers and streams, and now he wanted to help her any way he could.

"I know you don't like it here," he told her. "But this is the only place we'll be able to get our business done. You still want to get the tribes to limit the beaver catch in their lands, don't you?"

"Of course I do," Morning Swan said. "But it would be better if we could talk with the councils of each nation apart from the Long Knives and their medicine water."

"Most of the tribes we want to see are here now," Thane said. "It's best if we take advantage of that. Besides, it would be too risky leaving without traveling with a lot of company. The word is there are Blackfeet war parties camped near all the passes and they're waiting for stragglers."

Thane spent his time talking and smoking with the leaders of various tribes, explaining his concerns to them about the great depletion of beaver that was taking place in their lands, resulting in broken beaver dams and the loss of water retention throughout the mountains. He talked well and they nodded, but it was not as easy to keep their attention as he had hoped.

With the injury to his arm and shoulder, and his subsequent loss of size due to decreased exercise, his reputation was suffering. The warrior chiefs of the various tribal councils all asked him why he had lost his medicine. He had once been a strong fighting man and now his woman had saved his life. They wanted fighters in their lands and the Long Knives fought their enemies, the Blackfeet. They did not want to limit the number of beaver taken, for that could mean angering their white brothers. What they were concerned about was what would happen should the Long Knives go back to their own lands.

"The Long Knives will never go back into their own lands," Thane told them time and again. "See, I have taken a wife here and I will remain for the rest of my life. It is our concern that the beaver will all be trapped out and then the rivers will rush past and the waters will be gone. If there are no beaver there will be no water trapped by beaver dams to provide pools for drinking. The land is already used heavily by the many horses and the great buffalo herds; and when the water comes from the sky, it takes the good soil and puts it on the bottoms. Without the beaver dams to trap this good soil and spread it out along the bottoms, it will all wash away to the great waters at the edge of the lands. When there is no more water and no more good soil on the bottoms, the land will die."

"Come back when your medicine is good," the various chiefs all told him. "Then we will listen."

Rendezvous continued with the usual gambling and horse racing, fighting, wrestling, and assorted pastimes, none of which Thane went anywhere near. He instead spent his time watching, something very new for him. His shoulder pained him continually, and he knew if he entered any contests, he would likely be shown up and have to suffer humiliation. A number of trappers tried to goad him into shooting matches but he told them he had nothing with which to gamble. They didn't believe him, and soon there was talk that Thane Thompson had lost his stuff.

Note of this was taken by those present, and the various tribal councils nodded and smoked and felt good with themselves at having not taken Bear-Man seriously about the regulating the beaver catch. The medicine of the once-powerful Bear-Man was now gone. Thane and Morning Swan could only grit their teeth in frustration and prepare to leave the rendezvous.

But the Crow warriors who had come were having a good time and many did not want to leave. A decision was made to remain a short while longer, as it was not a good idea to break up the force. In fact, the talk was of joining a large brigade of trappers headed north so that large forces of Blackfeet could be dealt with.

During the next few days a rumor began to develop. The talk spread from among the various council members of the tribes who had spoken with Thane. They felt that perhaps the medicine shield he carried with him, the one belonging to the Piegan war chief Rising Hawk, had somehow turned its medicine and had now cursed him. There was talk among trappers and Indians alike that this medicine shield could bring bad luck to one who stole it, not to mention the one from whom it had been taken. And what about those in camp at rendezvous?

It had been reported at one of the other two camps that rabid wolves were in the area. It was said horses and men had been bitten; one man, during sleep, had lost one side of his face. It was an odd and harrowing thing to see, and to some the only way it could be explained was bad medicine.

There was one among the trappers who had been waiting a long time for a circumstance such as this. Wild Jack Cutter, whose odd eyes gleamed in the light of a bright fire, called to all who would listen to tell them he thought Thane Thompson had brought them all bad luck and that the only way out for them was death for Thompson. Toots had found another horn somewhere, a longer one, and began to blow notes and laugh. The more Cutter talked, the more the other trappers and the Indians listened. Cutter said he knew where Thompson was and led a group to where Thane was oiling Gulliver. Eli had been in another camp and had overheard Cutter talking. He rode in just ahead of the mob to warn Thane.

"We'd best skeedaddle," he told Thane and Morning Swan. Sir John, who was reading nearby, stood up and hurried over.

"Cutter's got the whole of rendezvous up agin us," Eli continued. "Gotten 'em to think you and your shield caused the rabid wolves. And I ain't much help with this bad arm."

But Cutter was already coming into camp with his crowd and they surrounded Thane.

"It's time you got yours," Cutter said to Thane, sounding like a growling dog.

"No," Morning Swan said. "Do not do this."

"You just stay outta the way," Cutter told her. "When I'm finished here, I'll show you a real man."

Without another word, Cutter rushed Thane, a large Green River knife in his right hand. Thane met the charge with his left arm and side, shielding his right arm as best he could. The two men came together hard and bounced off each other. Thane reached for his own knife.

"I'm goin' to do it this time!" Cutter slurred, circling Thane.

Toots stood just inside the circle of men that had formed.

"Cut him, Jack! Cut him, Jack!"

Eli stood helpless with Morning Swan and Sir John. They could only watch as the circle of men awaited the outcome to see if indeed Cutter was right in saying Thane had brought them bad luck. If Thane won, then it was Cutter who was wrong. But to interfere could bring death to them all.

Sir John had a fierce look about him. Just as during that first spring on Green River with the Shoshone, he saw how Thane's medicine shield could help them. He left to get it and his place was taken by someone else. It was Runs-in-Water.

"Bear-Man is a true warrior," Runs-in-Water told Eli and Morning Swan. "His medicine is bad now, but it will again be good. He does not deserve this."

The fight continued and the onlookers shouted, "Cut him, Jack!" Toots continued to scream, "Please, Jack, cut him up for me!"

Cutter lunged again and Thane grabbed the big man's knife arm. They rolled to the ground, kicking and fighting for position. As the two men came to their knees Thane's grip was fastened tightly around Cutter's wrist, but he could not maneuver his right arm to bring his own knife into play. He fought the intense pain in his shoulder as much as he fought Cutter's strength and, finally, as Cutter brought his head up to lunge forward, Thane slammed his head into Cutter's face.

Blood spewed from Cutter's nose and he gasped. Thane thrust forward with his knife. It was then that Toots hit him across the back of the head with the horn. Thane fell forward and his knife, instead of plunging into Cutter's chest, glanced off his ribs. Cutter roared and slumped sideways on the ground in a big ball. Thane shook his head to clear his senses and Toots again raised the horn.

Eli brought his rifle around in a wide arc and the butt slammed into Toots's head, shattering the wood and sending Toots into a headlong sprawl, which ended in the fire. He screamed, his buckskins ablaze, and rushed in crazy circles around the area while everyone scattered to get out of his way. Toots finally fell to the ground and began to roll. One of the trappers who had been watching the fight began to laugh and poured whiskey over Toots, igniting him into a blast of flame.

Thane was holding the back of his head and Runs-in-Water, his own knife drawn, came over to help him up. Sir John now had the medicine shield and was holding it up in front of the onlooking Indians and trappers. He was talking medicine to them, the medicine that was protecting Thane. The Indians immediately began to back away, praying to their spirit helpers for their own protection. Morning Swan was helping Runs-in-Water with Thane, and in the confusion no one saw the wounded Cutter come to his knees.

Runs-in-Water was just taking Thane's arm to help him up when the blade entered his abdomen. Cutter ripped with all his might and Runs-in-Water came open like a sack, his bowels whooshing out in a bloody mass. It was then that the pack of rabid wolves entered the camp.

One of them jumped an onlooking trapper, tearing at his hands as he brought them up in front of his throat. Two others, snarling, began to snap and bite at anything or anyone they saw, rushing through people like evil black shadows. Runs-in-Water was bent over on his knees, his face in his own blood, singing his death song.

Thane shook his head to clear it and helped two Crow warriors turn Runs-in-Water onto his back. The warriors were weeping and singing mourning songs, trying to stuff Runs-in-Water's entrails back into him. But he was dead and all they could do now was take him back to the village and console his family.

Morning Swan was sickened and angry. She had her bow armed with an arrow, and if the Long Knives and other Indians hadn't been scattering from the rabid wolves, she would have surely shot until her quiver was empty. Thane and Eli both worked to calm her down, finally making her realize that it was over now and there was nothing more that could be done.

Morning Swan continued to look on bitterly as the camp began to settle down. The wolves had either been shot or were gone and trappers and Indians alike were gathering to gamble at the hands game or to tell stories and drink more around some fire. The excitement of the wolves and the fight was past.

A few of the Crow warriors wrapped Runs-in-Water

in one of his own buffalo robes and tied him across his favorite horse. Morning Swan and Eli gathered belongings and, with the rest of the Crows, prepared to leave. Sir John was beside a fire, writing furiously in his journal.

Meanwhile, Thane looked for Cutter. He passed fire after fire and no one dared look at him. No one wanted anything to do with him now, no matter what his medicine. One wrong move and Thane Thompson would smash them to pieces. While looking, Thane did not bother to ask when he found someone resembling Cutter. He would simply pull the trapper's head up by the hair to get a look and that man would say, "No, no, I'm not Cutter. Just leave me be."

Thane continued to look, but Cutter had escaped somehow. Thane knew his knife had not done that much damage to Cutter's side, so the man was not likely to die on his own. Thane looked under every pile of robes and in every lodge. But Cutter was gone and there was no telling where he had run to. Finally, at dawn, both Eli and Morning Swan convinced him to give up so that they could all leave and go back up to the Crow village.

As light creased the eastern horizon, Thane mounted Whistler and made ready to head back north. He rode one last time through the camp. There was little to show that the previous night had been any different from any other. A baby cried from a nearby lodge, but otherwise it was quiet. The grounds were littered with all sorts of items—from clothes and weapons to horse tack and cooking utensils—and strewn with very drunk trappers and Indians who lay passed out in heaps among their robes.

The only signs of anything unusual was that at one end of camp lay a bloody, gray-furred hump. Two others lay at various places, their mouths open slightly, grinning oddly in death, their long fangs exposed. And in the center of the camp lay a charred human figure. Nearby lay a battered horn.

Twelve

THE JOURNEY BACK TO THE CROW VILLAGE WAS DIFFICULT for Thane. He blamed himself for Runs-in-Water's death and the sorrow that hung so heavily over everyone. No one blamed him, though; everyone thought instead that Runs-in-Water had proved himself strong and brave to come to Thane's aid under the circumstances.

It angered them that one of the Long Knives, supposedly their white brothers, had run a knife through a Crow warrior. Thane explained that not all Long Knives were as wretched as Cutter and the now-deceased Toots. It so happened that Cutter detested all Indian people and most everyone else as well. It was hard to imagine what pleasures, except killing, he got out of life. Thane made all the Crow warriors understand that Cutter would have been no match for Runs-in-Water in a fair fight and that their brother warrior had died a proud death and was surely enjoying himself in the next life.

Though everyone tried to get Thane to realize that he was not responsible for what had happened, he nevertheless felt that had he exerted himself more during the fight with Cutter, had he forced himself to somehow be stronger, he might have ended things for Cutter before all this happened. His mind seemed blocked against the notion that Toots and his horn had interfered. But Toots was no more than a mass of charred flesh and bone now and Thane thought only of someday finding Cutter.

Morning Swan and Eli talked extensively with him during the journey, assuring him that what had taken place would not make him unwelcome among her people. She knew he felt incompetent for not having won his own battle and thereby causing the death of Runs-in-Water. This mental anguish, coupled with his intense physical pain, was tearing him down emotionally day by day. His shoulder bothered him constantly during the trip back and merely lying on it the wrong way at night would bring him awake with a start. Morning Swan realized now that time was not going to make his shoulder come back to normal, but might instead make it worse. She had to, in some way or another, figure out a means by which to help him regain his health.

In the village, there was sadness and mourning. Runs-in-Water's father was an elder named Cuts Plenty. Thane gave him five good horses and picked out two apiece for each brother and uncle. Thane vowed to Cuts Plenty that he would someday avenge the loss of his son. Cuts Plenty was saddened but surprisingly not greatly angered. He told Thane that he knew his son would likely die young, because of his brash behavior and his tendency to get himself into trouble. He seemed relieved in a way to learn that in the end Runs-in-Water had brought honor to himself, and was proud to know that his son had died with a good heart. Cuts Plenty then smoked with Thane and told him he would always be his friend and helper.

The only joy for both Thane and Morning Swan was Rosebud and Jethro. The two children had missed them a great deal and were so happy to see them that they did not fight between one another or misbehave for nearly a full day. Though they seemed happy enough to see their parents, both Rosebud and Jethro looked at their father closely, hoping to see that his health had returned. Both had been very concerned about this, and Jethro in particular had been suffering.

Jethro, it was learned, had spent his time in their absence stealing great quantities of meat from the village drying racks and fighting with some of the other boys. Some of the fights had been fairly serious and Jethro had broken one boy's nose and sprained another's hand. Stealing discreet amounts of meat was expected and no one was ever concerned about a few pranks, but fighting other boys with such anger was another matter.

Morning Swan learned from Little Bird that Jethro was becoming quite hostile towards the other boys in the village. He was sulking and would not discuss his feelings with anybody. Rosebud had found him hard to deal with as well, and finally had left him alone. Morning Swan discussed it with Thane and told him the problem was with him, his father.

"How can that be?" Thane asked, his tone indignant.

"You are his father," Morning Swan said. "He looks up to you. For some reason he is having problems with himself about that. I think it is because of your bad shoulder and losing power among the men. He sees this and it bothers him. You and he will have to get it straightened out. Already three mothers have complained they are afraid he will hurt their sons."

"Tell them to keep their sons away from him," Thane said. "Besides, it can't all be Jethro's fault."

"I'm sure it isn't," Morning Swan said. "And that is what I told the women who confronted me. But Jethro has to get over his anger or there will be more trouble."

"He wants to go hunting," Thane said. "We will leave tomorrow and I will get to the bottom of this."

Thane left with Jethro early the next morning to hunt in the hills above the village. Jethro knew where a herd of deer had been watering each morning at a spring and wanted to sneak up and see how close he could get to them. He was not yet old enough to have a bow that would kill meat, but it was good to learn how to get close. And he had just received a special buckskin hunting cape from his grandfather, Bear-Walks-at-Night, complete with head and antlers, and he was anxious to try it out.

While they rode in the early light of dawn, Thane talked with his son.

"Is there some reason why you are fighting so much with the other boys?" he asked.

"They make me mad with what they say," Jethro answered. "They are saying that you have lost your medicine and that you are becoming weaker. They laugh and say that soon their own fathers will be stronger than you."

"You can't let that bother you," Thane said. "It's just talk."

"But why do you hold your arm funny most of the time?" Jethro asked. "I know you can't use it like you should. Is your arm going to be that way always?"

"No, Jethro, it isn't." Thane said it with conviction, so that he sounded assured of himself. This was something that was going to happen, and soon. He wanted Jethro to quit worrying and he wanted to be sure that he had no other opinion himself on the matter.

"How soon will it be better?" Jethro asked.

"Soon. My arm will be as good as new very soon. Instead of beating up all the other boys, you tell them that your father is going to be stronger than he ever was before. You tell them that you will bet them your finest weapons against their that this will come true, even before the next snow comes."

Thane realized he was putting pressure on his son as well as himself, but he knew this would cause him to seek some kind of guidance to heal his shoulder once and for all. It was no longer a matter of pride, but necessity as well. If he failed to come through, for his son's sake as well as his own, he could never live with himself.

And there was Morning Swan and Rosebud to consider as well. Morning Swan had already lived with a man who had been injured, then slowly lost his self-esteem and disintegrated both mentally and physically. This had taken its toll on her emotions and she still expressed guilt over it at times, wondering what more she might have done to help him.

This man—who was Long Hand of the Piegans—had become desperate to regain his former self and had died trying to gain it all back at once. Thane did not want to put Morning Swan in the same situation once again, though she was already there and was showing signs of deep concern. Thane decided he was not going to allow this to happen. He realized that now he must make himself mentally ready to somehow get himself physically strong once again, for desperation was also staring him in the face.

The sun was starting to climb, a rim of gold in the east. Jethro was anxious to reach the spring and sneak up on the deer. He had brought some blunt arrows, so that he could shoot a deer but not wound it and leave it in pain. He was anxious to show his father how much he was learning about hunting and what a good stalker of game he was. It troubled him to think that his father could not hunt buffalo with the other warriors, and in the back of his mind he was telling his father that, if need be, he could soon provide the meat for the family.

They left their horses and proceeded on foot, the wind in their faces, just a breeze that came in tiny gusts and moved the drying blades of grass. There had been no rain in the passing of a full moon, which was normal here at this time of year. The sun shone hot during the day, and down on the bottoms close to the

river the nights remained very warm. It was the
extreme opposite of the cold moons, when everything
bundled up against the cold. Now all things worked to
fend off the heat and wished for the return of the days
just before the snows, when the land was once again
given rain and the days were fresh with life.

But now it was the middle of the warm moons, and
with the rains of spring past, the time for seeds to fall
had come. Thane saw that the grass had opened the
sheaths in which the seed had been developing. All of
them looked different now, each species delivering
offspring that would eventually find their way into the
soil to germinate. The grass that during the early part
of spring grew up in bluish bunches along the slopes
and hills was now a deep brown, the small hair-like
projections on the tiny seeds turned sideways, meaning the seed was ready to fall. The grass with the long
stringlike projection on each seed, called needle-and-
thread, was also dry. The seeds stuck to hair and
clothing, and when they fell to the ground, they waited
for a rain. The water would curl the long hair-like
projection on the top of the seed, and when the sun
again came out, the projection would dry and the seed
would corkscrew itself into the soil.

When Thane and Jethro spotted the deer drinking
from the spring, they got down on their hands and
knees and Jethro placed the hunting cape over himself. Thane stayed back and watched Jethro while he
worked his way closer to the deer. He did not move
directly toward them, but in a circular pattern, acting
as if he were grazing. The deer spotted him but paid
him no attention. Soon he was within shooting distance and placed an arrow against the side of a small
spike buck.

The little buck, more startled than hurt by the blunt
arrow, bounded away from the spring with the other
deer and up a hill. Soon they all stopped to look back.
Jethro had dropped the skin and was running over

toward Thane, jumping with joy at his success. Thane was next to Jethro congratulating him when a large buck joined the other deer.

"Oh, Father! That is a great big one! Shoot him with your rifle."

Thane looked up at the deer. Massive antlers branched out high and wide.

"Do it, Father! The meat will have his strength and the antlers will have power."

Thane brought Gulliver to his shoulder while Jethro continued to urge him to shoot. He steadied the rifle and the blast echoed through the trees. The deer all broke into a bounding run and the big buck stumbled, then fell.

"You got him!" Jethro yelled in triumph. He ran toward the hill where the massive buck lay.

Thane saw a million stars in front of his eyes as his shoulder burst with pain. He was aware that Gulliver had slipped from his fingers and into the grass at his feet. He wanted to reach down before Jethro noticed but it made him dizzy to move. He began to teeter and then, when he tried to step forward, he fell to the ground.

When he awoke, Jethro was rubbing his face with cold water from the nearby spring. Jethro's eyes were wide with concern, and though he had seen others lose consciousness, to him it meant they had lost life for a time.

"You died, Father," Jethro said. "You died for a time. What happened?"

Thane brought himself to a sitting position. His head began to clear but the pain in his shoulder was intense. He tried to hide it from Jethro, but the boy could see it plainly.

"I don't know how to help you," Jethro said, shaking his head. "And I don't want you to die."

Thane got to his feet. "I'm not going to die, Jethro. I'm going to get better and stronger. I told you that.

Now let's get that deer skinned and dressed out so we can take him back down to the village."

They were camped again at the Rotten-Sun-Dance-Lodge-Creek when a crier rode through the village and announced that scouts had located a large herd of buffalo along the lower stretches of the Bighorn. The time for the fall hunt had come. It was then that Morning Swan approached Thane and told him if he wished to regain his strength and the use of his shoulder, he must not go on the fall hunt. He must allow her to secure winter meat for their lodge and remain behind at this place instead to face a most critical test.

Morning Swan told him he must now leave his fate in the hands of her father if he wished to be healed. There were tears in her eyes as she spoke and though Thane asked her what was disturbing her, she would only say that it now lay in his hands and that he must talk with her father, Bear-Walks-at-Night. Morning Swan would say no more no matter how hard Thane tried to question her.

After he thought about it over the next few days, Thane decided he would do what she asked and then later he would get her to explain her sorrow. The children were doing well and no one in the entire village was sick. In fact, everyone was unusually happy about the hunt. In Thane's mind there was no need for her to be acting this way. She told him she was not fearful for his safety or that he might die. In fact, she felt better about his health now than she had in a long time.

Thane could think of no reason for Morning Swan's behavior. It disturbed him that she would not confide in him and discuss what was causing her sorrow. Was it a problem with him? Was there something between them he should know? Another man? Morning Swan would only tell him that nothing of that sort entered into her sorrow. He must either decide to go to her father and talk about his shoulder or decide not to. After he had made that decision and spent time with her father, only then would she consent to discussion.

But Bear-Walks-at-Night had been gone to the mountains for a number of days. Morning Swan would only say that he was preparing for his time with Thane. The village was getting ready to move toward the Bighorn and Thane was instructed to remain behind and follow the waters of Rotten-Sun-Dance-Lodge-Creek to where it flowed from the Beartooth. Bear-Walks-at-Night would be waiting for him there and he would tell him what to do.

While the villagers prepared to move down to the Yellowstone and across to the Bighorn, Sir John completed packing his own belongings. He had been watching Thane for a long time since he'd injured his shoulder and he was concerned that, in addition to the physical pain, Thane might be suffering considerable mental anguish as well. For the first time in a long while, Thane had declined to work with him on parts for various plays. Sir John saw this as the first stages of mental breakdown and hoped he might be able to do something about it.

His tasks for the move now completed, Sir John took the raven, Joker, perched on his arm, and began to look for Turtle. Turtle could hardly be considered a boy now, as he was already one of the better horse tenders in the village and would before long go into the hills to seek a medicine dream. Sir John found him talking horses with a number of adolescent men and called him aside.

Though Turtle found Sir John to be quite interesting, the general consensus throughout the village was that Sir John was unpredictable, possibly possessed of evil spirits at times, and generally one to avoid as much as possible. Those with strong medicine, warriors and elders who had proved themselves, were not in fear of Sir John, but others in his company might have reason to worry. For this reason, Turtle wanted this conversation with Sir John to be brief.

"I have to go out and help move the herd very soon," Turtle told Sir John at the outset.

"Yes, I understand," Sir John said. "I merely wanted to return your bird to you. He has served me well."

"But why?" Turtle asked. "I thought you liked him. And he certainly enjoys it when you wave your hands and talk to him."

"Yes, but I have no more need for him and I cannot care for him where I am going. So please, take him back."

"But you paid for him," Turtle said. "And I don't want to give up the horses and my lionskin quiver."

"You need not give up anything for him," Sir John said. "Just take him and treat him as well as you once did."

Sir John left Turtle with the bird on his arm and looked for Thane and Eli. He found them at the stream that ran past the village, talking seriously about Thane's upcoming appointment with Bear-Walks-at-Night.

"I hope I am not interrupting," Sir John said.

"Join us," Thane said.

Eli scowled but continued talking to Thane. "This is one of those things," Eli was saying, "that happen in the Injun way. It happens and nobody can explain it. You just let it happen and that's all."

Thane knew by now that Bear-Walks-at-Night intended to cure his shoulder injury by means of his medicine, the grizzly bear. Bear-Walks-at-Night had once been a medicine man, a *shaman*, but had not practiced for many winters. There were other medicine men in the village, but none with the medicine of the grizzly bear. Thane had seen one medicine man cure a boy who had accidently been shot in the side with a trade rifle. The boy had been near death and this medicine man, whose medicine was the otter, took the boy into the river and held him underwater. After what had seemed a long time to Thane, the boy and the medicine man surfaced and a dark fluid ran from the wound in the boy's side. An otter then surfaced and, before swimming away, dropped the rifle ball from its mouth into the medicine man's hand.

Thane had seen this so there was no reason to question it. He knew he would never understand what had happened, but he had seen it. Now something similar was being prepared for him. There was no doubt this was the case, as the villagers would no longer talk to him but only pointed and talked among themselves. Only Morning Swan and the children spoke to him, and acted as if nothing were wrong. But something was going to happen to him and he realized now, thinking back to his experience with the Little People, that he must accept whatever was to come.

"I'm not afraid," Thane said to Eli. "If that's what you mean."

"I'm only sayin' that you should figure to see some strange things," Eli answered. "That medicine shield you took from Rising Hawk that first fall. Well, maybe that has something to do with why I'm still alive and maybe it doesn't. I only know there's something about it, something that's there that I can feel. You've got to believe in what you're going to do. Otherwise bad will come of it. I seen it before, good and bad alike."

Thane nodded. "I understand. You don't think for a minute I would do this and have doubts about it, do you?"

Sir John then spoke up. "Thane, I intend to take a steamboat down to Fort Union and then go back to civilization. Come with me. Allow yourself medical attention from a competent physician. And when your shoulder is healed we can amass ourselves a fortune.

With the material I have gathered out here, we can formulate theatrical performances unequaled in any part of the world."

"John, I'm not an actor," Thane said. "And I told you a long time ago I have no intention of returning to the East. I didn't know you intended to go back yourself."

"I have seen what I came to see of this land and the people here," Sir John said. "Now it is my duty to take it to the people who have yet to learn of it."

Eli wrinkled his nose. "If you think playactin' what you seen out here will make you somebody special, then think again. It's my notion that you didn't do it before you came out and you won't do it when you get back neither."

"My good man," Sir John said, setting his jaw, "it is men such as you that would discourage the world from turning, I'm afraid. Well, so be it. Your kind are a part of the overall picture and it is my duty to portray you in such a fashion, which I will do."

Eli was giving him a funny look. "You never did talk sense and I don't figure you ever will. Just the same, I wish you good luck back in the white diggin's."

Sir John bowed, removing his Robin Hood hat. He then turned to Thane. "It disappoints me that you are wasting such a talent," he said. "Perhaps some day you will reconsider."

"Perhaps," Thane acknowledged, "but I doubt it. I wish you success."

Thane shook Sir John's hand and the English actor was gone. He would travel with the village to the Yellowstone and then find his way to the port just below where the main camps were always placed. There he hoped to find a steamboat headed downriver.

After telling Eli he would join them on the Bighorn, he met with Morning Swan. She had just finished preparing the lodge and belongings for travel. Rosebud was helping her and Jethro was nearby, shooting arrows through a rolling hoop. They all came together and Morning Swan again had to blink back tears.

"I wish you would tell me why this bothers you," Thane said to her.

"It does not bother me in the manner you think," she told him. "I will be happy to see you on the Bighorn, when your shoulder is good once again."

Rosebud, now far too big to hold like a child, nevertheless wanted him to take her in his arms. He went to one knee and after they had hugged for a while, Rosebud nodded and smiled.

"It will be a good time for you, Father, a sacred time," she said. "I am happy."

"You watch the hills and take care of your family," Thane said to Jethro. "Listen to what the warriors tell you."

Jethro nodded. Ever since learning his father was once again going to be well, he had become his old self. Though he was not fighting with the other boys, he was still raiding the meat racks. But he didn't yell as loudly now when the women caught him and scolded him.

"You know the way to go," Morning Swan said to Thane. She was in his arms and his embrace made her feel that the world would soon be right again, though there was a price to pay.

"Listen to my father and do whatever it is he tells you," she added. "Do exactly what he tells you."

Thane nodded. "I will. It won't be long until your father and I will meet you on the Bighorn."

Again Morning Swan's eyes filled with tears. "Go now," she said. "Go up into the Beartooth and find my father. He is waiting."

The wind was gentle, as if calming Thane for what lay ahead. He rode Whistler up the switchback trails toward the top of the high Beartooth. All during the journey he thought back to the days of spring spent up there trapping, and his encounter with the grizzly and the ordeal of the long walk back home. His mind recalled what he had felt each step of the way as Whistler took him along the same trails.

Toward the top, Thane reached the spot where he had seen the Little People. Scattered through the trees on the side hill were the remains of the elk, bones that had been picked clean by wolves and the skull with the huge rack of antlers. A sudden, odd feeling overwhelmed him and he wished to hurry past there.

Each cliff and group of large rocks he saw from then on seemed to move with the force of something he could not understand. He expected to see them again at any time, but there was only the call of ravens overhead and the wind that came in gusts as he neared the top.

The plateau was as he remembered it: a vast panorama of high wilderness peaks and sloping meadows of matted grass and alpine wildflowers. Scattered clumps of evergreens showed the effects of constant wind and the scattered lakes were deep and chill blue. Again he saw scattered herds of elk, and bighorn sheep grazed and stared at him as he found his way across and finally to the edge of a small lake. On its shore stood a single lodge with a large fire crackling outside.

"I knew you would come," Bear-Walks-at-Night greeted him. He was holding a long pipe made of red stone. There was a certain curious determination about him, a strong-willed expression in his eyes.

"My dream is finished," he then said to Thane. "Was it Morning Swan who told you to come?"

"Yes," Thane answered. "I knew it was for my shoulder but she was very sad and she wouldn't tell me the reason why."

"I know why she is sad," Bear-Walks-at-Night said. "I asked her not to tell you, for I feared if you knew you might not come. Now, you must sit and smoke with me. We have much to do."

Thane could see that the inside of Bear-Walks-at-Night's special lodge had been set up in an exact way.

There was the aroma of various medicine plants, including sage and ground juniper, and there were pots of special herbs sitting behind the fire. A large bundle wrapped in skins hung from the center pole. This was a special medicine bundle, Thane knew, that contained the articles to be used by Bear-Walks-at-Night in treating his shoulder. What was in the bundle was impossible to say, as Bear-Walks-at-Night had put items there based on his dream.

Thane waited for Bear-Walks-at-Night to seat himself and then followed his example with the red stone pipe, pointing it first skyward, then toward the ground and the four directions, praying for good fortune during this ordeal. They smoked for a time without speaking, each taking his turn with the pipe. Finally, when the time was right, Bear-Walks-at-Night told Thane they must begin.

"You know why you have come," Bear-Walks-at-Night said. "Are you ready to do this thing?"

"I am ready," Thane said.

Bear-Walks-at-Night looked directly into Thane's eyes. He was pleased. They were strong and unwavering. This man who had married his daughter realized the importance of having the right attitude at this important time. It pleased Bear-Walks-at-Night even more to know Thane was willing to undergo something that could prove awful so that he could again be strong of mind and body and a respected warrior among the Kicked-in-Their-Bellies, that he would do this without question at the request of Morning Swan. And he didn't insist on knowing the reason for Morning Swan's sadness. This proved he trusted in what was to come and thus made him a trustworthy man in his own right.

Throughout the day, Thane and Bear-Walks-at-Night labored to build a sweat lodge. It was important they build it together, and as they worked, Thane took note of the many prayers offered by his father-in-law. They would cut long willows and then smoke the pipe

before laying them into place. Once the willows were
in place, Bear-Walks-at-Night then covered the small,
rounded structure with many grizzly bear skins taken
during special hunts over a number of years. Bear-
Walks-at-Night told Thane he had cached them here
in this high wilderness many winters past, when he
had been told in a dream they were to remain there
until a special time came. That special time was now.

When completed, the sweat lodge was furnished
with a number of rocks that had been heating in a fire
nearby. Thane watched while Bear-Walks-at-Night
used a forked stick to transfer the white-hot stones
into a small pit in the center of the sweat lodge. They
adjourned for a time back into the special lodge,
where they ate from three different bowls and smoked
the pipe. Then they removed their clothes and Thane
followed Bear-Walks-at-Night back over to the sweat
lodge, where he measured cupfuls of water and poured
them onto the hot rocks.

All through the night and for the following three
days Thane and Bear-Walks-at-Night sat in the sweat
lodge fasting and praying. There were times when
Thane felt he would suffocate from the steam, but he
persevered and as time passed he felt himself losing
the fusion between mind and body. He no longer
knew night from day and his body felt rinsed of all
that pertained to human mortality. In the sweat that
flowed from him was all that had once held fear and
strain.

The wounds in his shoulder and leg now seemed
detached and without consequence. It was if his body
knew no bounds and that his being consisted only of
spirit and could float to any destination. Finally, as
the sun lowered itself again, Bear-Walks-at-Night led
him from the sweat lodge and to the edge of the lake.
They dove together.

Thane knew only the sudden impulse of mortality
again as the cold water struck the air from his lungs.
He rose up and stood with the water beading on his

body, then running in tiny rivlets down the scars on his back and shoulder. The trees and grass were all the most brilliant of green and the stars that were showing themselves in the early night sky popped out like flashes of hot white.

"He is waiting," Bear-Walks-at-Night told Thane. "Bring your thunder stick."

They remained without clothes and in a short time reached the tree in which Thane had been carving his name when the grizzly had scared Whistler from under him. On the trunk were the letters THANE THOMPSC, with part of the O still open and the N totally absent.

"Finish carving your name," Bear-Walks-at-Night instructed. "You can stand on my shoulders."

Bear-Walks-at-Night held Thane steady and he finished carving his name and then the date. He was aware that his shoulder was becoming stiff but he continued to work. As he finished, he got down from Bear-Walks-at-Night's shoulders and stood facing the huge grizzly once again.

The bear was walking toward them in a straight line, not veering one way or another, as if following some preordained trail. Thane felt a strange fear suddenly well up inside of him, but held his position. Bear-Walks-at-Night had his arms outstretched toward the grizzly, as if welcoming a relative. Then the bear stopped and rose onto its hind legs.

"Shoot him through the heart," Bear-Walks-at-Night said. "Straight through the heart."

Thane forgot about his shoulder and the fear and aimed Gulliver. The blast shook him and his shoulder reacted again with pain. He was aware of his own determination and did not drop to his knees or lose consciousness. Instead he watched as the huge bear stood motionless for a moment before falling sideways in death.

Bear-Walks-at-Night said prayers and walked around the fallen bear a number of times. Twilight was a deep ochre streak across the west where peaks ripped thin streaming clouds. Thane continued to watch his father-in-law, unaware of the oncoming chill of night and his aching shoulder. He watched as Bear-Walks-at-Night worked with his knife and then reached into the chest of the great bear. He removed the heart, through which there was a small hole, and held it to the darkening sky. Then he cut a piece from it and handed to to Thane.

"You will have his heart and his strength," Bear-Walks-at-Night said.

Thane ate the piece of heart, chewing it hardly at all and swallowing it nearly whole. He watched Bear-Walks-at-Night place the rest of the heart into a small parfleche, praying as he did so. Thane then took the parfleche from him and held it in front of his own heart for a time.

Bear-Walks-at-Night then lit three torches he had brought along and together with Thane skinned the bear. They left the head intact with the skin and with great difficulty dragged the hide and head together through the darkness back to the special lodge. Thane found himself covered from head to foot with the grizzly's blood, and Bear-Walks-at-Night told him some of it had gone into his body so that it would mingle with his own blood.

For the remainder of that night and throughout the next day, Thane and Bear-Walks-at-Night spent their time in the sweat lodge. During that time, Thane made a small medicine bundle that he would from this time on wear around his neck. It was cut from a small piece of grizzly hide that Bear-Walks-at-Night had brought up with him. Thane placed various articles inside of it, including the elk teeth he had taken the night of the Little People, some grizzly teeth, and pinches of the herb mixtures Bear-Walks-at-Night had given him to eat and drink.

As nightfall again approached, Thane was instructed to wait in the sweat lodge until he was summoned to the special lodge. Before long Bear-Walks-at-Night appeared and Thane walked behind him, naked, into the special lodge.

Thane took a seat cross-legged in front of the fire. Bear-Walks-at-Night handed him a large pot to place on his lap and instructed Thane to hold it there and not to let it move no matter what might happen. Thane situated it so that it rested on his ankles, where they crossed between his thighs. He felt anticipation such as he had never known and worked to force himself into a state of total release, so that what was to come would occur without problems.

Again Thane's mind felt detached from his body and he knew his time in the sweat lodge had brought him into another dimension, where he was to remain until Bear-Walks-at-Night was finished with him. He had not jumped into the lake as before and he had not eaten since partaking of the grizzly's heart. Now he sat cross-legged in front of the small fire in the special lodge and watched Bear-Walks-at-Night scrape slivers from the claws and teeth of the bear into a stone bowl. He ground them and put the powder into another bowl and mixed in powdered herbs and meat and the bear's blood. When Thane was finished eating this mixture, Bear-Walks-at-Night began to pray once again. Then he left the lodge.

When Bear-Walks-at-Night returned, Thane froze with fear. He could not tell if it was a grizzly he was seeing or if Bear-Walks-at-Night had donned the hide they had taken from the fallen bear. It did not matter for whatever was there had the mind and voice and actions of a bear. There was tremendous growling and snarling and Thane fought every instinct of self-preservation so he wouldn't bolt and run from the lodge.

He sat rigid, prepared for whatever might happen. His mind was now even more removed from his mortal self and he felt as though whatever it was Bear-Walks-at-Night had prepared for him to eat was now boiling just below his heart. It was a strange sensation, the odd movement deep within him that seemed to have life of its own. His hands, which held the bowl in his lap, seemed not a part of him at all, but rather detached limbs that held onto an object he thought now was spinning.

As he continued to listen to the growling and the snarling, it began to come to his ears in a sort of rhythm or pattern that tended to numb him and put him in a kind of stupor. He now watched and waited, as if apart from what was happening, yet in the center of everything. He saw the bear figure in front of him circling him now, as if he were a form of prey. Strange sensations of helplessness now overwhelmed him as the middle of him continued to roil and work up higher. Then he felt the fangs on his shoulder.

He opened his mouth to scream but no sound would emerge. He found himself paralyzed and unable to move. The growling continued and the strange sensation of the fangs on his shoulder seemed to change something within him and he suddenly felt his shoulder moving inside. An odd blood streaked with yellow trailed down from his scars and from his open mouth came wads of the material he had eaten, also streaked with yellow. It fell from his mouth and into the bowl in front of him.

Then, as suddenly as a snake strikes, Bear-Walks-at-Night's hand streaked out and dumped the contents of the bowl into the fire. There was a strange roar followed by an ugly hiss as the flames suddenly blew upward, as if pulled from the top of the lodge. The flames continued to roar and took on the shape of a bear that clawed and fought through its death throes, its claws slim lengths of fire that reached out toward Thane but could not touch him.

Thane stared and saw eyes that were red coals within black holes in the fire. There was sharp cracking and popping followed by horrible drippings of white where a mouth appeared and teeth fell out, one by one, as liquid into the fire. The claws that were lengths of fire then dripped off to nothing and the roars lessened. The fire then receded and fell into a dense black smoke that filled the lodge.

Thane felt himself being pulled to his feet. He was running and soon reached the lake, black and cold in the night, and jumped in.

He jerked as the chill slammed into him and he rose from the water, gasping. He somehow felt lighter and his shoulder moved freely, without pain or stiffness. He yelled for joy, the heavens blazing with stars and the trees jagged and black against the sky absorbing his echo. He looked for Bear-Walks-at-Night, thinking he had joined him in the lake. But he was not to be seen.

Thane emerged from the lake naked and cold, yet alive in a way he had not felt for a number of years. Now he felt a strange mixture of elation and confusion. He called out for his father-in-law. There was no answer. He called again. Still no answer. Then he turned toward the special lodge and saw it was aflame, bursting into the night in streaks of fire. He yelled and began to run toward the lodge, calling out Bear-Walks-at-Night's name.

While the lodge burned, Thane stood back and shielded his eyes from the heat and intense light. He was sure Bear-Walks-at-Night had set the fire but could not make himself believe he was still in there. There was no way to see into the flames, which seemed to be fueled by some intense and all-consuming force.

Thane stood near the lodge until way past dawn, looking into the ashes with total bewilderment. He had forgotten his shoulder was as strong as the day he had first looked out from the huge butte at the edge of Piegan country. He seemed not to notice that the air temperature was near freezing and that his breath condensed in the pink light of the oncoming day. He stood without any means of understanding anything that had taken place and began to wonder if he was awake or merely dreaming.

As the morning progressed, Thane dressed and continued to wonder at what had happened. His clothes were cold and yet he did not feel them on his body, so great was his confusion and concern. The strange mystery of what had taken place the night before was now in the distant background of his mind. Instead he concerned himself with the whereabouts of his father-in-law and why the lodge had burned.

He cut a long branch from a nearby aspen and began to rummage through the smoking ashes where the special lodge had stood. He could find nothing but soft gray flakes that burst into powder at his touch. There was no sign of anything that had once been there, no pieces of pottery, no scraps of the bear's hide, no bones. Nothing but feathery ashes.

Thane walked the surrounding area and continued to wonder what had taken place. Bear-Walks-at-Night's horse continued to graze peacefully with Whistler, yet all the belongings he had brought were gone, even the saddle. This seemed odd, as Thane could not remember that Bear-Walks-at-Night had taken his horse tack into the lodge; and it certainly was not now resting beside his own saddle and other belongings, as it had been the night before.

Deciding there was nothing more he could learn from the camp surroundings, Thane went to the tree where they had killed the bear. He found his name and the date preserved in the tree, but the grizzly's carcass was missing. There was no sign of blood or entrails, and no remains from the grizzly's death. There was only grass mixed with the tiny blossoms of a small white flower.

Thane turned suddenly, feeling a presence near him. He saw nothing and heard only the wind brushing the tops of the pines. Overhead a raven flew cawing toward some distant hill. In a distant stand of aspens tiny birds chattered to each other. But there was something he couldn't explain. And it told him it was time to leave for the Bighorn.

What would he tell Morning Swan? What would Little Bird think of him for leaving his father-in-law, her husband, after he had cured his injuries? Thane knew somehow that the answers would have to come from Morning Swan. He sensed she had known what was to take place and that, in the end, she realized she would never see her father again. This, Thane surmised, had been the reason for her tears. Had he known this in the beginning, Thane then thought to himself, he likely would not have come up into the Beartooth.

Thane saddled Whistler and prepared to leave. He accepted the fact that he would never fully understand what had occurred and that he was not meant to. His was to accept it and to do so in good faith. What had happened to him, in Eli's words, was something that can't be explained, but just is.

With a strong shoulder and two good horses, Thane was not concerned about getting over to the Bighorn country. He was not concerned about Blackfeet, as they were likely on their own fall hunts and would be concentrating their efforts upon making meat for the upcoming winter before turning to the task of killing their enemies. He saw his trip as merely a leisurely ride through a country colored with the splendor of late fall.

And from the first moment of his trip down off the Beartooth and across the country toward the Bighorn, Thane knew he was right about having a safe trip. There appeared to him each morning, usually while he went out to greet the rising sun, a large form in the early light, watching him from some distant hill. The form would remain only for an instant before leaving. And Thane knew he would watch and give thanks

each morning from that time onward to his spirit
helper, the giant white bear, the grizzly.

Thane stood in the darkness on the crest of a hill
above the Bighorn River and looked down into the
Crow village. With his shoulder healed, he felt reborn.
He was anxious to see Morning Swan and the children
once again. It was the night of November 12, 1833.

The night was cold and the stars a crystal white. He
studied the various constellations, formed in the
Crow way of thinking by persons who had once lived
on earth and now came out only after dark. Stories
were told around campfires mainly during the cold
moons, because it was during this time that the
Morning Star could best be seen. The stars in their
immense proportion seemed always to be the same,
shining on like the light of eternity. But there was
nothing that remained the same, Thane realized,
watching a star plummet in a fleeting trail of white.

The entire village came out to greet him and the
pots were filled with meat. Morning Swan, though
losing her father as a result of his return, welcomed
him and cried in his arms. The children did likewise,
each hugging him for a long period of time. Jethro was
so happy to see his father's shoulder healed that he
climbed a tree and began to shout to the heavens.

They had tried to wake Eli up, but he was stone cold
in sleep after drinking a large quantity of whiskey. He
was sure Thane had died somewhere in the high
country and for some time had been drinking his grief
away. After he was sure that Eli could not be awakened, Thane went back among the people and looked
for Jethro, who was still up in the tree shouting praises
for his father's return.

Thane was laughing, Morning Swan and Rosebud
standing beside him, when the night suddenly exploded. The sky came aglow with balls of light that fell
to earth like burning white campfires. From his formal
education in Virginia, Thane knew them to be mete-

ors. There was an incredible shower of them and Jethro fell from the tree, spraining his ankle. The Crow people all began to sing their death songs, hustling their children into the lodges. Some men brandished their weapons, singing war songs, thinking they would surely die but would be killed as a warrior should be.

Throughout it all Thane tried to calm them. He tried to get Morning Swan to bring the children out from under the blankets and out of the lodge so they could see a wonder that came only once in a lifetime. She screamed at him to take cover so that he might not die. It was crazy to have gone through what he had just lived through and then stand out where the fire spirits would surely kill him.

The stars continued to fall in steady streams. Thane marveled at the sight, wondering at its cause. He wished everyone else might see the sight for what it really was. But try as he might, he could not subdue the terror that burst like a fever through the Crow village that night. He tried to talk to the warriors but many of them were frozen in fear, their eyes on the falling fire in the sky. The village was a deafening chorus of death songs and chants to the spirits for protection. Finally, while the women sobbed over their children and the men tried to control their urges to hide with their families, the meteor shower ended. Thane stood looking into the sky, calm and unafraid.

Now everyone looked at Thane. He was in the center of the village with his hands folded across his chest. Thane called the people together to tell them that the night was again safe and they no longer needed to fear the sky. They all believed, to a person, that Thane had driven away the evil burning spirits. It had been his powerful medicine that had saved them. The one they called Bear-Man, the one who had returned from the Beartooth with his strong medicine just in time to preserve them from death, would forever be their protector.

The Crow people all gathered around him that night, reaching out in turn to touch this man who had been sent from his medicine dream to save them. Jethro, indifferent to his injured ankle, beamed with pride; his father had not only regained his medicine, but was now even more powerful than before. Even Morning Swan now looked upon him with awe, thinking she had learned something more about her husband than she had ever dreamed possible. Thane realized there was no way he could tell them that the meteors had come and gone without any action on his part.

Eli finally awakened to learn he had missed something.

"Not only did I sleep through you getting back into camp," Eli said, "but it appears I missed some big medicine."

Thane told Eli what had happened and continued to look into the night sky, thinking about himself and his family, and the upcoming times ahead. It occurred to him that this night would bring change. As surely as the sky was rearranged, so would be the earth. Things would be different. The Crow people, all still staring at him in wonderment, would expect great things from him. His stature as a warrior would be greater than ever before and he would decide with the council what was best now for the Kicked-in-Their-Bellies, of the Crow Indian nation.

Part Three

1835-1838

Thirteen

SINCE THE NIGHT THE STARS FELL, THANE HAD CONTINUALLY grown in stature among the Crow people. With his strength fully returned, he presented a massive frame of muscle and power that impressed all who looked upon him. He was considered a warrior come from the spirits to keep the Crow lands safe from enemies and rich with game. His influence had spread far and wide across the mountains.

The Kicked-in-Their-Bellies band was now well known not just among the people of the Crow nation, but among the other tribes as well. They were strong and dressed well, as was customary for their people, but now they stood out for other reasons as well. This particular Crow band had a reputation as a fierce and warlike group, feared and respected, and it was due mainly to the Long Knife who had the medicine of the great white bear.

Though Thane still kept Rising Hawk's medicine shield in a special place, he had made one of his own. It was a symbol of his personal medicine, the grizzly, and it was made from the heavy neck hide of a bull buffalo, in the tradition of the Crow medicine shields, and then lined with grizzly fur and eagle feathers. At its center was painted a bear with long teeth and claws, and dark hair tipped with white.

The Long Knife, Bear-Man, was a strong leader and it was said he possessed powers that no other man possessed. Bear-Man had carried the pipe three times against Crow enemies. In a raid that had lasted but one day, the Lacotah had lost two war chiefs and a hundred horses to him. Twice the Blackfeet peoples had suffered losses at the hands of Bear-Man and his raiders, who took horses and scalps, driving war parties north and away from Crow country. Care was now taken among enemy war parties to be sure that they came nowhere near the lodges of the Kicked-in-Their-Bellies, least the warrior called Bear-Man release his strange and powerful medicine against them.

Now that the Blackfeet people were joining forces against the Long Knives who continued to trap beaver from their streams, they were ever more aware of this different Long Knife who lived among their bitter enemies, the Crows. The Kainah, called Bloods, had been the ones who had suffered the most at the hands of Bear-Man, and they swore to one day cut his heart out. Among the Piegans the warrior Rising Hawk had once been great and respected. Since he'd lost his medicine shield, it was said that he sat continually in the hills, crazed, his eyes now nearly burned out by the sun.

Even among the white traders in the mountains, Thane Thompson was considered dangerous and unpredictable. He was an Indian in his heart, who cared about the Crow people. He never came to rendezvous anymore, but those who visited the Crow told stories that he now had a mission. It was said his eyes held anger for anyone who would not listen or did not care about what was happening in the mountains. He had made it his sole purpose in life to save a land that had once flourished but was now falling to abuse. He was

tired of talking, it was told, about how the fur trade
was dead, and how the trappers should leave and give
the land its life back. He and his Crow wife, the
Woman-Who-Had-Counted-Coup, Morning Swan,
were thought to be immortal. Among their people,
they were highly honored.

Since arriving in the village the night of the meteors, Bear-Man had grown to be as strong as any
warrior who had ever made his name in the mountains. The Kicked-in-Their-Bellies knew this man
would help keep them free of enemies as long as he
was with them. He had become a true Crow and he
cared about his family and the good of the people. He
was a member of the council and had joined the
Kit-Foxes, a warrior society. He was lean and strong
and, except for his light hair, he might have been born
in a special lodge. Though he still wore the broad-
brimmed hat, there was no longer an owl feather in it.
Instead it was trimmed with porcupine quills and red
beads and the band was made from strips of thick
grizzly fur.

But as strong as his reputation was, Thane felt
helpless against the changes that were happening in
the Crow lands. Now the land was receiving a great
deal of grazing pressure from not only the Crow
horses, but also the horses of the many Long Knives
who were building forts along the rivers. Near these
forts were great herds of horses which could not be
moved to new pastures during the course of each
summer. There were too many horses for the amount
of forage available and the animals grazed the grass to
the roots, causing dirt to blow in the wind.

The elders watched this with their hands held over
their mouths. They looked to Thane, the powerful
warrior Bear-Man, to stop it. But he told them he
could not, that it would now be very difficult to put an
end to something that had started years before and
was gaining in momentum. Thane told them he could

not stop the dust. Only the sky spirits could bring the rain, and this would not help if the grass was grazed off and could not grow.

This was something many of the elders looked upon as a bad omen. They had never seen the spirits raise specks of dirt to blacken the sky. This meant the ground spirits were angry at having the grass stripped off and not allowing it to grow back. And now there were few beaver dams to stop the onrush of melted snow and spring rains. As a result the rivers began to get dark with this dirt and great numbers of fish could be seen floating belly-up along the shores.

Other warning signs appeared, among them the lowering of the water tables throughout the land. The rivers roared in the spring and blew torrents of water down from the mountains. Streambeds and river bottoms were forever altered and torn away by the powerful rushing water. Trees were uprooted, taking valuable soil from the bottoms, and steep banks began to develop along the edges of the rivers. In many places there was no sign that beaver dams had ever existed. Where pools had once lasted throughout the hot months of the year, now only dry streambeds remained, their gravels bleached in the blazing sun. The deltas that had once formed from beaver dams that caught sediment loads began to erode down and dump their fine soil particles into the streams and rivers, to be carried away forever.

With the many forts and horses and the various bands of Indians that began to camp around the forts, the buffalo herds moved out from the river bottomlands and onto the open plains. The Yellowstone Valley was affected as badly as any other and the Kicked-in-Their-Bellies followed the herds in order to kill food for the lodges. This winter they were camped not along the Bighorn where the warm waters flowed, but farther south and east, along the waters of the North Platte.

This was a land more open than the hills and valleys of the Yellowstone. There were not the vast groves of aspens and willows that served as prime beaver habitats and thus attracted numbers of trappers. Beaver could be found in scattered locations here, but the plains broke out vast and wide from the mountains and the land was huge. Buffalo herds grazed everywhere here, free for the most part from the interference of the fur trade. More and more, though, traveling bands of both Crow and Shoshone came to hunt.

From one of these bands came a new husband for Little Bird, who had not remarried since Bear-Walks-at-Night had gone into the Beartooth to help Thane regain his power. Since that time she had been living in Thane and Morning Swan's lodge. Though she had been content, this older warrior, He-Walks-among-Them, had captured her heart and her imagination.

Little Bird was sure that Bear-Walks-at-Night wanted her to do this. He-Walks-among-Them was much like Bear-Walks-at-Night had been, though his medicine was the golden eagle and not the grizzly. It was a good union and Little Bird again saw life as she once had, but Thane noticed a difference in her. It was subtle, as if the passing of Bear-Walks-at-Night was the end of a time in her life that could never be recaptured. It seemed almost that she was entering a new time in her life, as were her people.

Thane continued to wonder about the future of the Crow people as the wind grew warmer and he watched another star fall. There were a lot of buffalo in this country, but he wasn't happy being down here. He understood that the herds were scattering more and more and that the various bands would have to do likewise to keep themselves in food, but he did not like the idea of splitting off too far from the Yellowstone and the other Crow bands. Though one of the other bands, the Sore-Lips, was camped a ways to the north along the upper reaches of the Powder River, there were still too few Crows in this territory to wage a defense against an enemy attack.

For this reason Thane now worried about remaining this far down from the Yellowstone. He enjoyed taking war parties out from the village to raid, but like the other parents, he feared an attack against the village. Women and children could be killed more readily than warriors, and if they were not taken as captives, their lives were not spared. Thane had seen too many Crow people in mourning already and he didn't want Morning Swan or himself to join them.

Life with the children had so far been very good for both Thane and Morning Swan. Rosebud had matured unbelievably and was the object of many a young warrior's attention, including that of Turtle. He would bring his pet raven by while Rosebud worked hides and have the bird whistle and then cover its head under a wing. Rosebud would try to hide her smiles, but when Turtle was there she was amused, and he would have the bird go into other antics. It was said that he was making a bone whistle with which to play songs late in the evening. But he would have to wait to get very serious about Rosebud, as he had yet to count a coup.

Jethro was fast shaping up into an outstanding young man. He was fast afoot and strong for his age, owing to the fact that he felt he had to compete with his older sister. She was quicker than he at grabbing rocks and sticks from one another's hands and it didn't seem to make him feel better to hear from Thane or Morning Swan that he shouldn't be ashamed, for his sister was a lot older than he. He worked that much harder to catch up to her skills. As he grew, he would challenge her more often and always with the same results. Even though she would give him gracious leads in footracing, she could catch him.

None of the other boys made fun of Jethro's competition with Rosebud, however, for the first one that would laugh was always challenged to a race and immediately humbled by him. And in addition to his physical development, his mind was broadening at a rapid rate. He was two years older and all that much more curious about life now. Eli, in a crude way, was teaching him to be a musician.

Eli, who still touted himself as the boy's grandfather, had traded a passing trapper for an old banjo. Eli had replaced the worn hide backing with finely tanned cow buffalo and had various trappers he knew bring out fresh strings from St. Louis each summer. He had worked to learn to play it himself, and Thane would often ask if he and Jethro wouldn't go out a ways from the village to play and stop scaring the horses.

In addition to plunking on Eli's banjo, Jethro had learned to read the primers that Stretch Tipson had left for him, which made his father happy, and he wanted to read new things now. Crow was his first language but English came as easily to him. And as with his sister, his mother had taught him the Blackfeet tongue as well. Besides this, he was learning two other languages.

It was here that Jethro could torment Rosebud, for she knew only Blackfoot in addition to Crow and English. A boy just older than Jethro, whose mother was Shoshone, was teaching him that language, and he was learning some French from a half-breed boy who had been taken into a family as a child. Now he would call Rosebud names in French or Shoshone and she couldn't understand him, which infuriated her. Morning Swan and Thane would often get tired of the bickering, but there seemed to be no real way to eliminate it.

Over the years Thane had learned to speak fluent Crow and Blackfoot, and was learning the Lacotah tongue from a brother warrior in the Kit-Foxes who had spent three childhood years as a slave. Thane was pleased with both Rosebud and Jethro for taking an

interest in knowing as many languages as possible.
Rosebud and Jethro had both remarked that they
didn't want to fall behind the other young people,
many of whom knew as many as five languages now.

This people, with their thinking so vastly different
from the way Thane had been raised, was on the edge
of change. It was not for the better, Thane realized, for
even the most aggressive of warriors would not fight
unless there was honor to be gained from the victory.
Thane knew that the whites, especially the newer
strain that was coming to reap the profits of a land just
beginning to be exploited, had no qualms about
utilizing any means possible to acquire wealth. Coins
that were round and held in the hand held no value to
the Crow people.

It was early morning when Thane realized his
concerns were becoming reality sooner than he had
expected. The wind that had come up during the night
was blowing strong and the snow was melting. He and
some of the other warriors had returned from the hills
above camp, where they had been saying morning
sunrise prayers, when village Wolves returned with
news of visitors. The Wolves reported them not to be
enemies, however.

From downriver came a group of men on horseback
and the village was gathering to greet them. They rode
in a long line, reminiscent of the old brigades that
went out for beaver. In the middle of the column was a
white wagon covered with canvas. Thane recognized
the two men in the lead from years past, and though
these two eyed him suspiciously, Thane welcomed
them and told them to join him and the other warriors
in council.

Morning Swan had been watching ever since the
Wolves had ridden in to announce the visitors. She
knew that there were now many different trading
houses around the mountains and that these men
must have come from one near here. It seemed to her
that the method of securing furs from the streams had

gone in a full circle from when she had first met Thane: the Long Knives had come out to trade with the tribes, had gone to trapping themselves, and were now going back to trading supplies in return for robes of every kind. Morning Swan knew in her mind that these forts were permanent and that the land was then considered to be owned by the forts.

"These men come to take from us," Morning Swan said. "Why do you welcome them?"

"It is my duty to welcome them, in behalf of your people, who consider them brothers," Thane reminded her. "I know you don't feel that way yourself, but we can't act on our own behalf."

Morning Swan continued to scowl. "They are not brothers. They do not come as true brothers."

Thane calmed her. "They won't like what I have to tell them," he said. "I don't know where they came from, but they will be gone before long."

Eli stood beside Thane. "Looks like a group out to buy robes and furs and such," he said, "seein' the number of presents and all they got. And damn, it's Sublette and Campbell. They'll be workin' against the company down here, if my guess is right."

There were a number of men, all traders and trappers, whose main leader was a trapper named Bill Sublette. With him was a small man Thane knew as well, named Robert Campbell. Both had been in the mountains a long time and knew the etiquette of smoking and eating before formal discussions of any kind. They knew both Thane and Eli well from past rendezvous and hoped their longtime acquaintance would do them good.

Sublette and Campbell took their places to the right of Thane, as guests, and waited for him to pass them the pipe. They noticed the grizzly claw necklace and the small medicine bag that hung around his neck. They saw that he had become true Indian.

While they smoked and ate, members of the Crow council recited war deeds against their enemies.

Sublette and Campbell, in turn, followed with stories of warring against the Blackfeet. Sublette had a Piegan scalp he passed around for all to inspect. When it was time for Thane's presentation, he told about the night the stars fell and how he stopped the fire from falling. Sublette and Campbell said nothing. They both realized how much influence he held among the Crows.

"Now," Thane began the discussions, "tell us why our brothers have come this day."

Sublette told him they were building a fort they called William not far away, at the confluence of the Laramie and the North Platte rivers. He told Thane it would make his heart glad if he could trade with the Crows, but that he had sent men into the Black Hills to talk to the Oglala Sioux. They wanted the Sioux to move into the Platte River country and kill the buffalo for them. Buffalo robes were getting to be very profitable.

Thane looked questioningly at Sublette. "Why do you come for our trade when you've got Lacotah enemies coming as well?"

Sublett shrugged. "Move your camp up to Powder River. When you come to trade, let me know and we'll see to it the Sioux don't bother you."

Eli looked at Thane and they both laughed. It was hard for either of them to imagine that a seasoned trapper like Sublette could be so muddled in his thinking. This came, Thane reasoned, from the heated competition between Sublette and the American Fur Company as they fought for the newly established buffalo-robe trade. Those out for the trade would do anything to get it.

"You can't tell me you're serious," Thane said. "You know you'll have blood all over your new Fort William. What makes you think you could keep warring Indian nations apart when they're camped less than two days' ride from one another."

Sublette then had Campbell order the other traders

to unload the trade supplies. The Crow women and children crowded around to gather up blankets and beads and cloth and various trinkets, while the men were given a number of items including knives and awls and hoop iron to melt for arrowheads and other weaponry. Then a number of kegs were unloaded and Sublette smiled.

"There's enough whiskey to keep everyone happy," he remarked.

"No Crow will drink it," Thane told him. "You know that."

"Anything can change," Sublette said.

Thane took a hatchet and walked over to the kegs. One by one he burst them with the blade and the contents flowed into the melting snow. Eli watched Sublette grow angry. Sublette and Campbell and the other traders then all looked at the Crow men, who were laughing. The Crows knew well that the medicine water made them do foolish things and caused problems among them. Those Crows who had partaken before had been shamed by the others and no one wanted to lose his dignity.

Thane then walked over to Sublette. "If I didn't have a wife and family, I'd go burn down your fort right now. With or without help, I'd burn it to the ground."

Sublette finally recovered and said, "You think you're God a'mighty, don't you?"

"I'm not in the trade business any longer, Sublette, that's all."

Sublette gathered his men and got them ready to leave.

"I'd move camp today," Sublette said. "The Oglalas are on their way."

As Sublette and the others rode away, Thane thought about making good his desire to burn the fort. But other warriors in the council told him they did not wish to do it, for it would surely mean killing some of the traders. It would not be a good thing to kill any of the Long Knives.

Councils were held daily to decide whether to stay or to leave the area. Thane and the other council members eyed one another continually, each knowing that the women were weeping in the lodges for fear of an attack and the loss of fighting men and possibly themselves and their children. Now that the snow moons were leaving there was less to worry about from the weather, but the food supplies had been exhausted over the course of their stay and there would need to be buffalo killed and meat dried to prepare the camp for moving.

So it was decided to move the village farther north, possibly as far as one of the old traditional camping areas at Lodge Grass. But first it would be necessary to have a hunt and kill enough buffalo to make the jouney. This would mean waiting for a time until the ground was either frozen again or free of snow and dry. Hunting on muddy ground was treacherous and even the most sure-footed pony could tumble its rider at any time.

As the days continued to go by the weather grew ever warmer, but the skies brought snow showers and occasional rain. Herds of buffalo wandered within easy hunting distance but the fear of falling beneath the hooves on a slick flat made the attempt far too dangerous to consider. Nearly a full moon passed, and it seemed as though the skies would never clear. The grass came and grew as the rain fed its leaves and flowers burst their colors across the wide flats and along the wooded draws.

While the village waited for the sun and dry ground for the hunt, Rosebud would listen each evening to the sound of a bone whistle. There was a large grove of chokecherries just behind the village along a draw above the river. For the past three evenings the music had carried from the chokecherries until late at night. Finally on the fourth night, Rosebud waited until she thought everyone in her lodge was asleep and stole out to the chokecherries.

"I thought you would never come," Turtle told her as she came into the chokecherry grove.

"It is cold and damp up here," Rosebud said with a giggle. "You are foolish to be out here."

"Yes, but you have come," Turtle said with a laugh. He drew Rosebud close to him and began to run his fingers through her hair. "Do you think I am worthy of you?" he asked.

"Of course," Rosebud answered. "You have counted seventeen winters, but you cannot have me yet. You have not counted coup and you have no wealth."

"That will all change soon," Turtle said. "And I will be given a warrior's name."

"What do you mean?" Rosebud asked.

"I cannot tell," Turtle said. "I cannot spoil it."

"Don't do anything foolish," Rosebud warned. "I will wait for you to gain honor."

Turtle held her tighter. "There are many young warriors in this village who want you for a wife. And it is said there are also many from other bands who even as these warm moons come would travel the lands to find your family and offer much wealth for your hand. They are all fine warriors; and what a great thing to have Bear-Man as a father-in-law. That would be something to brag about."

Rosebud pulled away from Turtle. "Do you care about me or only that my family has great honor?" she demanded.

Turtle pulled her back close to him again. "I am only saying that I want to gain honor before I lose you to another. That is all I am saying. Can't you tell that I've wanted you to be with me for a long time?"

"Yes, but all you have done so far is make that silly raven of yours do tricks."

"That silly raven is all I have. But that will change soon."

Rosebud felt his lips meet hers and she allowed herself the pleasure for a moment. Then she stopped him and her voice showed her concern.

"I don't want you to take any chances. Do you hear me?"

Turtle laughed in the darkness. "Do you think I am weak? Do you think I cannot prove myself? If I am to be a man, the time is now. You wait for me. And do not worry, for I know my time of honor is near."

Turtle left her and was gone in the darkness. The rain came again and pattered against the chokecherry leaves and made little thumping sounds when it struck the ground. Then there was a call, like one of the small prairie wolves, almost a laughing yap. Rosebud hurried down toward the lodge and worried that Turtle had become too confident in a land filled with enemies.

While the sun crossed four times they traveled afoot, keeping to the draws and below the ridge tops, eating only pemmican and jerky. During the day they would get what rest they could by holing up among the trees and rocks above the valley floor. Then, with darkness, they would creep as slowly and surely as the short-tailed cat with spots, whose eyes are made for the night. They would reach the new Fort William very soon, and though none of them had yet seen eighteen winters, this was to be their time of manhood.

Turtle and four other young men tried to think only of their mission and the glory that awaited them should they succeed. Within their minds they fought the knowledge that their mothers were now weeping and their fathers and brothers worried about them. Turtle could still hear Rosebud's soft voice begging him not to be foolish. Turtle realized as well as the other four that they should have waited for an experienced leader to bring a war party together, and then ask to go along as apprentices.

But Turtle was not willing to wait. He wanted Rosebud. The other four wanted to prove themselves as well. Now was their greatest opportunity.

Each had an extra pair of moccasins and a knife at his side. They wore only breechclouts and thin hide shirts against the weather, shirts they hoped they could decorate with the stories of war. By the end of this day they would be where they wanted to be, preparing for the night and their raid. Now they were working their way down the upper reaches of the Laramie River to where the fort should be waiting for them. Turtle was pleased. As leader he had planned the trip well—moving along the swollen waters of the North Platte and then moving out into the wooded hills above the valley to cross the upper reaches of the Laramie drainage. The waters rushed swiftly through the rivers now and to take stolen horses home they would have to stay to the uplands.

They looked down into the valley where the Laramie joined the North Platte. The smoke from the fires looked thin and gray as it rose into the late-day sky above the new Fort William. Turtle and his small party watched from a good distance upriver. They had found the fort and yes, there were Lacotah camped there. By this time tomorrow, Turtle thought, these Lacotah will have lost horses and will be hiding their faces in shame before the Long Knife traders who had brought them to these lands.

Turtle and the other four awaited darkness, sharpening their knives and rehearsing in their minds the plan for the upcoming raid. They would not worry about meeting again, but each would hurry with his catch back to the village. Since they were so few, they would have to be fast and clever. Each would have to do his part so that they could all escape without losing anyone. It was not important to steal a great many horses. It was important, though, to take at least twenty, and possibly some other articles from the Lacotah camp.

Turtle worried the most about the camp Wolves, who would likely be out in the hills now scouting around for signs of enemies near the fort. For this reason it was important they remain hidden and speak as little as possible to one another. If they were discovered now their plan could never take shape and they would not be likely to escape with their lives. Death to even one of their party would be death to them all, for any survivors who made it back to the village would have to hang their heads in shame forever.

Darkness fell and the five disbanded to go their separate ways. He who travels alone is far less likely to be discovered. Each would take whatever horses he could from the herd and drive them as slowly as possible out of the river bottom and onto the flat that ran to the west. They would meet later in the low mountains above the Laramie River. It would be much easier to outrun pursuers if there was no rushing water to cross.

Now that the time for his test had come, Turtle took a deep breath and asked the spirits to guide him. The rain had stopped and the air was fresh with the pungent smell of sagebrush. Overhead, rushing clouds hid Sun-of-the-Night and the sky was a mantle of black. Turtle did not worry about sound as much as he would have had there not been so much rain. The ground was soft with flowers and fresh grass, and trickles of water sounded from little springs among the rocks and draws along the bluffs. Crickets, the night-singers, chorused from every leaf and twig. In the distance the calls and yaps of small prairie wolves echoed and the night settled in peacefully.

Turtle went to his hands and knees in the darkness and eventually to his belly as he neared the fort. The bottom was filled with Lacotah lodges and everywhere fires burned merrily while dancers moved their feet to drummers seated at various locations. Scattered among them were Long Knives who passed out jugs of the medicine water that made the mind crazy. Turtle recognized the two that had come to the village during the late part of the snow moons, and had been driven away by Rosebud's father, Bear-Man.

Instead of doing the wise thing and dumping the medicine water, the Lacotahs were falling victim to its evils. The Crow people had for a long time kept themselves free of the medicine water. All the elders realized that they appeared foolish to everyone when they drank it. But there had been some quarreling that day when Bear-Man had broken the kegs of medicine water. Turtle had overheard some of the younger warriors saying they did not think the medicine water was so bad.

Turtle could see now by watching that it was mostly younger Lacotah men who were drinking, while the elders sat back and smoked and shook their heads. These young Lacotah men were even giving it to their women. They moved around the village, laughing and yelling, drinking from the jugs. Often they would transfer the medicine water mouth-to-mouth so that their friends and loved ones could experience the feeling from one another.

This went on for some time and Turtle found it all confusing. The entire village seemed to be enjoying a celebration and there seemed to be no one on watch anywhere. It was as though the Lacotah were in a different world where there were no enemies, only the medicine water to make things perfect. Turtle remained where he was for some time, looking around to be sure there was no one on watch. It all seemed too good to be true.

The horse herd was at the far end of the village, scattered up and down the valley. Earlier they had been bunched together so that they could more easily be watched and herded. This told Turtle that there were few horse tenders on duty and he knew from his

own experience that these young Lacotahs were likely
having a hard time keeping the horses close to the
village.

Turtle then came upon someone crawling toward
the horses. He drew his knife but then heard the call of
the nighthawk, the sign they were using to locate one
another. Turtle then found one of the young men who
had come with him and they shared a laugh. Neither
could believe what was taking place in the Lacotah
village and both decided they would gather as many
horses as each could manage to steal. Glory this night
would be as easy as shooting an old bull. They parted
with eager desire to fulfill their dreams.

It then came to Turtle that he would gain even more
glory should he return to the village with a special
buffalo pony. The best horses were tethered in front of
the Lacotah lodges. Deciding he could gather other
horses later, Turtle made his way forward cautiously.
He worked his way to a lodge at the outer edge of the
village, and after deciding there was no one in the
lodge, he took position to watch and decide what he
would do.

The Lacotah singing and dancing continued and the
men passed even more jugs of medicine water between them. Turtle spotted a buckskin in front of a
lodge not far into the village. The lodge was covered
with buffalo, each carrying many arrows. A good
buffalo pony without question. Turtle was tempted to
creep into the village toward the pony, but decided to
wait when he saw three Lacotah men approaching.

Two of the Lacotah men had the third between
them, his arms over their shoulders. He was yelling
and talking in a crazy manner, as if delirious. He was
trying to get to his knife but the other two were
holding his arms tightly and yelling at him. Turtle
moved back into the darkness as the two Lacotah men
laid the third inside the lodge.

Turtle was now startled. He had learned enough
Lacotah from a friend to know that the crazy man was

talking about a dream in which a number of horses were taken from the village. The other two men were telling him it was only the medicine water and none of his dreams ever came true.

Turtle took this as a bad omen and was ready to give up and leave. Then a commotion began in one part of the village, attracting everyone's attention. A number of men were quarreling about something and one of them was on the ground. The camp police moved in to establish order and Turtle saw his chance to get the buckskin.

Quickly he moved to the lodge, cutting the reins that held the horse. Turtle then spoke softly to the pony and rubbed his nose with sweetgrass. He told the pony that he was a friend and that he wanted to be carried swiftly away. Turtle was ready to mount the horse when he suddenly heard yelling directly behind him.

The Lacotah warrior who had been taken to the lodge was stumbling toward him, shouting at him while he fumbled to fit an arrow to his bow. Turtle moved instinctively. He charged the startled warrior, his knife drawn. He was quick and plunged his knife once, then twice into the Lacotah's chest. The warrior gagged blood and whiskey in a tremendous gush that sprayed Turtle's arm and the warrior's front.

Turtle turned and saw the commotion farther in the village was still in progress. The Lacotah was on his knees singing his death song through a garbled mixture of blood and air. Turtle took a lock of the dying warrior's hair in his left hand and cut a circle across the warrior's head with his knife, then ripped. The scalp came free with a sucking, tearing sound. Turtle grabbed the Lacotah warrior's bow and took it and the dripping scalp back to the buckskin.

Some in the village had by now discovered him and there was shouting as Turtle kicked the buckskin into a run outside the village. Lacotah warriors were mounting their ponies to chase him but many of them could not stay on and fell off in their drunkenness. Turtle knew he would have no trouble escaping and headed the buckskin through the darkness toward the mountains to the west.

As he rode, he felt a mixture of elation and shame—the shame coming from killing the Lacotah warrior who had been almost helpless in his drunkenness. It might have been different had the village not been under the influence of the medicine water.

But that was not the way it had happened this night. Turtle and the other young men would from this night on be considered warriors and be given new names—names worthy of warrior status. Across the top of the hills in the west, flashes of lightning shot down like hot white fire. His power had come on this night; the storm had brought him glory. With his head held high in the darkness, he rode toward that distant storm.

Fourteen

OF THE FIVE YOUNG MEN WHO HAD GONE ON THE RAID,
Turtle gained the most glory. He had stolen but one
horse, the buckskin, but had counted coup against an
enemy and had returned with a scalp and a weapon.
Though his mother was still angry with him, his new
name was being used in a war song and there were
drums pounding in his honor.

Turtle's name was changed to Takes-a-Bow, in
honor of the coup he had struck against his Lacotah
enemy. The singer of the war song was an uncle on his
father's side, whose own father had taken a lance from
an enemy warrior in times past. Takes-a-Bow and his
family would also receive additional honor, for they
chose to host a celebration for those young men who
had followed Takes-a-Bow on the raid. All the young
men would receive new names. They had achieved the
status of warriors and could now go to war as respected men.

The other four were happy for Takes-a-Bow and
gave him a great deal of credit for keeping their group
together and arranging the plan to raid the Lacotah
village. Between the four of them, they had returned

with seventy Lacotah horses. From the markings on
some of the ponies, there was no question they had
been taken from Crow villages in times past. These
ponies would be given back to their original owners
among the Crow people, bringing even more honor to
the four who took them. Takes-a-Bow, casting off his
adolescence forever, handed the buckskin's reins to
Thane and told him outright that he wished to marry
Rosebud.

"I will bring you many more buffalo ponies in
time," Takes-a-Bow promised. "But I want you to
have this pony now so that when I do get the other
horses, you will understand why I will also give them
to you."

"You are a worthy man," Thane told Takes-a-Bow,
"and if Rosebud is willing, she will become your
wife."

This talk was held in private and Takes-a-Bow left
to join the dancing as happy as any time he had ever
been in his life. Even escaping with the buckskin and
the bow and scalp from the Lacotah village, then
rejoining his comrades who had all been safe and had
all taken Lacotah horses, could not compare with the
feeling he now had. He would join the dancers in the
center of the village and he would dance for Rosebud.

Rosebud watched from the edge of the circle as the
dancers moved around the scalp Takes-a-Bow had
taken. There were other scalps taken from past fighting, but Takes-a-Bow's scalp was placed in the center
upon a coup stick made especially for him by his
uncle. Her fear for his safe return had finally abated
and all this seemed unreal somehow, as if it might not
really be happening. After coming down from the
chokecherries on that night, she was sure she would
never see him alive again.

But now she was elated at his glorious return. She
knew this meant they would be married and that their
lives would now become as one. She knew also, as she
watched him join the dancers, glancing in her direc-

tion, that he had been talking with her father about having her as his wife. From the way he danced, Rosebud was sure things had gone well.

When it was the women's turn to dance, Rosebud joined in and worked herself to the inside of the circle, where she took it upon herself to dance close to the coup pole where the scalp hung. Takes-a-Bow stood back and noticed this. It made him feel all the more like a strong warrior and, finally, in control of his life as a man and a Crow warrior. He knew that his life with Rosebud would be a happy one. It would not be long until that life could begin.

During the dancing, while Rosebud was resting and eating, Little Bird approached her. Little Bird was smiling. This woman, whom Rosebud loved dearly, had always been there to help with anything and everything. Rosebud knew how much her mother thought of Little Bird, and had come to realize what a help this woman had been to them both when they first returned to the Kicked-in-Their-Bellies from the Piegan village now many winters past.

Little Bird wanted Rosebud to know that she and He-Runs-among-Them were both overjoyed to know she would soon be wife to Takes-a-Bow. Little Bird wanted permission to be part of the ceremony and to be allowed to speak in behalf of Rosebud at that time. She would give Rosebud a new dress and a lot of material to sew on the dress. And she would show Rosebud a favorite pattern she used for quillwork.

Later during the night, Takes-a-Bow found Jethro standing beside him, asking him about the raid.

"You must have been strong to have killed a Lacotah," Jethro said. "Were you afraid?"

"I cannot lie to you," Takes-a-Bow told Jethro. "Anyone who says he isn't afraid when he faces an enemy cannot be human. He who is not afraid is a spirit. And I am not a spirit."

"But you were strong," Jethro said with a admiring smile. "And you gained honor."

Takes-a-Bow thought of telling Jethro about the medicine water, but thought better of it. It would be something Jethro would not be able to understand unless he had witnessed it for himself. He would learn about such things himself, Takes-a-Bow concluded, before much more time in his life had passed.

"I am going to give you a present," Takes-a-Bow told Jethro. "I am going to give you my raven, Joker. You could teach him many things."

"Your raven?" Jethro asked, seeming a little downcast. "I was hoping for something like a knife, or a lucky arrow. But that bird? Are you sure he's a present?"

"You can give him to the first son Rosebud bears me," Takes-a-Bow said. "That is, if the bird is still alive."

"Oh, with my luck he'll live forever," Jethro commented.

The marriage would take place once they returned to the camp at Rotten-Sun-Dance-Lodge-Creek, likely just before the hot moons came. Though tonight was festive, in Morning Swan's mind it only meant more time until they could be away from this place. Like the other mothers and the elder warriors in the village, she knew there was imminent danger with each passing day they spent in this place. The Lacotah would surely come for their horses and to avenge the loss of their brother warrior. They would come in great force and there would be much death and suffering. It was certain they would be outnumbered and any delay after tonight would cost lives.

"Why couldn't we have waited to celebrate?" Morning Swan asked Thane while they watched the dancing. "What's going to happen when the Lacotah come back for blood?"

"It's my feeling," Thane said, "that they will be a while in coming, if they ever do come."

"That is a strange thing for you to say," Morning

Swan told him. "How do you think our warriors would react if the same thing happened here?"

"The same thing didn't happen here," Thane said. "If what Takes-a-Bow and the other four told me is true, the Lacotah are just beginning the end of their lives as a strong nation. They were all filled with whiskey is what Takes-a-Bow told me, and stealing from them was like taking meat from an old woman's drying rack."

Morning Swan looked hard at Thane. "You mean the Lacotah offered no resistance?"

"They tried to resist," Thane said, "but they were all drunk and sick from whiskey. Takes-a-Bow was almost ashamed of how easy their raid was. He said the Lacotah men and women alike were drinking so much they paid no attention to what was going on around them. Takes-a-Bow said the warrior he killed could hardly stand up. I think the traders there at Fort William will persuade the Lacotah to stay and get their revenge later. They'll pour more whiskey down them and get them to think about trading and avenging their brother when the rest of the Lacotah nation moves down to join them. If any come, it will be young, drunk hotheads who will be easy to defeat. It won't be a large force."

"So you think we're in no danger?" Morning Swan asked.

"I think we should move tomorrow as planned," Thane said, "but I see no real reason for loss of sleep. Our camp Wolves will be on watch and as broad as this valley is, they'll see anyone who approaches."

The festivities went on late into the night, but with the coming of the sun, the village was awake and everyone was preparing to move. Rosebud worked with Morning Swan, humming a song as she spun a daydream through her mind about Takes-a-Bow. He was young and strong and brought forth her desires as a woman. After much persuasion from him over time she had found herself giving in to his sexual advances. The previous night they had been together. It did not matter to her that she had gotten little sleep; her life as wife and perhaps mother would begin shortly.

Once on the move, no one thought much about the Lacotah. Three days of steady traveling had put them up among the foothills of the mountains named for the bighorn sheep, the wild sheep with the broad, curled horns that survived so well along the rocky slopes of the mountains. They were a small yet majestic range of mountains and a favorite of many favorites among the locations within Crow country. These mountains, especially along the southernmost slopes, appeared as shelves of rock and timber that had been turned on end by some huge and powerful force in ages past. These mountains held spiritual powers and the Crow people never passed through this area without special prayers.

When they reached the camping area at Lodge Grass, they found a number of Crow bands already camped there. There were many lodges along the river, but instead of celebration for the arrival of the warm moons, there was widespread mourning.

It was learned that during the last of the cold moons, a number of Crow men had gone to the camp of a group of Long Knives at the mouth of the Clark's Pork on the Yellowstone. For some reason the Crow men had partaken of the medicine water offered to them by the Long Knives. As a result, Crow men, women, and children had been killed by their own people in drunken fits of rage.

Warriors had fought one another over old feuds and quarrels thought long forgotten. Men had beaten their women, and in some cases wives had killed their husbands, for reasons that the medicine water had brought out in each of them. It was a bad time for the Crow people in this village. It was a confusing time. Enemies took lives and the people banded together in their sorrow; but when people of the same tribe fought and died, the mourning was not the same.

After seeing what had happened, Morning Swan grew angry. She talked of wanting to go somewhere to live, far off, somewhere that problems such as this could not reach.

"There is no place we can go to escape this," Thane told her. "It is something the Crow people will have to work out among themselves. Now, more than any time before, the tribe will have to look within itself and we will have to forgive one another for what has happened." Thane, as he talked, wondered if the Lacotah people were not facing the same situation at this very time.

"My concern is that this means the end of my people," Morning Swan said. "Falling into the trap of drinking the medicine water has placed us under the control of the Long Knife traders. We will be no more than animals coming to the call for food—a liquid food that controls the mind."

Thane knew Morning Swan was right. It seemed there was nothing that could be done to change that, for the tide had risen already and nothing would keep it from getting worse. It was a disheartening thought and Thane found himself growing more despondent over it than Morning Swan. He knew what it did to people, educated or not, who became addicted to it. Out here in the mountains there were few things that gave pleasure and each one was partaken of heartily. Alcohol was something that could make the senses climb, then plummet in little time. For Indians, who had few inhibitions as it was, drinking dropped them to a state of no control.

Councils were now held regularly to discuss what steps to take to avoid the problems they had witnessed among the other bands. It was only a matter of time until the Kicked-in-Their-Bellies were in the same situation as the others. Already feelings were mixed among the young men about the values of having a good time. Some of the young warriors from the other Crow bands were saying the drinking had not bothered them, just others who had no control anyway.

During the time in the Lodge Grass camp Thane gave a great deal of thought to this problem, as well as to the other distinct changes that were taking place in the mountains. Though the migration had just begun, there would soon be a host of wagons headed for the Oregon Territory that promised such a rich and exciting future to anyone who went there. Values from the East were spreading like fire into the West and there was no way to stop it.

Thane thought of his children and—they would certainly come sooner than he would like—his grandchildren. Their future, he determined, could not be contained within the old ways. Like the coming of the horse, the arrival of the white culture would make things vastly different for the Crow people, as well as every other Indian nation. The trick, as Thane saw it, was to plan ahead.

He approached Morning Swan late one morning while she was scraping the hide of a freshly killed buffalo cow.

"We'll grow tobacco to trade," Thane said. "I grew up doing that. We'll establish our own business among the Kicked-in-Their-Bellies and take the hides cross-country to St. Louis each year. All the Indians in this area will want tobacco, big tobacco like I can grow."

"What are you talking about?" Morning Swan asked. "Why do you speak of doing a trade when you have for so long talked against taking the beaver?"

"The beaver trade is virtually over," Thane said. "Now they want buffalo more than anything. The Indian people out here are going to trade them with somebody and it might as well be us. We could have a tremendous business."

"My people are not interested in what you call

'business,' " Morning Swan reminded him. "They will never take an interest in something like that."

"It is time they *do* take an interest in something like that," Thane argued. "This country will someday come under control of the whites and it will be better to already have established some power that they can understand, some monetary power. I can open an account in St. Louis in the name of our band and—"

"You are talking crazy," Morning Swan broke in. "Aren't you listening to me? My people do not want to live that way. *I* do not want to live that way. And I thought you left your white ideas back in the eastern lands where you came from."

"Yes, but those ideas are coming out here now," Thane pointed out. "They're coming far faster than we realize. You've already seen the preachers and ministers coming out to bring the white man's religion. That ought to tell you something. Take it from me. When you see churches sprouting up, that's the groundwork for everything else."

Morning Swan could see that Thane was speaking with sense. Yet she could not accept it, and no matter what he said to her she would resist his logic. She knew that all the tribes, including the Crows, were beginning to think that the white religion was superior to their own. After all, didn't the Long Knives have powerful medicine: better weapons and better clothes and more food of various kinds? Weren't those with the white skin better able to withstand the powers of storms and make fire inside boats that traveled the rivers? All of this seemed true, as many of the Long Knives often laughed when her people hid from lightning and thunder.

"No matter what comes to these lands," Morning Swan told Thane, "the old ways will always be the best. The old ways are the most reverent. The more a person knows about the powers that be, the more power that person thinks he has. It is not good and it will lead to destruction. I do not want any of it."

"We can't stop it," Thane said.

"Maybe not, but we don't have to be a part of it. Nobody is going to tell me I have to become part of this new culture. And I don't want my children to have anything to do with it either."

"They're not just *your* children," Thane said.

"They are my children!" Morning Swan snapped. "You should know that by now. They were born into my mother's clan, which is my clan, and to that clan they belong. You are only the father."

"Doesn't my being their father mean anything? Am I not to take an interest in their future?"

"Their future must be one of strength and character," Morning Swan said. "I do not want them going crazy on medicine water and living for the sake of the white man's money. That is crazy."

Thane realized he was not going to have Morning Swan's approval to go ahead with what he knew would be beneficial in the years to come. No matter what she thought, he felt in his own mind that the white ways would someday prevail, and since he already knew the white ways, he could provide for his grandchildren at least. He pondered the idea of beginning a tobacco plantation of sorts up along the Yellowstone. There was no question that tobacco would be a good trade item. It was worth pursuing.

The camp at Lodge Grass was moved before very long, as Wolves scouting out from the village reported the movements of a large number of Lacotah out from the Black Hills. Oglala and possibly other divisions of the Sioux, Thane realized, on their way down into the North Platte River country to establish trade with Sublette and Campbell. News might have already reached them about the raid for horses led by Takes-a-Bow. They would want to avenge the loss of their fallen brother and the odds would be greatly in favor of the Sioux.

Thane saw that he and Morning Swan could fight

until the moon turned blue for the cause of conserving the mountain resources, but no one was going to listen to them. Trading posts were back in vogue. Whiskey was a luring commodity, and in time the Indians were going to do the job of killing buffalo and other animals off themselves just to have furs to trade for whiskey.

Thane's thoughts went back to early that spring, when Sublette and Campbell had come to visit the Crow camp on the upper North Platte in hopes of establishing trade. Sublette had been right in saying his new post was going to be an important one. The fort was already gaining notoriety. Some trappers who had come through the Crow village just a few days past had stopped to talk with Thane and told him they already knew of the post they were all calling Fort Laramie. The American Fur Company knew about Fort Laramie also, and Thane knew it would only be a short time before the Company either owned the post or the post no longer existed.

More than anything else, the gripping bite of the Company's operations in the mountains angered Thane. It made him think of William Chapman and how he had murdered his father in order to gain control of the plantation, so that he could have enough wealth to buy out surrounding plantations. Total control; a monopoly if at all possible. Now it was happening within the mountain fur trade. The larger the American Fur Company became, the more strength it exhibited. Already Fort Union at the mouth of the Yellowstone was a stronghold and a major stumbling block for any competition trying to go up or down the river. In addition, other posts were being established up and down the major drainages to secure the trade in all areas.

It was at the mouth of the Bighorn River that the Kicked-in-Their-Bellies decided to make temporary camp. Smoke twisted into the sky from behind the pickets of a fort, above which flew the U.S. flag and the flag of the American Fur Company. Around this

fort were pitched a number of Crow lodges, ill kept
and ratty in appearance. Women wandered about
from lodge to lodge, seemingly not doing much of
anything, while a number of men were lying in the
shade of nearby trees and against the outside walls of
the fort.

Antoine Lavelle was among those camped along the
river near the fort. He looked haggard and worn in a
buckskin shirt and a worn and dirty cotton shirt. He
had been living with another *berdache* in another
band's village for some time. They had lived in
relative happiness, as none of the other villagers had
bothered them. But during the night of the medicine
water, Antoine's friend had nearly been killed by an
angry Crow warrior. Now Antoine was trying to nurse
him back from a severe knife wound to the stomach.

Eli, as usual, wanted nothing to do with Antoine.
During that first year in the mountains, the old
trapper had teased Thane about him. But now he
found no amusement at all in Antoine. Thane and
Morning Swan talked with Antoine for a time and
decided the Crows were now beginning to suffer as
greatly as all the other tribes.

"My friend did nothing to harm anybody," Antoine
explained about the stabbing incident. "He was not
even among those who were drinking with the Long
Knives. The warrior who hurt him just did not like
him and decided in drunken anger to stab him. That
sort of thing went on all over the village."

"Why are you camped here?" Thane asked. "Why
are any of you camped here? That's a bad sign, you
know."

Antoine nodded and shrugged. "You can see the
hangover sickness and unhappiness all around here.
But many of them continue to drink and trade, when
they can barely walk over to the fort. My friend is too
badly injured to move, so I'm just staying with him
until he dies."

Morning Swan told Thane she wished they would

leave right away, before something bad happened. Already warriors from the Kicked-in-Their-Bellies were expressing an interest in trading inside the fort. Thane and other members of the council met and decided to find out what was happening at the fort and to try then to get their people to move camp with them.

Thane found a man named Matson in charge of the fort. "He just come out from under a rock," Eli said to Thane under his breath. The usual head man was a trader named Samuel Tullock, whom the Crows called the Crane—because of his long neck. Matson said Tullock was on a trip downriver to Fort Union and wouldn't be back for a few days. Matson was a small man with ratty black hair and shifty eyes and only half a nose, one nostril being only a scar where a knife had likely carved through.

There were other Company men standing around watching, one a huge Frenchman with a shaved head and a large ring in his nose. He watched Thane closely, looking him up and down. Matson kept eyeing Thane with an odd smirk on his face, and it made Thane wonder if they had been somehow waiting for the Kicked-in-Their-Bellies to eventually show up, since they were one of the last bands to come to any fort to trade. Thane knew very well what was being planned and he called Matson aside right away.

"Whatever you've got here," Thane said, "we don't want any of it."

"Maybe you don't," Matson said, "but what about the others?"

"Did you hear what I told you?" Thane said.

"You're a big man," Matson said, "but I know you can't speak for the rest."

The employees at the fort were handing out presents to the Crows, little twists of tobacco for the men and various cuts of bright cloth and pouches of beads and tiny mirrors for the women. Everyone was eager to get a gift of some sort. While the employees

scattered around among the Crow people, the big
Frenchman remained nearby and continued to watch
Thane, his nose twitching and the ring in it moving up
and down.

"I've heard stories," Matson went on. His eyes were
squinting at Thane while he spoke and his cut nose
slanted with his frown. "They say you're wilder than
any Injun ever born for sure. They say you chase men
out of streams and throw their traps into deep water."

"Nobody traps right," Thane said. "Too greedy.
Nobody wants to save some beaver for new stock.
Streams without beaver become washout gullies."

Matson shrugged. "Well, I don't know about that,
but we here at Fort Cass are mainly interested in
buffalo."

"Don't tell me that," Thane said. "No matter how
poor the price, as long as there's beaver and money to
be paid for them, you'll take them from this country."

Matson looked over at the big Frenchman and then
back to Thane. He felt uneasy standing so close to this
man whom everybody feared. Thane Thompson had
his light sandy hair roached in front in Crow fashion
and trailing loosely behind. His eyes showed no
measure of fear whatsoever, and he had looked at the
Frenchman just once and no more. He was as
dangerous-looking as the stories had conveyed, with
huge bulging arms and a face that bore black paint
marks on each cheek, marks that resembled the claws
of a bear.

Matson swallowed and tried to ease closer to the big
Frenchman.

"Well, mainly we want buffalo hides," Matson said.
"Surely you ain't worried about them bein' wiped
out."

"There was nigh as many beaver at one time," Eli
said, speaking up. "Don't see many now."

Matson had managed to move closer to the big
Frenchman. He grunted and his little smirk of a smile
returned. "Buffalo don't live in streams."

"No," said Thane, "but rifles and arrows work faster than traps."

Morning Swan had come from the village to see what was taking so long. She was in a hurry to get going again. She came up to Thane and her eyes were narrowed at what was going on around her. Jethro was with her and he was watching everything with interest.

"I told you to stay back with the other boys," Thane told him. "Now go ahead and get back to the camp. Stay with Takes-a-Bow and Rosebud. We'll be over there in just a short time."

The big Frenchman eyed Jethro. His nose jumped and the ring in it pushed out. He moved slowly toward where Jethro stood. Eli saw him and stepped between him and Jethro. Thane noticed the move himself and worked to control his anger. Thane then told Jethro forcefully to go back to the others outside the fort.

After Jethro left, Matson eyed Thane nervously. Thane was glaring at the big Frenchman. The Crows now were wandering around the fort while employees continued to show them the things they could get for buffalo robes they brought in. There were various types of flintlock rifles, the percussion kind that made firing faster and easier but, Thane knew, not necessarily more predictable. Among other commodities were various kinds of blankets and capotes for winter wear, as well as the usual tools and beads and cookwear for women.

"Thompson," Matson said suddenly, hoping to distract him, "do you remember Wild Jack Cutter?"

Thane turned to face Matson. "What about him?"

"You just missed him. He went with Tullock to Fort Union. He's got a Blood for a wife and he's a good Company man. He's told me about you."

"That's good," Thane said. "If he were here now, I'd cut off his head and stick it up on your flagpole, along with this Frenchman's here. We'll hang his head up sideways, by that ring he's got in his nose."

The big Frenchman eyed Thane, but showed no interest. His nose continued to twitch with the ring moving in it.

"I want to go now," Morning Swan said. "I wish we could get everybody to go now."

It was then that some of the *engagés* came over and talked to Matson. He nodded and soon they appeared with tin cups and jugs of whiskey.

Thane glared at Matson. "You'd better have them put that away," he said. "And right now."

The *engagés* stopped pouring and looked at Matson, who looked at the huge Frenchman. They finally ignored Thane and began to pour.

Thane jumped among them and threw two of them to the ground, spilling the whiskey, before turning to meet the big Frenchman. The Frenchman was predictable, coming head-on with his fists flying. Thane took a glancing blow off the shoulder and slammed a heavy fist into the side of the Frenchman's ear. The Frenchman straightened up and shook his head while Thane leveled another blow flush into his nose and mouth, driving the ring through his upper lip. The big Frenchman yelled and fell backward against the wall.

Matson watched Thane work on the big Frenchman, but did not move. Morning Swan had her eyes on him and her right hand on a knife at her side. Matson's face turned white as Morning Swan ordered him back from the fight.

The big Frenchman was sliding slowly down the fort wall, his lip sliced into pieces by the ring. Two *engagés* were being held at bay by Eli's rifle, but two others came at Thane from another direction.

"No need to worry," Eli told Morning Swan. "Thane'll blow out their lights easy."

The two *engagés* jumped Thane. One tried to hold him from behind but Thane easily pulled him off and slammed him into the other *engagé* who'd come forward. The two men tumbled over one another, then got up and ran away.

Matson continued to stand and watch, his eyes glaring hate.

"Now you fight him," Morning Swan said to Matson, pointing toward Thane. "Go ahead."

Matson shuddered and shook his head no as Thane approached him. Matson continued to back away as Thane told him he had better change his trade practices or have his fort burned to the ground.

"Thane!" Morning Swan yelled suddenly.

Thane turned and moved just in time to avoid an ax that was swung by the huge Frenchman. Instead of slicing Thane's back, the blade sunk itself into Matson's face, splitting his head like a block of wood.

Thane had been angry before, but now he became enraged. He turned on the Frenchman and began to beat him unmercifully. After repeated blows to the face and body, Thane turned him sideways and drove him head-first into the fort wall twice. The Frenchman, face scraped raw and the ring now torn from his nose completely, flopped unconscious into the dirt.

"We'd just as well finish it all now," Thane then said. "I don't care for this bunch at all."

"Best let it go from here and leave," Eli warned. He was shaking his head. "It'll get us in trouble out here if you go to burnin' their fort."

"Look what's happened." Thane was pointing to where some of the Crows who had been there before were breaking into the whiskey supplies. A good number of Crow men were now drinking and passing jugs around. Other *engagés* at the fort were either standing back away from Thane, or had already run away. But by now many of the Crow men were already drunk. They gathered around, clapping Thane on the back, laughing at Matson's split head and rolled-up eyeballs.

Some Crows who were not drinking worked with Thane and Morning Swan trying to persuade the others to stop and get ready to leave. Fights broke out. There was heated disagreement now between those who wanted to leave and those who were not yet ready. After lengthy arguing it was decided that whoever wished to stay could remain behind and travel on later to the new campgrounds on Rotten-Sun-Dance-Lodge-Creek. Those who were ready to leave would go now and set up camp.

Morning Swan became greatly unsettled. She found Little Bird and He-Runs-among-Them in a hot dispute. He-Runs-among-Them was determined to stay and he told Little Bird she would do the same. He-Runs-among-Them was getting his first taste of the medicine water and he was enjoying himself.

Rosebud joined Morning Swan and the two tried to comfort Little Bird. It was difficult, for Little Bird was angry and saddened at the same time. It was impossible for her to understand how the medicine water could have made He-Runs-among-Them such a different person. She had never seen anything like it and it frightened her. This medicine water altered minds and thinking permanently. She was now afraid He-Runs-among-Them would never go back to being what he once was.

"It has finally happened," Morning Swan said to Thane sadly as they prepared to leave. "Our band has finally become ruined by the medicine water as well. Things will never be the same."

"My heart is very heavy," Rosebud added. "Little Bird is so happy for Takes-a-Bow and me, but she is now unhappy for herself."

"They'll catch up before long," Thane said, hoping to cheer them both up. "They'll grow bored with just nesting here in front of this fort with nothing to do. Soon they'll be trying to catch up with us, and maybe they'll bring these others along with them."

"I'm worried that if we don't all stay together, something bad will happen," Morning Swan said. "It always does."

Thane frowned. Morning Swan always thought of the practical things. There was no doubt they would be in danger if they waited very long to break camp and move up from the fort to join the main village. This was the time of year when war parties left for major raids. What was even more disturbing was the thought that they might never move up, but remain around the fort as had others. It did seem, as Morning Swan had noted, that times for the Crow people were going to become bad.

The journey up the Yellowstone to the camping site was a quiet one for all the people. At various stages along the way, others would turn back to join their relatives who had stayed behind at the fort. Some hoped to persuade them to move, while others grew indifferent and seemed not to care what happened from here on.

Morning Swan worried continuously about Little Bird. She knew things with He-Runs-among-Them would be very difficult now. Takes-a-Bow and Rosebud thought about joining some of the others as they left to go back to the fort, but Thane and Morning Swan persuaded them not to. Jethro added, "You've got to help me with this raven, Takes-a-Bow. He's more than I can handle."

Though the early summer sunshine was warm and the wildflowers fragrant, there was not the usual gaiety and joking as camp was made on Rotton-Sun-Dance-Lodge-Creek. A good number of the Kicked-in-Their-Bellies were now behind at the fort and no one knew when they might be coming to join the village. In fact, there was no certainty that they would. Some of them would likely become like those they had first seen camped outside the fort: lost and forlorn, dependent on the whiskey from the fort traders and reduced to a wretched life.

Morning Swan and Rosebud discussed Little Bird constantly. They wondered if she and He-Runs-among-Them would finally agree to leave the fort and come up to the village. Similar discussions were taking place all over camp. Life among the Kicked-in-

Their-Bellies had been changed forever. Families had
been broken apart and war brothers had spoken harsh
words to one another. Fathers had left their families
so they might remain behind to drink and sons had
paid no attention to the words of their fathers and
mothers, so that they might call themselves independent and frolic under the influence of the medicine
water.

Takes-a-Bow and Rosebud were now worried about
their wedding ceremony. It would seem strange to
have Little Bird missing. They wished it were a
happier time; but in any event, they wanted to
announce their union to the village. Morning Swan
and Thane met with Takes-a-Bow's parents and exchanged gifts, and Takes-a-Bow gave Thane five more
horses he had traded for earlier. Despite the sullen
atmosphere of the camp, both families were happy
and the people offered their congratulations and best
wishes.

During the feast, everyone sat around a fire and
Takes-a-Bow told Thane that he would provide well
for Rosebud. He could no longer speak directly to
Morning Swan, but instead told Jethro to let his
mother know that he would kill a mountain sheep
with the next cold moon season so that she might have
a new dress.

"Forget about hunting," Jethro said quickly. "You
two had better have a baby. And it better be a boy. I
need someone to give this crazy raven to."

Everyone laughed for a time. It was the first such
expression of happiness that Jethro could remember
in a long while. Maybe it was a good sign. He was
hoping this bad cloud that kept blocking out the fun of
the village would soon dissipate and be lost. There
was certainly no future in continuing things the way
they presently were: before long everyone would have
collapsed from depression.

Jethro had spent some time thinking about what
was happening to the Crow people, and in his young

mind he could formulate more than the older people gave him credit for. He was always of the opinion that adults made life far too complicated and looked for problems, rather than just enjoying things as they came along. This matter with the medicine water seemed to be somewhat silly. He had at one time sneaked a taste himself and found it was hard on his stomach, and made him sick. In fact, he was of the certain opinion that if a person wished to make a habit of indulging in it, he or she would have to work up a resistance to getting sick from the stuff.

It seemed to Jethro that this medicine-water thing was mostly a matter of doing what everyone else was doing. The older warriors had no real use for it. They had experienced a lot of life already and there was nothing that could enhance things all that much. No matter how you felt when you drank, sooner or later you would be through drinking and things would go back to normal again. The chances seemed good too that you would do something that made you wish you hadn't felt the need to drink.

It was the younger warriors, those near Takes-a-Bow's age, that felt the need to be different. Jethro could relate to that. He felt the older people in the village were too stagnated in life and the way they lived it. There was no reason to be so similar in pattern and nature to one another; there was no reason not to be a little reckless once in a while. Drinking medicine water was the height of being reckless, though. Jethro was afraid that once you started, it changed your mind forever and made you crave it—like food and water.

As the days now passed, Rosebud remembered Jethro's remark about giving the raven to her son with a smile. She too hoped she would someday have a boy. But now the fate of her people concerned her. She knew the deep emotions her mother felt: the anger and grief that mixed and produced so many different feelings inside. There was little she could do, she realized, except continue to pray to the spirits that Takes-a-Bow would never drink the medicine water.

Takes-a-Bow watched Rosebud each day, thinking about what Jethro had said. A boy would make him very happy. He hoped by the time his son was born that things would again be good for the Kicked-in-Their-Bellies. He hoped the scourge of the medicine water would pass by that time and families would once again be back together, war brothers would again be close.

It was especially painful for Takes-a-Bow, since two of the young men who had been on that first raid against the Lacotah were now behind, drunk outside the gates of the fort. Takes-a-Bow had wanted to drag them away, but one had pulled a knife and so Takes-a-Bow had released him. It was not like any of his friends to do that and it made him realize what evil spirits were inside the medicine water.

As the afternoon of a midsummer day wore into evening, Morning Swan decided she would travel above the village to her favorite place, the meadow where the aspens grew.

By early evening she was there. But the area was far different now and she looked around in surprise. Where she had come for so long to speak to the trees was changed so that she hardly recognized it. The aspens would not answer. They could no longer talk to her. Morning Swan stood among them, above the creek at her favorite place, and looked at the branches. The buds were hard and dry and had never swollen to pop leaves with the coming of the warm moons. There were only scattered, sickly leaves among the aspens, and only those trees in the center of the grove showed any leaves at all. The smaller ones on the edge were bare, and when Morning Swan twisted their limbs, they snapped and broke free.

This favorite place, this grove of trees she had come to know and love as a child and frequent even as a grown woman, had become a graveyard.

Morning Swan was struck with remorse. For a time she walked among them, talking, telling them not to die but to try to hold on. Tears formed in her eyes as she walked among the oldest of the trees, with large trunks that had been refuge to her for so long. She could no longer hear the soft rustling of tender leaves and the calling of small birds as they gathered nesting materials. Now there was only the sound of wind through coarse branches, lifeless branches that would now wait for time to bring them to decay.

Filled with hurt and anger, Morning Swan made her way down the slope and to the bottom. It was as she had feared: the beaver were gone, their dams up and down the creek for as far as she could see washed out, the branches and wood cuttings mostly swept away with the rushing waters from melting spring snow. There were no more pools of clear, still water, brimming with the speckled fish that jumped and swam together in large groups. There were no more turtles that sunned themselves on rocks and old logs. The speckled whites and reds of delicate bog flowers were gone. Instead the banks of the creek had been eroded down and the rushing waters had ripped them apart and carried the soil far down the valley and into the river.

Now the bed of the stream was far below its original level and the scarred banks showed it was cutting even deeper. The water table in the gravels of the stream that had reached back under the banks to give life to the trees and shrubs and flowers along the valley floor had dropped far down and the plants that needed that water to live, including the grove of aspens, were dead or dying. In just a few winters more, Morning Swan realized, this little meadow once filled with sparkling pools and bright-colored flowers would be a totally dry and desolate place.

Morning Swan began to walk away from the scene. She wanted to turn back to look and see that it was all a terrible dream, that the beaver were still there, slapping their tails against the water and pushing mud and sticks together to catch the precious water that the land so badly needed. She wanted to see the fish jumping once more and the flowers waving softly in the morning breeze, and see the little birds flitting from branch to branch in her aspens.

But it was all gone and she dared not look back. Something inside of her was sick and part of her was on the ground back there below those aspens, where they had lost their lives. Part of her heart was there and she felt if she looked she would have to turn back, and perhaps she would remain there and die herself.

Morning Swan began to walk faster, tears blinding her. She started to cross the stream and as she went she tripped and fell and she looked to see a steel trap, rusted and muddy. Caught in the trap was a beaver's front leg, long ago chewed off, now only bone and decayed skin. Morning Swan lurched to her feet and screamed. She took the trap in both hands and began to slam it against a rock, yelling out her anger. She slammed and slammed and the bones broke into fragments and the dead skin scattered, but the steel remained intact. The rock chipped and the edges of the trap, the rust flying from it, bit into her hands.

Finally, she took the trap by its chain and flung it far out across the bottom, where it thumped into a stand of dead willows. Morning Swan sank to her knees and began to sob. Blood from her hands streaked her face and mixed with the flow of tears. In the stand of aspens up the hill, another delicate leaf slipped from a branch and settled into the dry grass.

The Small Robes band of the Piegan Blackfeet prepared to move their village. They would travel north and join with various bands of their brothers, the Bloods and the Northern Blackfeet, the Siksika. There would be a large number of the three divisions of Blackfeet people gathered together and there would be much talk of what to do about the many Long Knives

that were continuously coming into Blackfeet lands
and the Crow people who had allied with them.

Rising Hawk had prepared himself to remain behind and travel toward the great mountain in the
Backbone-of-the-World, the Going-to-the-Sun Mountain. It would be a hard and dangerous journey and
the chances were good he would die along the way, for
his ribs could easily be seen and his eyesight was very
bad. Many seasons of prayer to Sun and the spirits and
little sleep or food had made Rising Hawk a walking
skeleton.

It was Rising Hawk's desire to make it to the
summit of Going-to-the-Sun Mountain and pray from
there for his medicine to once again become good. He
was determined to do this, or die trying. A great deal
of time in his life had been spent mourning over the
loss of his medicine shield and there was no point in
continuing if it would do no good. It was not fair to his
family, his mother and father, who now paid him no
attention because he had asked them not to. He had
lost everything of value but one horse, and now there
was but one woman left in his life.

Yellow Tree loved him as much as she ever had, but
she'd become ever more confused over what was
happening to her husband. Her two sisters, both
younger, had gone to other warriors to bear sons and
be wives. They had told Rising Hawk they could no
longer live with him the way he was. Yellow Tree could
not understand herself what was happening: why was
Rising Hawk driving himself into the next life this
way? Since he was surely killing himself, wouldn't it
be far simpler and certainly more worthy of honor to
just ride into Crow lands and fight until he was killed?
The way he was treating himself now would kill him
in time as surely as a Crow arrow.

When she thought of the Crows, Yellow Tree
thought of the woman who had been captured as a
girl, Morning Swan, who had been raised among the
Piegans. This Morning Swan—though Yellow Tree

had never really known her—was someone you never forgot. Now she was a Crow again, this woman who many among the Piegans had thought was special.

Yellow Tree thought it was because of Morning Swan that a lot of this misery had started. Perhaps, thought Yellow Tree, this woman had been sent by the bad spirits to cause trouble among the Piegans. After all, Morning Swan rode a horse and used weapons like a warrior. And she had counted coup against the Blood people by killing warriors in a fight in which she had saved the life of the Long Knife, Bear-Man.

In her mind, Yellow Tree blamed Morning Swan for the whole situation. Had Morning Swan not been so independent and so very lovely, Rising Hawk would have taken no interest in his brother's wife nor desired her so badly when his brother had died. Rising Hawk would likely have attained an answer to his prayers long, long before now if it hadn't been for Morning Swan. If she had not tempted him with her beauty, he would not have acted as he had against his brother and wanted her for his own after his brother's death.

In a way, Yellow Tree wished Morning Swan had not run away from the village after Long Hand's death. Even though she would likely now be in the lodge with herself and Rising Hawk—and possibly even be his sits-beside-him-wife—at least Rising Hawk would be healthy now and not near death. Morning Swan would still be a Piegan and not a Crow once again, and would not have had the chance to save Bear-Man's life. That battle with the Blood warriors would have turned out differently and the Bloods would have brought back Rising Hawk's war shield.

Try as she might, Yellow Tree could not change the past. She could only hope for the best in the future. She longed to bear Rising Hawk a son. But he was usually too weak to engage in anything but sleep, and when he did enter her, his efforts were not good and she had not yet conceived. Perhaps, Yellow Tree thought, if I could have a son Rising Hawk would look at his life far differently and have something to live for.

Yellow Tree fought tears now as she worked to get their lodge taken down and prepared for the journey. She could not keep her eyes off the hills above the village, where Rising Hawk was riding toward the Backbone-of-the-World and his last days in this life. She had tried to talk him out of going up there, but she had received only harsh words from Rising Hawk and finally had spoken no more. His mind was as hazy as his eyes and he had growled whenever she'd tried to help him, even when he'd tripped and stumbled on open ground. He was going up there to die, no matter what she thought.

She had just finished packing belongings when she heard a voice calling to her from behind her. She turned to see an old warrior making his way toward her. Rain Maker was coming toward her and she didn't know whether to be glad or afraid. He was stooped and aged and considered one of the Special Ones among her people. His dreams were often visions of what was to come and for this reason he was a *shaman*, a medicine man.

"Yellow Tree," he said to her, "do not be afraid of me. Instead be happy."

"Do you know something about Rising Hawk?" Yellow Tree asked him.

Rain Maker nodded. "I must speak to him. Has he left yet?"

"He has. Is it too late to stop him."

"No, you must stop him. He is the only one who can help me."

Yellow Tree was startled. "Help *you*? I thought you might help Rising Hawk."

"It is possible we can help one another." The old warrior was staring out into the hills where Rising Hawk had disappeared. "But you must go and find him. I have spoken to one of Rising Hawk's uncles and he will give you a horse, a fast horse, though I doubt if

Rising Hawk is traveling very fast." Rain Maker then
handed Yellow Tree a flat rock with a face painted on
it, a blank face on which there were numerous black
paint marks. "Give this to Rising Hawk and tell him
Rain Maker must speak with him. He will feel the
power and believe you. I will await your return."

That afternoon, Yellow Tree caught up with Rising
Hawk and showed him the flat stone. Rising Hawk
brought it close to his face so that he could look at it.
He gasped and dropped the rock. A look of fear
appeared on his face.

"How did Rain Maker know of my dream?"

Yellow Tree was still very confused. "Rain Maker
did not speak of any dream. He only said to bring you
back so that you could help him. He gave me the rock
for you and said you would feel its power. All of this
makes me afraid."

Rising Hawk began to lose his fear, and for the first
time in many seasons Yellow Tree saw him smile
broadly. He gathered new strength and gave her a hug.
Yellow Tree felt tears rolling down her cheeks. She was
happy and she didn't know why. She only knew that
things would now be better for Rising Hawk and
herself.

"What is all this about a dream?" Yellow Tree
asked.

Rising Hawk shook his head. "That is something I
cannot speak of at this time. Once I have spoken with
Rain Maker, perhaps I can tell you what has been
happening to me. But now I am very happy and I feel
my medicine will again become good. And I want to
thank you for staying beside me all this time."

After hugging Yellow Tree, Rising Hawk lowered
himself and found the stone on the ground. He
squinted his eyes to study it more.

"I want my eyes to become better," he told Yellow
Tree. "When we reach Rain Maker I want to be able to
see his eyes when he tells me what is now to become of
me, and how I will once again regain my power."

Rising Hawk ate greedily from a pouch of pemmican that Yellow Tree gave him. He was ecstatic at learning about Rain Maker's desire to talk with him. Yellow Tree could feel the sudden change in her husband and it gave her renewed hope for his recovery and return to his old self. After the passing of so many seasons Rising Hawk now felt he would not have to die in order to regain his power.

That night they lay together in their robes and Rising Hawk showed so much strength in his love-making that Yellow Tree thought him completely recovered. Though he was incredibly thin and emaciated from his ordeal, he was mentally alive again and wanted to think he was physically back to normal. He wanted to be the man he once was in only a few short moments of time. Yellow Tree, now as happy as she had ever been since the day of her marriage to Rising Hawk, said prayers of thanks to the spirits and asked them to forgive her for her lapse of faith. Though she understood none of the reasons why all this was happening—the dreams of both Rain Maker and Rising Hawk, and Rain Maker's desire to see Rising Hawk—Yellow Tree nevertheless accepted this as a time of change for the good.

In three days they reached the Small Robes. The band was spread out over a good distance, traveling toward the east, where they would establish camp along the Big Muddy River. Rising Hawk was frustrated at not being able to see clearly, but felt confident his eyesight would improve over time. His worry now was mainly over time and how much of it would pass before he once again was in the good graces of the spirits and had regained his personal power. His dream, apparently seen also by Rain Maker, would be the key to his recovery.

Fifteen

RAIN MAKER WOULD NOT SPEAK WITH RISING HAWK UNTIL the village settled along the banks of the Big Muddy River, just upstream from a large Gros Ventre village. Nearby was a Blood village and also a Northern Blackfeet village. There would be other bands that would come before long. The valley of the Big Muddy River would soon be completely filled with the Blackfeet people and their allies, the Atsina—the Gros Ventres. All the people were coming here this early season of the warm moons for talk and the Sun Dance ceremony.

Rising Hawk felt good that his eyesight had improved, even if ever so little. Everything was still hazy and spots flowed before his vision, but the outlines of the trees and the horses and the lodges were becoming more distinct. He could walk better and he was eating more and more so that his body was growing stronger. Yellow Tree made love to him nightly and her touch made him glad he had found her to take for a wife.

Finally, when Rain Maker had spent time in the hills praying and felt he was ready, he sent for Rising Hawk. It was a sharp morning in which the last crisp touches of the passing cold moons lingered in the air. This huge valley bottom, flanked by rising bluffs and badlands, was alive with the barking of dogs and the laughter of children. Life on a day like this was at its best.

Rising Hawk, though somewhat anxious about this meeting with Rain Maker, could barely contain his exhilaration at seeing the last of his ordeal. He knew it was over. In his mind he was sure there was an end in sight and that he would once again have his powers. This made him want to shout for joy and declare his new feelings to the world.

Rising Hawk followed Rain Maker out of the village and into the gray hills beyond. The old man carried a rolled-up skin and a pipe with a large pouch of tobacco. Rising Hawk carried his own bag of personal articles and his small medicine bundle around his neck. He hoped it would contain new powers after this day.

Though Rain Maker was ancient, he walked briskly and Rising Hawk worked to keep up. He kept his eyes to the ground, now becoming slightly clearer with each day, and enjoyed the trip. Mumbling mostly to himself, Rain Maker stopped now and again to complain that his joints bothered him and that his women didn't want his man-part as often anymore. There was little wisdom, he concluded, in thinking that any of the younger women would want to see it for any reason. He wondered aloud what good a man-part was to an ancient if no one wanted to partake of it.

Above the village, the day broadened into clear blue. The noise of the village was muffled by a soft breeze that flowed along the steep hills and came to rest in the branches of scattered pines and junipers. Their odor was strong here and, mixed with the smell of sage and fresh grass, it made a blend of new life.

As they neared the summit of a rocky hill, Rain

Maker became very sullen. Rising Hawk knew he should not speak until Rain Maker asked him to. He took a seat beside Rain Maker and watched the old man build a fire of sage and ground juniper. When it was lit and dancing in the morning air, Rain Maker added sweetgrass to the flames, then said prayers and smoked the pipe before passing it to Rising Hawk.

They smoked for some time without speaking. Rising Hawk listened to the prayers and periodically squinted into the sky. He could hear the screech of his medicine helper, the red-tailed hawk, while the bird circled through the morning sky. This exhilarated him even more and he could hardly contain himself. There seemed little question in his mind that this day would be very special.

Finally, Rain Maker was ready to speak. He had finished smoking the pipe and set it down next to him. Though Rising Hawk could not see his eyes plainly, he could hear a distinct tone to his voice.

"Rising Hawk," Rain Maker said, "I am afraid."

Rising Hawk was taken aback. He did not expect Rain Maker to announce that *he* was afraid. At first Rising Hawk feared this meant his medicine would not return and that he would have to still go up onto Going-to-the-Sun Mountain to pray. Now Rising Hawk felt foolish. There had never been anything to suggest he would become strong once again. He was afraid he had taken it all for granted and that this was a cruel joke being played upon him by the spirits. He didn't know how to respond to Rain Maker.

"I know this confuses you," Rain Maker continued, "but you have to realize that I cannot understand what I have seen while sleeping for a number of nights. And I know you have seen the same things, for you were in my dreams and you spoke to me. You told me the medicine of a powerful Long Knife had entered your body and for this reason you would not die. I do not know of any such medicine and I want to know from you if your dream told you of this medicine."

"My dream was only images and I could not determine what they meant," Rising Hawk said. "I did not know if it meant I was supposed to die or live. That is why I decided to go to Going-to-the-Sun Mountain."

"It is good that I told Yellow Tree to find you," Rain Maker said. "It is good that she caught up with you."

Rising Hawk nodded. He pulled from his bag of personal articles the flat stone with the odd paint markings on it.

"I hoped that all this meant my ordeal was over," Rising Hawk said. "I was sure that my medicine would return and I would be forgiven for losing my medicine shield. Now I feel like a fool."

"Do not lose heart, Rising Hawk. It is certain that your medicine will someday return, but only after you have faced a far greater ordeal that you have already lived through. That I am certain of."

"I do not understand," Rising Hawk said. "If I fasted any longer, I would die."

"No, you are not to fast for this ordeal. You must eat and make yourself strong, far stronger than you ever have before. You will face an enemy like none other you have ever seen before. He is human and he is a Long Knife. Surely you know that from your dream."

"I saw a Long Knife in my dream," Rising Hawk acknowledged. "I saw him, but not clearly. It was as if he and I were the only ones alive among many hundreds, even more, as their bodies were scattered over a great distance. This Long Knife was hazy in my dream and I could not make out his face. I could only see that he was very powerful. But I am sure he is the one the Crows call Bear-Man, the one who stole my medicine shield."

Rain Maker nodded. "He is the one. But there was

something in my dream that I could not understand, and you see it there on that rock I gave to Yellow Tree."

"The spots are what made me understand you knew of my dream," Rising Hawk said. "I saw this rock and these spots in my dream. Did you also?"

"I saw that rock with those spots," Rain Maker said. "That and many other things."

Rain Maker unrolled the skin he had carried up to reveal a large drawing of his dream. There were images of men traced in charcoal and colored with paint. The drawing illustrated many bodies falling upside down from the sky, all covered with unusual spots. In the middle of the falling bodies stood the figure of Rising Hawk with his shield in one hand and the other arm extended out. Blood flowed from a wound on his wrist. Another figure stood beside him. This was the figure of a Long Knife, who also had a medicine shield. Upon the shield was painted the form of a huge bear with large teeth and claws. The grizzly, the white bear. This man's other arm was extended toward Rising Hawk and his wrist was also bleeding. Neither Rising Hawk nor the Long Knife was spotted like the others.

"At first I thought the spots were holes where the little round balls from the thundersticks of the Long Knives had entered," Rain Maker said, "but now I am not sure. I thought the Long Knives had come in huge numbers and had killed us all with their thundersticks. I do not think now that the spots were from thundersticks."

"What are the spots then?" Rising Hawk wanted to know.

"Something bad," Rain Maker said. "Very bad. You must eat and regain your strength. As you now realize, you will be a part of it and you will not see the spots."

Rising Hawk knew this was all he would hear from Rain Maker on the matter for now. The old medicine man, for whatever reasons, chose not to share the secret of the spots with him. Rising Hawk knew better than to insist on an interpretation of the drawing, but instead had to be content with following the ancient's directions, whenever they came.

"I am poor and cannot pay you now for your help," Rising Hawk told Rain Maker. "It will not always be this way. I will pay you in time."

Rain Maker nodded. He relit the pipe. "I am in no hurry for payment at this time. That can come later. For now you must remain humble and regain your physical and emotional strength. You are a chosen one."

For a time after Toots's death at the 1833 rendezvous, Wild Jack Cutter had found himself lost. Fight it as he might, he had missed Toots in an odd way and somehow craved the half-wit's dependency on him. The sexual gratification didn't effect him all that much, for it was Toots who had taken the perverse pleasure in seeing someone's guts roll out on the ground. Cutter had merely benefited in a take-pleasure-in-whatever-measure-you-can sort of way from Toots's crazy lust afterwards.

But there was something about Toots Cutter had missed for a long time afterward and he wasn't sure if he would ever figure it out. Though Cutter didn't like to think of himself as an oddball, he had to admit that what Toots had given him while alive he would likely not get from anyone else. The little ratty man had been more trouble than he had ever been anything else, always goading people into fights by blasting his horn, then turning to Cutter for safety. Maybe it was that segment of the relationship he missed more than anything: coming to Toots's aid and seeing the cold fear that would then show itself in those men's eyes, that sheer terror that they could not stop a crazed animal like himself if brought to the test.

There was only one man who was not intimidated by him, who was perhaps crazier in a way than he was.

Thane Thompson, the one the Indians called Bear-Man. Young and strong and with a nice smile, but underneath ready to tear the heart out of a man who did him wrong. Cutter finally knew that night of the rendezvous what it felt like to know fear, to think your life would soon be gone. Cutter realized he was lucky Thane Thompson hadn't killed him. That would have happened if that Crow hadn't stepped in and paid with his own life as a result.

There wasn't a day went by that Cutter didn't think of Thane Thompson and plot the means by which he would surprise him and kill him. It would have to be surprise, total surprise, for Cutter knew if Thane Thompson ever found him again, that would be the end. Cutter realized, in fact, that he was lucky to be alive even now. The knife wound inflicted by Thompson had taken slivers from his ribs and infection had grown in the wound almost immediately. After he had escaped that night, he had found himself alone and weakening with each day. He might have finally died had he not showed his collection of scalps to a war party of Bloods and told them he wanted the heart of Bear-Man.

Now he had the best of both worlds in his quest to get Thane Thompson. He was an agent for the American Fur Company, which had established inroads in trade with the Blackfeet nation, and now used this position to incite more and more hatred against Thompson and the Crows. He boasted continuously about killing Crows and other Long Knives who disliked the Blackfeet people and who did not trade with the Blackfeet and their allies, the Atsina, whom the Long Knives called Gros Ventres. The Blackfeet had come to know him as Broken Mouth—for the scars and the row of missing teeth—and were pleased to know how badly he wanted to kill Bear-Man.

And Cutter had taken himself a woman, a Blood woman who was used to beatings. She was a three-

time widow without children, a castoff to be avoided.
He couldn't even remember her name; he just called
her "Woman" and made her tend to all his needs
whenever he demanded. If her pace was not sufficient
to suit him, he used a length of willow cane on her. It
was a special sort of weapon that he was proud of, cut
from the lower growth, thick yet limber, to produce
good stinging power. He kept it tied to his side, as a
commander would his sword, and had worn off the
bark at one end from using it so much on the woman.

Heavy Breast Woman saw each day as another
nightmare for her, filled with lashings and terrible
pain. She could not remember the last time she knew
happiness. Her parents and most of those in her clan
had died from a coughing sickness they had brought
back from trading in the Saskatchewan. She had been
a small child and had been left home with friends,
who'd then raised her. She had grown to be heavy as a
young woman and didn't marry until much later than
other girls, and for very little value. After three
husbands, all killed in battle, no one had wanted her
and she might have died if this man, Broken Mouth,
had not called her to him.

At first Heavy Breast Woman had been happy to
have a man. There was no one who really cared about
her and she felt lucky her people hadn't banished her
from the band. After so many husbands who had died
in war, she had gotten a reputation as bad medicine.
With the coming of this big Long Knife, she had
hoped her status would change. She'd made herself
believe that the odd color in his eyes was nothing to be
afraid of and had told herself she would now have a
man to please and someone to bring meat for the
lodge.

Heavy Breast Woman had learned very quickly that
Cutter, the evil man called Broken Mouth, took a
great deal of pleasure in inflicting pain. His odd eyes
would sparkle and his crotch would get big whenever

he held his willow switch. He would lash her repeatedly and smile. Then, when he was finished, he would
force her to satisfy him with her mouth.

It made her sick, but she could do nothing, and she
knew if she didn't perform he would kill her. Never
had she known anyone so cruel, so terribly cold and
heartless. If only she had someone to run away
to—even one brother or an uncle—she would go. But
she had no one and she feared if she ran away and
Broken Mouth caught up to her, he would kill her by
slicing her entrails out of her body. Her condition now
was worse than if she had been banished and left to
starve. Now, Heavy Breast Woman thought each day,
she wished that had happened.

She now found herself riding with him and a
number of Blood warriors toward the fort called Cass.
They had been at the big fort, Union, and were on
their way back upriver. The head of the fort called
Cass, a Long Knife with a long neck named Tullock—
called the Crane—had journeyed with them but remained apart, ignoring Cutter and the Bloods.

Broken Mouth was acting like a strong warrior and
she didn't want him to get wild and start to whip her
later. Broken Mouth was getting to be big medicine
among her people and she couldn't understand why.
He wasn't particularly brave; he would much rather
backshoot a man, or slice him with a knife when he
was helpless or not looking. Heavy Breast Woman
didn't know why her people had come to like this man
at all, unless it was because he hated the Crows and
the one white warrior they called Bear-Man.

Since this was Crow country, a large number of
Bloods were traveling in the party. There were few
women and children, most of them remaining up in
the village along the Big Muddy River. Some warriors
had brought their younger wives and a few of the
women, like Heavy Breast Woman, were older. There
were Wolves out in every direction to scout ahead for
signs of enemies. There could be Lacotah or Cheyenne

as well as Crow in this area, now that the big Fort
Union was so popular. Mostly there were Assiniboins
and Crees and Dirt Lodge People who traded at the
large post, but all the Indian nations had gotten into
the spirit of trading now.

Besides coming down to trade, the Bloods wanted
to steal horses if they got the opportunity. Crow
horses if at all possible. They were sure the Crows
were in this country and it was the Crows they wanted
to kill if they could. For as long as anyone could
remember there had been war between their peoples,
and there always would be. Past atrocities against one
another had caused the songs of mourning to never
cease and the fires of vengeance to burn at all times.

This pleased Cutter, and as he rode at the head of
the party with a warrior named Many Robes, he
realized his life had taken a dramatic turn for the
good: he could exercise his will to kill and do whatever
else he pleased, and have the support and security of
the entire Blackfeet nation behind him. He never
missed an opportunity to discuss Thane Thompson
and to point out how many Blackfeet warriors he had
killed. This white Crow, Bear-Man, was a deadly
enemy and Cutter felt he would some day see the
fruits of his dream to take the head of Thane Thompson.

Cutter was hoping to get the support of the American Fur Company as well, but his meeting with
Tullock and the small ruler of Fort Union, Kenneth
McKenzie, had not gone as well as he would have
liked. Cutter had hoped to be given a position at a
soon-to-be established post high on the upper Missouri, similar to Tullock's position at Fort Cass, if and
when the Company opened that post. Tullock had
spoke in Cutter's behalf and Cutter himself had talked
about what a good leader he was.

But McKenzie had not been so easy to convince.
When Cutter was finally finished, he had asked the
details of the incident at the rendezvous back in '33,

when he had sliced open the stomach of a Crow warrior who was helping Thane Thompson during their fight. McKenzie had stressed that he wanted the trade of the Crows as well as the Bloods and other Blackfeet, and he didn't want warfare if there was any way to avoid it. Profits were built on trade, lots of it, and when Indians were busy killing one another off, that left less time for hunting and trapping.

Cutter was aware that Tullock had paid him little mind during the trip, but Cutter didn't despair. Instead, he built up bitterness within himself. Tullock could plot against him if he wanted, it didn't matter. Cutter knew the Bloods cared about him and he was going to strengthen his position with them. This McKenzie at Fort Union figured he had a lot of power, and that he could have Tullock do what he wanted. McKenzie was powerful, but he couldn't rule over everybody. Especially somebody like himself, who got things his own way eventually, one way or another.

At length they were in the vicinity of Fort Cass and Cutter's thoughts were interrupted by the arrival of the Blood Scouts, who reined up and pointed toward the fort.

"Crow lodges, just outside the fort," one of them told Cutter and Many Robes. "It will be a day of victory for us. We will take many horses and many Crow dogs will die."

"Are there no Wolves of their own watching the camp?" Many Robes asked.

"We did not see any. Let us kill our enemies."

"Wait," Tullock said. "They have come to trade. They are not there to fight."

Cutter laughed at Tullock. "The Bloods will kill Crows first, then trade. That's how it will be."

The Bloods painted themselves for war and advanced upon the Crow camp outside the fort. It was as the Wolves had reported—even better. The Crows were certainly not prepared to fight and it would be a day of easy victory.

Antoine Lavelle was on a hill saying prayers to his spirit helper when he saw the Bloods approaching. He began to run from the hills toward the fort, crying out in anger at having gone so far out to pray, and on foot. After running to near exhaustion, Antoine realized he would not be able to warn them. Even at this distance he could hear the Blood war cries and the screams from the Crow people. He began to sing mourning songs for the *berdache* who was his friend and companion, and all the other Crows, who would now lose their lives. When he had finished his singing, he calmly walked to the edge of a huge sandstone cliff that overlooked the river below, and without further ceremony, jumped over and onto the rocks below.

When she saw them coming, Little Bird could only yell in horror. Ever since Bear-Man and Morning Swan had left with the Kicked-in-Their-Bellies, Little Bird had shared her days between fear and intense anger. She had tried to tell He-Runs-among-Them that they shouldn't stay many times, but he would not listen. All he ever wanted now was the medicine water. There was always medicine water for the men and they had given up nearly all their possessions, besides their furs and robes, to get it and drink it. They got sicker and sicker each day, but continued to trade for it. This was not a good place to remain, Little Bird had known all along, with so little strength. They should have left here long ago.

Little Bird was attending to He-Runs-among-Them, trying to get broth into him so that he might regain his strength and get over being sick from the medicine water. There were many like him, younger warriors as well as older, who were in pitiful shape from the after-effects of their drinking. They were lying around in agony and when the Bloods rode down the hill, screaming war cries, there was no chance for anyone.

The camp dogs erupted in a loud round of barking and growling, but scattered like birds when the Blood horsemen bore into the village. Some of the younger warriors who were not as sick scrambled for their weapons. Some got to them and others were cut down as the Bloods ran their ponies through the camp and used clubs and battle axes and lances against everyone not armed. The war cries of the Bloods mixed with the screaming of women and children and the din became a high, steady blast that pierced Little Bird's ears like the blade of a knife.

Dust billowed up like heavy fog and through the haze Little Bird saw her people falling beneath the Blood horses and their scalps being ripped from their heads. Some of the smallest children were scooped up and carried away while those older, along with their mothers, were killed on the spot. It was as if the Bloods were raining from the skies, there were so many of them. Soon the wailing and confusion enveloped all the Crows so that they ran about in a frenzy.

The younger warriors who had gotten to their weapons managed to kill some of the Bloods with arrows and shots from the thundersticks, but soon Blood arrows and return fire from their own guns brought the Crow men down. Lodges went down and fires began to burn everywhere, adding to the dust and haze. Little Bird, who was singing her death song, tried to get He-Runs-among-Them to get to his feet and run toward the fort with her, where many of the others were now headed.

But He-Runs-among-Them was too sick and he was on his hands and knees vomiting, nearly oblivious to what was going on. A young Crow warrior ran past them, dropping his knife, and fell just a ways past, an arrow through his neck. Little Bird picked up the knife and held it tightly while she screamed at He-Runs-among-Them to get up. She tried to move him, but he kept falling down and could only get back to his hands and knees. Then through the haze of dust came a man on a horse who upon seeing He-Runs-among-Them helpless jumped down from his horse.

Little Bird jumped in front of him and saw that he

was a Long Knife. His eyes were strange and wild and his mouth was open in a yell, showing no teeth along one side. He pushed her aside and drove a large knife into He-Runs-among-Them's back, just below the base of the neck. He-Runs-among-Them jerked and tried to cry out, but was too weak.

Little Bird screamed. She took the knife and lurched for the big Long Knife, who was cutting at He-Runs-among-Them's scalp. With all her might she drove the knife at him. But he turned and caught her arm and laughed.

She felt his blade enter her stomach and rip across, like a stroke of fire. He pushed her back away from him and she doubled over and vomited. Food and blood together splattered on the ground before her and she saw herself coming closer to the mess she had made in the dirt as her knees buckled. She vaguely heard herself singing her death song as everything around her seemed to grow hazy and dark. She put the horrible pain out of her mind, kneeling there, and made herself glad.

She was going to the next life where all would be happy and there would be nothing like this to live through. No one would have to fight and there would be plenty of food and no cold moons. She saw herself joining Bear-Walks-at-Night and He-Runs-among-Them, and all her other friends and relatives who were dying this day. She would join those who had gone before her, whom she had never met. They would be glad to meet her and there would be a feast. She smiled. Then it was black for Little Bird and her body pitched forward.

Cutter, waving a number of scalps, headed his horse toward the fort. The *engagés* in the fort, who had watched the attack begin, scrambled to let Tullock inside and get the gates closed as terrorized Crows trampled one another in an effort to escape the Bloods. They climbed the walls and crashed the gates as Blood warriors tried to cut off their escape. Cutter tried to yell to Tullock to order the *engagés* to get out of the way and not shoot either at the Bloods or the Crows. Finally, when Cutter made sign language that the Bloods were ready to kill everyone, even the traders in the fort, Tullock and his men drew back from the gates.

The fighting continued inside the fort and the shrill chorus was deafening. Tullock and the *engagés* pressed themselves against the walls and locked themselves inside buildings while Crows and Bloods alike ripped one another apart before their very eyes, ignoring them completely. The Bloods were far superior in numbers and weapons and readiness, and as Tullock and his men watched helplessly, pieces of Crow bodies became strewn about the fort grounds like deadfall timber.

Tullock looked on and watched Cutter fighting Crows with the Bloods. This was not good for trade and now the Company would have a bad name among the Crows. Cutter didn't think of anything but killing and he was going to cost the Company a lot of profits. All the work the Company had done in the past to make inroads among the Crows now stood in jeopardy because of Cutter. Tullock would make sure McKenzie learned of this right away.

Finally it was over and there was a gradual chorus of excitement and triumphant yelling among the Bloods as they started to celebrate their victory. Cutter had Heavy Breast Woman attend to his sexual needs, pushing her down on him while everyone danced around them. Tullock, who was finally recovering from his concern that he and the *engagés* would be killed and the fort burned, found Cutter passing out whiskey to the Bloods.

"Who gave you permission to do all this?" Tullock asked Cutter.

"I allowed myself," Cutter said, staring with his cold eyes. "You think you got anything to say?"

"You're paying for the whiskey," Tullock told Cutter. "You can't just give it all away. We've given out the full free allotment already."

"How about if I tell these Bloods you don't want them to celebrate their victory?" Cutter threatened. His smile showed clearly the dark void where the teeth on one side were missing. "They'll burn this place down and roast you over a slow fire."

Cutter was sure he had the best of Tullock now. It was time Tullock stepped down a ways. Cutter thought Tullock was a good trader and got the most out of the Indians for what he gave them, but he was too much a Company man.

"Let me show you something," Tullock then told Cutter.

He took Cutter out from the fort to a grave marked by a wooden cross. The inscription read: "DOLE MATSON killed by Thane Thompson."

"Thane Thompson was here while we were gone," Tullock then told Cutter. "He passed through with his Crows and he didn't like what he saw here. Matson here and the big Frenchman got in his way. The Frenchman went downriver the next day and what's left of Matson is right here. They said his head was chopped in two."

Cutter laughed. "You afraid of Thompson?"

"Are you saying you're not?" Tullock asked.

"I can take him any time I want," Cutter said.

"Good, then just hang around here for a while," Tullock said. "When Thompson and the rest of them Crows find out what happened here today, there's going to be blood come pouring out of somebody someplace. And McKenzie won't like this at all."

"You can't even shit without his say-so, can you, Tullock?"

"Shit or no shit, I'm sending men downriver to tell McKenzie about all this," Tullock warned. "So you'd better figure on takin' these Bloods on north, and I mean tomorrow. There's more Crows up the valley than you could ever stand off, even inside of here."

"We'll leave when we're good and ready," Cutter said.

"Well, you had better soon be good and ready," Tullock told Cutter. "I wouldn't want to be you when Thompson and the Crows sound their war drums. The way I just heard it from some of the men, Thompson wants your head on a pole."

Cutter walked away thinking about what Tullock had just said. He looked around the country and wondered if Thane Thompson were out there watching somewhere, waiting for him and the Bloods to get drunk and helpless, so that he could come down with his Crows and wipe them all out.

Cutter watched the hills for the rest of the night while the Bloods drank and carved the bodies of the fallen Crows. They ran around with scalps and heads and limbs, and danced to the light of a number of big fires. Drums pounded so loud that Cutter wondered if they couldn't be heard throughout the whole valley. He wanted to tell the Bloods to stop and not allow what they had done to happen to them, but there was no way he could do anything but just hope Thompson and the Crows were far up the valley.

Tullock watched Cutter and grew ever more angry. Cutter had put his post in a great deal of danger now. He didn't want Thane Thompson putting an end to Fort Cass with a torch and a horde of angry Crow warriors. He was certain as he watched Cutter now that Cutter was ready to leave at any time. He would get the Bloods to break camp as soon as he could and take them back north. Cutter had better stay north, Tullock reasoned, for there would be Crows and Company men alike after him if he ever came back into the Yellowstone country.

When news of the massacre at Fort Cass reached the Kicked-in-Their-Bellies, there was widespread mourning. Nearly everyone had lost a close relative. Morning Swan was not surprised at the news, and though she mourned with the others, she seemed to feel that these bad times were to be expected and that there were more bad times to come—that this was just the beginning. After returning from her favorite place she had told everyone the land was dying and if it died, so would the Crow people.

But everyone else blamed the Bloods. The young warriors, Takes-a-Bow included, were ready to make war immediately. Wiser heads among the elders prevailed and it was decided that the Bloods would pay for their deed, but in time, when they were not expecting it. After this the Bloods would be on the lookout continually, expecting a retaliatory raid at any time. They would be ready and with their numbers and the numbers of their Piegan and Northern Blackfeet brothers together, they would be a more than formidable force to contend with. It was best to wait until such time as this had died down in both camps. It was very likely the Bloods would fight the Cree or the Assiniboin or the Lacotah sometime during these warm moons. When that happened, their minds would be off the Crows. That would be the time to strike.

Thane was ready to burn the fort, but it was learned other bands of Crows were already camped near the fort once again and trading was going on as if nothing had happened. The other Crows did not blame the traders, but the Bloods. It had not been the traders who had killed their people. This frustrated Thane and he wondered where Cutter had made off to.

News and talk of war had no impact on Morning Swan. In her mind there was nothing that could stop what was coming, and that was total destruction. As the summer progressed, her attitude remained the same. Prevention could have made all this suffering and sorrow unneccessary. She was bitter. She said openly that the Crows had no one to blame but themselves for their situation. Wasn't it true they had given in to every wish of the Long Knives, allowing all

the beaver to die out? Wasn't it true that giving in to
the Long Knives continually had not brought respect,
but only increased greed? How long would it take
before her people realized they were being used? It
didn't matter if they learned now, Morning Swan
decided, for it was already too late.

After a time of mourning, the Kicked-in-Their-
Bellies slowly returned to daily life. They knew in
time the Bloods would be paid back and that they
would be happy for their lost relatives when that
happened. Eli spent a lot of time with his banjo. He
had taken to playing it and telling stories to the
children. There was always a crowd of the younger
ones around him and he delighted them by picking
and reciting tall tales at the same time.

Thane spent the spring and early summer primarily
with Jethro, and the cold moons as well when they
finally came. During that time Jethro passed his
seventh birthday. He was old enough now to want to
be with his father. Though he looked a lot like his
mother, he wanted his father's medicine. They hunted
for the most part, and worried. Jethro commented
often that he thought his mother had changed in her
mind. She was no longer the happy and jovial mother
he had known as a small boy. Where she was once
open to new ideas and learning new things—she had
even learned to read a little—she was now adamant
about keeping things as they had once been. In fact,
she had gone totally in the opposite direction.

Where she once thought it a good idea for Rosebud
and Jethro and the other members of the Crow tribe to
learn to speak English and read English, she no longer
wanted to have anything to do with it. She spoke only
Crow and would not speak to anyone who didn't talk
to her in Crow. Jethro thought of how she yelled at
him now if she heard him speaking English or saw him
reading anything at all. He had heard his mother and
father in long and heated debates over what was good
for him and what wasn't.

Jethro found each day that passed to be harder for him. He didn't want his mother and father fighting continually, but he wanted to please them both. It wasn't a simple task: conforming to one parent's desires irritated the other. For a long time he had found himself thinking that there was something he was doing to cause the problems. But at length he decided that they fought about almost everything these days and that what he did or didn't do was but a small portion of their total unhappiness. His father had told him repeatedly that he should not consider himself to blame for their unhappiness—it simply wasn't his fault. That might be the case, but it didn't solve the problem of how to make his mother happy once again.

Thane was as concerned as Jethro, and though he had thought long and often about the problem, he had no solution. In discussing it with Morning Swan, he had found her to be almost apathetic to the rising of the sun each day; she was set on seeing the end of the Crow people and nothing could change that now. She pointed out how the land was dying around them and how, because of that, the Great Powers were angry with the people. Also, the people had fallen victim to the medicine water, as she had predicted, and because of that they were either being slaughtered by their enemies without so much as a fight, or fighting among themselves and destroying themselves in general.

Morning Swan put the blame on the changes that were coming into the lands and the rapid and unquestioning acceptance of these changes by her people. She argued as she always had that to ignore the land for the sake of making the Long Knives happy was going to cost the Crow people dearly. She said repeatedly that these things had already happened to the Indian peoples along the Big Muddy River—noting their relatives, the Dirt Lodge People, in particular. All Indian peoples were losing their old ways quickly. It was to her simply a matter of time until the Crow people suffered the same fate. Then all would be gone forever.

Jethro realized he was growing older and in so doing, was becoming more aware of those issues that affected adult decisions about the future of the people. Fighting their traditional enemies to keep their lands and gaining glory in war were still uppermost in each warrior's mind. But he could see how the matters his mother raised could effect that dramatically. There was no question the Long Knives had helped to fight the Blackfeet people when they had first come. But now they were trying not to fight them, simply to gain more in trade for their own people to the east in their own lands.

Though he could not fully understand why, Jethro noticed there were fewer and fewer traveling Long Knives that came to the Crow villages to visit and stay for the winter. He had learned from his father that the need for the beaver pelts had essentially passed and the large numbers of Long Knives trapping the mountains had dropped off as a result. They had left and the beaver were gone. Jethro had come to see that the Long Knives had spent time with the Crow people not because they liked them and were actually their brothers, but because the Crows protected them from the Blackfeet.

As time passed, Eli began a gradual change. He seemed to go into himself at times now, as if thinking he didn't belong anywhere anymore. Everything around him was changing, perhaps slowly and subtly to most, but rapidly and definitely to him. The old rivers and streams, as he had come to first know them, were no longer gathering spots for free trappers who laughed and shared stories and hump ribs over fires that burned until dawn. This type of man was vanishing. Beaver was down and the companies were talking of no longer needing the roving men who had come to make the mountains their home.

There were still plenty of their kind in the mountains, but they had little to look forward to. A man could make his way alone out here until he died—and most of them didn't want to go to work in trading posts—but life would never be the same.

Eli had taken to picking his banjo and thinking about the past. Jethro seemed to be the only one who could really cut through Eli's depression, and at times he got the old trapper to laughing and telling of how he had come to know this country as if it had spit him out from its womb. So dear to him were these mountains and valleys that he thought should they ever drop out of sight, he would vanish right behind them.

The cold moons came and the Kicked-in-Their-Bellies went into the Wind River country once again. Though the area seemed the same, the discussions around the fires were not in keeping with the older days. There was ever more talk of trading with the Long Knives at their forts, and of the many new things they were bringing up the river each year. These new things, many among the band argued, would make life easier for the Crow people. Now they did not have to spend as much time making knives and arrowheads and axes, for the forts had all these things. And a great many warriors had learned how to shoot the thunder-sticks.

When the warm moons came again, the Kicked-in-Their-Bellies moved from the Wind River down to the Yellowstone. The fall buffalo hunt had been good and there had been many killed, including a great number that had been skinned and only the tongues and hump meat taken for food. The extra hides were for trading. The men would get a lot of the things they needed for war and hunting, and the women would look pretty after visiting these forts. Also, for those who wanted it, there would be plenty of medicine water.

A great herd of buffalo was sighted on the upper Yellowstone and a hunt was organized. Morning Swan told Thane he did not have to kill but a few animals. As with the previous fall hunt, she knew there would be a lot of buffalo left lying and she wanted to make use of them.

Thane killed but one buffalo, a young bull in prime. But Morning Swan found herself skinning and cutting up meat continuously. Rosebud helped, even though she and Morning Swan were looked at strangely by the others in the village. Only the poorer people among them would go out and butcher animals killed by another. Warriors killed meat for their families and then allowed the lesser in society to have the fallen not claimed.

Neither Rosebud nor Morning Swan cared what the others thought of them; they butchered as many animals as fast as they could. But the sun was hot and a vast number of buffalo went to waste. Finally, when the village was moving and the carcasses of the unused buffalo became too spoiled, Morning Swan left angry with her family and the rest of the band.

Though it wasn't the first time Morning Swan had watched buffalo fall and only the hides taken, it served to make her feel all the more that bad times—even worse than what was now happening—would soon be upon them. She kept to herself more and more and was difficult to get along with. Both Thane and Jethro spent more and more time away.

Out from the village one day with his father, Jethro found himself contemplating the future of his family and their happiness. He saw this as all centered around his mother.

"I want to help her become what she once was," Jethro said with concern, "but I don't know how. Do you, Father?"

"I don't know what to do," Thane told his son. "Your mother does not let anything cheer her up these days, not even the news that Rosebud is with child. Maybe you and I together can think of something. It is hard to see her so unhappy."

Jethro had been thinking for some time. He knew

better than to feel that his mother had lost her love for his father simply because he was a Long Knife. It was true, she disliked most Long Knives but there were others, like Eli, the old one, whom she cared for a great deal. And he knew how much his mother loved his father. He was sure of what she had once had told him: love and color have nothing in common.

Over time, Jethro had discovered the practical relationship of women's emotions to life. As with his mother and Rosebud and the other women of the village, it was the small and seemingly unimportant things that made them happy: shells and elk teeth, even if only a few, for dresses; having their man comb their hair and paint a red stripe down the part; a small bouquet of flowers, no matter what their condition.

He remembered trying to make his mother happy one morning by bringing in a handful of blue and fragrant lupine flowers. Instead of seeing a smile, Jethro had seen tears before she turned away and went off. Later, as Jethro remembered, she had come back and thanked him for the thought. This made him think of the Place-of-the-Swan-Trees, the aspens his mother had loved, and the flowers there. Perhaps, Jethro thought, she had lost her will to be happy when she had discovered all her trees were dying. If that could change, then maybe her happiness would return.

"Why don't we go up to the Place-of-the-Swan-Trees?" Jethro asked his father.

"Why do you want to go up there?" Thane asked. "I saw that place when it was beautiful and I've seen it since, now that the beaver are gone from there. It's just not the same. I want to remember it as it used to be."

"Maybe we can make it like it used to be," Jethro suggested. "Or at least help the Powers make it like it used to be."

Thane thought a moment. He could see the possibility that the land might heal itself if given the opportunity.

"Let's go," Thane said to Jethro. "I don't know what we can do, but we can at least give it some thought."

Upon reaching the Place-of-the-Swan-Trees, Thane noticed that the land was indeed in the first stages of healing itself. A colony of beaver had moved in and there were dams here and there, once again retarding the flow of water. It would be a number of years yet before the change could bring the area back totally, Thane realized, but it was a start.

They walked along the bottom, among young aspens and willows that were yet very small, but shooting up where the life-giving water had returned. The dead trees were mostly gone, used by the beaver for dam construction. The habitat was returning but it would take time for there to again be enough food and shelter for the beaver population to grow substantially.

"We have to keep this place from being trapped any more," Jethro said. "See, the life is returning!"

Thane nodded. There was the familiar slap of wide tails against the water as they walked up the valley, noting changes for the good here and there. At the edge of a small, newly established bog, Jethro picked a handful of red flowers.

"These were not here last year," Jethro commented. "Mother will like these."

It was just before nightfall when Thane and Jethro returned to the village. Jethro had kept the flowers inside a bundle of wet swamp grass he had picked. The flowers were nearly as fresh as when he had first picked them.

Morning Swan was talking to Rosebud inside the lodge. They both looked up as Jethro and Thane entered. Jethro unwrapped the flowers from their protection inside the swamp grass and handed them to his mother. Morning Swan's mouth opened in surprise.

"Oh, where did you find them?"

"At the Place-of-the-Swan-Trees. There are others growing there once again. The beaver are coming back."

Morning Swan felt the tears roll down her face. She tried to blink them away when Jethro told her he loved her and wanted her to be happy again, as in the old days.

"Things will be better again," Thane told Morning Swan. "No matter what happens, we have to think they will eventually get better."

Morning Swan nodded. "It is a good sign."

Then, for the first time in a very long while, she smiled broadly. She held the flowers and looked at her son and her husband. She turned to Rosebud, whose stomach was swelling.

"I have been foolish to be so unhappy," Morning Swan said. "I have not been very wise. How could I have overlooked the love I have around me?"

They feasted that night and celebrated the beginning of the return of the Place-of-the-Swan-Trees. Eli ate with them and in his old eyes was a glint of relief that things were returning to normal with Morning Swan. Things were still not good with the Crow people in general, but at least circumstances would be easier to cope with as long as everyone was striving to make the best of things.

Morning Swan was anxious to go back up to her favorite place once again. It would take a long time to heal the place entirely and she realized it would never look just as it had before. No place really stays exactly the same, she thought to herself. She realized she could not hold her own happiness back because of what was happening around her. It was time to look ahead and make the best of whatever came. Perhaps in time the Long Knives would tire of taking robes and furs. The beaver would come back into the streams and the plains would remain black with buffalo. She had to think this would happen. If she allowed herself to think otherwise, she would again become downcast and her family would be unhappy.

What she had, she realized, was most important. She had the love of her family.

Sixteen

THE HOT PART OF THE WARM MOONS ARRIVED AND AGAIN the skies brought no rain. There was loud thunder that came often and brought the flashes of powerful light that sometimes started fires in the dried grasses and trees. It was the time when the people spent their days bathing in the river or doing their work in the shade of trees.

Each night brought a cool and welcome breeze down off the slopes of the mountains. The Kicked-in-Their-Bellies had adjusted to their changing life and were once again happy and carefree. There were those who had broken away to join other groups which wanted to spend most of the time trading. Those who did not wish to do this remained behind, stayed away from the forts along the rivers, and hunted far back in the foothills and mountains of Crow country.

Eli had found a favorite spot just a ways above the Place-of-the-Swan-Trees, where Morning Swan again found solace and peace. Eli's place was marked by a large pine, similar to the one he had befriended down in the Wind River country, on the Popo Agie.

"I'll lay odds the two trees are kin," Eli told Thane,

regarding his newfound tree and the other one on the Popo Agie. "No two trees could be so much alike and not have the same pa at least. That old boy down on Popo Agie must have shot it off in a big wind of some kind."

Thane had laughed. "The wind don't likely come up this far."

"That one did." Eli was certain.

It was during one late evening when Thane and Eli were discussing trees and pollen that could travel a long distance when a solitary rider appeared, alerting none of the Wolves on watch, for they knew the rider. There were no shouts of alarm, but only laughter. One of the Wolves made his way through the village and jokingly announced that Crazy Arms had returned and was crazier than ever. Minus his Robin Hood hat and wearing a worn cotton shirt and trousers, Sir John Preston rode a long-eared mule past the amused villagers into the middle of camp.

Thane and Morning Swan stood in wonderment and Eli squinted for a time before getting an amused look on his face.

"He ain't dressed for no playactin'," Eli observed.

Sir John dismounted and winced at the pain in his cramped legs.

"I have arrived not a moment too soon," he said with disgust. "I dare say I've been aboard this despicable beast for far too long and I shan't stand another moment of it."

Thane didn't know where to begin. "Sir John, where did you come from? I thought you were back in the East."

"My good friend," Sir John said, leaning against Thane for support, "mine is a story that would curl the hair on a dead rabbit's lip."

The remark seemed to Thane entirely out of Sir John's normal character. He wasn't sure even what Sir John meant. Eli took the remark more literally.

"Looks to me like your hair's been curled, then fried," Eli commented.

"Ah, but that is the point of it, old-timer, sheltered old hunter," Sir John said. "Life is to taste of the flames and give the moment its do."

Eli frowned and looked at Thane, who studied Sir John in the waning light. He didn't smell of drink, yet his senses seemed somehow dimmed, or at least altered.

"What do you mean by all this?" Thane asked. "Let's get you some food and you can tell us what's happened to you in the past couple of years."

Sir John took a seat next to Thane. They smoked and ate for some time, together with a number of other warriors in the village who were anxious to hear the story, and Sir John began.

"After I left you, I journeyed to the Yellowstone River but found no steamboats would come this far upriver. So I journeyed further with a large delegation of Crows off to visit and trade with their relatives of the domed, earth habitats downriver. There were a number of bands, led by Rotten Belly and another interestingly dressed gentleman named Long Hair. I must say, it was an interesting journey and it became even more interesting when we got farther down to where the dirt lodges of the Mandans and Hidatsas were situated."

"You had to travel that far to get to a steamboat?" Thane asked. "I thought you could find one at Fort Union."

Sir John nodded. "That was my intention. But I was informed there that the boat *Assiniboin* was en route and was spending time at the villages just downriver. We reached the villages and it was there that I met with some fascinating people indeed, including one Baron Braunsberg, named Maximilian, Prince of Wied-Neuwied; a servant of his named Dreidoppel; and a Swiss artist also in his employ named Carl

Bodmer. This Bodmer fellow was painting portraits of everyone he could entice to sit for him. Simply astounding."

Eli was sitting back, shaking his head. "Cain't understand that a'tall. Why the hell are them kind out here? Christ! Ain't they got enough to do paintin' back where they come from?"

Sir John shrugged, as if indifferent to Eli's viewpoint. In times past he would have clouded with anger and struck up an argument that would never have been settled.

Thane couldn't help but notice that Sir John was lacking his usual zeal for storytelling. His descriptions lacked enthusiasm and his tone was dull and flat, as if he were merely reciting facts he knew but cared little about. It was as if he had become a different man, one who had lost something within himself. It was odd enough that he still remained out in the wilderness but now he seemed a man trapped here, without the drive for knowledge he had had in the beginning.

"That must have been food for a lot of note-taking," Thane said to Sir John.

Sir John went to a large saddlebag and pulled out a ream of bound paper. He handed it to Thane. After thumbing through the sheets, Thane became confused.

"These sheets are blank," he said to Sir John. "I don't understand."

Sir John looked at Thane and tears suddenly appeared in his eyes. He covered his face with his hands and broke into wracking sobs. Thane and Eli looked at one another in astonishment. The warriors there did not know whether he was acting or if his emotions were real. They stared.

When Sir John finally regained his composure, Thane asked him what had brought on his terrible grief. Sir John's eyes were wide and somewhat glassy, the tears on his face shining in the light of the fire. He threw up his hands.

"All I have now is blank and empty reams of paper. My journals from all the years, they're gone, they're all bloody gone!"

Sir John then began to laugh, more to himself than as if sharing it with anyone present. He tilted his head to the sky and rocked to and fro as he laughed. He shook his head, as if he thought it a strange and unique kind of joke. Again Thane and Eli looked at one another. The warriors began to talk. While Sir John laughed, frowns appeared. Some of the warriors began to get nervous, and the longer Sir John laughed the more uneasy they became. At length the council disbanded and only Thane and Eli were left, with Sir John sitting silent and staring into the fire.

"The man's addled," Eli said. "He's plumb dropped all his rocks."

"Are you saying you don't have your journals any more?" Thane finally asked.

Sir John took a long time to answer. He seemed in some sort of trance that was broken only by Thane's question, which took time for him to face.

"They are at the bottom of the Missouri," he finally told Thane. "In that bloody, goddamned muddy nightmare of a river. Lost! God in heaven!" He raised his hands to the sky, as if waiting for the journals to descend down from the extreme vastness, intact and the way they had appeared when he'd last seen them. "I shall never again wonder at the nature of fairness. None exists."

"Would it help if you told us what happened?" Thane asked.

"None exists," Sir John repeated, his mind bogged down on the reality that his life was so unpredictable. "This world is a savage within itself," he finally said.

"John," Thane said, "I can't talk to you if you're going to be crazy."

"Couldn't talk to him before neither," Eli said. "Maybe that's why he got along so well with that raven—they both make noise and don't make sense."

"You, my good man, are wont to be ignorant," Sir John snapped at Eli, "and it shall always be thus. Perhaps you can perceive no more than what's necessary for mere existence, but there are many who have a taste for more than the routine."

Sir John turned to Thane. The fire flared into his angry eyes, angry, helpless, and hopeless. Nearly ten years of daily notes and discourse on the mountains and the Indians in them, the rendezvous each year and the men who had come out here, was all gone. Boiling waters had swallowed them. Angry waters exacting payment. Disturbed waters that cared little for the passengers frequenting her of late.

"I arrived at Fort Union," Sir John told Thane. "And I immediately embarked with this astounding gent, Maximilian, and his party and the American Fur *engagés* upriver to the location where the new Fort McKenzie was erected. It is near the Great Falls, which you know well. I will say in all frankness that I took almost as many notes in the two years I was there as I did the whole of the time previous. I watched men come and go and Indians of many nations trade and dance wildly at the fort walls. Yes, and I watched them fight until the grounds were so very saturated with blood as to become as a sponge. And there came a day when the Blackfeet and the Assiniboins met and the fighting was as I have never before witnessed. It was astounding to say the least, and the artist, Bodmer, stood in their midst and painted them as they tore the hair from one another's heads. Incredible.

"I had it all, in prose and verse and even rhyme. I must say it was a chronicle without precedent. Then, during the spring and summer last, I went back to Fort Union and from there was destined back to my city. I had twelve packs of journals, mind you, from every time and place since my coming into this wilderness. I had visions as broad as this land. I would bring this savage country to the heart of the cultured world.

Those people in my city, they would see and hear it from the stage. They would see and hear me as I portrayed a land and a life unbeknownst to those vast crowds. But it was not to be.

"It was the *Assiniboin*, the steamboat I journeyed upon. At the mouth of Heart River we went aground and the bloody boat sank before we could catch our breath. I was nearly drowned, had to remove every bloody stitch of clothing to get out of the muddy water. All my journals were lost forever, tumbled somewhere beneath that brown and slimy monster of a river. It held me fast like a giant serpent and I could do no more to retrieve my work than if I were reaching into the sky for stars. And those barbarian rivermen laughed from the shore. I will not forget that day. Even to my grave I will see it."

Eli was sitting silent, staring at Sir John. The old trapper was watching a lifetime slowly slip away into the clutches of the future, but Sir John had watched his life's work sink out of sight in but a few moments.

"Why did you come back upriver?" Thane asked him.

Sir John shrugged. "Had I continued onward toward my home, I would have felt I had come out for nothing. I could not go back and have empty hands to show for so long a period out here. I must reconstruct what I once had. I must do that."

"Do you think you can remember what happened from day to day?" Thane asked.

"Sure," Eli said. "Hell, I can help him. We'll all help him."

"But I once had it," Sir John said, his eyes growing large. "It was there, day by day—"

Sir John suddenly rose to his feet like a cat and kicked into the flames. Sparkles of fire in the form of burning coals and sticks danced across the ground and scattered villagers everywhere. Two lodges caught fire and shrieking people erupted from the doorways and under the lodge edges, tearing up the stakes and rushing away to avoid the flames. Both lodges were destroyed before the fires could be put out.

Sir John continued to kick into the fire until Thane restrained him. Camp police then showed up and Sir John was tied to a tree at the edge of the village to await a council's decision on his fate. Sir John offered no resistance as they hauled him roughly and bound him securely. Thane followed them and when they were finished tying him, Thane tried to get Sir John to raise his bowed head.

"What's done is done," Thane said. "You can't pull your writings up from the bottom of the Missouri."

"There is nothing left for me," Sir John said. "My future, my very life, was inscribed on that paper. I could have written a thousand plays."

"You still can," Thane said. "You didn't lose your hands in that steamboat accident."

"A decade of work has been lost," Sir John said. "One does not easily make up for that. Besides, I can never again face the people of this village, not after what I did tonight."

"A man is allowed to lose himself once in a while. It's not the end of the world."

"Tell them to kill me," Sir John said, bowing his head once again.

"Ahh! That won't solve anything. How are you to know things won't be worse in the next life?"

"Good God in heaven!" Sir John growled, raising his head. "Have you lost your Christian upbringing entirely? It is so. You are now but a barbarian hunter."

Thane's eyes flashed. He took a breath and looked away from Sir John.

Sir John ground his teeth as he talked. "I shall never withstand the loss of my memoirs. Never."

"Start them over," Thane said. "I plan to travel the country again before long, trading tobacco for buffalo hides. All over. Eli said he would help. We'll go to all the old places: Green River, the Great Salt Lake,

Pierre's Hole, all over the mountains. Together we'll remember what happened. You can do it again."

"Do you truly think so?" Sir John asked.

"Why, sure. You've just got to want to is all."

"I have no idea where to begin."

"You're making it hard for yourself," Thane said. "Remember that night on the Green River when we first talked for any length of time? When we shot at the beaver skull? If you can think back on that night, you can pull everything else together."

Sir John thought for a time. Finally he said, "Perhaps you are right. It would be incredible, but perchance I could recall most of that I have previously written."

"You can recall all of it," Thane said.

Sir John then got a look of concern on his face. "But what have I done here? What if they *do* want to kill me?"

"You didn't do anything worth taking your life over. You wrecked things pretty well, but you didn't cause any deaths. You will have to restore some property and likely live outside the village for a time, as punishment. But I can't see how they would want your life."

It was not as easy as Thane had first thought. The following day, Thane sat in on the council and argued until nightfall that Sir John was not dangerous to the village, but merely angry at having lost something he had worked at for a very long time. Thane equated it to having lost a lot of pictures painted upon robes and carved into rocks. The elders were not impressed by Thane's analogy and they wanted to banish him from the village forever.

"Let him stay and I will see that he does no more harm," Thane persisted. "He will help me take the tobacco into other lands for trade."

Because of Thane's position, Sir John was given another chance. He would have to live outside the village until the families which had lost their lodges and belongings to the fire were given restitution. He would have to hunt and kill buffalo so that they could make new lodges; he would have to provide horses in payment for the possessions lost in the fire. He would have to do these things or something else of equal value.

Throughout that spring Sir John resided in a lodge downriver from the main village, erected for him by Morning Swan and Rosebud. Thane and Eli shot buffalo and elk to provide meat and skins to the families whose lodges and belongings had been lost to the fire. Sir John sulked for almost the entire period, until Thane told him to begin writing again or head back to the East. There was no reason to remain with the Crows imposing on everyone if he wasn't going to try again.

Sir John realized Thane was serious. If Thane ceased helping him, he would have no choice but to leave. Sir John then began to take notes and organize his daily writings. As soon as he began, he got back into it and worked hard. He noted things he had heard but not yet seen, concerning the changing nature of travel and the influx of people coming out. It was in his mind now to correlate what he would see and hear firsthand with what he had already witnessed.

Sir John got back into his writing with a zeal, but ran into his first frustration right away—ironically, in the form of Thane himself. Seated near a breakfast fire early one morning, Sir John wanted to know what had happened those years past to allow Thane the use of his shoulder and arm once again. And he wanted to learn what this largely undiscussed topic about the Little People in the mountains was all about.

Thane nodded while he ate and thought how hard it had been for him to realize what had happened to him in both instances. He had certainly come to conclude he had experienced them, but he knew he could never truly understand all of it. The fact was no one, not even the most experienced *shaman* among the people, would profess to know all about any of the mysterious forces that surrounded them. They would merely accept the fact their bodies and minds could be used as an instrument for these forces.

Each time he prayed and gave thanks for life, Thane now remembered the gift he had been given by Bear-Walks-at-Night and the ultimate sacrifice his father-in-law had made. The grizzly was to Thane a sacred animal now. Over time he had come to realize how closely tied all elements of life truly were, and how interdependent they all were.

"I was healed by Bear-Walks-at-Night," Thane finally answered Sir John. "You remember how he went up into the Beartooth Mountains and I followed him. Well, the man's spirit is now in the form of the grizzly—which I have taken as my medicine."

"What do you mean?" Sir John asked. "That is impossible."

Thane then got up from the fire and told Sir John he needed to tend to some horses.

"Wait!" Sir John said, running after. "I thought you were going to tell me what I wanted to know."

"Maybe someday something like that will happen to you," Thane told Sir John. "But until then I can't talk to you about something you can't or don't want to believe."

Sir John thought about what Thane had said. He was torn between what he knew was real and what he knew others would perceive as witchcraft. These Indian people had a way of life and until the past few years when the missionaries came, they had no conception of the word "devil." Now the Crows joked among themselves, and whenever it would thunder and rain while the sun was out, they would remark that the devil must be fighting with his wife.

When Sir John wrote now, he merely noted the ceremonies he witnessed as customs and traditions. But he thought more each time he wrote something and realized that losing his original journals might not have been so bad after all: in effect, he had missed the point before of a lot of things he had documented.

Sir John's desire to act came back to him as well. And though no one paid particular attention anymore, Thane found himself falling back into his old roles and enjoying it. It brought back memories of the early years in the mountains. It also reminded him once again of his boyhood and the culture of Virginia, where he was raised. It also brought back the anger that had been dormant for a time. He could see William Chapman again and wondered if the man now owned half of the Virginia farming region.

Thane finally realized that if he were not careful, his anger could reach the level of that which Morning Swan had lived with for so long—until Jethro had given her the swamp flowers. Thane did not want that and resolved to realize his past was behind him and to look ahead and make it good. Time always brought change and it was important to be flexible.

During an evening when he sat with Sir John and Eli in front of a fire, Sir John mentioned the initial coming of various missionaries and settlers bound for this region, into what was now being called Oregon Territory. These and similar individuals, Thane remembered, had showed up at some of the rendezvous in the early thirties. They were already beginning to influence the increased flow of emigrants.

Eli sat toying with his banjo, listening to the talk.

"What business has white wagons got out in this country?" he suddenly blurted out. "It weren't made out here for such travelin'. But there's movement afoot now to change that. God A'Mighty, but it makes me madder than a wet hen to see what's on its way."

"It shall come nonetheless," Sir John said.

"Them folks what's comin'," Eli continued, "they don't know a Piegan from a Crow arrer and don't care to. Them days when I was first out here with the Major, old Andrew Henry—well, they be done gone now. Forever." He looked at Thane. "Even when we looked down on Rising Hawk and them Piegans from the Square Butte, well, that was country unspoilt too. Ain't going to be that way for long. No siree, things will get as rotten as my knee."

Thane was shaking his head. "I can't see how they'll ever get all this settled out here. It's too big. There's not enough here. You can't put a plow into most of this country. You have to be very selective."

Eli turned to Thane. "Do you still aim to grow tobacco?"

"I'm thinking about it more seriously than ever before," Thane said. "I've got plans to farm a spot of bottomland along the Yellowstone this year and seed tobacco next spring. If there's no way to stop the trade out here, then at least we can develop it for ourselves and maybe get a good head start for what's coming. Like Sir John says, like it or not, it's on its way."

"What's happened to you?" Eli asked. "Farmin' and tradin' don't cross paths, to my way of thinking."

"Well, maybe they do," Thane argued. "Tobacco is big medicine. A good supply is important. I'll have the biggest and the best tobacco crop you've ever seen. I intend to get the trade away from the Company if it's the last thing I do."

Eli shook his head. "I can't figure you a'tall. You come out here and go to farmin'?"

"I just need a little patch down next to the river," Thane said. "Someplace level out of the wind. I'll cut a ditch from upriver to get water to it. I wouldn't call that anything but an experiment."

Eli laughed. "Ain't no mules out here trained to harness. And I'll hate you till you die if you go to bringin' some in."

"There's a lot of pack mules out here," Thane pointed out. "And they can be trained to harness. When the crop is in, we'll go across country and set up our trade with all of the tribes. We'll hit the ones we already know real well, then go across the mountains and talk with the Flatheads and the Pend d'Oreilles, all of them."

"Is that the only way I'm goin' to get you to take me cross-country for one last look?" Eli asked.

"We'll be ready late next fall," Thane promised. "One year of fallow and then we plant. There'll be a tobacco crop you've yet to see the likes of."

Eli frowned. "I've yet to see the likes of a crop I liked."

Sir John then spoke. "I would be ever so willing to help you," he said, "maybe for payment of some of the tobacco. Not much, mind you, but enough to make restitution to those families whose lodges caught fire. How does that sound?"

Thane nodded. "I don't see why that wouldn't work out fine. But there's a lot to do and it's going to be hard work, different from anything you've ever done."

Sir John shrugged his thin shoulders. "Ah, but I was born to farm!"

In but a few days time, Thane began to implement his plan. Along the Yellowstone, just down from the mouth of the Clark's Fork, Thane found a nearly level terrace that would be excellent for a series of tobacco fields. It received full sunshine though it was behind the bluffs that rolled up from the river, so that the ever-present wind from the southwest would not dry the plants. It would be easy to cut a ditch in from above, leading from the Clark's Fork, to bring water for irrigation. It was in exactly the right place.

Thane realized the weather out here was far different from Virginia. But for his purposes, he needed only water, sunshine, and enough time to get good leaf development on the plants. He was not concerned with having the best crop for a market or pleasing buyers with whom he could count on trade for a profit. His sole purpose was to grow tobacco, which he knew would certainly get bigger and leafier than the plants that developed from the Tobacco Ceremony and subsequent planting the Crows celebrated each spring.

The terrace proved ideal for the project. It was large enough to grow more tobacco than the entirety of all the tribes in the region could smoke over a winter. Sir John, as he had promised, was a willing worker. In the beginning he got in the way more than he helped, and Thane would find himself turning around into him or bumping into him some way or another.

"I didn't say I was a farmer," Sir John remarked. "I said I was born to farm—it takes time."

Sir John wanted the Crow people to see him working among them and helping Thane, so that they would understand he had good intentions. He was sorry for his outburst, which had cost property and valuable possessions that could not handily be replaced. By helping with the sacred crop, the tobacco, he would be demonstrating his desires to make things good again with the Crow people.

But it was not easy for Sir John, and after a number of days pulling sagebrush plants from the field to go under plow and digging a ditch with the others from the Clark's Fork over to the field, Sir John found himself physically exhausted each night, nursing blisters and sore muscles. Eli, who would watch during the day while either playing his banjo or leaning on his cane, would shout, "Doin' good, John! Keep her up!" At length Sir John would look up from his work and wipe sweat from his brow, saying, "Get out here with that cane, my good man, and move some dirt!"

Thane spent his time constructing a crude plow frame from pine and rawhide, using buffalo shoulder blades for plowshares. He built harnesses and worked with a number of mules until they were fairly well trained. After numerous broken and replaced plowshares and a number of tumbles and spills, he had succeeded in getting the area initially broken.

"We'll need to soak this down for a time with

irrigation water," Thane then said. "It should make working it the second time a lot easier."

For a number of days Thane oversaw the flood-irrigation process that brought water from the nearby Clark's Fork and spread it over the field. After a time it was soaked down and when the surface had dried sufficiently, the plowing process began again.

"We've got to get this worked up real well," Thane said. "Next year we'll have a great crop."

Morning Swan had watched it all with skepticism.

"The Crow people go along with you because of who you are," she told Thane. "They will never do this sort of thing themselves. My people let the land grow what they eat."

Thane knew Morning Swan was still not interested in seeing a trade business begin. She deplored the idea of falling into the same position as the other companies, which were literally killing one another to gain a foothold. Thane worked continually to try to convince her he did not intend to do business as the other companies did and would allow the other tribes to make their own decisions about trading. Tobacco was all he would offer.

Morning Swan was not intent on arguing and told Thane that she only wanted to live in peace. She was concerned only with helping her people get back to a happy, normal life without the pitfalls of the medicine water and trading with the Long Knives in the forts. Thane was hoping to convince her that he would be taking his tobacco to them and not erecting forts. That way he could see them in their villages and they would not have to become dependent on him.

When the field was dry enough to plow once again, Thane set to work. He wanted the soil as loose as possible by the upcoming winter, so that new plowing and seeding the next year would be simple. Sir John, anxious to make good his agreement with Thane, insisted on taking the plow the first day.

"This orta be good." Eli chuckled. "Shakespeare on a plow."

Thane helped him get the mules harnessed and the plow steadied in an upright position. Once Sir John had the reins wrapped around his wrists, he was ready.

"Be gentle with the mules," Thane warned. "They're just getting used to things yet."

But Sir John had already yelled, "Go!" to the mules.

And they went. They bolted forward and the plow jolted sideways. Sir John tumbled with them and when he yelled, "Whoa!" they began to run.

Thane and Eli and the Crows who were watching doubled over with laughter as the mules in harness came loose from the plow and Sir John, his wrists wrapped in the reins, bounced along the field behind them.

Finally, Sir John got himself free and stood up, wobbly. Everyone was still laughing, but Eli had stopped and he was down on his knees breathing heavily.

"Eli, what's the matter?" Thane asked.

"It's my chest. It hurts a powerful bunch."

"Lie down and take it easy," Thane said. "Just take it easy."

Eli was shaking his head. "No, boy, no. Damn, this is it, I'm goin' under." He tried to smile. "At least the Blackfeet never got me."

"No, just take it easy," Thane was saying, helping Eli into the shade of a tree. "You'll be fine. You just need a minute."

Eli stumbled badly as Thane helped him. The old trapper tried to smile again.

"That John, he let them mules take him, didn't he? John ain't such a bad sort at that."

Thane eased Eli down with his back against a tree. But Eli wouldn't let go of Thane's hand. He held on tight and he made Thane look into his eyes.

"You been like a son to me," he said. "You been good to me all along. I've been lucky to know you . . . and Morning Swan, good woman that she is."

"Eli," Thane whispered, "just hang on now."

Eli's eyes were beginning to grow dull and the lids were beginning to droop. Tears welled up in them and spilled out onto his old cheeks. He groaned from the pain in his chest and continued to hold Thane's hand, gripping it as if struggling against falling somewhere. Speech was harder for him, and though Thane insisted he rest so that his strength would return, Eli continued.

"Them kids of yours . . . I wished I had spent more time with 'em . . . maybe hugged 'em once. I wished I'd have hugged 'em once. They won't forget me? You won't forget me, will you, boy?"

Eli was beginning to tremble, and Thane realized the old trapper was indeed dying. It was happening and he could not escape the fact. In just a short few moments, Eli would be gone.

"No, Eli," Thane managed. "No one could ever forget you."

Others were coming now. Sir John, who saw what was happening, was running up from the field. Jethro was coming from the village as fast as his legs could carry him, followed by Morning Swan, who was helping Rosebud along. She was holding her stomach, hurrying as fast as she could.

"That Jethro," Eli was saying, "he's quite a boy, he is. . . . Made of the old stuff . . . Tell Rosebud . . . tell her I wanted to see her baby."

Eli let his breath out completely and his head slumped forward. Thane caught him and pulled the old man to his chest, hugging him.

"Oh, Eli," Thane was saying, "don't go. Don't go."

Sir John, bruised and covered with dirt, arrived and slumped down. He knelt there a few moments, his head bowed, and then got up to walk off into the trees by himself, pulling leaves from the branches as he went.

Jethro was there asking what was wrong. Morning Swan and Rosebud knelt down and they all hugged one another, their tears flowing. Thane continued to hug and rock the old trapper and in the Crow village there arose songs of mourning.

It was spring once again before Thane returned to the tobacco field. His eagerness to farm had subsided with Eli's death and for a long time—throughout the rest of the summer and into the previous fall—Thane had felt as though a large portion of his life had suddenly fallen away. Try as he might, he couldn't shake the loss. Not until the birth of Rosebud's baby.

"We have named him Eli," Takes-a-Bow told Thane, "for the old Long Knife who was so dear to our hearts."

Thane realized the baby boy would likely carry other Indian names through his life as well, but the thought of naming him Eli was fitting. The old trapper, now resting under the big pine upriver, the pine he had once said he thought was kin to the big one on the Popo Agie, would always be a part of the stories the Kicked-in-Their-Bellies told of the first coming of the Long Knives. One of the very early American trappers, along with John Colter and Major Andrew Henry and the others, Eli Kleinen was the last of his kind.

At length Thane finally resolved to go back to his attempt to grow tobacco. Spring had passed into summer and the clouds that crossed the sky were rising thunderheads that showed many shapes and seemed to come and go with sudden quickness. With Eli's passing he'd become all the more aware that things were changing and the old times were swiftly departing. The trapping of beaver was still in evidence, but it would soon be totally a thing of the past.

With more trading posts springing up all the time there was a certainty that the old method of trapping and rendezvous was gone. It was time to realize that the roving brigades of free trappers would soon be nonexistent. It might be in but a few years or possibly much longer, but there would be something that would again—like the fur of the beaver—draw men to this region. When that happened, settlement would surely follow.

Thane realized he was now set back another year in his growing schedule, but he would continue and go ahead with his idea in hopes of providing a future financial basis for his family and the Kicked-in-Their-Bellies as a band. Again the Crows were willing to work with him, and Sir John wanted to continue in his quest to make amends to the families who had suffered from the fire.

One morning when Thane was overseeing the flooding of the fields, a group of Crow warriors rode up the river to change his plans again. They were representatives from other Crow bands and their message was that it was time to make war against the Bloods and the other Blackfeet peoples. There was news that their villages were scattered and they were in disarray. No one seemed to understand the reason why, but now was the time to strike and wipe them out, camp by camp.

That night Thane sat with the council, and after listening again to the Crow warriors who had arrived, they accepted the news and concluded that the time was indeed right. Their enemies, if the news were true, seemed to be having major problems of some kind. Thane and the other members of the council discussed at length the reasons for the Blackfeet troubles. There was the reality that the buffalo herds were scattered this year and hunting was bad. That would result in a breakup of the bands into smaller units. The visiting Crows mentioned that there were many Crow bands that were far out in Crow country looking for buffalo. Another reason was perhaps clan feuding, which had caused the breakup into groups. Whatever it was, it was a good sign for the Crow people, who intended to avenge their slain relatives.

Thane wondered what part Cutter had in all this. He wondered where the man was now and if he might still be with the Bloods. It was very likely. There was no reason to think this man could be anywhere else. He could fight whenever he wanted to and he would always have the support of a people who wanted the head of Thane Thompson.

The night before they were to leave, there was a long war dance. The sky was a fitting backdrop, with the sun falling behind a boiling tempest of white that spit lightning along the ridges above the village. The wrath of the spirits was with the Crow people, it was thought, and the power of the storm would be with them. This was especially pleasing to Takes-a-Bow, who felt his personal medicine would be great. With great confidence he retraced the jagged lines on his war shield with fresh white paint.

Thane and Takes-a-Bow danced with the others over scalps taken in prior years. Thane at last brought out Rising Hawk's medicine shield and war cries were voiced at it. All the warriors cried for victory and embellished their weapons with fresh war paint, feathers, and other signs of personal glory. Thane retraced the image of the grizzly on his shield and added fresh paint to highlight the outline. All the while he watched the warriors dance around Rising Hawk's shield, on a pole in the center of the village, now being killed like an enemy in a mock battle by Crow dancers.

Sir John wrote in his journals, his eyes wide in the light of the many fires. He saw this as an opportunity of a lifetime—to go to again see Indian warfare before his very eyes. They would join with other warriors from other bands and meet them downriver to form a large and powerful unit. They would travel into Blackfeet lands and with the coming of the time just before the cold moons, they would return with Blackfeet scalps and horses.

Jethro wanted to go as a horse tender, but Thane would not allow it. A smaller and less important time would be more appropriate. Rosebud wept at learning Takes-a-Bow would go along. But that was different; he was a proven warrior and if he wished to gain further respect, he must count more coups and gain more honor.

When the dancing was finished, Thane stared for a long time at Rising Hawk's medicine shield. A steady rain fell for a time and then let up, bringing a sharp freshness to the air. Water ran off the face of the medicine shield, dripping from the painted wings of the hawk on its front—like lines of clear blood.

It seemed strange to Thane that after so long this article of war still held its fascination and importance. He knew that with it he could gain at least some measure of mental superiority over any Blackfeet they might meet. If Rising Hawk were among them, it could prove the turning point in a major battle.

Morning Swan, knowing the importance to her people of what was taking place, asked nothing of Thane—except to be careful and remember her love for him. As with the other women in the village, there was a certain silence that came with goodbyes when men went to war—for fear that too many words would somehow keep them from returning alive.

Morning Swan asked Thane to be brave in the fighting, as she knew he would, and to look out for Takes-a-Bow so that he would return and not make Rosebud a widow. It was so very important that the war party do well, for it meant keeping the respect they had fought for over so long a period of time. To be defeated was to lose face in the eyes of the enemy and to eventually lose the land as well.

After Thane and Takes-a-Bow had prepared their articles of war, they said goodbye to their families. Takes-a-Bow had new confidence, now that his medicine shield was freshly painted with the zigzag patterns of the storm. Together with Rising Hawk's shield, Thane carried his own personal medicine shield—the image of the grizzly freshly painted again. He would ride the buckskin given to him by Takes-a-Bow. With the coming of the sun they left for Blackfeet lands while war songs echoed up and down the valley.

Seventeen

WILD JACK CUTTER HAD HIS HORSES PACKED AND HE HAD beaten Heavy Breast Woman once already that morning. He didn't want her saying anything to anyone about their leaving; and from the look of fear in her eyes, he didn't believe he had anything to worry about.

Since the massacre of the Crows at Fort Cass, Cutter had remained along the high Missouri with the Bloods. Besides Fort Cass, he had stayed away from all Company posts in the area, including Fort Union and Fort McKenzie. He was sure the Company wanted no more to do with him, not after causing a big loss in profits for them. He hadn't cared at the time what the Company thought, since his time with the Bloods had been good. But now he was sure that too was over.

A contingent of Bloods from another band, with some Piegans and Northern Blackfeet, had arrived late in the night. They had been trading far downriver at Fort McKenzie and now brought word of impending disaster for the Blackfeet people, disaster brought upriver by the traders on their fireboats.

Cutter had stood in the shadows listening to the

news. He had heard the messengers telling the Blood council about sickness at the fort—sickness that was killing off the Blackfeet people like the grasses that die before the snows. From the way they described the symptoms of the disease, Cutter was certain it was smallpox.

Now there would be an upheaval among the Blackfeet, and likely all the Indian nations in the region. Smallpox had killed them off before and they knew what was in store for them. They would want revenge against the Long Knives.

The messengers had brought other news to the village as well: they knew for certain a large war party of Crows was advancing into their lands. There were a great number of their enemy, and leading them was the Long Knife Bear-Man.

Cutter rode away from the Blood camp as rapidly as possible, drinking whiskey from a flask and worrying about what he would say to the camp Wolves on duty. When he met one of them he told the warrior that he wanted to go out and hunt, and had Heavy Breast Woman along to pack the meat. Cutter was known as one who did strange things at strange times of day and the warrior thought little of it. In the back of Cutter's mind was the concern that the messengers to the village had brought the smallpox with them and that he was getting himself away from the camp in time.

As Cutter rode with Heavy Breast Woman behind him, he hoped he would not have the misfortune of meeting Thane Thompson and the Crows. He had a plan in mind: he thought that he might possibly do well to try to reach Rising Hawk's band of Small Robes. They were far up on the Two Medicine River and had likely not yet heard of the smallpox. Cutter realized he had at least one thing in common with Rising Hawk: they both wanted Thane Thompson.

So Cutter made the upper reaches of the Two Medicine River his destination, a location he knew to

be a favorite camp of the Small Robes band of the
Piegans. This year the buffalo were spread out across
the upper plains and foothills so badly that the bands
were splitting up for a time to hunt. It was well known
that the valley of the Two Medicine River was good
for hunting almost any time of year.

Cutter and Heavy Breast Woman reached the Small
Robes' village after nearly a week's travel. Rising
Hawk, who was slowly regaining his strength after so
long a time fasting and praying, greeted Broken
Mouth and his woman and made them welcome. But
he could not understand why they were traveling
alone.

"It is my wish to live with the Small Robes," Cutter
said. "The Bloods are out hunting and there is news
that Bear-Man leads the Crows into this country. I
want to fight the Crows with Rising Hawk by my side.
I want him to know I would like to kill the Long Knife
dog they call Bear-Man."

"How do you know this?" Rising Hawk asked.

"Messengers came to the village and told of Bear-
Man and the Crows," Cutter answered. "I want to be
with Rising Hawk when Bear-Man comes."

Cutter and Heavy Breast Woman were given food
and their horses were cared for while Rising Hawk
went to Rain Maker's lodge. For a long time Rising
Hawk had been waiting for a sign of the time when he
would regain his lost medicine shield and he wondered if that time had come.

"I cannot say for sure," Rain Maker said. "But I am
afraid because of the dream and the painting on the
robe. I had the dream again just last night and the
images that were falling through the air again had the
spots on them. But this time the spots were much
bigger, and they were running with blood and white
slime."

Rain Maker held himself steady, but his manner
was one of deep concern. In his many years he had
seen a lot of things, and he knew from stories told by

those who had gone before that sickness came and went and took many of the people with it.

Rising Hawk's eyes widened. "What does that mean? Is it disease, as you told us in council after we talked?"

Rain Maker shook his head. "I cannot say, but I am afraid."

"Do you think I should lead a war party out to find Bear-Man? Broken Mouth comes with news that he is leading the Crows against us."

"How well do you know this man Broken Mouth?" Rain Maker asked. "He has the eyes of a mad wolf."

"I know only that he wants badly to kill Bear-Man, or see him killed," Rising Hawk answered. "That is the only reason I choose to be around him. He came to our village, he says, to tell of Bear-Man's coming. If this is true, then I am grateful to him."

"Bear-Man is strong," Rain Maker said. "And you are again strong. Bear-Man is in the dream. Perhaps now is the time to go against him."

"But what if your dream means there will be sickness among us?" Rising Hawk asked. "I do not want to go to war and return to find my family and friends all dead."

"We will know soon enough," Rain Maker said. "We will send warriors out to the other villages to find out."

"Our people are scattered," Rising Hawk said. "And if the sickness is not here, it would not be wise to bring it back."

"We have to know," Rain Maker said. "It is important that whoever goes understand not to be foolish. Death can be seen from a distance."

Rising Hawk nodded. His mind was troubled. He needed to regain his medicine shield and his power and he realized he must find Bear-Man to do this. He thought it very fortunate that Broken Mouth had come from the Blood village to tell him about Bear-Man and the Crows. Rising Hawk felt this was a good sign and might be his only chance to regain his power, as Bear-Man did not come into Blackfeet lands very often anymore. Bear-Man, like himself, was getting older. He likely had children of his own. But he had come into Blackfeet lands and it was important that he not leave alive.

Thane admired the country he had known during his first year in the mountains. Though it had been a number of years since he had been through here, Thane thought of this country as special to him. It was here that he had first met Morning Swan and Rosebud. Just ahead was the Musselshell River, through a stand of trees and over a hill. And despite the fact he was leading warriors into enemy lands to fight, he wanted to again see the place where he had first met his wife.

Thane brought the Crow warriors to a halt along the high ridge that overlooked the flow of the river below. His smile was slowly replaced by a frown. There was a large encampment of Bloods and Northern Blackfeet directly below, but there were no warriors riding out to do battle. Instead, scattered warriors from different lodges looked up and ran for their horses, looking back to see if the Crows were coming down the hill after them.

Thane stared. The Crow warriors screamed war cries and prepared to give chase.

"Wait!" Thane yelled. "Do not go after them. Something is wrong."

"Nothing is wrong," a young Crow warrior from another band shouted. "They are like children who run away, that is all. We should run them down and kill them."

"Look, there are bodies lying around in the village," Thane pointed out. "There are a lot of sweat lodges along the river. Children are wandering around lost. Something is wrong."

"I say we kill our enemies," the young Crow from

the other band shouted again. "They are getting away."

"Do what you want," Thane said. "I, for one, am not going. I do not know why some of the Bloods lie dead in their village and the warriors leave their women and children crying. I do not want to die the same way. It could be sickness."

"Those Bloods who are riding away are not sick," the young warrior argued. "And it is time they died."

The young warrior screamed a war cry and charged off toward the fleeing Bloods. Others followed though Thane shouted for them to stop. Takes-a-Bow and those who were Kicked-in-Their-Bellies stayed behind, along with some from other bands. But nearly half the war party was riding out toward the Blood warriors, now riding out from their village as fast as their horses could carry them.

Thane watched and saw some of the fleeing warriors fall from their horses. Some tried to rise to their feet and others lay still. It brought to Thane's mind the day Long Hand had come after him and had fallen from Whirlwind. There was no question now that some form of disease had ravaged the Blood village.

"We must leave here," Thane told Takes-a-Bow and the others. "We must go now."

"What about our brothers?" a young Crow warrior asked. "Are we to leave them behind?"

"We have no choice," Thane told him. "They would not listen to me and chose instead to endanger their own lives as well as the lives of their people. Stay away from them now and let them go back alone. You must all understand if you come anywhere near any of them after this, you will likely die. And you will spread it to your families. Look down into that village if you don't believe me."

"What are we to do?" another young Crow asked.

"Go back to your separate bands as soon as possible and go high into the mountains with them," Thane said. He was talking when from nearby came shouts

and screams of war. A half-dozen Blood and Northern
Blackfeet warriors who had worked their way up from
behind charged across the hill toward Thane and the
other Crows.

"Shoot them!" Thane yelled. "Shoot them before
they reach us."

The Crows fired a volley of arrows and shots from
their trade rifles. The Blackfeet warriors fell and their
horses turned away and down the hill toward the
village. Then a lone Blood warrior, who had taken
another position while his brothers mounted the
attack, screamed and came on alone. He was nearly
upon them when Thane yelled.

"Get back away from him! All of you get back and I
will take him."

Thane rode forward toward the charging Blood. He
had already fired his Hawken and held the barrel to
use it as a club. Thane's medicine shield, the bear on it
freshly painted, caught a ball fired from the Blood
warrior's fusil. Then as Thane raised his Hawken to
deliver a blow, the Blood warrior ran his pony directly
into Thane's buckskin. Thane dropped the Hawken
and struggled to stay on his horse. Crazed and screaming, the Blood warrior jumped him.

They fell to the ground and the warrior, seemingly
possessed of superhuman strength, tried to drive his
knife into Thane's throat. Then there was a shot from
behind and Takes-a-Bow jumped from his pony, holding his smoking rifle.

Thane rose quickly to his feet. "Stay back!" he
warned Takes-a-Bow. "This is one enemy scalp you do
not want."

The other Crows were now talking among themselves, their hands over their mouths. They knew the
enemy warriors had all chosen to die a glorious death
rather than fall to the sickness that was killing their
people.

Thane stood over the Blood warrior's body. He
spoke to Takes-a-Bow and the other Crow warriors as

a group. "All of you, return to your villages and tell them of the sickness. Tell them how your brothers have exposed themselves to death and that they must be left behind if the Crow people are to survive. Then go into the Bighorn Mountains and stay there until I have returned. I have fought with this warrior and may become sick myself. I will wait until it is over and then return."

"I cannot leave you here!" Takes-a-Bow yelled out.

"You have to," Thane shouted back. "Now go, and do not come in contact with anyone until you get back to the village. Do as I say."

"I will remain behind with you," Takes-a-Bow said.

"No!" Thane yelled. "You have a wife and baby son. I will not die. Now hurry and go, before the sickness gets to the village."

Thane stood and watched while Takes-a-Bow and the others hurried back toward the south. He knew Takes-a-Bow was reluctant to leave, but hoped he would have enough sense to think about it and not be foolish enough to come back later. It seemed to Thane that Takes-a-Bow could understand it meant his life, as well as the life of his family and possibly the entire Crow nation.

When they were gone, Thane felt relieved. He stood back from the fallen Blood warrior and stared down into the village, where all was total disaster. Children continued to wander around crying, and now and then someone would come out of a lodge and collapse on the ground. There were no drums sounding and no medicine men chanted, for they were far past that stage. Not many in this village remained alive, and Thane was glad he was upwind and far enough away that the horrible stench could not reach him.

Thane got back on the buckskin and rode upriver until he found a location next to the water where a number of war lodges had been erected. They were in good shape, likely used most recently by Crows or

Shoshones traveling through to steal horses or raid Blackfeet villages. This was where he would remain until he knew whether or not he had contracted the smallpox.

Thane stripped himself naked and covered his hands with mud and a thick layer of leaves. There were extra clothes and moccasins in a skin bag and Thane placed these and all other articles he would want later in a hole he dug in the ground. In the hole he placed his rifle, wrapped up tightly, and Rising Hawk's medicine shield and his own as well. He covered the hole and washed off the mud and leaves. Then he put the clothes he had been wearing back on.

If he lived, he would have to burn them. He would have to burn everything he had come in contact with, including those things he would take into the medicine lodge with him—and the medicine lodge itself. He could not afford to have anything he knew or even suspected to be contaminated. It would do little good to survive and then spread the disease and watch it destroy everyone else.

Now all he could do was wait. It was a strange time for him, wondering if he would die or live to see his family. He thought back into his own family's past and remembered his father telling a story about his grandfather having both cholera and smallpox, and living. "We're a tough breed, we Thompsons," Thane remembered his father saying at the time.

Perhaps that was true, Thane thought. He realized he must keep a positive attitude. That would not be easy; the vision of the ravaged village just downriver was etched into his mind. And now everything and everyone who had ever been close to him during his life grew in importance. Everything he saw reminded him of Morning Swan and his family. Along the hillside were clusters of flowers that opened their bright blossoms to the summer light and spilled their fragrance into the air. Birds flitted through the trees, the little chickadees who told him he was not alone, and various tiny colored birds that flashed from branch to branch in the chokecherries and the gray thorns of the buffalo berries. How long had it been since he had really noticed them?

In the distance, the meadowlarks held their heads up and gave their shrill and happy calls, while overhead the hawks of the valley soared against the deep sky. How long had it been since he had truly given thanks for all he had been given? For a healthy family, all of whom were strong and bright and a joy to be with each day.

Often a raven would fly low over the trees, looking down to see who was there, voicing a harsh, throaty squawk. Each one that passed reminded him of Jethro and his pet raven, Joker, which was growing to be an old bird but nonetheless interesting. Jethro, Thane would think to himself, my son, whom I want to see once again more than anything. All my family, if I live, will always receive my undevoted attention.

More days went by and Thane spent them looking out at the mountains and remembering the past. There was a hillside above the river that offered a good view of the country. The mornings would come in bright and the days would become hot; then the clouds would rise huge and white into the afternoon sky to rumble and bring isolated storms to the mountains and open plains. Thane would sit and while away the time and wait, and his mind would go back to those early years, to the color of the water in the lakes and streams and how he had watched the fish jumping and the ducks and geese floating, their young bobbing along behind like balls of yellow fluff.

He saw again the lines of elk that flowed into winter valleys in long trails of tan and dark brown against the white of the mountains; the herds of deer and antelope that moved on delicate feet through the grass of the plains and open valleys. And there had been that first herd of buffalo, an endless, swimming mass that trailed up out of the river and spread out like a dark blanket across the plains.

And there was Morning Swan. Thane could see her again, just down the river where they had first met, each equally afraid of the other. All that seemed like a thousand years ago—when he had first seen this country and its boundless horizons. A lot of men had come and gone during that time, and should he die, he would just be another one of the many.

Time now seemed to Thane like an irrational gift that came so easily, then was lost without a sound. It made him feel like one of the small stalks of grass that spread itself up from the ground around him while so many of its kind were doing the same thing along the same hillside and out across the land for as far as the eye could see. Each year they died back before the snows and were forgotten.

In just over a week, Thane began to feel sudden chills and nausea. He was not surprised and he was not afraid. If I die, he concluded, then it will be without endangering my family. Thane had prepared one of the war lodges by laying out robes within it and placing beside them water in skin flasks and pemmican he had brought on the journey. He was glad it was the summer season and did not have to worry about keeping the war lodge heated. He knew he must remain within the lodge until he had gone through the period where the pox worked its way out of the body.

As the fever grew worse, Thane worried about his family. He worried mainly that Takes-a-Bow and the other warriors had not reached the village in time to warn them of the smallpox. He hoped that if someone had to die, it would be himself only. Morning Swan could live without him; she was strong and took things in stride. Jethro and Rosebud would both be devastated for a time but they would recover. Rosebud would raise her son, and Jethro would grow up to be as strong as if his father had not died. That was the way of things: death came and life after went on. Those affected looked ahead. And in a land where life was so fragile, death was expected at any time.

Thane climbed the hillside to get one last look before he went into the lodge, to see it all again should he never come out. He realized that he might be overcome at any time and collapse but he went ahead and drank in the late morning air. He said a prayer that should he die, his family would carry on and not grieve long over him.

As he rose to his feet, feeling light-headed and much weaker, he made himself happy that he had lived as long as he had. Then, as he began his descent toward the war lodge where he would lie under the robes and await his fate, he noticed movement on the opposite ridge. He was growing more dizzy and he squinted to see. The figure seemed plain to him then—a large dark shape that ambled slowly, watching him. The great bear, the grizzly. Thane smiled. Now he was truly ready.

Morning Swan sat atop Moon Eyes and made no move to kick the small mare into a run. Takes-a-Bow asked her what they should do and she answered nothing. Jethro merely stared up the hill at the great number of enemy warriors. Their small party, out searching for Thane, was no match for the Blackfeet. Sir John, for the first time since coming into the mountains, felt he was surely going to die.

Rising Hawk and the other Blackfeet warriors began war cries, while Morning Swan made sign up to him that she knew where his medicine shield was. It would not be good if he allowed his warriors to attack.

Rising Hawk rode down the hill with three other warriors and they met between the two parties of Crow and Blackfeet.

"Why did you not take the Crow warriors with you

and try and run?" He asked. "You have a fast horse. I can see that she is bred from my brother's horse, Whirlwind."

"We did not come into your lands to fight you," Morning Swan said in an even tone. "And I have no reason to run away from you. You will not harm me, nor will you harm any of the others with me."

Rising Hawk raised his eyebrows. "What gives you that kind of confidence?"

"Because you want your medicine shield back and I can lead you to it."

There was little more to the conversation. Rising Hawk had to agree. He knew that to cause harm to anyone now would likely be bad for his efforts to regain his medicine shield; it could likely cause his death. After so long a time he was once again looking into the eyes of the beautiful Crow woman who had once been wife to his brother. She knew where she was going and it would be wise to let her lead the way.

When they reached the hill overlooking the devastated village of Blood and Northern Blackfeet people, Takes-a-Bow pointed down and told them all that it had been from this spot on this hill that they had first noticed the village had been struck by the bad disease.

Rising Hawk and his warriors were speechless for a time. Then they wept unashamedly. The village was silent and deserted, except for the ravens and magpies pecking at the remains of the victims not eaten by wolves and coyotes. Lodge door flaps hung loose and feathers that adorned the dead moved in the breeze. As they looked down, a black cloud passed in front of the sun.

"The sickness is everywhere," Morning Swan told Rising Hawk. "Now I must go and see if Bear-Man, my husband, lives or is dead."

"Is my medicine shield with him?" Rising Hawk asked.

"It is," Takes-a-Bow answered.

Takes-a-Bow had come back that day after leaving

with the other Crow warriors and had watched Thane until after dark. Now he led them upriver to where he had seen Thane preparing one of the war lodges. Just before they reached the hill overlooking the river, Morning Swan turned to Rising Hawk as they rode.

"I do not know what we will find, but it would be best if you remained back a ways. It is likely he has become sick. But whether or not he is still sick, or even dead, I will go to be with him."

Thane was on his stomach, drinking from the river, when he heard the sound of horses on the hill above. He stood up, a blanket soaked with disease and sweat wrapped tightly around him. His fever was breaking and it was his first day out of the war lodge. He had gotten only a mild case and would not be badly scarred. He gave credit for his good fortune to his grandfather, who had no doubt passed on some quality genes to his grandson.

But now was not a time to be rejoicing. Not yet. He recognized Morning Swan, Takes-a-Bow, and Sir John as they waved to him from the top of the hill. There were a number of Crow warriors with them, mostly cousins and various warrior members of Takes-a-Bow's clan.

"Don't come down here," Thane warned them. "I am not yet clean."

Sir John explained to Morning Swan and Takes-a-Bow that Thane was recovering from the smallpox but could still infect anyone he came in contact with. Morning Swan let the tears fall from her eyes. She was overjoyed, but also frustrated at not being able to see Thane.

"We made it back to the village in time," Takes-a-Bow shouted. "The people are in the Bighorn Mountains, away from the river."

"Jethro and Rosebud are fine," Morning Swan then shouted down. "Jethro will never forgive me for making him stay behind with his sister and the baby."

Thane let the words act upon him for a time.

Knowing everyone was safe relieved him greatly. He took a deep breath and spoke again.

"You know I want to come up and see you, but I can't. It will be a number of days yet until I feel safe enough to be with you all. How did you know where I was?"

"That day we found the village, I came back and looked for you," Takes-a-Bow said. "How could I go back and not know where you were?"

"What of the others?" Thane asked. "Those who would not listen and went after the fleeing warriors?"

Thane saw Takes-a-Bow shrug and tell him he had no idea what had happened to them. Sir John yelled down then and said he wanted to get an account of things since they had last been together.

"And I want you to know," he added, "those bloody fool mules have decided they will no longer pull a plow."

Thane then saw a number of Blackfeet warriors crowd up to the edge of the hill. Rising Hawk said something to Morning Swan and then looked down at Thane.

"I have your woman," Rising Hawk said. "I now want my medicine shield."

"I have your medicine shield," Thane told Rising Hawk. "It is buried so that it will not become infected by the smallpox. In time I will give it to you and you can go back to your people and we will go back to ours. There has already been enough dying."

Rising Hawk was silent for a time. Finally he yelled down, "How long a time?"

"Sun must cross the sky at least five more times," Thane answered. "It is not in my heart to give your shield to you and have your people die."

Rising Hawk did not speak for a time. He looked down at his enemy, and though he had never known this man at all, he could now see that he was truly a warrior of honor. It would seem he would like for the

Blackfeet people to die, whether it was from sickness or by any other means. But there was no honor in that sort of death and there was no honor in killing an enemy by a means such as that. This man they called Bear-Man had survived this terrible sickness and he was not afraid to say he would not give the medicine shield back until he was ready. His heart was truly strong—of the great white-tipped bear.

But this man was still an enemy. No matter what kind of honor he possessed, he was still the man who had stolen his medicine shield and his power, thus disgracing him before his people, the Piegans, and all his brothers of the Blackfeet nation. No words of honor, no kindness, no deed of any kind could change what had happened. Rising Hawk was resolved that Bear-Man must die for his honor to return.

"It is good that you do not want my people to die of the sickness," Rising Hawk finally said. "But I am not sure that you do not want to keep my medicine shield. If you truly wish to return it to me, you will come to the village of the Small Robes on Two Medicine River before the next moon begins. I will take Morning Swan and the other two with me now, and if you are not there when the next moon comes, they will die."

Thane thought about negotiating with Rising Hawk. His medicine shield was buried at the bottom of the hill and could be dug up now, which would mean it would become contaminated. But Thane realized that if Rising Hawk saw that he could not get his medicine shield back without contamination, he would feel he had nothing to lose in killing Morning Swan and the others. Thane knew he was not realistically able to stop Rising Hawk from doing whatever he wanted. His concern now centered on what the Piegans might do to Morning Swan and the others once they got to the village.

"I will come to your village," Thane finally yelled up to Rising Hawk. "And at that time I will trade your medicine shield for Morning Swan and the others. If any harm comes to them, you know it will be bad for you."

Rising Hawk sat his horse for a moment and then yelled down, "You must keep your word. If you do not come, they will die."

Thane watched helplessly while Rising Hawk and his warriors escorted everyone away. When they were gone, Thane jumped on the buckskin and rode to the top of the hill. He could see them riding into the distance, soon to be swallowed up by the mountains. It was almost harder now than when he had waited for the sickness. There was nothing he could do for a time, and that time would go very slowly.

After five days had finally passed, Thane was ready to begin his journey toward the Two Medicine River. The fever had broken without complications and he felt remarkably good. His strength was returning rapidly and the sores were healing without infection. He was ready for whatever lay ahead, and after he had burned the lodge and all the blankets and other contaminated articles, he left with the smoke at his back and rode the buckskin at a slow lope toward the Two Medicine River.

Nothing crossed Thane's mind but his destination, across the small divide at the headwaters of the Musselshell and then along the Missouri until he broke away from it and headed straight northwest along the main range of the Rocky Mountains—the Backbone-of-the-World, as the Indians called it. The Two Medicine River was deep in Blackfeet country, a distance above the Great Falls, territory that until Fort McKenzie had been built was suicide for intruders.

It was again suicide country, Thane thought, for the smallpox had without question come from Fort McKenzie and spread out through this region. Further down on the river—at Forts Cass, Clark, and Union —there was no doubt widespread death as well.

Blankets and other trade articles would most likely spread the infection, and without question the Indian tribes throughout the mountains were now looking at the traders as the cause of this disaster among their people.

Thane did not know what to expect once he reached the Piegan village. Rising Hawk would likely not have harmed anybody yet, but it remained to be seen what he would do once he got his medicine shield back. He would have to save face in some way, and Thane felt sure that would mean by either killing him or dying himself.

Upon reaching the village, Thane was met by Rising Hawk and a contingent of Piegan warriors. Rising Hawk immediately took back his medicine shield and inspected it thoroughly. Thane recognized Cutter with them, as he maneuvered his horse forward to get close to Thane. Cutter had his same strange eyes, and when he raised his rifle, a Piegan warrior near him grabbed it and Rising Hawk commanded him back into the village, under penalty of death.

"I didn't know he lived with you," Thane said to Rising Hawk.

"He does not live with us," Rising Hawk quickly corrected him. "He still lives with a band of our brothers, the Bloods. He brought news of your coming into these lands and I am grateful to him. But he cannot kill you. It cannot be he that kills you."

Thane did not have long to wait to find out what Rising Hawk's thoughts were. Rising Hawk and the other warriors escorted him to a large tree that grew just back from a high bank over the river. There were two rawhide ropes tied to the trunk of the tree that hung down off the steep bank. They were pulled up to reveal a painted log at the end of each rope: one depicting Rising Hawk in victory and the other had the image of Thane, with a knife in his heart.

The villagers now began to come out in excited groups, talking and pointing, taking positions for the

event that had been planned. Thane knew he would
have to fight Rising Hawk to the death. The reason
was plain: Rising Hawk had lost a close family member, his brother, to an enemy—and his medicine
shield as well. Rising Hawk had been doubly shamed,
and not to try for satisfaction against the very enemy
that had shamed him would make Rising Hawk a
coward in the eyes of his people.

Rising Hawk then went to the top of the nearest hill
with his medicine shield. Thane watched with the
other Piegan warriors while Rising Hawk offered
prayers. The hot, windy day pulled thermal currents
down off the face of the nearby Rockies and red-tailed
hawks soared through the sky all across the valley.
After a time, with his medicine shield raised aloft,
Rising Hawk rode back down the hill and declared
himself ready to kill Bear-Man.

With the fight inevitable, Thane was concerned
about how Morning Swan and the others had been
treated. But he was not allowed even to know if they
were here or still alive, or what their condition was.
His only way of knowing they were in the village was
when an old warrior Rising Hawk called Rain Maker
stepped forward and gave Thane a war club—Takes-
a-Bow's own war club.

"You son-in-law says it possesses power," Rain
Maker told Thane. "You will need it."

"Has Rising Hawk told you the story of how he
found me? How Morning Swan led him to me?"
Thane asked.

Rain Maker nodded. "Rising Hawk also told me
that you could not give him his shield until after you
had fully conquered the sickness, so that the shield
would not bring the sickness to our people. You are a
man of honor. But that cannot stop what must take
place this day."

"Then you know and Rising Hawk knows," Thane
said, "that I have already cheated death once—that

the sickness could not kill me. Perhaps that means the spirits will not let me die."

Rain Maker knew Thane was doing this to give himself an advantage in the fight against Rising Hawk, for Rising Hawk was right there, listening to every word. But the old warrior also knew that nothing must stop Rising Hawk from removing the shame from himself. Rain Maker did not want Rising Hawk going into battle with this man thinking the spirits were against him.

Rain Maker shook his head with force. "The sickness does not have the power that Rising Hawk has. And Rising Hawk has spent many winters without his medicine, which means the spirits have always been with him. They will be with him on this day also."

Thane smiled. He wasn't finished. He pointed out the zigzag marks on the handle, indicative of the power of the storm, and then raised his hand to the west, where thunder clouds were mushrooming into the early afternoon sky.

"Rising Hawk should be happy he is alive and has his medicine shield back. He should not be so foolish as to give up his life now."

Rain Maker ignored him. "You know how it must be, Bear-Man. Enough talk."

"It is now for me to take your life with the medicine you once stole from me," Rising Hawk told Thane. "Because of you I spent many winters in distress; I might have died. And you caused the death of my brother. It is time you paid for all of that."

"You have survived all of that," Thane told Rising Hawk forcefully, "just to die this day."

Rising Hawk stared at Thane. He and Thane stripped together for battle and there was silence. The entire village had come to watch, lining the bank of the river up and down. Each of the rawhide ropes was pulled up and a noose tightened under the shoulders of each man. Thane and Rising Hawk would now be lowered to hang suspended above the river, each by his rope, to fight until the death.

Morning Swan, bound tightly inside Rising Hawk's lodge, knew Thane and Rising Hawk had begun their fight. With the village almost totally silent, she knew everyone had gone to watch. Since their coming, all she had heard was how Rising Hawk would kill her husband. She had been kept a captive in Rising Hawk's lodge ever since that time, away from Takes-a-Bow and the others, and she had had to listen to Yellow Tree constantly bragging about Rising Hawk.

Though Yellow Tree had never once tried to physically harm Morning Swan, there was a lot of verbal abuse, none of which affected Morning Swan in the least. Yellow Tree should have tired long ago of trying Morning Swan's confidence, for Morning Swan would always get the best of her in the end by saying, "Bear-Man took Rising Hawk's medicine shield and stole his power; nothing can change that."

Rising Hawk made his final preparations and Thane was allowed to paint himself for battle and speak to his medicine helpers. When he was finished—his face and chest covered with black and yellow claw designs, his wounds from the grizzly highlighted by vermilion —the people of the village stared at him with their mouths covered. They pointed and spoke and wondered at the red blemishes that stood out all over, the markings of the healing smallpox that looked every bit as foreboding as the war paint itself.

Each man had a war club and his shield, plus a knife at his side. The clubs were secured to each man's wrist by rawhide thongs. The knives were to be pulled and used at the discretion of each fighter. Should one or the other drop his knife into the river, he would likely be marked for death. Should either of the fighters cut the other's rope so that he fell into the river, he would be drawn up and killed.

Thane, as he was lowered down on the rope over the river, knew he would see Morning Swan and Takes-a-

Bow and Sir John and the others alive now. Rising Hawk had not harmed them. If by no other sign, Thane knew this to be true by the actions of the old warrior Rain Maker, no doubt a *shaman*. This old medicine man was without question Rising Hawks's mentor, and had been throughout the time he had been without his shield. There was something in the old warrior's eyes that told Thane he already knew the outcome of the fight but would not say.

At Rain Maker's command, Thane and Rising Hawk began their fight. Dangling like two jumping fish, each at the end of a line, the men swore and struck at one another repeatedly. Most of the blows were defected by the war shields, both of which immediately became scuffed and marked up, the fringed edges tattered and ripped. Thane's left arm soon grew numb from the incessant pounding. If it weren't for the shield's thickness and slight curvature, he might have suffered a fracture.

Often blows struck by Thane and Rising Hawk would glance off an arm or shoulder. It was most important in the minds of both men to protect the head and throat. A direct blow either place would be stunning and result in more blows and certain death. Once Rising Hawk got his legs wrapped around Thane's middle and tried to squeeze the air out of him, but Thane slammed his legs with the war club and Rising Hawk released his grip.

The fighting continued and both men grew weary, spinning and kicking and striking out at one another, while the rope under each man's arm dug raw grooves in their armpits, bloodying their sides. Each man worked to position himself so that he could pin his enemy against the steep, rocky bank over which they hung. But neither allowed himself to become trapped, and the fighting was a struggle of intense exertion with little real effect.

There were scrapes and abrasions from the war clubs and sore and cracked ribs from direct strikes. In

time both were dark with sweat and blood that mixed
with dirt from the bank, coating them in a layer of
thin, lumpy mud. The Piegan people continued to
cheer for Rising Hawk, hoping he could strike a fatal
blow soon. But the white warrior, Bear-Man, was like
a powerful spirit; the stories about him had been true.

Then both men struck at one another at the same
time and their war clubs met in midair, snapping both
handles in two. Thane reached for his knife, as did
Rising Hawk, and the two exhausted men tried to stab
one another, cutting awkwardly. Slashes appeared
along their arms and across their shoulders. Both war
shields became a mass of crosshatch carving designs
as each man worked to gain the advantage over the
other. They both wheezed for air and shook their
heads to restore oxygen to numbed brains. The river
below had become a rushing, dizzying mass, which
neither dared look down at for fear of confusion.

Finally, Rising Hawk plunged his knife downward
and Thane got his war shield up just in time. The
blade became stuck in the thick hide shield and Thane
saw his chance.

Thane ripped underneath at Rising Hawk. The
blade caught Rising Hawk along the inside of his left
arm, slicing deep. But despite the wound, he gripped
Thane's wrist in his right hand and twisted with all his
strength.

Thane felt his fingers open and saw his knife drop
down into the current below. Rising Hawk grabbed
for his own knife, to wrest it from the hide shield, but
Thane, in turning the shield away from Rising Hawk,
slammed it into the side of the bank and the knife
bounced free and out into the air, where both men
watched it fly down into the water.

Both men hung, bleeding, gasping for breath. Neither had any weapon but their hands and both knew it
would be impossible, unless they dropped the medicine shields also, to fight to the death in this manner.
They hung for a time, each swinging at the end of his

rope, the water rushing below them. Then they felt themselves being pulled up and over the bank. They lay exhausted on their backs, the people all closing around to stare at them. Finally they came to their feet and Rain Maker brought them together.

"The spirits are with you both this day and neither of you was meant to die," the old *shaman* stated. "You have crossed blood between you and you have both fought with honor. Your medicine is as one. It is something that the spirits have decided."

Rain Maker had Thane grab hands and touch arms along their length with Rising Hawk, so that each man's blood might flow into the other. If neither was to die, the old *shaman* then told the people, then they must be considered as one. They are equals in the eyes of the spirits and also in the eyes of the Piegan peoples.

"You will be allowed to leave our lands with your woman, Morning Swan," Rain Maker said, looking at Thane. "But it is for the council to decide what will happen to the others. You will be held until that decision is made. And you must live with it."

"I have fought this day," Thane said, "so that they *all* might go back with me. It is not right that we should not be allowed to leave now. All of us together."

"You have fought well and it would not be good to kill you," Rain Maker said. "But you are our enemy, as are the others. Piegan people have died by their hand and so they must die. That you will have to accept."

Eighteen

TO GET TO THE HORSES, HEAVY BREAST WOMAN HAD TO GO past the edge of the village and cross behind the captives' lodge. In going past the lodge, Heavy Breast Woman could hear Broken Mouth yelling. The bruises on her body still hurt from the whipping she had taken when Broken Mouth had not been allowed to kill Bear-Man right away. His voice instilled cold fear in her and she visualized what would happen if the Wolves took her back to camp and did not kill her. She would become as good as leavings for the scavenger birds if Broken Mouth found out.

Then Heavy Breast Woman had a sudden thought. She began to wonder why she couldn't make everyone angry at Broken Mouth. She suddenly felt elated. She would work things so that Rising Hawk and everyone in the village became angry at Broken Mouth. This would be a way to rid herself of this horrible man forever. She wondered to herself why she hadn't thought of this before.

The more she thought about it, the more Heavy Breast Woman was sure that she could turn the village against Broken Mouth. She would make it appear that

Broken Mouth was now worried about the sickness the Long Knife traders had brought into Blackfeet lands. She would tell Rising Hawk that Broken Mouth wanted to free Bear-Man and the Crow warriors and help them escape so they could all leave together, knowing the sickness was coming soon.

She hurried to Rising Hawk's lodge. She politely called from outside and was allowed in. Rising Hawk was sitting just inside and Yellow Tree was dressing his wounds, reapplying fresh poultices of herbs and medicine plants. Morning Swan—the Woman-Who-Counts-Coups and wife to Bear-Man—was sitting at the back of the lodge with her hands tied. Heavy Breast Woman stared at her a moment before speaking to Rising Hawk once more.

"Thank you for receiving me," she said. "I have come to warn you that Broken Mouth, the man who owns me, is trying to help the captive Crow warriors to escape."

Rising Hawk stood up quickly. "What do you mean?"

Heavy Breast Woman stood up and pointed outside the lodge. "I heard him talking to Bear-Man. I heard him saying that he would free them."

"I thought Broken Mouth wanted Bear-Man to die in the worst way," Rising Hawk said.

"Broken Mouth does not want to stay here," Heavy Breast Woman said. "He believes the sickness will come to us like a cloud of fog. That is why we left my people, the Bloods. He wants to free Bear-Man so that they might all escape."

"Are you certain of this?" Rising Hawk asked.

Heavy Breast Woman nodded. "He has brought horses to the edge of the village and they are hidden in a grove of the big trees."

"Why don't you let me finish with your wounds?" Yellow Tree put in. "You can act on this when I am finished."

"This can wait," Rising Hawk said.

In the captives' lodge Sir John looked at Cutter and said, "*Double, double, toil and trouble . . .*"

Cutter turned from Thane and stared at Sir John. "What?" he asked.

"*Fire burn and cauldron bubble.*"

Cutter went over and glared down at Sir John now.

"What did you say?" Cutter asked.

"You should go into acting," Sir John said. He had thought of something that would divert Cutter's attention from Thane. He watched Cutter twist his expression into puzzlement.

"Why certainly," Sir John continued. "Followers of the Shakespearean works would find you incredible. You would make an alarming Christopher Sly. Or better yet, Macbeth. You might appear in the cavern with the three witches. Yes, that's it. You could jump up out of the caldron."

Sir John began to smile. Then he bellowed and rolled over on his side, shaking with laughter. Cutter's strange eyes were dancing with hate as he pulled his willow whip, as if drawing a sword, and yelled. He began to slash at Sir John's head and shoulders. Thane quickly came to his feet and kicked Cutter soundly in the ribs. Cutter stumbled sideways and caught himself against the side of the lodge. He turned on Thane and pulled his knife.

There were shouts from outside and Rising Hawk pushed his way into the lodge, followed by Heavy Breast Woman and the warrior who was supposed to be guarding the door, plus some of the other police warriors in the village. Heavy Breast Woman began to speak rapidly and nod her head.

"See, he is trying to take them away. It is as I told you."

Cutter glared at Heavy Breast Woman. He was as confused. Thane looked to Sir John and Takes-a-Bow. The best thing for them was to be silent and go along with whatever Heavy Breast Woman was trying to do.

It was plain from the look in her eyes, the intense hate, that she had put some plan together to get Cutter into trouble. And she was so intent that she actually believed what she was saying herself.

Heavy Breast Woman squinted at Cutter. "I told you it was not a good idea to try and escape with these Long Knives. But you would not listen."

"What the hell are you talkin' about?" Cutter blared. He started for Heavy Breast Woman but Rising Hawk cut him off.

"What is happening here?" Rising Hawk demanded.

"I'm just stopping them from getting away," he answered. He was getting worried about the intense anger in Rising Hawk's tone.

Rising Hawk turned his attention from Cutter to the police warrior who was supposed to be on guard. "Why did you let him in here?"

The warrior hung his head without speaking.

"Did he pay you to let him in?" Rising Hawk asked.

The warrior continued to hang his head and Rising Hawk told him to leave and go to his own lodge; he would be dealt with later.

"You say they were trying to escape?" Rising Hawk asked Cutter.

"Yes, trying to escape," Cutter nodded. "I got here just in time to stop him. He and the others were going to run out and try to escape."

"With their hands tied?" Rising Hawk said. "They were going to run away with their hands tied? I see only your knife here. What knife would they have used?"

Cutter looked around the lodge. "They must have one in here somewhere," he finally said.

"Why are a number of ponies tied in the trees near here?" Rising Hawk demanded. "I see enough for you and Heavy Breast Woman and these captives."

"What?" Cutter said. "I didn't put no horses in the trees."

"They are all your horses," Rising Hawk said. "And some others that belong to warriors here. Could it be that you were hoping to take these captives away? And did you know anything about the terrible sickness before you came here with Heavy Breast Woman?"

"No," Cutter stammered. "I didn't know nothin' about the smallpox. And I didn't plan to take them anywhere. I didn't."

Cutter had no idea what was happening and he couldn't understand what Rising Hawk was saying about horses being tied in the trees near the village. He knew this was all Heavy Breast Woman's doing. But there was no way he could get to her now. There were two police warriors with Rising Hawk and he could hear the whole village assembling outside the lodge.

Two of the police warriors grabbed Cutter and took him outside the lodge. He knew he would be foolish to resist; it was just some sort of lie concocted by Heavy Breast Woman and he could get things straightened out shortly. He did not know where they were taking him and it bothered him to see the villagers pointing. In their eyes was a sudden and sincere dislike. Heavy Breast Woman must have told Rising Hawk all about the smallpox. Surely they would not take her word over his.

Heavy Breast Woman watched the camp police take Broken Mouth and tie him to one of the tree trunks at the edge of the village. He was not struggling against them and this puzzled her. She thought surely he would be very angry. No matter, Heavy Breast Woman thought, she would have to go over there and kill him as soon as she could. Somehow, she thought, Rising Hawk would find out that she had been lying about the horses. Then they would all be angry at her.

Whether or not Rising Hawk decided to believe anybody, Heavy Breast Woman knew she had taken herself past the point of no return with her plan. She must see that Broken Mouth died. She no longer cared what happened to her as a result. Banishment, or even death, was much better than being with this man. She had no life with him and if she must die, then she would gladly accept that.

As the night progressed, Heavy Breast Woman saw Rising Hawk and other warriors go to where Broken Mouth was tied and talk briefly. They were in council and she knew they were trying to understand what was going on. Twice she had avoided a crier who had been sent for her, so that she might talk to the council. She did not want them to learn she had lied; she only wanted a chance to kill Broken Mouth.

It was then that there came shouting from just outside the village. All the people turned their attention to three riders who burst into the village and then up to the circle of warriors holding council in front of Rising Hawk's lodge. It was a serious and rude interruption but the camp Wolves, who had been on lookout, were with the three warriors. Breathless, they all jumped down from their horses. The three visitors were warriors from other bands: one was Northern Blackfeet, one a Blood, and the third a Piegan.

"All the people of our nation are dying," the Piegan said to Rising Hawk. "It is the sickness that brings blotches to the skin and sores that break out into puss. Many have already gone to the next life."

Rain Maker now looked at Rising Hawk and the others in the council. "You have all seen the drawing I made on the buffalo robe. Now we know what my dream and the drawing means. Perhaps the Long Knife, Bear-Man, was right in telling us we should go back away from all our people and remain there."

All three of the arriving warriors began to move toward the tree where Cutter was tied. Their faces were lined with intense anger. They drew their knives and asked permission to kill Cutter.

"Why do you want to kill him?" Rising Hawk asked.

"It was one of the fireboats that come to the forts

that brought the sickness," the Blood warrior said. He was glaring at Cutter while he talked. "He knew this and lived among our people, but said nothing. The blankets and all the other trade items had death upon them. Now our people are dying."

"Wait!" Rising Hawk stepped in front of them. "There are other Long Knives here as well. And there are Crow warriors. We have them in a captive lodge. We will kill them all together."

Rain Maker looked hard at Rising Hawk. "I do not think that would be wise," he said. "You know that Bear-Man is standing upright with you in my drawing while all the others are falling upside down. That means he will live, not die. Killing him would anger the spirits."

Rising Hawk thought a moment. Everyone was watching him. There was not a one among them who wanted any of the Long Knives to be freed now.

Rising Hawk shook his head and spoke to Rain Maker. "They must all die. They are killers of our people."

Rain Maker turned and went back toward his lodge. The people made way for him while Rising Hawk approached Heavy Breast Woman.

"It is good that you told us Broken Mouth was going to run with the other Long Knives. They did not want us to know about the bad sickness and that they brought it. But why did you not tell this to the council?"

Heavy Breast Woman searched for words. Finally she said, "I have lived very badly at the hands of Broken Mouth. No one cared about this. I thought it was time that I kill him or some day die by his hand. That is all I can say."

In late afternoon, a special fire was built in the center of the village. It was decided that death should come first to Broken Mouth, who would have tried to escape without telling anyone of the sickness. That was worse even than trying to free Bear-Man and the

Crow captives. He was a white trader and responsible for many Blackfeet deaths.

For Broken Mouth, it was decided that death must come slowly. The others would die in a bad way also, but Broken Mouth must be made to suffer terribly— as the sickness made the people suffer. He was dragged to a pole near the main fire while drums pounded and songs of victory were sung. His clothes were cut away, without particular care, and he was left standing naked to await his fate, his strange eyes wide and crazy.

Heavy Breast Woman looked into the sky and saw that the storm she had been watching had come. She sang with the others and looked on with satisfaction while warriors brought sharpened pieces of pine wood and jammed them roughly between his ribs and into his body, leaving a short piece of each splinter protruding out. Cutter tried not to show pain, knowing that would make it worse on him. The splinters were not long enough to kill him, like a knife, but just long enough to go a few inches past the bone and muscle tissue into the body cavity.

"Stick some of them into his stomach also," Heavy Breast Woman suggested.

Cutter screamed as splinters were pushed into his stomach and abdomen. The splinters were then all lit with embers from the main fire. The splinters would burn until they reached his skin and went out, but the pitch in the small pieces of pine would then carry the heat on through the wood deep into his body.

The splinters burned quickly and Cutter moaned in agony as the flame scorched his skin and then carried through in the pitch to the inside of his body. Screaming, Cutter learned, only brought Blackfeet people from the circle of dancers in to poke him with sharp sticks or bounce rocks off his head. The Blackfeet knew what they were doing: the pain was meant to be intense, without the relief of passing out.

Heavy Breast Woman was not satisfied. He was not

yelling loudly enough, but only moaning and whining like a small child. She went forward and sliced his chest with a knife. Already delirious with pain, Cutter stood hanging away from the pole, his skin twitching with each quick pull of her blade. His pain was already far too great to yell in rage. But Heavy Breast Woman still was not satisfied. The women and children and warriors all chanted while she then pushed porcupine quills into his eyes. Finally, she did the same thing to his genitals.

Thane and Morning Swan were then brought out to watch while Takes-a-Bow and the other Crow warriors were tied to trees nearby. Sir John told the warriors he wished to be the first to die, to show his courage. He asked them to allow him to take some of the splinters out of Cutter's body and push them into his own.

Standing next to the dying Cutter, Sir John looked first to Thane and then to the sky, where the clouds had begun to roll and thunder. He smiled as flashes of jagged lightning split the dark ceiling above. Cutter was slowly going unconscious and Sir John turned to the Blackfeet warriors who were waiting for him.

"This dying man," Sir John told them in Blackfeet, "he says he will give his spirit to me."

The Blackfeet warriors looked at Sir John and frowned. Sir John smiled and nodded. The Blackfeet warriors looked from Cutter to Sir John and backed away slightly.

Sir John then pulled splinters from Cutter's body and rolled them across his face, leaving little tracks of gore. With his hands he scooped blood from Cutter's knife wounds and in front of the gasping Rising Hawk and all the other Blackfeet present, he smeared his face and chest, leaving globs of Cutter's blood hanging from him. Then Sir John held his stained hands out to the crowd with wild eyes and screamed.

The drums stopped and the chanting hushed as the people stared at Sir John. Rising Hawk looked to Rain

Maker and began to mumble. Rain Maker raised his hands to the sky and began to chant, his old hands trembling.

Sir John screamed again, his eyes turning even wilder. Then in the Blackfoot tongue, he spoke from the ghost scene in Shakespeare's Macbeth:

Blood hath been shed ere now, i' the olden time,
Ere humane statute purged the gentle weal;
Ay, and since too, murders have been perform'd
Too terrible for the ear: the time has been,
That, when the brains were out, the man would die. . . .

Sir John watched the people as they stood frozen. He laughed and pulled Cutter's slumping head back and plucked a quill from a bloody eye. Sir John let the head fall forward again and held the quill aloft and stared at it. Then he lunged toward the crowd of hushed Blackfeet, their hands held over their mouths. They jumped and mothers grabbed their children to keep them away from the crazed man in front of them. Rising Hawk stood paralyzed, remembering Rain Maker's words about not making the spirits angry. He turned, but Rain Maker was gone.

The thunder grew louder as the storm moved in over the village. The Blackfeet people looked up and gasped, and some began to hold one another, as if feeling the cold that brewed in the dark clouds overhead. Thane and Morning Swan stood motionless, waiting to see what Sir John would do next.

Cutter, seeming somehow to come to life, raised his head back, the porcupine quills protruding from his swollen eyes, blood and matter dripping from their sockets. Sir John kissed him and then dropped himself to the ground, as if in death, and slowly came to his feet, running his bloody fingers through his hair. He fell back again and rose again, then continued with the lines from Macbeth:

. . . And there an end; but now they rise again,
With twenty mortal murders on their crowns,
And push us from our stools: this is more strange
Than such a murder is.

Overhead, the clouds broke and thunder clapped like a monstrous drum, while Blackfeet people, old and young, screamed and ran from the scene, dashing in crazed lines out from the village. Rising Hawk stood staring, unable to move, while Thane cut Takes-a-Bow and the other Crow warriors loose. Takes-a-Bow and Morning Swan then worked to keep the other Crows from running away as well.

"Crazy Arms has the spirits with him," Takes-a-Bow told his fellow warriors. "He is our protector this day."

They left the village in a driving thunderstorm. Rising Hawk had gone to a hill with his medicine shield and held it aloft to the storm. Out from the village, the Blackfeet people hid in stands of thick chokecherry and bottom brush, hoping the crazy Long Knife and the spirits would not kill them.

They rode day and night until they got past the Musselshell River. They were concerned that Rising Hawk would assemble his warriors and be after them. But it was finally certain that they were away from danger—at least from Rising Hawk and the Blackfeet.

The smallpox had passed through the land and its devastation was everywhere. In their travel they came across scattered Blackfeet villages, all deserted, littered with corpses. They found not only Blackfeet, but Assiniboin and Cree villages as well, as they had traveled south and west from their homelands to try to outrun the death. Along trails was sign left by traveling bands hoping to escape the disease, telling of widespread death among all the Indian people—of many hundreds that were no longer among those in this life.

It did not matter to Morning Swan, nor to the other

Crow warriors, that these dead people were all enemies. In their eyes at this time they were all people,
like themselves, who had friends and families and did
not deserve to die in this way. Morning Swan's tears
were not just for these that they passed by, but for the
many, many more that were certainly scattered
throughout all these lands—the Indian peoples of this
region who had no defenses against an enemy that
crept upon the air into their lodges.

When they finally reached the Yellowstone, they
learned what had happened to the young Crow warriors who had foolishly rode off after the fleeing
Blackfeet some time back. Thane remembered telling
them not to go, and Takes-a-Bow remembered his
sorrow at seeing some of his close friends riding away
from him, knowing he was seeing them for the last
time.

They did not have to ride down into the large
encampment of Crows along the river to understand
that the smallpox was killing them off. The village was
along the river at a favorite camping place, where
immense sandstone bluffs shielded the valley bottom
from driving winds.

Morning Swan and Takes-a-Bow, as well as the
other Crow warriors, wept openly at seeing another
band of their people in such a state. It was late
afternoon and drums sounded in the village, along
with wails of mourning and chants from the *shamans*.
Sweat lodges stood all along the river banks and the
sick and dying were everywhere.

Then Morning Swan pointed to a huge sandstone
cliff above the village, where a number of young Crow
warriors on horseback were sitting their horses with
their arms raised to the setting sun. They prayed for a
time before tying strips of cloth around their horses'
eyes as blindfolds. Then, like a stream of buffalo over
a *pisken*, the warriors rode at a gallop to their deaths,
tumbling down onto the rocks at the river's edge.

"They are sacrificing themselves to save their loved

ones," Morning Swan told Thane through her tears.
"They do not know that they cannot stop the sickness
that way."

Thane worried even more now that the Kicked-in-
Their-Bellies might have contracted the disease as
well. He did not want to have to face seeing Jethro and
Rosebud—with her baby—and all the others, dying
as had so many others. Life would hardly be worth
living should they find something like that.

This was on everyone's mind as they made their
way up and out of the Yellowstone Valley and into the
Bighorn Range. They rode day and night until at last,
during late evening, they saw the lights of many
campfires high in the mountains.

The Kicked-in-Their-Bellies were joined with members of the Sore-Lips and the Whistling Waters clans.
They welcomed Thane and Morning Swan and the
others with a loud chorus of cheers and shouts of joy.
The disease had not come into the mountains, and
since the cold moons would come before too long, it
was thought the sickness would pass through and be
gone by the coming of the next warm moons.

Jethro and Rosebud were never so glad to see Thane
and their mother as they were now. Not even when
Thane had gone into the high Beartooth had Jethro
been so concerned about his father. For many days
after that he walked by his father's side and sat beside
him, and hunted with him when the people made the
fall hunt, just below the mountains. Morning Swan
held Rosebud's baby and played with him each passing day without fail. She held him up so that she could
see him and pressed him to her bosom so that she
might hear his heart beat.

"When will he be old enough to have a raven?"
Jethro would ask periodically. Often he would turn to
Sir John and say, "You started this whole thing by
giving him to Takes-a-Bow before he was a warrior.
Maybe you should have him back."

"I'm afraid he wouldn't care for life in the city," Sir

John would always say. "For that is where I am bound when the occasion to leave arises."

The cold moons were spent again where the warm waters bubbled from the Bighorn River, the traditional camping area, and the people again were happy. There was plenty of meat from the fall hunt and the snow was not deep nor the cold too biting. Many new stories were passed around the fires, including the feat of Sir John in the Blackfeet village. It became a favorite among children, who wished to hear it just before going to bed, so they could hide themselves in their robes and make strange noises to scare one another.

At the advance of the first formation of rain clouds, the Kicked-in-Their-Bellies made ready to move once again from the upper Bighorn to their traditional spring hunting areas. Buffalo had come back into the valley of the Yellowstone. This was a sign that good times for the people were ahead, and the spring ceremonies were celebrated with great zest.

The hunt was successful and the people felt times ahead would be as they had been in earlier days. The traders were still there, but not in the same numbers. Fort Cass had received the new name of Fort Van Buren and had then been burned to the ground. No one among the people knew who had burned it, but no one really cared either.

Rosebud announced she was again with child and Jethro commented he would have to catch another raven. At the Rotten-Sun-Dance-Lodge-Creek camping area, all the people gave thanks for their many blessings and new marriages were announced.

They had not been in camp very long when a delegation of white adventurers rode into the village, led by a man who called himself Lord Oliver Stone. Their guide was a mixed-blood Iroquois named Minelle, who spoke fluent Crow, as well as French, Blackfoot, and five other Indian languages.

Stone and the others had been in the mountains

over the past year, hunting and gathering information
about passes and transportation routes through the
area. It was their intention, when the weather was
more predictable, to move on down the Yellowstone
and then back down the Missouri to tell what they had
found and plan accordingly. Stone seemed to know
every story in the mountains and had come to the
village just to meet Thane and judge what kind of man
he was. He promptly asked Thane if he would be
interested in guiding him, should he return and desire
his services.

"I can't say at this time," was Thane's answer.
"That's something I would have to give thought to. If
you make it back out here, maybe then I'll know."

Thane at this point wasn't sure about anything in
his future, except happiness with his family and the
Crow people. He had, for now, decided against advancing with his plan to grow tobacco. To do that, he had
concluded, would bring the seeds of change into this
land far more rapidly than he wanted. Instead, he
wanted to enjoy this lull in the rapid transformation
of this country, to allow himself to see what he found
here now—at this time—and hold it forever in his
thoughts. He wanted to watch the huge grizzly, his
medicine animal, travel the lands; he wanted the geese
that crossed the skies to stay in his mind forever,
without thinking he might some day look up and not
see them.

Sir John decided he would travel back with Lord
Stone and then on to New York, for certain this time,
and begin his life anew where his culture had preordained his character and future. He was glad to have
found someone with whom to discuss more sophisti-
cated topics while he journeyed to his home.

Lord Stone and his men remained with the Kicked-
in-Their-Bellies until they were ready to move on. Sir
John told Stone he had one last matter to attend to
and, on an evening when the wind was soft and the
last of the snows were being pushed from the slopes,

Thane and Morning Swan found him up at the Place-of-the-Swan-Trees.

Life was returning to the small valley. Orange and red-stemmed willows were showing new growth and the dogwood and wild plum were arrayed with snow-white flowers. There were a number of aspens with leaf buds that had popped, revealing tender leaves in tight rolls, waiting for successive days of warm weather to bring them out fully. The delicate catkins—the seed-bearing part of the trees—hung like long, fuzzy Christmas ornaments, moving slightly in the breeze. The new trees had grown tremendously and were now well over Thane's head.

Again the creek was filled with deep beaver ponds where fish jumped and rose to the surface along edges of soft ice that broke away in small chunks and floated with the current. Along the slopes, following the melting snow up the hills, were blankets of delicate flowers, yellow and blue, that the sun made colored carpets of in the last hours of the day.

Morning Swan smiled. "This valley will someday be as beautiful as it once was, but in a different way, and with the beauty showing in different places."

The beaver dams, now built in different parts of the creek to adjust for the past erosion, had caused a shift in the location of wetlands and boggy areas. The result would be the same, however: retardation of the rushing spring flows that were sure to come, holding the precious water back for use by plants and animals during the hot moons.

It was up near the head of the little creek where Thane and Morning Swan found Sir John. There were a number of fat groundhogs who sat a distance away watching him. He had dug a tremendous hole among the rocks in one of the hillsides and had a number of large skins he was preparing to bury.

"That's a big hole," Thane commented. "What do you intend to put in it?"

"My journals," Sir John answered. He was wrapping them tightly in hides that had been smoked first and greased heavily on the outside to prevent water damage.

"Why, in God's name, are you doing that?" Thane asked.

Sir John stopped his work for a moment. He was breathing heavily from his work and in the late afternoon air, his breath came out in clouds of steam. He looked out to where the sun was descending over the Beartooths and then back down to his journals, as if burying a son.

"This is the place for them," he finally said, "at least for a time. If I persist in the notion of taking them back with me, I fear I would just lose them again in some brown and scummy river. They might as well remain here until such time as I have grown older and can understand what I have written. Perhaps I shall return and collect them at some future date—perhaps not. At least if I never see them again, it will be by my own hand and not by some quirk of fate. Far and away a more gratifying experience, don't you think?"

"You've nearly gotten killed because of those journals any number of times," Thane said. "You came to the village after losing them on the *Assiniboin* and you were crazy enough to nearly burn down all the Crow lodges over it. Now you bury that work in some hole, just like that?"

"It's my work to bury, now isn't it? Besides, there is not a soul on this earth would ever believe I could have seen such things and heard such things and felt it, and . . . well, I just am better off for now without these nuisance records. It makes me freer to tell it the way I would like, you know."

"Aren't you going to write plays when you get back?" Thane asked.

"I cannot in reality say at this moment," Sir John answered with a frown. "I have come to realize that it has all been written. In one form or another, each dream and each scheme has been touched upon. Even out here among these savages, there is nothing that has not been conceived of and brought to bear fruit that hasn't tasted the morning sunshine, or drunk of a deep rain, many times before.

"It is only a different form of human being that is doing it, don't you see?" Sir John continued. "Those with different skins and different paint and different clothes, but all made up the same inside. All crying out for help in this world where laughter and pain are but a pinhead apart. Those across the seas have spoken thus before, and written the same. It will become thus in the new world that is here, far sooner than you think. And I dare say by writers with far more talent than myself. I shan't begin to top them."

"But you can't think that way," Morning Swan said suddenly. "The time will come when my people wished they had the words of their elders to look at and reflect upon. It is people like you, who put words down and make them real, who will tell people not yet born what has happened."

Sir John smiled. "Well, maybe that is it, then. Perhaps I feel that the words on these papers are from others, that nothing is my own. They will be here for those who want to know. They will be here when it is time to dig them up and learn the way things once were."

Sir John finished his work while the air grew colder and the sun fell. That night clouds filled the valley and a soft, heavy snow fell. The snow continued through the next day. Thane and Morning Swan and Sir John talked of the old days and the events that had, in such a short number of years, shaped their lives so drastically. After another day of snow, the sun came out and the land was a glaring white. Piles of snow grew soft and the creeks gurgled with fresh, crisp water.

By the next morning, the snow was melted and the land was bright and clean. Sir John spent his last few hours watching the clouds rise off the jagged peaks of the Beartooths. Then he said goodbye to all and left with Lord Stone and his men.

Thane prepared to go on a hunt with Jethro, while Morning Swan helped Rosebud with the baby. The sun rose up, a gold ball, and the sky was a sweep of blue from horizon to horizon. Wisps of green grass that had appeared before the storm showed again and took on a deeper hue. The tiny spring flowers, their stems now dark from the frost, turned their leaves to the fresh light, drinking in the warmth that gave them renewed life, and opened up new blossoms that colored the hills and bottoms.

Across the expanse of open sky a broad V of geese flew northward where the ponds and lakes would soon be free of ice and the grass high for nesting. And from pine trees all around the village came the voices of the tiny chickadees, singing, "Summer's near, summer's near."